W9-CHS-072

ONE NIGHT OF LOVE

Snow fell, obliterating all but the backs of the dogs as they ran. Cara buried her face in the furs to keep the stinging ice out of her eyes. Behind her, Tall Dancer watched the trail.

The dark afternoon deepened into night before they stopped. Tall Dancer unhitched the dogs and turned the sled over to cover the load of furs. His knife flashing, he cut down branches and erected a shelter. "We will be in my village tomorrow," he told her. "After tonight, we will have no more time together."

The unspoken suggestion in his words, the passion building in his eyes, made Cara's heart jump into a rapid beat. "I know," she whispered. *I want to spend these hours in your arms . . .* Cara closed her eyes, knowing the depth of his need and the answering need within herself.

His mouth captured hers in a kiss that bruised her lips and sent her blood roaring in her ears. He picked her up, his mouth never leaving hers. The fragrant cedar bed crackled as he laid her onto the bear pelt. Lowering the skin that covered the opening of their shelter, he cast them into the ghostly glow of the fire.

She laced her fingers through his hair. A sense of power filled her as he trembled at her touch. . . .

BOOK YOUR PLACE ON OUR WEBSITE AND MAKE THE READING CONNECTION!

We've created a customized website just for our very special readers, where you can get the inside scoop on everything that's going on with Zebra, Pinnacle and Kensington books.

When you come online, you'll have the exciting opportunity to:

- View covers of upcoming books
- Read sample chapters
- Learn about our future publishing schedule (listed by publication month *and author*)
- Find out when your favorite authors will be visiting a city near you
- Search for and order backlist books from our online catalog
- Check out author bios and background information
- Send e-mail to your favorite authors
- Meet the Kensington staff online
- Join us in weekly chats with authors, readers and other guests
- Get writing guidelines
- AND MUCH MORE!

**Visit our website at
http://www.zebrabooks.com**

RAVEN'S BRIDE

Kathryn Fox

Zebra Books
Kensington Publishing Corp.

http://www.zebrabooks.com

ZEBRA BOOKS are published by

Kensington Publishing Corp.
850 Third Avenue
New York, NY 10022

Copyright © 1999 by Kathryn Fox

All rights reserved. No part of this book may be reproduced
in any form or by any means without the prior written consent
of the Publisher, excepting brief quotes used in reviews.

If you purchased this book without a cover you should be aware
that this book is stolen property. It was reported as ''unsold
and destroyed'' to the Publisher and neither the Author nor the
Publisher has received any payment for this ''stripped book.''

Zebra, the Z logo and Splendor Reg. U.S. Pat. & TM Off.

First Printing: November, 1999
10 9 8 7 6 5 4 3 2 1

Printed in the United States of America

Chapter One

Southeast Alaska—1801

Cara Tarakanov crouched and faced the masked figures that circled her. Weaving and dipping, they danced, their lithe bodies silhouetted against leaping flames. Abalone shells embedded into the eyes of the killer whale and raven masks glistened, giving dual life to the dancers now circling closer.

"Leave me alone!" she shouted in broken Tsimshian, frantically trying to put together the difficult words. The pounding drums thumped into the center of her aching head. Backing away, she stumbled and fell over a cedar limb. She seized the branch, scrambled to her feet, and brandished it at the masked men.

"Get away from me, I said." The dancers paused and glanced at each other. The drummer faltered, then increased the rhythm. A lone dancer twirled toward her, his mask a grinning octopus. Its carved tentacles waved in the air. Furiously yanking on the strings that controlled the mask's arms, the dancer leaped at her.

"Kill her!" a voice boomed.

The drummer stopped pounding. The dancers stilled, then parted to allow Klaida, the old chief, to squeeze through the line and walk toward her. His long robe of woven cedar fibers dragged across the ground, leaving a trail in the mud. Lines furrowing his brow hinted at the depth of his anger.

Cara cringed at the rage on his face. She was ruining his potlatch, destroying the celebration meant to honor his recent marriage.

"Kill her!" He thrust out his arm and his long, jagged fingernail grazed the skin between her eyes.

The dancers surged forward. Cara raised the branch and whacked one on the knee. He howled and hopped away, holding his leg. She darted toward the space made in the crowd, but it was quickly filled by another warrior. Klaida snatched a slave-killing club away from one of the chagrined dancers.

"I'll kill you myself," he said through gritted teeth, "and you will cause no more trouble."

Towering over her, he raised the club to its apex and looked down into her face. She dropped the branch and met his gaze. At least her death would have some dignity. Closing her eyes, she waited for the blow that would end her enslavement.

After a moment, she opened one eye. Puzzlement filled Klaida's face as he stared down at her. Raising the club higher, he paused, and Cara knew he was waiting for her to plead for mercy. Edging her chin forward, she stared back at him. Clouds scuttled across the full moon, casting the village into sudden darkness. Voices rumbled warnings about omens and superstitions.

Klaida looked over his shoulder at his new wife, Palina. She nodded encouragement to her husband and flashed Cara an arrogant, tight-lipped smile.

"Why do you not drop to your knees and beg?" he asked.

"Because I do not fear death."

He lowered the club slightly and frowned.

"Death will be a welcome end to my service to you and Palina."

He lowered the club another inch. "To die at your master's

potlatch is an honorable thing. All these guests will appreciate that I am a wealthy man, that I can afford to sacrifice my slaves.'' He waved the club toward the people crowding closer.

"Then kill me, Klaida, and be quick about it."

Wary voices rumbled louder about the dangers of angering the spirits. A puff of wind blew snowflakes across Cara's face.

"Kill me," she ordered. "Why do you wait?"

He hesitated again and slid his gaze away from hers. The north wind blew the clouds aside and the ceremonial ground was flooded with bright moonlight. Klaida lifted the club, grinned triumphantly, then . . . a hand grabbed his arm.

Cara's breath caught in her throat and Klaida's mouth fell open.

"Tall Dancer, why do you interfere in this?" Klaida asked, slowly lowering the club.

"The host of so fine a potlatch would offer a guest the thing he desires most, Klaida," the tall warrior answered in a deep, satiny voice.

Cara tore her eyes away from the club and focused on the frightening mask in front of her. The front was the carved image of a man, his teeth bared in anger. A salmon with eyes of sparkling shell and teeth painted brilliant red sprawled across the figure's head.

"What of mine do you wish?" Klaida asked, relinquishing the club.

Tattoos of the raven and the whale covered the warrior's long, muscular legs. A brief bark apron hung from his waist to midthigh. Spidery tattoos covered the muscles that bulged from arms, and the skin of his thigh muscles strained against more inky images of whales and ravens. His chest, sprinkled with coarse black hair, was marked with romping otters and soaring eagles.

"I wish her." Tall Dancer dropped the club to the ground and pointed at Cara.

Klaida laughed nervously. "She will only bring you trouble, Tall Dancer. She is disobedient, and my wife beats her regularly."

He studied her wordlessly. Cara strained to assess this man bargaining for her life, but his eyes were hidden by the mask.

"She will obey me." His voice was rich with authority.

Cara peered closer. The warrior's black eyes snapped at her through the holes in the mask. Suddenly, he grabbed her wrist and hauled her against his chest. Grabbing a handful of her short, cropped hair, he yanked her head back.

Then he loosened his grip and his fingers glided down her neck, out onto her shoulders, and down her arm. His touch was gentle, warm, almost tender, yet he smelled of the urine men anointed their bodies with in honor of the potlatch celebration, a scent she had learned to hate.

Scratching and biting, she launched herself at his face. Caught off guard, he stumbled backward, and she bolted for the fringe of dense cedars beyond the firelight. She could smell the pungent scent of the deep forest when he grabbed her and spun her around. The eyes behind the mask now snapped with anger.

Gales of laughter and crude remarks erupted from behind him. He bent down, scooped her up, and tossed her over his shoulder. Her feet dangling, Cara kicked and squirmed and beat on the small of his back with both fists.

"Be still," he hissed in Russian, his fingers digging into her thighs.

Cara stopped, stunned. How did this Tlingit know Russian? Better yet, how did he know she spoke it?

"Are you sure you can handle her, Tall Dancer?"

Cara recognized Palina's voice and craned her head around to see the young woman approach them, her hips swaying suggestively.

"Yes. I have work for her," he answered.

Palina sidled closer. "She never obeyed me even though I beat her every day." She ran her hand down Tall Dancer's arm. "Will you train her like one of your sled dogs?" Another step and Palina pressed against Cara's legs and smiled slyly into Tall Dancer's face.

"If you two are through, put me down." Cara struggled against arms that tightened around her like an iron band.

"Be still," he hissed again in Russian.

"I won't be still. Put me down."

"If you don't be still, I'll—"

"You'll do what? Kill me?" Cara's head throbbed from hanging upside down.

Palina frowned. "What language is it you speak? It is no dialect I know."

Cara felt his muscles tense and knew she had gone too far. Why hadn't she just kept her mouth shut?

"She speaks the Da Nene. It is common near my people at Yakutat."

Palina paused for a moment, considering, then giggled and swayed off. Cara felt her captor relax, but his grip tightened and he strode toward the ceremonial ground. Would he kill her himself?

They passed the first line of long plank houses, and people tittered and made suggestive remarks. They reached what she judged to be the center of the village, and Cara was surprised when her captor entered a house crowded with people. Her head bounced as he plopped her onto her feet.

"Sit here." He shoved her to the ground near two raven totems that guarded the door. He yanked a thong of leather out of his belt, quickly encircled her wrists and ankles, then tied her to the totem. "Stay there," he ordered. Reaching down into a sealskin bag she hadn't noticed before, he pulled out a fringed dancing shirt and pulled it over his head.

"Dance for us, Tall Dancer," Klaida shouted from across the circle of people, the confrontation apparently forgotten.

The crowd echoed his words. Tall Dancer glared down at Cara, then padded to the center of the circle.

At the first strike of the drum, he crouched, and the drumbeats grew louder and quicker. With two feathered wings in his hand, he began to dip and weave. Hushed, the crowd sat spellbound while the fringed trim on his dancing shirt swirled around him. With his mask pulled low over his face, he became the terrible figure that grinned from the cedar wood crest on his forehead. Children in the front row huddled against their mothers and buried their faces in ample bosoms. The drum thumped louder and his dance became angry, demanding.

Each drumbeat shot through Cara as she watched, entranced by the story he wove with only arms and legs. The music built to a climax, and he danced faster and faster. Cara felt herself drawn into the dance, into the story, into him. With a jolt she realized her thoughts had drifted to the feel of his skin against hers, the pressure of his chest against her legs, the firm caress of his fingers.

The dance reached a crescendo with his last leap, and the house roared to life. Choking on the cloud of dust churned by the people rushing to congratulate him, Cara coughed and sputtered, wanting to hate him with each gasp.

Then he was beside her. He sliced through her bonds with a knife and unceremoniously threw her over his shoulder again.

"Are we always going to travel like this?" she asked, cringing as he ducked to pass through the low door. His only response was a grunt.

Watching the ground recede, she bobbed along until they approached the edge of the village. She raised her head to look forward, and his fingers bit into her.

"I just wanted to see where we were going."

He made no response, then kicked open the door of a long plank house guarded by two elaborate whale totem poles. He set her on her feet and pushed her into the blackness. She stumbled over a bundle and fell to her knees. The soft fur of pelts squeezed between her fingers.

Glancing over her shoulder, she saw he had moved inside, away from the doorway. She sprang for the opening. Splinters gouged under her nails as she dug into the rough wood.

Freedom was only inches away when he grabbed her shoulders and pulled her backward. Coarse male hair prickled her back and his breath ruffled her hair. He whirled her around, then firmly sat her down by a cold firepit.

Her chest heaving, she raised her gaze to the shadowy figure that stood over her, one leg on either side of her knees. Then he squatted down and she followed his gaze to the scars striping her legs.

Although she had long ago grown accustomed to wearing few clothes, she was suddenly overcome with modesty under his hot gaze. The meager rags that hung from her shoulders offered little covering for her body.

His hand touched her leg. She flinched away, but his fingers inched up her leg dangerously close to private areas. When he neared the edge of the material barely covering her hip, she lunged away again, but he grabbed her before she could clear the bed.

"Are you going to stay there, or do I have to tie you?"

His voice was rich, deep, and threatening as he spoke the Russian syllables. Easing back against the furs, she reassessed her enemy while he studied her leg. He was tall and powerful and could probably crush her with one hand.

How much about her did he know? How had he known she was Russian, and what was he going to do about it? He was Tsimshian or Tlingit, she guessed. That made them enemies— deadly enemies. Would he take her away, kill her somewhere away from the eyes of the village?

The edge of his breechcloth gave her an intimate view of firm thigh as he rose and whirled away. With dismay, Cara watched the sliver of light disappear with the closing of the door.

Total darkness, so deep she couldn't see her hands, surrounded her. Her senses heightened as she waited for some action from him. The acrid smell of long dead fires and the sharp scent of grease clung to the air.

Soft rustlings came from the firepit a few feet away. A tiny flame sputtered, illuminating two human palms cupped around the glow. Soft moss caught and filled the area with a fragrant smoke.

The hungry blaze grew until it lit the center of the windowless house. In the firelight, her new master squatted by the stone hearth, one knee supporting his weight. Head turned, he removed his mask and shook loose a mane of black, shoulder-length hair.

He stood and stared down at several packs at his feet. She was at his mercy. Maybe if she did what he expected, if she made his supper and readied his bed, maybe she could survive until the morning, then wait for another chance to escape. She scrambled to the fire, hands bound, and rummaged through the sealskin sacks for preparations for a meal.

His hand closed around her arm and he gently pulled her to her feet. The fire behind him flickered and caught larger wood. She stared into dark, ebony eyes sheltered by bushy black brows. Tiny bones dangled on a leather thong through one ear lobe. Slowly, the corners of his mouth lifted into a smile, softening the lines of his slim face.

"You do not have to do that," he rumbled. "You are not my slave."

"I'm not?" Cara searched his face, ready for a ruse. "But Klaida gave me to you."

Without answering, he gently guided her back to the pile of furs and firmly pressed on her shoulder, indicating for her to sit. If she wasn't his slave, then what was she? Cold fear again flooded through her as her gaze traveled up his body to his face. She closed her eyes against the fleeting images that flashed into her mind, images of another dark, close room and another naked male body.

"What are you going to do to me?" she squeaked.

"Feed you." He turned back toward the fire. Squatting down, he pulled a skin-wrapped bundle out of one of his packs. "How long have you been here with Klaida?"

"I don't know," she said, and shrugged. Cara's mind spun back over the past. The passing images, the many faces ran together in a collage of terror. She glanced at him.

His dark eyes studied her closely, watching for any flicker of an untruth, she imagined. She couldn't tell him who she was or where she came from. If he knew she was the daughter of the Butcher, he'd kill her before morning. She'd have to invent some story, some lie he would believe.

"Where were you captured?" he asked, opening the small parcel.

Cara's mind flew. "I don't know."

He cocked an eyebrow at her, then picked up a piece of dried salmon. "Was it inland? Along the coast?" He popped a piece in his mouth and chewed. Cara couldn't concentrate on her story for thinking about the food. Days had passed since she'd eaten.

"I told you, I don't know."

His fierce look made Cara sorry she had snapped. After all, she was in no position to anger this man.

"Were you captured by the Tsimshian?" he asked, rubbing his chin and frowning.

"No. The Haida. Then I was traded."

"To Klaida?"

She shook her head. "To another band. Then another." Too many memories and too much time made it impossible to explain. She closed her eyes and tears squeezed out from beneath her lids.

He held the dried salmon up, popped another piece in his mouth, then offered some to her. She snatched it out of his hand and crammed it into her mouth. Chewing slowly, she savored every bit of the strong fish flavor.

He ate another piece and offered her more. She grabbed every morsel for fear he would change his mind.

"Where are your people?" he asked.

Icy fear crept into Cara's veins. Her people were probably at Fort St. Michael, planning the end of the Tlingit nation. "They're all dead. Drowned in a shipwreck."

"Hmm." He stroked his chin and looked at the carved beams overhead. "I heard nothing about a shipwreck."

Cara swallowed, her eyes glued on the last piece of fish poised on his fingertips. She prayed God would give her an answer, just drop it into her head. The saliva in her mouth was choking her. "We were exploring along the coast when a storm blew in."

"Exploring what?" He handed her the last morsel.

"The coastline." She grabbed the fish and jammed it into her mouth.

"What is your name?"

Panic gripped her throat, making it impossible to swallow. "Cara."

He stared at her a moment, then stood, retrieved the mask and set it on his head. "I have to go back to the potlatch." Squatting down, he gently took her ankles and bound them with a soft leather thong. "I do not like to do this, but you must not escape." He tugged the strap and tightened the knot. "Too tight?" he asked.

Cara shook her head. Did he know she could easily untie the knot? Surely he did. Was this a trap? What would happen if she ran?

"There is extra wood within your reach. Water is there." Tall Dancer indicated a small wooden vessel at her side. "I will return later." He pushed to his feet and walked out of the light. Cold wind swept in as he opened the door, then closed it.

She sat for a few moments and listened to the wind buffeting the corners of the house. A storm was approaching, one the village had talked about for days. The shaman had predicted deep cold and heavy snow. Her chances of escape were diminishing.

Chanting and wailing filled the air around the village as Tall Dancer headed toward Klaida's house. A blast of wind whipped dry leaves around his feet and jingled the shells and bones attached to his dancing shirt. Wishing he had brought his bear fur, he wrapped his arms around himself.

What had he gotten himself into? What had possessed him to ask Klaida for such a pitiful slave, especially a Russian woman? He shook his head and wondered if Klaida knew he held one of the hated *promyshlenniki* in his very house. Probably not, or the girl would have been killed long ago.

Villagers huddled before the plank house the old chief shared with his new wife. Klaida's relatives were already ushering high-ranking individuals into the graduated wooden benches marching from the firepit to the roof of the house when Tall Dancer arrived. A man in a woven spruce hat directed him to a bench down near the front of the group. Klaida must have done much loaning this summer to have achieved all this wealth, Tall Dancer thought, eyeing the tall pile of blankets.

Then Klaida entered the area around the fire. He yanked aside the top blanket covering a mound of furs piled on the lowest bench. Carved dishes, mats, spoons carved from mountain goat horns, tobacco mortars, and shell jewelry loaded another bench.

Klaida strode to the front and vainly adjusted the tall headdress interwoven with spruce roots. Tall Dancer counted fifteen roots and chuckled. Klaida had given fifteen potlatches in his time, and this was Palina's first. The old man had done well to capture such a prize in a wife. There would be a baby to bounce by the fire before next winter if he were any judge, Tall Dancer thought, watching the way Klaida eyed his young wife.

"Friends, you all know my name," Klaida began, strutting back and forth. "You knew my father and his father before him. You know what they did with their property. They killed or gave away their slaves; they burned their war canoes in the fire of the feast house; they gave away all their blankets and cut to pieces all their sea otter skins, all their fine bearskins."

The guests rumbled and nodded.

"My father and his father before him were not common men," he continued. "They were true chiefs. I will not block the path of my father or his father. I am descended from my father, and he from his father."

Again, heads bobbed in agreement while Klaida traced his ancestors back through the generations. Tall Dancer watched the response. If Klaida had enemies here, they would contradict his lineage and revenge would be in order.

"I have many names and am linked to many tribes. I have many chiefs as ancestors. There are no lower chiefs in our family. Who can approach what was done by those chiefs, my ancestors?"

No one commented. Klaida went into another speech about his ancestors, and Tall Dancer's attention wandered from the monotonous tone. The trip back to his village would be a long one, but not long enough.

He sighed, thinking of the fate that awaited him. There were many furs to retrieve from his hiding places along the way. Then he, too, would be expected to give a potlatch in celebration of his marriage. He glanced back at Klaida, who had put his arm around his wife's waist and was already looking at her as if he wished he could make the other guests disappear.

Tall Dancer wished he could make his wife-to-be disappear. He shifted his position on the hard bench. Thoughts of Kaskoe made him uncomfortable. He hadn't seen her since she had been shut away with her grandmother two years ago. Even then, while still a child, Kaskoe had an evil disposition. *Has womanhood changed her?* Tall Dancer shifted again and gained a curious glance from the man beside him.

Palina walked across in front of her husband. She reached down and picked up a wooden bowl from a large stack. She told how she had worked many hours on the carving and hollowing out of the utensils. Tall Dancer's thoughts went back to the girl he had left in the house. He glanced at Palina's pile of jewelry and saw pieces made from braided red hair.

A queer pain shot through to his heart as Cara's face flashed before him. Dirty and disheveled, beaten and abused, she had found the spirit to stand off old Klaida and ruin his potlatch. Yet, standing there, her green eyes snapping with anger, she had struck a chord in him, something he had never felt before. *She's Russian,* he reminded himself. The thought dashed his lightened mood. Russian traders came to Tlingit territory for one thing—sea otter pelts. And they took them any way they could—trade, theft, or murder.

He shifted again, thinking of the women of these men standing at the railing of the tall ships, raising squares of cloth to their noses whenever the canoes full of Tlingit men came too close. Somehow Cara didn't fit that picture.

He thought back over their conversation. If a Russian ship had wrecked, surely he would have heard. That was something that would have been talked about, and rumors would have spread. No one he met had mentioned it. Even when he reached the Haida nation, there was no talk of a white slave.

The sound of feet plodding on wooden planks jerked him back to reality. Klaida was handing out the gifts. An old man from a neighboring clan received Klaida's prize possession, a huge, round copper worth many blankets. Someone shoved blankets into Tall Dancer's arms. Others piled spoons and mats on top. Jests about his upcoming marriage shot back and forth. Lastly, Palina handed him a necklace hung with an amulet of red hair.

Tall Dancer trudged back across the now empty grounds. The load of blankets shifted and he stumbled, then regained his balance. Pushing the door open with one foot, he dropped his load of gifts.

The fire had died to a few small flames and Cara lay curled in a ball on a huge bear pelt, the thong still around her ankles. He smiled. She could have easily untied it.

One fist tucked beneath her cheek, she slept fitfully, jerking and twitching. He moved quietly to her side, knelt down, and looked closely at her. Despite the obvious signs of abuse, her skin was smooth and pale. Dark lashes quivered on her cheeks, her lips parted, and she moaned softly.

"What did they do to you, little one?" Tall Dancer murmured, ruffling the stiff, ragged ends of her hair. He touched her cheek. *So soft.* He allowed his fingers to linger on her face. The warm scent of her swirled up as she moved in sleep, and he longed to lie down beside her.

The remains of her tattered dress had risen up to her thighs, exposing more scars crisscrossing her legs. Moving aside the rags that lay across her back, he found more ugly scars. Rocking back on his heels, he fingered the hair amulet and remembered Palina's expression when she gave him the necklace.

He pulled Cara's dress down and covered her with more furs, letting his fingers linger on the soft white skin of her neck. A woman of her courage was rare. Surely somewhere a man awaited her return.

Rising, he crossed his arms over his chest and moved toward the fire. What had made him interfere in her death? Was it her courage? He could explain his interference no other way. Whether or not Klaida killed his slaves was none of his concern.

But what would he do with her now? The thought struck him like a thunderbolt. The nearest Russian settlement was Fort St. Michael, more than a month away. He glanced over at her again as she turned in her sleep.

If he wanted to keep her alive, no one must guess her heritage. Skirmishes between the Russians and the Tlingits had intensified over the last several years as the *promyshlenniki* carved up the Tlingit's homeland, claiming all land, game, and furs for themselves.

At the door his packs sat, ready to leave tomorrow. He'd have to take her back to his village and keep her there until next fall. He sighed. By then he'd be married.

Chapter Two

Soft movements woke Cara. Tall Dancer gathered his belongings and stuffed them into one of his packs. He still wore the dancing shirt trimmed in beads and shells, and a long furry robe hung across his shoulders. Cara glanced down. A blanket lay across her that had not been there when she went to sleep.

Smoke filled the house as he kicked sand over the embers.

"You're awake," he said, straightening.

Motionless, Cara watched him come toward her. He extended his hand, but she did not take it. With a soft sigh, he grabbed her forearm and pulled her to her feet. Reaching into his pack, he produced a long, narrow strap. Rolling the leather nervously between his fingers, he hesitated, then looped it around her neck.

"I'm sorry," he whispered and tightened the knot. Slinging his pack across one shoulder, he started forward. Cara set her heels and hauled back against him.

"Come," he commanded and gave her another yank.

She stumbled out into the light of a frigid, snow-covered morning. On the porch of the house, snow piled six inches against the wall. In the forest beyond, morning sun crowned every tree branch with jewels. The wind promised more snow.

Tall Dancer jerked on her arm, sending her stumbling down the steps and into knee-deep snow. She floundered, trying to step in his wide tracks. The bottoms of her bare feet were soon numb, and her steps faltered.

Klaida's guests were beginning to filter out of their houses, calling good-byes to each other. Tall Dancer pulled on her arm insistently, hurrying her along. As they neared the edge of the village, Klaida and his wife came outside. Tall Dancer stopped in front of them and abruptly gave Cara a rough shove that sent her stumbling. When she regained her footing, she yanked hard on the strap. He stopped his conversation and leveled a chilling look at her.

Palina regarded her with a disapproving stare, then lowered her lashes and turned her gaze on Tall Dancer. They talked, and Cara stared at her feet, catching an occasional word of the rapid conversation. Then Palina and Klaida turned and reentered their house. Tall Dancer gave a quick yank on her leash, and she staggered behind him as he hurried her along to the outskirts of the village. All the pleasant thoughts she had had of him since waking fled.

Leaving the well-trodden path, they pushed into a thicket covered with rapidly thickening snow. The brush shook, and something in the tangle whined. Cara stopped and strained against the thong, which was tied securely around his waist.

Tall Dancer parted the brush and silvery forms leaped out at him. Cara shrank behind him in fear. Her memory instantly flashed to the timber wolves she had seen, how they chased and caught their game, ripping it to shreds with their sharp, white teeth.

Pushing more of the brush aside, he revealed a sled in the depth of the thicket. While the dogs leaped up on him and licked his face, he wrestled the sled out into the open and threw his packs and furs into it.

In a few minutes, he had the dogs harnessed. He threw an old fur across Cara's shoulders and, without a word, stepped on the runners and spoke to the team. They lunged forward, nearly jerking Cara off her feet. Both hands grasping the collar around her neck, she ran behind to keep up. She lost the blanket at the edge of the camp, but couldn't stop to recover it.

He neither looked back nor spoke to her until they had lost sight of the village. Then he pulled the sled to an abrupt stop and scooped her up in his arms. His warmth felt good for the instant he held her before dumping her into the sled and covering her with furs. Offering no explanation, he again stepped on the runners and spoke to the team.

The sun had climbed high in the overcast sky before they stopped again. His hair, soft as spun silk, brushed across her cheek as he bent over her. "I'm sorry I had to do this," he said, removing the strip of leather from around her neck. His rough fingers massaged skin that burned to the touch. "Are you all right?"

Cara eyed him suspiciously. "My feet burn."

He looked at her toes, then scooped up handfuls of snow and massaged her feet. "Is that better?" he asked, rolling each toe between his fingers.

The intimacy of the action caught her off guard and she tried to yank her foot away, but he held it firm.

"I had to convince Klaida and Palina you were my slave, or they might have killed you anyway."

Why is he helping me? she wondered, fighting the warm feeling his gentle touch was awaking. "Why did you ask for me if I am not your slave?"

"I do not keep slaves," he snapped and stood.

With long strides, he went to the head of his dog team. He squatted, smiled, and spoke to each animal, all the while picking up and examining every paw. Cara snuggled deeper into the nest of furs and pulled them up around her chin, studying the mysterious man and wondering if he would make her walk.

She expected him to speak to her, but instead he stepped onto the runners, spoke softly to the dogs, and they were off again.

* * *

They traveled until dusk, when he stopped the sled, unloaded his packs, and ducked beneath the branches of a group of young cedars. He left her in the furs while he cut down feathery branches and piled them against a wooden frame for a shelter. The wind whined through the trees around them, and spits of snow fell as tiny frozen balls. He scraped the snow away from beneath the shelter, laid down a layer of dried leaves, then spread furs over them.

"We're in for a blizzard tonight," he explained, draping skins across the top and down the sides to the ground. He paused and looked at the sky, where gray, boiling clouds hurried by. "How are your feet?" He pulled aside the furs covering her and cupped her foot in his hand. "Still cold?"

He crouched down and rubbed her foot with more wet snow. "Tonight I will make you boots."

She watched his hands kneading her feet, felt the gentleness in his touch. Closing her eyes, she let the warmth he generated move up her legs and into the rest of her body. How long had it been since someone had touched her gently?

When her skin glowed bright pink, he stopped, shook the snow off his hands, and lifted her into his arms. Snowflakes fell on his shoulders and melted into wet droplets on his sealskin shirt. Heat from his body warmed her as he moved quickly to the shelter. The dried leaves crunched as he laid her on the bed of furs, then ducked back outside.

Through the opening of the furs, Cara watched the snowfall soften into occasional flakes. Tall Dancer quickly made a fire and skinned a rabbit he had caught earlier. The sweet meat sizzled and popped and dripped grease onto the flames. She was so hungry her stomach felt hollow by the time he crawled under the cedar canopy and handed her half. Aware that he watched her, she tore into the meal like an animal.

"How long were you with the Haida?" he asked suddenly.

Cara slowed her chewing. Her mind whirled. He was trying

to trick her. She was so tired, he might succeed if she wasn't on her toes. "A few months."

"And then you were traded?"

"Yes."

"To the Athabaskans?"

"Yes."

"Traded outright. No potlatch?"

Cara carefully went over her previous answers. "Yes. No potlatch."

He chewed in silence and Cara watched him from the corner of her eye. Why was he so persistent? Did he suspect she was lying?

He finished his meal, carefully licked away the grease, then rose and left the shelter. Cara sat in the furs and waited—for what, she didn't know. Darkness fell rapidly. The snowfall diminished, and the wind died. She peeped outside and looked up at a hazy waning moon obscured occasionally by drifting clouds.

Out in the forest, there was no sign of him. No tracks, no sound, only the cracking and sputtering of the fire's fight for life against the snow.

Slowly, she let the fur drop back into place and realized for the first time how tired she was. Pillowing her cheeks with her hands, she lay down and slept.

Tall Dancer ruffled Buck's fur where he lay in a hollow in the snow. The big dog rolled his eyes up, but didn't move his muzzle from the furry protection of his tail. Sure his team would weather the storm, Tall Dancer pulled his leather pack from his sled and returned to the circle of firelight. All was quiet. He pulled back the fur cover. She was fast asleep.

Dropping his pack by the fire, he threw on another branch. The wood crackled and hissed and popped off a shower of sparks as he placed a bag of water close to the flames and dropped the fur from around his shoulders. Pulling his shirt over his head, he poured a little of the cold water in his hand,

and splashed it across his chest. Some of the tattoos on his arms melted away, but a large, black picture of Raven remained splayed on his shoulder and across his chest. Watching the soot trickle down his body, he smiled, thinking of his mother's horror when he had refused to be permanently tattooed like the other boys.

The bark apron slipped easily to the ground, and he stood naked before the fire's heat. The bite of cold felt good against his skin. Stretching his arms over his head, he strained to touch the stars above. The shallow snowfall had taken some of the bite out of the wind, and he put off dressing. Crossing his arms over his chest, he stood by the fire, letting it warm him in front while the cold nipped at his back.

Glancing down at his body, he thought of the Russian blood running through his veins and felt a surge of anger, then a stab of guilt. His father had been a good man, one who saw the corruption the *promyshlenniki* were bringing to the Tlingits but was powerless to stop their invasion.

Cara moaned in her sleep and a sudden blast of cold air bit into his back. He picked up the small skin bag of water and sloshed more onto a piece of soft skin. He watched it roll down his arms and spill across his tattooed chest. Rivulets of water ran down his legs, where whales were etched into his skin.

Raising one hand, he sniffed his forearm. Finally, the last scent of urine was gone. He hated that custom more than any of the others associated with a potlatch, he thought, shrugging into a set of worn sealskin pants and running his palms down the smooth leather.

A howling wind whipped the snow into a low fog. He grabbed his long fur coat and crawled into the shelter with Cara. She slept buried beneath wolverine skins, her back now to the opening. One hand gripped the edge of a hide. Tall Dancer propped his head on his hand and watched the rhythmic rise and fall of her side.

What would his mother say when he brought her home to their village? He had no other choice except to pretend she was his property. Going back to Fort St. Michael meant retracing his steps, going back to the far end of his trapping territory, missing the summer fishing season, and putting his mother's supply of food at risk for the coming year. No, he couldn't take her there now. She'd have to wait until next year. Then he'd take her to the settlement and see she got home—wherever that was.

He reached down, touched her tortured hair, and thought how beautiful she must have once been. He let the hairs slide through his fingers, imagining what it must have been like when it was long and silky. She sighed and snuggled close to his warmth.

Blue circles shadowed her eyes and long lashes rested on her cheeks. She kicked one leg out from beneath the furs, revealing the ugly, puckering scar he had seen last night. Tall Dancer sat up, frowned, and traced the scar with one finger. What could have caused such an injury? How had she survived?

Beneath her lids, her eyes moved rapidly. Her lips pursed and every few seconds she whimpered. Each mewl went straight to his heart as she struggled with her nightmare.

He leaned down and gently kissed her forehead. She murmured and moved closer. He kissed her again, moving down to her cheek, painfully aware of the reaction of his body. The urge to take her into his arms was suddenly overwhelming. She frowned and mumbled.

His arms were nearly around her when her eyes flickered open. She stared straight at him for a moment, then her eyes drifted shut and she sighed in her sleep.

Tall Dancer lay back, her head nestled on his shoulder, her breast warm against his side. He wanted her, no sense in denying it. He had never wanted a woman the way he wanted her.

In fact, there had been no other woman. He was a virgin, as chaste as the maidens of his village now shut away with their grandmothers and aunts learning the art of womanhood. He was years past marrying age, and the dirty, drunken whores at Fort St. Michael had held no attraction for him. Then his inexperience hadn't mattered. Now it did.

Carefully, he removed Cara's head from his shoulder and sat up. Clasping his knees with his arms, he shook his head.

What a mess he had gotten himself into. Had he thought he could come home to the village with her in tow and everyone would understand his need for a beautiful slave? Had he thought the elders would understand? They wouldn't. They would expect him to give her away and honor his impending arranged marriage.

Cara awoke to a stiff wind whipping snow against the cedar boughs over her head. She peeped over the edge of the furs covering her. At her side lay the big bearskin he had worn yesterday. She pulled aside the skin covering the shelter's entrance. A man in sealskins sat huddled by the fire, his shoulders hunched against the wind. She glanced out at the forest, assessing her chances for escape. Gentle though he was, he was, after all, a man.

As if in response to her thoughts, he turned. "I see you're awake. Are you hungry?" He smiled.

Cara stared at him, unsure for a moment he was the same man. The eerie tattoos had been replaced by smooth, light brown skin. She frowned. Was he Kolosh?

She drew her legs beneath the furs, reluctant to give up her warm nest. But the aroma of roasting meat wafted on the air before it was snatched away by the wind. He watched her for a moment, then rose abruptly and left the fire, returning in a few moments with a skinned rabbit, which he held over the flames.

Cara crept from the furs, keeping one pulled around her, and sat down by the firepit. The woods beyond were a blur, and the snow was deeper by several inches from last night. Everywhere tree branches sparkled.

Tall Dancer removed the meat from over the fire. Cara didn't wait for him to take it off the stick. She grabbed it out of his hand. He watched her with a smile on his face, but she didn't care if he laughed at her. Licking her fingers for every trace of grease, she devoured the meat and sucked the bones clean.

"What are you going to do with me?" she asked. Her tongue flicked the last morsel off her finger.

Tall Dancer raised his head and looked at her, then lowered his eyes. "I'm going to take you with me to my mother's village."

Fear niggled at the edge of her consciousness as she felt the question well up in her. "Are you Kolosh?"

"Yes," he answered.

Panic rose in Cara. Vivid memories of death rained on the Kolosh by her father flashed into her mind.

"Do you live there, too?"

Again, he avoided her eyes. "Part of the year. The other part I trap."

"Will I be your slave there?"

He smiled, crinkling the corners of his dark eyes. "You will not be my slave either here or there."

"Then how will you explain me?"

His eyes darted away from her face and panic rekindled in her. Something about the situation wasn't right. What was he hiding?

"I do not know, but we will worry about that later. You will stay with us until next fall. Then I will take you to Fort St. Michael, where there are other *tsatyka*."

Cara frowned and looked him over, from his brown hair to his light skin. "You're white, aren't you?"

Her words hit him like a thunderbolt. Except for his height, he had always passed for Tlingit, though no one at Fort St. Michael knew that. The Russians there tolerated him, assuming he was another Russian hunter of unknown background, taking advantage of the bounty available. If they knew he was half Kolosh, they wouldn't be so eager to take him into their confidence.

"Half. My mother is Tlingit. My father was Russian."

His voice had changed when he mentioned his father, and sweat dampened her palms. She couldn't go back to her father and she couldn't go into a Tlingit village. Although Tall Dancer seemed tolerant of her background, probably because of his own, that didn't mean the other members of the village would be.

She certainly couldn't survive alone. Anyone she might contact in the wilderness would take her captive. It was hopeless.

He turned his face away from the fire, and she seized the chance.

Scrambling to her feet, she grabbed the bear pelt and plunged toward the forest. The deep snow slowed her steps, and she knew her flight was useless, but desperation drove her on. Behind her, she heard curses, then a crack and another string of oaths. Glancing back over her shoulder, she saw him fall backward and lie still.

Once the camp was out of sight, she knew she was lost. Thick snow had changed the appearance of everything. She lost her bearings and wandered aimlessly. *Where will I get food? Why didn't I wait and stash away food and at least a knife?*

The hours of the short day passed as she stumbled on. Darkness lowered like a curtain and the cold deepened. Numb from the toes up, Cara sighted a thicket of small cedars. Something scurried out when she crawled in, but she willed herself not to think of what might be sharing her shelter. Inside, only a dusting of snow covered the thick mat of leaves and needles. Wrapping the pelt around her, she burrowed into the leaves.

An owl's lonely hoot awoke her. The moon that had been just above the horizon was now straight overhead, and the stillness of predawn pervaded the forest.

An eerie feeling crept over her, and the hair along the nape of her neck stood up. Something moved outside her hiding place, something that stealthily and deliberately circled.

She sat up and put her hand down on a small, furry object. It squealed and darted away. The thing outside galloped in pursuit. Cara stood and parted the thicket in time to see a wolf catch and snap the rabbit's neck in the bright moonlight.

Tears welled up in her eyes. The rabbit had sought protection the same as she, and she had given away its hiding place.

Covering her ears to shut out the sound of cracking bones,

she sat back down in the thicket. Something else warm and furry brushed against her bare leg. Another rabbit. She squinted in the faint light and saw several of the creatures cowering amongst the leaves.

Just as she was wondering if the wolf would come back, soft steps rustled the leaves outside. The wolf moved closer and snuffled at the bushes separating them, seeking a way through. Then the sounds stopped behind her. Something was shoving its way through the undergrowth. He was coming in! Realizing that it was the rabbits attracting him, she sprang to her feet and dashed into the open, praying he wouldn't follow.

Blood spattered across the churned mantle of snow beneath her feet as she dashed in the only clear direction. She heard the relentless thud of the wolf behind her. Her breath came in gasps, but still he gained on her. Branches tore at her face and bare arms. She dropped the pelt, hoping to confuse him and buy herself enough time to escape, but he didn't give the skin a sniff.

She rounded a thicket of cranberry bushes, and another wolf, a silvery one with large yellow eyes, stepped into her path. She slid to a stop and turned. The first wolf saw the second and slowed his pace to a jarring trot, but didn't stop.

Cara threw her hand over her mouth and screamed. The silver wolf bunched his muscles and lunged at his opponent.

The two animals collided in mid air, each struggling to grip the other's throat. They churned the snow and filled the still forest with terrible growls and yelps. The first wolf wrestled the second to the ground, his teeth tightly clamped around a foreleg.

A blur raced past her. Ax drawn, Tall Dancer swung at the first wolf, catching it in the rib cage. Yelping in pain, the animal flew through the air and landed a few feet away, jerked once, then was still.

Tall Dancer approached the other wolf and Cara recognized Buck, the lead sled dog. Tall Dancer knelt, and the dog rolled to his feet and hopped to his master, head hung in misery.

After running his hands through the dog's fur, he stood and

looked in Cara's direction. His face contorted in anger, his eyes snapping fire, he stepped toward her. She backed away until a pile of fallen branches was at her back.

He came nearer, and Cara snaked her arm behind her, feeling the wall of limbs. Her fingers closed around a dead branch. It broke free easily, and she hid it behind her back.

"What were you thinking?" he asked through gritted teeth. "You have no food, no weapon. You are stupid, ignorant like the rest of the *tsatyka.*" He spat the words and reached for her.

A scream tore from her throat as his hands closed around her shoulders. She raised the piece of wood hidden behind her and slammed it into his side. As she whirled, she heard the breath go out of his body, and he fell to his knees.

Intending to flee again, Cara took two steps before the pain in her arm flooded her. He had grabbed the last scar Palina had inflicted, a deep jagged cut that had failed to heal properly. Bright spots danced on the surface of the snow, and her vision tunneled in. Soft coolness rubbed her face as she sank into it.

Vlad Tarakanov paced the sea-drenched deck of his ship anchored in the harbor at Fort St. Michael. Snowflakes pelted him as the wind whipped the snow into a blizzard. The ship moaned and rolled beneath the onslaught of the storm. He paused by the rail and searched the murky night for a light.

Where is Baranov? He scanned the low fog that obscured the shore. The governor of the Russian-American Company had better learn to keep his appointments, Tarakanov thought, again scanning the fog for the governor's boat.

A dim light appeared off the bow. Bobbing and dipping with the angry sea, a lone *baidarka* emerged from the fog. Two Aleut men, one hunched low in the front and another in the back, pulled on the paddles, laboring against the wind. The small craft stopped alongside, and Tarakanov tossed over a rope ladder.

Between the two Aleuts stood a man swathed head to foot in fur. The boat shifted and he braced his legs apart to keep from pitching overboard. Stumbling, he reached for the rope and stepped on the first rung.

A large wave shoved the *baidarka* from the side of the large ship and left the man dangling in space. Tarakanov reached over the rail, grasped the man's forearm, and hauled him aboard.

Aleksandr Baranov threw one leg over the rail and tumbled to the deck. Quickly, he stood and shoved his fur hat away from his face. "Damned *Aliaska* weather," he cursed, reaching out to shake Tarakanov's hand.

Tarakanov smothered a smile at the sight of the governor of the Russian-American Company floundering around on his deck like a landed salmon. Well-decorated and well-compensated by the homeland, Baranov was the darling of the tsar—for the moment. Word was that Baranov was meeting problems with the native population. *Handling them too easy,* Tarakanov thought as he looked into the little man's eyes. "Have you any news of my daughter?" he asked.

Baranov shook his head. "No. My men have found nothing. No one has seen a red-haired girl. I fear she is lost."

"Bitch," Tarakanov swore under his breath. "Perhaps you could send out another search party," he suggested, watching Baranov's eyes dart to the door leading down into the warmth of the ship's belly.

"I don't know." He hesitated, again glancing toward the door.

"Would you like to go below and join me in a drink of vodka? We can discuss this further."

"Yes," Baranov answered, sidling toward the cabin. "I'll think about it while we drink."

Tarakanov ushered the governor down the steps and into his cabin. A single lamp burned, throwing a dirty yellow light against bleak walls. Maps and papers littered the floor and the desk. Hastily, Tarakanov poured two glasses of vodka and handed one to Baranov, who removed his gloves and snatched the glass away, then emptied it in one gulp. Wiping his mouth on his otter fur sleeve, he handed the glass back to Tarakanov.

"I must insist you search again for my daughter, Governor,"

Tarakanov said, refilling the glass. "The sea was calm, although cold, and she is a strong swimmer. I can't sleep thinking of her in the clutches of some savage."

Baranov sipped the second glass slowly. "Perhaps I could send some men to Ska-out-lelt's village. His is the nearest. Perhaps she crawled ashore and found her way there, although God help her if she's in the clutches of the Kolosh."

"I hope that is true." Tarakanov lifted his glass in salute.

"Tell me, Vlad, why did you bring your daughter here?"

Tarakanov raised his eyes and saw that Baranov stared directly at him. What did he know? Had some of his men talked? Hardly, he told himself, if they valued their lives. "There was no one I trusted to leave her with," he said with a shrug.

"Her mother is dead, then?"

Again, Baranov stared at him and the room seemed smaller.

"Yes. She died when Cara was very young."

"And your daughter has accompanied you on every voyage since then?"

Where was this questioning going? "She has sailed with me since she was not much more than a child."

"Well." Baranov set his glass on the table. "How did she fall overboard if the sea was calm?"

Tarakanov itched to loosen the neck of his shirt. "That, Governor, is a mystery. She went up on deck for some reason. One of the crew saw her standing alongside the rail looking out over the sea. Then she was gone."

"No splash? No one went in after her?"

Tarakanov moved around the desk until he stood at the governor's side. "No, the men did not hear her go overboard."

"Odd," Baranov said, stroking his chin. "It almost seems she slipped away for some reason, doesn't it?"

Tarakanov searched the governor's face. "Why would someone dive into these frigid waters of their own accord?"

"Why would a young woman *want* to go ashore alone in this savage land?" Baranov questioned.

Tarakanov shrugged. "She is headstrong and had been nagging me to take her ashore to see the savages. Perhaps she decided to go on her own.''

''Or maybe she was running away from something.'' Again, the governor leveled that steady gaze at him. ''Have you sent men to look for her?''

''Yes. They scoured the coast the next morning and found nothing.''

Baranov set the fur hat back on his head. ''I must say, you don't seemed overly upset.''

''I have been worried sick about her, Governor, but now I must consider the possibility she drowned. After all, why would she leave the safety and warmth of her home and go abroad in a strange and dangerous land?'' Tarakanov watched Baranov glance quickly around the dirty, cluttered cabin. ''The water was freezing and the wind would have snatched her very life away were she wandering about in wet clothes. No, she fell overboard. I only held out hope she would be found alive.'' Tarakanov ducked his head and hoped he looked heartbroken.

''I will send out another party in the morning.'' Baranov emptied the second glass, set it on the table, and covered the top with his hand, indicating he had had enough. ''I have another matter to discuss with you, and I regret having to bring it up at this time.''

Tarakanov cursed silently and raised his face.

''It is about your treatment of the Kolosh. Another group of them came to the fort today and complained your men robbed their village and raped their women.''

Tarakanov poured himself another drink and gritted his teeth. ''The men refused to hunt for me. You know the rules.''

''I agree we can't let them think they have the upper hand for one moment, but we can't tyrannize them as you have. They will fight back eventually, and I don't want a war. I want the settlement of Fort St. Michael by our people to be orderly and without violence.''

Tarakanov hated the condescending tone the governor used with him. ''Violence is the only thing they will understand.'' He turned from the table and paced the room to control his temper. "I beg your pardon, Governor, but must I remind you that it is ships' captains like myself who are out among the Kolosh every day, and not yourself?"

Baranov's face reddened as he yanked on his gloves and turned to leave. He stopped at the door, one hand on the latch. "You are sure you have told me the truth about the girl?"

"Yes. Every word."

"And you will speak to your men?"

"Yes, yes."

Baranov raised the door latch and paused in the hallway. "Do you know what they call you?" He nodded toward a carved mask hung at a tilted angle on the wall.

Tarakanov shook his head.

"The Butcher. And I expect you have earned the title."

Chapter Three

Cara opened one eye to study the tangled branches over her head. Confusion clouded her thoughts as vivid memories of the wolves flashed into her mind. The last thing she could remember was cold snow sliding into her mouth and nose. Where was she, and how had she gotten here?

Someone moved next to her, brushing against her skin. The musky odor of sealskin mingled with the sharp smell of cedar wood, and someone placed a warm cloth on her wounded forearm. Blinking to focus better, she recognized the shelter. Tall Dancer leaned over her, his black eyes watching her intently while he held a compress to her arm.

She jerked away, flailing out at him, and he winced and whitened. Her gaze traveled down his body to his bare waist, surrounded by a soft skin strapped in place with thongs.

"I know now why Klaida was so quick to let you go," he said, easing himself backward out of the shelter.

She watched through the flap as he hobbled toward the fire and placed the skin into a steaming basket, wrung it out, and turned back toward her. A half-remembered image flashed before her, a foggy dream of a naked man standing before the fire. His muscles had rippled as he stretched his arms over his head, the copper flames reflecting against the perfect dark hue of his skin. He turned, revealing a magnificent raven tattoo that spread across his shoulder and down his chest.

"It's a whiteout," he said, ducking back inside the shelter, shaking loose the icy particles that clung to his hair. "The wind picked up about an hour ago." Groaning, he dropped to his knees and crawled inside.

"How did I get here?" she asked, again eyeing his middle.

"I carried you." He placed the poultice on her arm again.

"Like that?" She pointed to the wrap.

"If I had not carried you, we both would have frozen." His answer was simple and flat. She studied his face, trying to guess the extent of his anger.

"We will have to stay here until the storm passes." He nodded, indicating the thickening snow outside. Then he stretched out beside her, his body skimming against hers. All was silent except for the soft pat of snowflakes.

"Your father," she said, sliding a little farther away. "Tell me about him." Anything was better than silence.

He opened his eyes and shifted to face her. For a moment he did not speak, then he sighed and shifted his gaze up to the roof. "Long ago when the *promyshlenniki* first came to Tlingit land, his ship came to trade with our people."

The soft glow of anger returned to his eyes, and Cara felt a prick of fear. "You say 'our' people, as though you are not part of him."

With a grunt, he turned onto his side and propped up his cheek with his palm. "Vasili Zaikov was a good man, not like the rest of the greedy *tsatyka.*"

Cara closed her eyes against bloody memories of her father's conquests: dozens of Tlingits slain on the beaches, their blood slowly draining into the sand.

"At first, we were glad to see the Russians. They brought beads and copper pots in return for our pelts."

He paused as if waiting for her to say something. When she didn't, he continued. "Then they became greedy. Trading for our pelts was too slow to please their chiefs. They came ashore and hunted themselves, took too many of our otters and seals. Soon there were none left for us.''

Her father's hold was always full of the otter skins he referred to as ''gold.''

''Father was once one of the *promyshlenniki* who hunted our coasts and killed our people. He did not like what the *tsatyka* were doing. One day during a hunt, he hid in the forest and did not return to the ship. Eventually, after much hard work, he was adopted into our clan, married my mother, and I was born. They decided to raise me here.''

''What happened to him?'' Cara inched further away as his breath stirred her hair.

''He was killed years later by hunters.''

He closed his eyes and Cara saw the skin tighten over his jaw. Anger edged his words with tightness. Who were these people to whom he was taking her? Did they hate the Russians as much as he? Did death await her there?

Tall Dancer opened his eyes and watched the emotions playing across Cara's face. Even in the dark, her eyes were suspicious, as wary as those of a trapped animal, and he understood her fear. He was taking her into the very heart of a people who wished all Russians dead. With each passing year, his people's hatred of the Russians grew. As he stared into her frightened green eyes, the desire to protect her became overwhelming.

''What will happen when we get to your village?'' Her voice was barely a squeak over wind that had angered from a sigh into a howl.

He had put off thinking about arriving at his village for several reasons. He had not yet figured out how he would explain Cara's presence to his uncle Noisy Feather, or to his mother. He would have to convince them she was his slave. That would be his only explanation for letting her live. Somehow, before they reached home, he would have to win her trust and convince her to go along with his plan.

The other reason would not be so easily solved. His marriage had been arranged many years ago. The union was not to his liking, but both families would suffer if he were to refuse to take Kaskoe as his bride. He reached over Cara and lifted the flap.

As he stared out into the whirling snow, he tried to envision Kaskoe's face. He remembered her as a child who never laughed, who ordered other children around, who never participated with the others. He could only guess at the woman she had become.

For the last two years, she had been shut away with her grandmother, whose task it was to instruct her on the passage from childhood into womanhood. She was of one of the highest ranked families. She would be a good match for him, except for the fact he did not love her.

"What will happen when we reach your village?" Cara asked again.

Her voice jerked him back to reality. "I do not know." The fear in her eyes wrenched at his heart. "I am going home to be married."

Cara jumped up, banging the cedar boughs and loosing a fine sifting of snow onto their heads. "I'll take my chances out here." Fists clenched, she shrieked at him over the voice of the storm. "I won't have another mistress like Palina."

Her sudden reaction took him by surprise. "I will take you to my mother," he soothed, grasping her arm. "You can live with her until the fall."

Cara's face whitened and he eased his hold. "No." She shook her head violently. "Take me to the white settlement."

"I can't. It would take us a month to reach it. Another month back. I would miss the summer gathering, and my mother would suffer for it."

"So I'm to be your gift to your new wife. Is that it?" Her green eyes blazed her anger. "I won't do it, I tell you! I don't care how much you beat me. Death would be better than another master."

Sadly, he watched her rant at him, her eyes filled with tears, her hair standing up all over her head in little irregular tufts. How he wished he could make her believe he would set her free. Until then, she needed his protection. One look at her face told him she'd never understand his words. Only deeds would impress her.

Hours later, the storm still raged. The sun had been a light disk behind the curtain of blowing snow all day. Now it was an orange glow low over the horizon. Tall Dancer left the shelter once to check on his dogs and stoke the fire, then quickly returned, concerned about Cara.

She had fallen into an exhausted sleep when her anger was spent. Curled into a ball and covered with skins, she shivered, and he worried she was not warm enough, that the wind whistling in through the branches of their shelter would freeze her before his eyes.

As night closed in around them for a second time, she roused herself from sleep and sat cross-legged in front of him. Dim light filtered in from the campfire, highlighting the spikes of hair covering her head. What kind of hell had she been through? His fingers found the amulet around his neck and caressed the strands of braided red hair. He reached toward her, and she jerked away.

"Let me cut your hair all one length so it will grow back at the same time." His hand touched her hair and she trembled, but didn't jerk away. Her eyes were locked on his, telling him she would meet whatever he had in store for her with as much courage as when she had challenged Klaida.

Gently, he moved his hand across the sharp spikes. "I won't hurt you."

Tears filled Cara's eyes as she fought the impulse to enjoy his gentleness, but experience whispered in her ear. He was not to be trusted; she had to remember that above all else. Still, he hadn't tried to hurt her—yet.

She pulled her attention back to his face. His eyes followed hers, watching her closely, but no malice gleamed in them, none of the lust she had seen in other men's eyes. She closed her eyes for a moment, diverting her attention to his hand running through her hair, his skin caressing hers.

Just as she relaxed, his hand faltered and slowed. Her eyes snapped open. In his hand gleamed his war knife. She slapped his wrist, sending the weapon flying, then she leaped at him, knocked him to his back, and straddled him. He caught her wrists as she attempted to claw his face.

"Wait! I was going to cut your hair." Tall Dancer glanced over their heads. The shelter teetered precariously. Laden with snow, its strength was tenuous enough, but her sudden movements had knocked loose one of the supports.

Hands flailing, she came at him again, pure malice in her eyes. With a loud crack, the cedar boughs came crashing down, covering them with needles and snow.

Cara scrambled from underneath the wreckage. Snow pelted down, drenching her hair. He crawled out and rose to stand beside her. Recoiling in anticipation, she waited for him to strike her, but he didn't.

In fact, he didn't say a word, only gave her one of his dark looks, turned, and began to reassemble the shelter. She sat down on a log by the fire and watched him jerk branches out from beneath the pile while snow whitened his dark hair.

Maybe, she thought with a twinge of guilt, she had been too hasty. He'd had plenty of chances to hurt her and hadn't. Maybe he *had* intended to cut her hair. Her hand went to the top of her head, and she fingered her tortured locks again. No, no man bore that amount of compassion.

He shook the snow out of the pelts and spread them back beneath the new shelter. She could tell he was furious by the set of his back, and her heartbeat rose when he squatted down in front of her. Gently, he took one of her hands in his and looked into her face. "I'm sorry I frightened you. I thought if I cut your hair, it would grow back even and you would feel better."

The sincerity in his voice startled her. His eyes were warm and friendly, and something in her relaxed a bit.

"I promise you I will not hurt you. I only want to return

you to your people, but you must come with me until then. Do you understand?''

She nodded, and he kneaded her fingers.

"I have an idea of what you've been through."

She watched his face and believed he did know.

"And I will do nothing to remind you of that."

She nodded again. "Can we go back inside now?"

He stood and led her to the opening. Dropping to her knees, she crawled in, and he followed. She lay down on the furs and he lay down behind her. Outside, the wind howled and the snow pelted. Occasionally, the fire snapped and popped. Their breaths came in unison, easing into relaxation with this uncomfortable compromise.

But his breaths did not slide into the rhythm of sleep and she knew he lay awake, as she did. Turning over, she faced him. His dark lashes rested on his cheeks and his long, straight fingers stretched out on the fur at his side. Cara touched the back of his hand, feeling the coarse black hair against her skin. He didn't move. Their combined body heat warmed the little shelter, and she felt her lids droop. Carefully, she laced her fingers with his.

Cara stretched and opened her eyes. The spot next to her was empty, but the fur bore the imprint of his body. She rolled over and peeped out of the flap. The day was clear and still. The wind had stopped, and a foot of new snow lay on the ground. Today they would leave for Tall Dancer's village. Apprehension tightened her throat.

Sharp barks echoed through the forest and she crawled out and peeped over the edge of the shelter. Tall Dancer stood in the woods feeding his dogs pieces of a rabbit he had snared. They jumped and leaped around him, snatching bits of meat from his fingers. A cold chill crept over her. The white dogs the Haida had kept for their fur were wild and had snapped and bit at her when she fed them. More frightening still were the timber wolves—beautiful phantoms of the night. She watched

Buck hobble forward for a piece of meat, limping on legs wounded defending her.

As Tall Dancer waded through the snow, she recalled how he had looked the night of the potlatch—a head taller than any other warrior, his voice steady and gentle as he stopped Klaida from killing her. Like the timber wolves, he, too, was a wild thing, as easily at home in the forest as in the center of a potlatch.

"They won't hurt you," he called. "Come pet them."

Cara shook her head.

"We will be together for many days. You should get used to them."

He had a point. Clutching his fur coat around her, Cara reluctantly moved toward the team. When she neared, they ran to her and began to sniff at her hands—all except Buck.

"They recognize my scent on the clothes you're wearing." He caught Buck by the leather thong around his neck and led him over to her. Patches of missing fur marred his silvery coat, evidence of his encounter. He didn't jump and scamper like the rest of the dogs. Instead, he regarded her with an almost human assessment.

Tall Dancer gently took her hand and placed it on Buck's fur. Memories of the wolf's teeth shredding the rabbit came to mind and her hand began to shake. He tightened his grip and guided her fingers across the dog's stiff hair. Buck stood patiently, his yellow eyes following her movements. Then, as she relaxed, the end of his tail swished back and forth slightly.

"We have to leave today," Tall Dancer said, pulling a black bear fur tighter around him as they walked back to their camp. He yanked off the roof of the shelter. "The ceremony is only a few days away, and I have to stop along the way and collect my furs for the potlatch."

Cara jerked her head around.

"Don't worry," he said, slanting her a glance. "I'm not giving away any slaves."

* * *

Snow stung Cara's eyes and the brisk scent of sea air buffeted her face as they skimmed across the snow-covered beach, avoiding jutting rocks and flirting with the fringe of cedars that hugged the shore. Beyond, the ocean glimmered and swelled beneath a cold blue sky.

For two days they had traveled the coastline, and Cara nervously watched the horizon for sails. She couldn't shake the feeling her father was following her, that somehow he would find her, even here among tens of thousands of acres of wilderness.

She glanced back over her shoulder and caught Tall Dancer watching her, a frown knotting his dark brows together. Looking away, she vowed to be more careful in her observations. No one must know her father was The Butcher.

She snuggled deeper into the bed of furs he had provided for her. He stood on the sled runners, the wind whipping his sealskin shirt and pants close to his body, and she wondered how he could stand the cold.

"Are you cold?" His lips brushed her ear so the wind would not snatch his words away.

"No!" Cara shouted, turning her head toward him.

He straightened and swung the sled abruptly into the forest.

"Why are we stopping so early?" Cara asked as the team halted.

"I thought you might like a surprise for supper." He stepped off the sled, unhitched the dogs, and started work on a shelter.

While he worked, Cara yanked low, dead branches out of the surrounding trees. Sweeping an area clear of snow with a cedar branch, she laid a fire and sat down on a rock to watch him tie cedar boughs into a home for the night.

How much did he know about her? she wondered. How much had he guessed? Despite her inner voice, she was beginning to trust him. That was dangerous. He was Kolosh, and if he found out exactly who she was, what would he do?

"Come." He stood before her, holding out his hand. She laced her fingers into his and followed him out onto the beach. Leaving two trails in the snow, they walked down to the edge of the churning surf. Bits of green seaweed roiled in the water. Tall Dancer bent down and scooped up some. "Brought in with the storm," he explained, placing the plant in a skin pouch at his side. They walked down the beach, and Cara glanced at the horizon.

"Why do you watch the sea?" he asked, bending to retrieve another bit of greenery.

Cara shrugged. "I like the sea."

"There is fear in your eyes when you look out over the water."

He stopped in front of her, blocking her path. Fear poured into Cara's veins, and her knees threatened to buckle, but he did not touch her. Slowly, she raised her eyes to his. He studied her face with a concerned look absent of anger. "Do you watch for someone?"

How easy it would be to tell him. "No. There is no one."

He moved down the beach again, and Cara heaved a sigh of relief.

When they returned to camp, he cooked the seaweed, seasoning the mix with dried salmon and fruit. Hungrily, Cara finished every morsel, now used to the glint of humor in his eyes when she ate ravenously.

He took their wooden dishes and wiped both clean with snow. After storing them in his pack, he moved to sit beside her.

"You are Russian?"

His words were a question and a statement. There was no anger in his face, no hatred in his eyes. Slowly, she nodded and awaited his reaction. Emotions flickered in his eyes, then he squeezed her hand and smiled. "See, you are still alive."

"I thought . . ." She let her words drift off.

"That I would kill you? No. I knew you were Russian that day at the potlatch, Cara. I wanted to see if you would tell me yourself."

She liked the way her name sounded when he said it. "We have done so much."

"Yes." He rose from the rock and moved to the fire. "Your people have done much to mine. But"—he turned to face her—"you have done nothing to me."

"What will you do with me now?"

He paused for a moment before he answered. "I will return you to your people in the fall, as I said."

"But won't it be dangerous for you to go to them? I mean . . ."

He turned his back to her. "The men at Fort St. Michael do not know I am Kolosh. They think I am a Russian hunter."

Cara did not answer. He stepped over to her and dropped to his knees so he looked her in the eyes. "See," he said, picking up her fingers again. "Now you know my secret, and I am at *your* mercy."

Cara touched his cheek, suddenly hungry for the feel of another's warmth. His skin was warm and rough, and she let her fingers graze across a scar on his cheek. A light flickered in his eyes, and she quickly dropped her hand.

The moon shed dim light on the rolling ocean waves. Tall Dancer stood on the shore and looked toward the silvery horizon. Who was coming for her? Whom did he fear? The wind cut through him as he shed his sealskins and stepped out into the surf.

Chills tightened his skin, and he rejoiced in the sensation as he waded deeper. Diving under the breakers, he soon swam out beyond the roaring water to where the ocean swelled and fell with each passing wave. He lifted his feet and let the water buoy him.

Closing his eyes, he saw Cara's face. She wavered before him as in an apparition. His chest tightened, and he tried to change his line of thought, tried to remember the face of the woman waiting for him. Try as he might, her image would not come. Even the cold water did little to ease his longing. Flipping over onto his stomach, he swam for shore, dreading another night of temptation.

As he picked up his clothes from the moonlit beach, a black dot against the far horizon caught his attention. He frowned. What was a ship doing so far north so late in the season? He sat down on the rock and watched as the ship slowly moved out to sea. He remembered Cara's covert glances at the horizon, her halting answers when he questioned her. With a feeling of dread, Tall Dancer made his way back to camp.

"How long have you had the dogs?" Cara shouted back over her shoulder. The wind snatched her words away, and she wondered if he had heard her. They were speeding along the coastline through sparse trees near the beach. Sunlight dappled the snow and blobs of it fell from the trees. She was breathless from the speed and the exhilaration of the ride.

"What?" His breath was hot on her neck as he leaned down.

"I said, how long have you had the dogs?"

He called out a command and the team slowed to a trot, then stopped altogether. "I was in Fort St. Michael for a time," he explained, stepping down off the runners and coming around to the front of the sled. "I met a man there who had traveled from far up north with these dogs. It was magic the way they worked with only his voice to guide them."

The respect and wonderment he held for his dogs was evident in his voice as he reached down and checked a harness. "I questioned him some more, then bought these dogs from him. I have never regretted my decision. *'Atle's* village doesn't understand, and the dogs frighten them whenever we go home."

"Who?"

" *'Atle,* my mother."

Again Cara was reminded of her destination, but she pushed the fear away. The day was too beautiful for bad thoughts. "The dogs frighten them more than they do me?"

Months ago, she never would have guessed she would feel so happy skimming along the surface of the snow at speeds she could only have imagined. She smiled up at him and watched his slender fingers straighten a harness and pat a dog's head. A warm feeling crept through her and she wondered if this was what it felt like to be safe and secure.

He smiled back at her, then mounted the sled and spoke a command. The sled jerked forward and again they were racing through the snow.

She glanced over her shoulder at him as he shouted a left turn to the dogs. His long hair fluttering, he leaned with the turn and the dogs swerved toward a high pile of rocks.

"Are you going to stop trapping once you're married?" she asked, clinging to the sled and fighting down the urge to shriek with glee.

"No," was his short answer.

Cara turned around. His jaw was set in a straight line and his good humor had disappeared. A sting of jealousy pricked her for the woman waiting to become his wife. *I wonder if she knows how lucky she is?*

Snow flew up from the rear of the sled and rooster-tailed onto Cara as Tall Dancer dragged one foot to stop. The pile of rocks towered over them. Nervously, she watched the mound of snow icing the top boulder, certain it would tumble down on her. He spoke softly to Buck, who promptly sat down. The other dogs followed suit.

Tall Dancer paced to the bottom of the boulder, turned, and paced east. Then he dropped to his knees and began to dig. Soon, a fur-wrapped bundle emerged. He untied the leather thong holding it together and beautiful black ermine furs tumbled out. He ran his hand over their softness, then retied them and put them carefully at Cara's feet.

"Hike!" he shouted to the dogs, who leaped forward again.

"What are those for?" Cara shouted.

"Gifts for my in-laws and for my uncle."

Again, Cara felt a stab of jealousy. She closed her eyes against the images that rose of Tall Dancer and a beautiful woman standing arm in arm, giving away these rich furs to their wedding guests.

"How many more stops?"

"Many!"

"How do you get so many furs?" Cara asked when they made the next stop.

"The dogs make it easier to get around. I can cover more distance than a trapper on foot."

As he tossed another bundle on the sled, Cara studied his face. The nearer they got to the village, the more glum he looked. Was it her imagination, or was he as unhappy about the marriage as he seemed?

"What is her name?"

He bent over the dogs to straighten a tangled harness. He jerked up his head. "Who?"

"The woman you're going to marry."

Concentrating on the harness, he waited until he was through before wiping his hands down his pants and moving toward her. "Kaskoe," he answered.

His face looked so stormy, Cara turned away.

Kaskoe.

She gave the name a picture in her mind—a beautiful woman with long, silky hair, standing at the edge of the water, waiting. He would arrive, jump off the sled, and take her into his arms. Cold sweat popped out on Cara's skin. The thoughts of what might happen next were terrifying. She closed her eyes and again felt cold hands sliding down her body, slithering across her skin.

"Are you ill?" He knelt at her side, peering into her face.

"No." Cara felt a blush creep into her cheeks.

"For a moment, you were very pale."

Cara stared into his warm brown eyes and again felt the flood of well-being he generated in her. But she knew it was to be short-lived, and her good mood disappeared.

In several days, the pile of furs in the sled was so high that Cara had to peek over them just to see the trail ahead. Nights around the fire, Tall Dancer had made her shoes, pants, and a shirt from two deer hides and he fashioned a coat from two wolverine skins. She had never seen so many pelts belong to one hunter. Even the men in Klaida's village were not this skillful.

"Will you give all these away?" she asked one morning as he was digging a bundle out from beneath another rock.

"Some go to Kaskoe's family as an engagement present. Others we will use in our home. The rest will be given as presents at our potlatch."

"Do you love her?"

Cara asked the question with such innocence and directness that it caught Tall Dancer by surprise. "It is expected of me to marry her," he answered shortly.

"You said that before. I just wondered if you loved her."

She was staring at him with eyes that made him feel he had no secrets. How could he tell her loved her, not Kaskoe? How could he tell her he had fallen desperately in love with a woman who should be his enemy, whose people held captive the fragile future of his own—and yet, despite all that, he was still going to do what was expected and marry the woman chosen for him?

From the first night in camp . . . no. From the first time he saw her shaved head and dirty face, saw her fending off warriors twice her size, he had known she would always live within him. But there could be no future for them. Commitments to his clan had to be kept, and Cara had to be returned to her own world. An insult to Kaskoe's family could mean war, but the prospect of living the rest of his life with her was becoming increasingly dreary.

"No, I don't love her," he answered slowly. "We marry for the good of the families involved, not for love as the white man."

"But you're white, too. Don't you want to marry someone you love?"

Tall Dancer could not answer her without giving his feelings away. She must never know how he felt. It would only confuse and frighten her, and she had had enough of both. He returned to covering his hiding place, feeling her eyes on his back.

Chapter Four

They were being followed. Tall Dancer knew it by the prickling on the back of his neck. Warriors, as best as he could make out, two of them, and not from his clan. Each day they traveled, despite the speed of the sled, their mysterious stalkers drew closer.

He stopped the sled for the midday meal and the dogs whined and milled about, tangling their harnesses. After unloading the sled, he motioned for Cara to follow him beneath the spread of an ancient cedar.

"What are you doing?" Cara asked, ducking to avoid a low-hanging branch.

"Someone is following us and has been for some time," he whispered. "Now they are coming closer. We will put your strap back on. Take your coat off." In urgent whispers, he instructed her to place the leather strap around her neck, then tied her hands behind her.

"I'll chance their questioning those," he said, nodding at her shoes. He gave her some furs to stuff under her clothes as insulation against the cold.

Resuming their journey, he slowed the dogs to a walk. Whoever was out there, he wanted to draw them closer. Each time he rounded a blind corner or stopped the sled for a cache of furs, the hair on the back of his neck bristled and the dogs whined.

By nightfall, his patience had grown thin. He had long ago discounted a chance meeting and had purposely kept to the open beach as much as possible. In the back of his mind, there was always the black ship that periodically appeared on the horizon, then faded into the sky.

They made camp that night as close to the beach as the cold wind would allow. He instructed Cara to sit on a log by the fire, her hands and feet tied and the thong around her neck. Hunched over, holding a ptarmigan over the fire, he glanced up at her and met her large, terrified eyes. So deep was her fear that the image of the mysterious ship surfaced again.

As the meat sizzled and popped, his eyes constantly flickered to the shadows beyond the firelight.

The dogs suddenly began to bark and two warriors stepped into the circle of light. Tall Dancer tried not to appear startled. To do so would admit to not being alert. Calmly, he laid aside the roasted bird and rose to his feet.

"We want to share your fire." One of the men pointed to the firepit, his eyes lingering on the speared bird.

"You are welcome." Tall Dancer waved in the direction of the camp, and the two men brushed past him.

Without ceremony, they sat down cross-legged by the fire and laid aside their bows and arrows. Cara stared at the patch of ground between her feet. Their conversation with Tall Dancer was rapid and short, and she caught only a few phrases of what they said. They pointed to the large pile of furs, and he calmly explained about the wedding. They nodded. One rose, moved to the pile of furs and fingered one.

"A good winter," he said with a grunt and let the thick ermine pelt fall. "What about the woman?"

Cara looked up and he pointed straight at her.

Tall Dancer didn't blink. "She is my slave."

Their comments were rapid and short, then she caught a phrase.

"How many blankets for her?"

Her blood turned to ice. She raised her eyes to the man's face and he grinned at her with yellow, broken teeth. Tall Dancer's face didn't change. He glanced at her nonchalantly, then turned his attention back to the man.

"One hundred blankets."

The men responded in a burst of chattering, far too rapid for Cara to follow. She turned hot with anger. So he did have a price.

"Too many blankets," the warrior said with a shake of his head. "Why so much?" He leveled a suspicious glare at Tall Dancer.

He blurted a rapid answer Cara didn't catch. The two strangers stared at him a moment, then burst into laughter, shaking their heads. They became more insistent, pointing, gesturing, and babbling. Tall Dancer crossed his arms over his chest and shook his head. Finally they shrugged, moved to the fire, and spread out their blankets.

Tall Dancer came to where she sat and spread a bear pelt out over a pile of dried branches.

"What did they want?" Cara asked as he quickly untied her hands and ankles.

"They want to buy you."

"And you made them an offer." She snatched her hand away as he removed the last thong.

"I set the price too high and hoped they'd refuse."

"But you didn't know."

He looked down at the strap in his hands. "No, I wasn't sure."

"What would you have done if they had accepted your offer?"

He raised his eyes to hers and she thought she saw a hint of mischief there. "I would have had to steal you back."

"What reason did you give for my price being so high?"

He flushed and looked at his hands. "I told them you . . . satisfied my needs."

She glanced at the two silent warriors, closely studying them both.

"So the bargaining is over?"

"Unless they think it over and decide to take me up on my offer."

"How could you put me in such a position?" Anger heated her cheeks.

"There was nothing else I could tell them. I had to give a reason." He took her hand in his. "I won't hurt you," he whispered. "Trust me and do what I say."

All through the evening meal, Cara held out hope the two visitors would tire of watching them, but they didn't. Even while they ate the roasted rabbits Tall Dancer snared, they watched, licking the grease from their fingers. As darkness closed in, it became obvious the men intended to share their camp for the night. They lay down on their unrolled blankets and turned on their sides facing Cara.

Tall Dancer fiddled with the fire, with his packs, and with his dogs. All the while, Cara cringed under the scrutiny of the two warriors as she sat cross-legged on the bearskin just beyond the circle of firelight. Even across this distance, she could tell the two men were suspicious of them. Branches cracking behind her made Cara jump.

"Promise me you won't try to get away," he whispered next to her ear as his knife sliced through the thong around her neck. "No matter what happens."

Cara craned her neck to look into his dark eyes and decided to trust him. What other choice did she have? "Where would I go?" she answered, shrugging.

He shoved the knife into a leather pouch hanging on his side and pulled her down with him to the furs. The steely taste of fear filled her mouth as her body sagged against his. His breath ruffled the short pieces of hair around her ear. He had promised he wouldn't hurt her. Cara stretched her legs out beside the soft fuzziness of his sealskins.

He had promised.

She hung onto those words desperately as he slid his arm beneath her and cradled her head against his chest. His heart was pounding nearly as wildly as hers.

"Who are they?" Cara whispered against his shirt. It smelled of dead leaves and the outdoors.

"I've seen them before," he murmured into her hair. "They belong to the Kagwantan clan." He rolled his head toward the men. Cara peeped over his chest. Both men lay with their heads propped on their hands, still awake, still watching.

"I don't think they believe us," he whispered. "They want a performance."

"Can't you just tell them again?"

"There's no reason for not parting with a slave. It would be rude."

He turned toward her, his face inches from hers. He cupped her cheek in the palm of his hand and she couldn't keep her eyes off his full lips. "I promise I won't hurt you."

His hand moved across her waist and around to her back. He rose up on one elbow and leaned over her. "We're going to have to give them what they want." His voice was husky, and something in it sparked new fear in Cara.

"What do they want?" Her breath was coming in short gasps and she felt like he was smothering her.

His hand, resting intimately on the small of her back, began to stroke up her side. His eyes darkened like the storm clouds that rolled in off the sea. "This," he growled, and suddenly pushed her over onto her back.

Cara writhed beneath his weight, pushing at his shoulders as he slid on top of her. His breath was hot on her face as he whispered, "It's dark here. They won't be able to see what we do."

The two men calmly watching from beside the fire were the least of her worries. Terror choked her as his lips pressed hot against the base of her neck. He slid his arms beneath her head and brought her face up toward his as his black lashes swept his cheeks. Cara squirmed beneath him and shoved at his chest, trying to throw him off.

"Be still," he whispered against her lips. "I'm not going to hurt you."

Cara closed her eyes against the panic rapidly consuming her. She was at his mercy. He could do anything he chose to her.

"Relax," he whispered in her ear. "Put your arms around my neck."

Slowly, she laced her arms behind his head.

"Now open your eyes," he commanded.

She stared straight into his and saw no evil, no lust.

"I won't hurt you," he promised again. "Don't be afraid."

His eyes swept closed, and his lips brushed hers, as soft as a butterfly. He drew back, closely observed her face, then winked. "That wasn't so bad, was it?"

Cautiously, Cara shook her head. He kissed her again, but this time he let his lips linger on hers and gathered her closer. Tendrils of hair clung to her cheeks and he brushed them away with trembling hands as his heart hammered against her chest. Cara entwined her fingers in his hair and pulled the thong loose. His hair fell forward, shutting out the two men watching them.

A strange warmth shot through Cara when his kisses deepened. Her heart began to pound in time to his. Vaguely wondering when this had ceased being a game, she ran her hands through his long, silky hair and let it fall across her face. His shoulders trembled as he caught one corner of the blanket in his hand and rolled them onto their sides away from the fire and into the darkness. He rested his chin on the top of her head, his breath coming in short gasps. His broad back shut out everything except the two of them.

With no words exchanged, they lay side by side, entwined in each other's arms.

"I think they're satisfied," he whispered after a few minutes, his voice breaking the spell.

Cara peeped over his shoulder. The two Tlingits rustled their bed of dry cedar boughs as they turned their backs to the fire and pulled their blankets up around them. Tall Dancer rolled away from her to lie on his other side.

He watched the fire consuming itself into embers and fought to control the passions burning at his center. How could her kisses affect him so? he thought as his heart began to slow. She turned on the blanket behind him, and he hoped she wouldn't touch him. One touch, and he'd be no better than the men who had abused her before.

Tall Dancer's sudden rejection jerked Cara back to reality and a wash of new emotions flooded through her. As Tall Dancer's breathing evened out, Cara knew he slept. The thumping of her own heart began to slow and guilt settled heavy upon her. How could she have allowed this to happen? She had wanted him and he had wanted her. Stars twinkled in an inky black sky above, leaving Cara to lay on her back and wonder at what point during their charade her fear had turned to passion.

Icy mist slapped Tall Dancer in the face as he shed his clothes on a beach barely tinted with the pink of dawn. Swimming in water cold enough to stun was a measure of manhood, a tradition long held by his people, and one he embraced.

The cold wind caressed his skin as he moved across the sand toward the surf. Taking a deep breath, he dived into the churning water and began to swim. Once he was past the breakers, he bobbed to the surface and floated on his back.

Fingers of light were inching across the eastern sky, promising a clear, bright day. He closed his eyes and saw only Cara's face. The surge of a wave swept over him. There wasn't enough cold water in all of the ocean to cool the flames burning within him.

Flipping over onto his back, he plunged his face into the water and wondered if she had noticed. Probably not, or she would have fought like a lynx.

As the sky lightened from dawn into full daylight, he began

to swim toward shore with long, leisurely strokes. An unusually warm wind caressed his bare back, the mysterious shift of the weather's temperament that so characterized his homeland. A wind cold enough to cut through layers of skins and furs could abruptly turn mild, as fickle as a woman's heart. A game of the trickster Raven, the old men explained.

Something off to his right caught his eye. Against the blue horizon floated the ship with the black flag. Tall Dancer stopped swimming and treaded water, watching the ship move toward him under full sail. Although the craft was still far away, he swam rapidly to shore, grabbed up his clothes, and bolted for the forest.

Dressing just inside the tree line, he watched the ship pass, its solid black flag floating out in the wind. Men scurried about on the deck. He watched until it went around a bend, then quickly made his way back to camp.

Cara stretched and opened her eyes. The two warriors were gone, leaving only their impressions on the soft ground. So was Tall Dancer. She reached out toward the place he had slept and skimmed her hand across the ruffled fur.

Sweet memories rose, quickly dashed by caution. She sat up, clasped her knees with her arms, and felt a flush creep across her face as she remembered every detail of his kisses. Shaking her head, she rose and began to roll up their furs and blankets.

A step in the forest startled her, and Tall Dancer walked out of the tangle. Cara smiled at him, but his face was set in a frown, and he was silent as he packed their belongings into the sled and hitched the dogs. Without a word about the night before, he motioned her into the sled, spoke to the dogs, and they dashed away.

As midday neared, temperatures warmed until the snow beneath the sled runners was soft and slushy. Cara now walked beside Tall Dancer to ease the burden on the dogs, who strained at their harnesses to pull the sled.

A distant rumbling passed overhead, vibrating the air and bringing a sense of wariness. The sound could have passed as thunder, but Cara knew better. It was a ship's cannon discharging, and nearby, too. Quickly, they moved into the trees. The sound was coming from straight ahead.

"It's the black ship. I saw it this morning when I swam," Tall Dancer said shortly.

Familiar fear washed over Cara, now tinged with a sense of loss.

"Are we near your village?" Cara asked the question burning in her mind and dreaded the answer. When he didn't answer, she turned to look at him. His face was a strange mix of expressions.

"No, not that close." His eyes met hers.

Cara turned around and felt tears start in her eyes. Shame, fear, and confusion all crowded in on her as he spoke to the dogs. They jerked the sled forward and the wind dried the tears that squeezed out, drawing the skin tight beneath her eyes.

At sunset, they rounded a point of land, and the blackened bones of a village jutted up like the rib cage of a long dead whale. Bits of wood lay scattered up and down the small cove's narrow beach. Tendrils of smoke drifted up into an orange-streaked sky, and skeletons of houses stood where homes had once been.

Tall Dancer stepped off the sled and stumbled forward, his shoulders sagging. Bodies littered the snow-blotched sand. Men, women, and children lay across each other, their blood soaking into the snow.

"Oh, my God." Cara covered her mouth with her palm as her nostrils picked up the scent of death. "Dear God, please don't let this be his home," she prayed, scrambling to follow him.

He stopped before what had been a large plank house. Now a gaping hole yawned where the roof had once been. The totems by the door were splintered into dozens of pieces. Ransacked bodies had been thrown on piles on the porches, and household goods lay strewn out the doors. Tall Dancer turned to look out over the cove. There was no sign of the ship, but between the bodies were dozens of boot prints.

He gripped the splintered totem until his hand trembled and his knees sagged. Beyond the door, inside the mangled house, were more bodies, horribly defiled.

He felt his face pale as he turned away and headed for the beach and a breath of fresh air. Standing in the edge of the surf, he let the waves lap up on his shoes, vaguely aware of the frigid water soaking through the leather.

Cara's hand slid up his back. When he looked down at her, her eyes were full of sorrow. He wanted to reach out and draw her near, enclose her in his arms to remind himself there still was life and warmth, but somehow, she was part of this. He didn't know how, but she was connected to the carnage before him.

He frowned, and her expression quickly veiled. She dropped her hand. He sensed she wanted to say something, but she turned and headed back toward the sled.

Dusk deepened into night. Cara sat down beside the dogs and watched Tall Dancer stack one body on top of another at the edge of the shore. The moon rose and illuminated the eerie scene with its cold, unfeeling light.

Burying her head in arms folded across her knees, Cara wondered how long it would be before Tall Dancer learned the black ship belonged to her father. She shivered at the thought, calling to mind how fearsome Tall Dancer had looked the night he claimed her at the potlatch and the extent of his anger. How would he treat her if he knew?

The acrid smell of burning flesh worked its way into her nose and she raised her head. Tall Dancer stood by a roaring fire, flames leaping over his head, as he burned the bodies of the dead. By morning, the fire would be out and the ashes would be washed to sea by the rising tide. She glanced at the horizon and squinted.

Then he turned toward the ocean, lifted his arms to the sky, and shouted something. Although she didn't understand the words, the intent was clear. He was issuing a challenge to The Butcher.

Days passed before he spoke beyond grunting a necessary word or two. They were further north now. Nights grew colder and the snow refroze. The days were overcast, made drearier because of his silence.

Then a bright day dawned and Cara rejoiced. As the sled flew down a deserted stretch of beach with abundant snow cover, the breeze was almost warm as it caressed her face with salty spray. A small cove dipped into the coastline and Tall Dancer swung the sled inland. They stopped on a stretch of beach where the water deepened so gradually the cove's bottom could be seen for some distance.

With more enthusiasm than she'd seen in days, Tall Dancer unhitched the dogs, then strode into the forest. He came back with a long, narrow cedar branch, which he sharpened on one end.

"Fish for supper?" he asked, holding up the limb and grinning.

He waded out into the water and tiny ripples moved out from his body as he eased along. Carefully, he studied the bottom as he waded. Cara moved up the hill and sat down on a dry spot of sand, far back from the edge of the water. He stopped and stood completely still. Then he lunged forward and lifted a wriggling fish above his head.

Cara smiled and waved, but he motioned for her to come to him. She shook her head and he motioned again, more insistent. Moving to the edge of the water, she glanced at him, then rolled up the legs of her sealskin pants and waded into the water. Surprised that the water was cold, not freezing, she picked her way along as Tall Dancer tossed the fish onto the beach.

"Come. I will show you how to catch fish."

She moved to his side, and he turned her so her back was against him. He put his arms around her and placed her hands on the lance. "Stand still and watch," he whispered, his breath moving the hair at her ear.

Cara stared into the water, trying to concentrate on the fish and what he said, but all she could think about was his chest pressed against her back, the strong beat of his heart, the warmth that came through her clothes.

"See?" He pointed down into the water, where a fish swam by their legs. With minute movements he raised the stick, then stabbed with lightning speed.

Cara squealed and turned away from the icy water that splashed in her face. The fish darted to safety. Tall Dancer looked so surprised, she couldn't resist. Scooping a handful of water, she threw it into his face and ran for shore.

He swore, then laughed as he splashed after her. His arms clamped hers to her sides and he swung her around. Sparkling droplets clung to his dark hair and lashes and his eyes danced with humor.

But Cara's laugh faded as his eyes darkened and he kissed her. His skin against hers, his warmth as he pulled her into his arms, the sense of safety she felt pressed against him all struck Cara at once and she suddenly wanted him with all her being. His quick intake of breath told her he'd read her kiss and her wants. He pulled her against the length of him.

A thunderous roar split the air and they broke apart, both panting for breath.

"What is it?" she shouted, covering her ears.

Tall Dancer pointed to the black ship at the center of the cove. Grabbing her arm, he charged out of the water and up the hill toward the forest, then dove behind a fallen log and tumbled her beneath him.

"Are you all right?" he asked, as he crawled to the edge of the log.

"Yes." Cara stared over the log at the ship and a chill poured over her. On the deck, dozens of men scurried to attend the guns. Why would he waste ammunition firing on them? she asked herself, then movement across the cove caught her attention. A trading party was scattering for the forest. Piles of furs lay near the water.

"A trading party from deep inland," he said through clenched teeth. "Murdering bastard."

The comfortable feeling between them vanished, and Cara felt a bone-clinging cold take its place.

Chapter Five

The ship's cannon belched out another ball. With a shrill whine, it sailed into the tops of the trees and exploded in a hail of wood splinters. The cries of the wounded and dying echoed across the water.

Cara covered her ears and sank down with her back to the log. Tall Dancer crouched at her side, watching the massacre across the water. Acrid smoke drifted on the breeze and Cara's throat tightened. With a sideways glance, she studied the angry set of his jaw and the way his fingers gripped the log's rough surface.

Time after time, the ship's cannon delivered fire and death until there were no more screams. Cara turned and peeked above the log. Two small boats dropped into the water and the men in them hauled against wooden oars, headed for the shore.

She watched the deck of the ship for a glimpse of her father—but maybe it wasn't his ship anymore. Maybe he had lost favor with the tsar by now. Maybe . . .

The eerie feeling of being watched worked its way into her mind. Slowly, she turned her head. Tall Dancer stared at her, a peculiar expression on his face.

Her eyes searched his, and he wanted with all his heart to believe she knew nothing about the ship assailing the coastline, but she did. He was more convinced than ever when she turned to face him, fear, guilt, and sadness in her eyes. His blood rushed warm when he thought of the kiss they'd shared only minutes ago, and his hands ached to touch her, but the thought that she was somehow part of the carnage he'd seen in the last few weeks stabbed him deeply. Slowly, she turned away before he could form the question he wanted to ask: *What are you to the* promyshlenniki *that they would follow you so far?*

Voices on the shore drew his attention back to the ship. The men were rifling through the pelts abandoned by their owners. They held them up, examined them, then threw over their shoulders any they rejected as worthless.

"Otter. They're only after sea otter," he murmured.

The black ship rode at anchor in the cove until nearly dark, when the men returned laden with the belongings of the dead Tlingits as well as their pelts. Against the lavender dusk, the ship arched her sail into the sky. An evening breeze caught and filled the canvas. Slowly, the ship turned and sailed out of the cove, disappearing into the dark horizon.

Wrapping her arms around herself, Cara edged toward the campfire. Her bearskin pelt lay next to her, but freedom from its weight felt so good she decided to endure the cold a little longer.

Squinting, she looked beyond the firelight. Some time ago, Tall Dancer had left the camp, saying he was going for a swim. He still hadn't returned, and Cara was beginning to worry.

She sighed, threw the heavy pelt across her shoulders, and headed for the beach.

Moonlight sparkled on the surf that lapped at the shore, and an icy wind promised more snow tomorrow. As she emerged onto the beach, the moon flirted with clouds silhouetted against the sky. At the far end of the beach, a massive rock formation hunched near the lapping waves. She squinted and saw a slight movement there. Staying close under the shadow of the trees, she approached the large boulders.

"Cara?" His voice beckoned from the dark.

She moved into the light as Tall Dancer stepped from between two of the stones.

"Over here," he said.

He had been swimming, as he had said. Moonlight reflected off droplets of water caught in the length of his dark hair. Her traitorous heart began to thump as he stepped closer, and she remembered the warmth of his touch.

As she moved to his side and looked up into his face, he crossed his arms over his chest and tucked his hands firmly under his arms.

"Do you see that?" he pointed out toward the ocean.

Cara followed his finger. Against the far horizon, a dim light bobbed, barely visible except for its reflection against the dark, glassy sea.

"What is it?" she asked, even as the answer thrummed through her.

He shifted away from her and leaned one shoulder against a boulder taller than his head. "It's the ship. It's been there since the fight this afternoon . . . waiting."

Even in the dark, she could see him turn toward her, feel his eyes drilling into her, trying to pull out her deepest secrets.

"Why is it there, Cara? Why does it wait?"

She swallowed, and the dread that made her stomach roil turned into a knot of fear. "I d-d-don't know," she stammered, hating the uncertainty in her voice. Had her father followed her here, or was his presence a coincidence? Was he simply ravaging the coast for more furs, or was he looking for her? Either could be true, but only if Vlad Tarakanov would profit.

Tall Dancer gripped her by her forearms and pulled her to him. "Tell me who you are," he demanded between clenched teeth. "That ship has something to do with you, doesn't it? What have you brought to my people?"

Panic arced through her like lightning. His face was twisted in fury, and for an instant she feared he would hit her or fling her onto the damp sand. Then her temper overcame her fear.

"What have I brought to you?" She put her hands on his chest and shoved him away. "You are the one who brought me here."

He stumbled backward, then regained his balance, but he didn't draw closer. "Yes, and I think that may have been a terrible mistake," he growled.

The chill between them clung to her skin like the early morning mist, coiling around and through her.

"You belong to him in some way." He nodded toward the horizon.

"Belong to whom?" Cara stared at him as her mind whirled. Did he truly know who she was? Had he known since that night in the Tsimshian village when he took her against her will, all under the guise of a rescue?

"The man who captains that boat, the Butcher—he has come for you. Are you his wife? His daughter?"

All the air left her lungs in one great whoosh. Although she was sure he already knew the answer, she knew when she spoke the words whatever tender thread had bound them together these last few days would be gone forever.

She raised her eyes to his. They were dark and unreadable, and Cara realized her feelings for this man were deeper than she had known. Her lips twitched with a suppressed smile at the irony. Only now, when she stood to lose it all, did she realize what his care and protection had returned to her. He had eased her fear and won from her a hesitant trust, something she had given no one in a long, long time. Her next words would erase it all.

His dark eyes mirrored her image and she wondered how he would see her from this moment on. "His daughter," she whispered.

Tall Dancer clenched his fists and banged one on the lichen-covered ledge of rock. Planting his arms on the rock's surface, he hung his head between them. "Did he send you here so he could seek out more villages to plunder?"

"No. That's ridiculous. How could he have known you'd rescue me?"

"I don't know." Shoving away from the rock, he walked to the edge of the surf. "The *promyshlenniki* have many ways we do not understand."

Cara stood behind him and watched the moonlight play on his bronze skin as another cloud floated past the moon's face. He was angry, very angry, and she should be afraid of him, but something pulled her toward him.

She moved a step closer, her feet crunching in the sand, but he appeared not to have heard. Another step and she stood close behind him. She touched his shoulder and felt him tremble.

"He must love you deeply to come so far."

The absurdity of his words almost made her laugh. Her father felt many emotions for her, but love was not one of them. Lust, maybe. Domination. Hatred. But never love.

"No, he does not love me," she said softly. "He comes to claim me."

Tall Dancer turned and looked down into her face.

"Vlad Tarakanov never gives up what he owns." She nodded toward the bobbing light, now dead center in a path of moonlight leading from the shore to the ship.

At daylight they broke their camp and moved toward the body-littered beach on the opposite side of the cove. A cold wind whipped the surf into foam and sprinkled the air with snowflakes.

As they emerged from the woods onto the beach where the men had been attacked, the dog team slowed, stopped, and refused to advance when they caught the scent of death. Tall Dancer stepped off the sled and moved to the bodies. He squatted down, and his shoulders heaved as he gagged at the sight of the severed hands and fingers strewn about the bodies. He stood, picked up a body by the heels and tried to drag it away. Again he gagged and ran a shaking hand over his eyes.

Cara threw aside the furs, climbed out of the sled, and

approached a scene all too familiar to her. On her father's raids
of the coast, his men often made a game of disfiguring the
bodies of the Tlingit they killed. Red with blood, they would
return to the ship with trophies of their cruelty.

She drew in a deep breath when she reached Tall Dancer's
side. He was staring down at a disfigured body, his face pale
and beads of sweat dotting his forehead.

"His name was Paddles-Toward-The-Shore of the Can-
kuqedi clan. I have often attended potlatches in his village."

Cara looked down into a face no longer recognizable and
wondered how he knew.

"There." He nodded toward another body missing a hand.
"That is Man Sealion. He and I speared a killer whale one
time." His voice quivered and rage emanated from his body
like heat.

Cara picked the body up beneath its arms and waited. He
studied her for a moment, then picked up the feet. Together
they moved the body to the edge of the water and laid it down.
The head lolled to the side, its sightless eyes staring up at the
threatening sky. Tall Dancer threw her a questioning glance,
but he accepted her help without a word.

Despite the grisly nature of the job, Cara felt satisfaction as
they stacked the bodies to burn. Her father had left the men to
rot, and she was interfering with his plans. That gave her a
sense of revenge, small though it was.

As the evening sun dipped into a gray, roiling sea, Tall
Dancer stuck a burning brand to the pile of cedar boughs stacked
around the bodies. The tentative flame hesitated, then caught
and roared to life, urged on by a cutting wind. The smell was
overpowering, the heat intense before both were whipped away.
No ship bobbed on the horizon tonight, and Cara's satisfaction
was incomplete. She had hoped her father lurked just in sight
of land, that he would see the flames and guess someone had
given the bodies a decent burial.

The scent of burning flesh curled and trailed around them,
permeating their clothes and their hair. Tall Dancer threw off
the pelt across his shoulders when the heat became unbearable,

but he was determined to see the last of the bodies consumed into ashes. He swallowed, the bitter taste of bile still in his mouth.

Glancing at Cara's face, her lips curled into a slight smile, he wondered what she thought as she stared out to sea. Was she mad? Had The Butcher, in his own insanity, abandoned his daughter to the people he murdered?

No, she didn't appear insane to him. In fact, she was one of the sanest of the *promyshlenniki* he had met. So why had she helped? The thought had nagged him all afternoon. Did she hope to absolve herself of some guilt by helping with the burial?

The fire had burned down to a few embers covered with a thick coating of gray ash. The moon was straight overhead, alone and dominant in a clear night sky, and Cara knew it was late. Behind her flickered the flame of their campfire, but beyond her, out on the beach, Tall Dancer stood alone, watching the rolling surf. He thought she was asleep, rolled tightly into her thick bear pelt, but she had followed him and now sat on a rock, watching.

A full moon turned the sand into silver and the stillness of predawn pervaded the forest. He stood, arms crossed, staring out to sea. Abruptly, he yanked his shirt over his head and kicked off his pants.

She was so close she could see every outline of his body as he stretched his arms over his head and strode toward the churning surf. A large wave breaking on the rocks quickly consumed him and his dark head disappeared from sight.

The stillness of the night became loud and lonely. Cara sniffed at her arms. The scent of burning flesh clung to her. She stood and moved down to the water's edge.

Stopping just short of the nibbling surf, she saw his clothes in a pile at her side. Kneeling down, she picked up his shirt and rubbed it against her cheek. It, too, smelled of burning flesh and held his body heat. Far beyond the breakers, he lay stretched out on the surface of the water, floating with the rise and fall of the sea.

Seized with a sudden impulse, Cara dropped her skin wrap,

shed her own clothes, and quickly wrapped the skin around her nude body. The wind cut through her like a knife, but the cold was invigorating, making her feel more alive than she had in weeks. She squatted down. Windblown mist dampened her face as she dipped her clothes into the water, thinking of the warm fire that would dry them later.

A wave sprang at her from the darkness, its attack so sudden her scream drowned in her throat as the salty water choked her. Like an invisible hand, it swept her out into the numbingly cold water, churning her further and further from the shore. Occasionally, her head cleared the water and she had the choice of either screaming for help or breathing. She chose breathing. Then, her lungs filled with the painfully cold air, the sea would yank her back to its bosom, pressing her deeper and deeper into the dark depths.

The unpredictable ocean flung her out of its grasp against a rock. Her head cracked against the stone and her thoughts slowed and wandered. The water swallowed her again and spit her out once more.

This time the rough surface of the rock grated against her skin, raking it from her body. Salt water stung the cuts, clearing her mind, but the waves surged over her head, filling her mouth and nose.

A strong arm passed under her chin and clasped the back of her head. Someone pulled her, dragging her behind a swimming body that occasionally rubbed against hers. Not until her feet touched the rough sand in the shallow surf did she realize Tall Dancer held her naked body in his arms.

His dark hair was plastered across his face and water ran in rivulets down his body. Cara slumped in his grasp, grateful for the warmth of his skin against hers as uncontrollable shivering consumed her.

"Cara?" Gently, he eased her down onto the damp sand and knelt at her side.

She coughed and a spurt of water shot from her mouth. Rolling to her side, she coughed up more water, and then precious air filled her lungs.

Sand ground against her skin as he scooped her into his arms, caught up their clothes, and hurried toward the campsite. Once there, he laid her on her cedar bough bed and piled furs on top of her. Cara stared through bleary eyes as he hurried to the fire, threw on more branches, then pulled on his clothes.

Sleep rushed to claim her as a numbness spread through her limbs, making raising a single finger seem an insurmountable task. She was vaguely aware of a cold draft as a warm body slipped beneath the furs with her and drew her close.

Warmth crept through her and the numbness receded, replaced by a lethargy that soothed worries and encouraged peaceful sleep.

When Cara awoke, the sky was still dark, but a sliver of pink overhead predicted dawn. She raised her head, then sat up. Tall Dancer sat by the fire, combing his fingers through his long dark hair. Her clothes were spread out by the fire to dry.

He'd saved her again.

Her near drowning was little more than a fuzzy memory, the most vivid part being the contentment she'd felt at being drawn into his arms, even if it was only to save her life.

His hands paused and he wrenched around to face her. "How do you feel?"

Cara pulled the furs higher over her bare chest. "I'm fine. Are you all right?"

He nodded, watching her closely. Then he stretched to his feet and came to sit unsettlingly close to her. He pushed the hair away from her face, his eyes narrowing in study.

"Why did you help with the bodies?" he asked unexpectedly.

Cara sat up and held the fur to her chest. "I wanted to help you."

"The sight of death did not frighten you?" His stare was unnerving.

"No."

"Are you accustomed to seeing your father's bloody leavings?"

Cara tilted her chin up, determined not to let him disarm her. ''Yes,'' she answered, as bluntly as he'd asked.

His eyes darkened, and she braced for his rage. Instead, his expression gentled. His fingers grazed her cheek, then his thumb brushed the moist corner of her mouth.

''What other evils have you endured?'' His words were more a musing than a comment meant for her ears.

Tears filled her eyes at his unexpected gentleness. She wanted to tell him her secret. The words stood poised on the end of her tongue. How good it would feel to tell someone, to share her pain with a compassionate heart. Did she dare trust him with the truth?

Quickly, she glanced away from his intense gaze. ''I saw many terrible things aboard my father's ship.''

''And felt them as well?''

Cara's gaze returned to his face. ''What do you mean?''

He yanked aside the bottom half of the pelt to bare her legs. ''Some of these scars are old, older than your time with Palina. Did your father do this?'' He traced a long scar until it disappeared beneath the pelt just below her hips. Something in the pit of her stomach fluttered at his touch.

''Yes,'' she whispered.

''Is that why you left?''

She stared at him as a thousand questions raced through her mind. He knew more about her than he was saying. Yet how could he know anything of her? She remembered his saying he traded in Fort St. Michael and that he was believed to be Russian, not Tlingit. Perhaps he had heard of The Butcher and his daughter. Her father's reputation always preceded him.

''There was no shipwreck, was there, Cara? Your father is a violent and evil man, yet he searches the coastline, killing and maiming, to find you. Such a man is not capable of loving a daughter.''

Cara felt her cheeks color under the pressure of her hoarded shame. ''I couldn't stand the killing any longer. He murdered the Tlingit, many of them women and children. It mattered little to him. All Kolosh are the same to him, obstacles in the way of his distinguishing himself in the eyes of the tsar with shiploads of sea otter furs.''

She watched Tall Dancer's face closely, expecting to see his eyes grow cold and dark, expecting cold dread to fill her chest and steal her breath, but neither happened.

Instead, he reached out to touch her, and she flinched away. He persisted and his palm cupped her face. "And he used his daughter as well.''

Cara lowered her eyes as remembered shame heated her cheeks and her inner struggle between guilt and pride began anew.

"What did he do to make you so afraid of a man's touch? Beat you?'' he asked as his fingers skimmed her face.

"Sometimes. Sometimes worse.''

He frowned and paled. "You are not your father, Cara, and I do not blame you for his wrongs.''

His breath was warm on her cheek as his lips brushed hers unexpectedly. He touch, his scent had become familiar, spurring to life a reaction in her, something over which she had no control. Fighting the panic his touch evoked, she raised her arms to his neck, letting the pelt covering her slip away, pushing away the voice nagging at her and asking if she was insane.

His intake of breath was sharp against her mouth as her bare skin touched him. A tremor passed through him and into her. He pressed her into the cedar boughs with his weight and caressed her arms with rough, callused, wonderful hands.

He pulled back, and Cara lay still and watched his face as he quickly scanned the naked length of her, now goose-pimpled under his gaze. As she watched his face, she wondered where the warning bells were, the tiny clanging sirens in her head that tried to keep her from harm. She shivered, as much from anticipation as from the cold snaking and coiling around her. Then he replaced the furs, tucking them gently around her.

"I am not the man who will teach you the ways of love.'' He rose to his feet and looked down on her again, then turned and walked out into the dark forest.

The pounding of the surf became a whisper before he stopped

and leaned his forehead against a moss-covered cedar tree. Hot fire raced through his veins and the terrible unnamed longing returned. Clenching his fists at his side, he willed himself not to return to camp and do what his body urged. Cara's words echoed in his mind, and the horror of what she had said settled on him. The Butcher was more than a murderer.

He was a devil.

Chapter Six

Snow fell fast and furious, obliterating all but the bouncing backsides of the dogs as they ran. Cara buried her face in the furs to keep the stinging ice out of her eyes. Behind her Tall Dancer stoically watched the trail, his face as unreadable as the mask he had worn the first time she saw him. They had exchanged few words since the previous night and spoke only enough for him to tell her they neared his village.

Soon they would go their separate ways. He would become a husband and she would become a slave. Many months would pass before she would see another friendly face, months spent watching him and his wife begin their life together.

Angrily, Cara wiped away a tear. Why had she let herself fall in love with him? How could she have been so stupid? He was little better than the men who had captured her and no better than those who had abused and imprisoned her. So why had her heart led her down this path of pain? *Because he is different,* an inner voice replied.

She knew the voice was right. He was a gentle and honorable man, a man of his word. She would see civilization again, but until that time, she would have to watch the only decent man she'd ever known marry another woman.

He leaned down to reposition a bundle of furs and brushed against her arm. Their eyes met. In that brief instant, her heart leapt into a wild beat and she damned him again.

The dark afternoon deepened into night before they stopped beside a small cove carved into the coastline. A stand of tall cedars growing close together protected the ground beneath them and a sparse layer of snow lay deep within their branches. Tall Dancer unhitched the dogs and turned the sled over to cover the load of furs. He plunged into the heart of the thicket and stomped out a rounded area. His knife flashing, he cut down branches and erected a shelter while Cara watched, rubbing her arms to stay warm. When he finished with the shelter, he laid a ring of stones for the fire and stacked in branches and dry twigs.

"We will be in my village tomorrow," he said as he pulled the skin off a ptarmigan.

Cara's heart sank at the reminder, for once they passed the boundaries of his village, he would belong to someone else—and so would she.

"Cook this, and I will return." He handed her the carcass speared through with a green branch, stood, and moved off into the night.

A bitter wind swept through the thicket and Cara huddled by the fire while the meat roasted. The snow fell thickly outside their warm nook. Where had he gone for so long?

A distant rumble grated across the heavens, then a brilliant flash lit the forest. Cara stood and dropped her wrap. A thunderstorm was rolling in off the ocean, and with it brilliant lightning that defied all earthbound things to challenge it. Watching such displays from the deck of her father's ship was one of the few pleasant memories she held of her former life.

As she stepped out of the trees and onto the beach, lightning stabbed a fiery finger into the ocean, illuminating the roiling surface. In the brief light, she saw Tall Dancer standing shirtless beside the swirling surf. Always amazed at his taste for the bitterly cold water, Cara approached him and watched as he gazed out over the storm-tortured water. His arms were crossed over his bare chest and the muscles on his back were tense. Something far away claimed his attention, or else something in his mind.

She laid her hand on his shoulder. He whirled around. Dark ringlets curled against his face, evidence that he had completed his swim.

"I came to see the storm." Cara pointed out to sea where another bolt of fire struck, closer than before.

"The Thunderbird comes from the mountains," he said, turning back toward the ocean. "He flaps his wings and makes the skies bellow."

Thunder rumbled so loudly that the ground shook beneath the percussion. "It's beautiful, isn't it?" Cara asked as another flash turned the ocean red and spidery fingers of fire darted out of the cloud.

"It will snow tomorrow," he answered.

"And I will leave you tomorrow." The thought, and the regret that accompanied it, had come unbidden.

He turned toward her, the fury of the storm mirrored in his eyes. "After tonight, we will have no more time together."

The unspoken suggestion in his words, the passion building in his eyes, made Cara's heart jump into a rapid beat. "I know."

I want to spend these hours in your arms.

The truth slammed into her with the force of the storm growling over their heads. As if a corridor opened between them, she suddenly knew his thoughts, knew the depth of the passion and love he felt for her, no matter that it made no sense.

For a moment, the world seemed to stop and bow to the fury of the storm. This was their time. Like the storm raging over their heads, this moment, once spent, would never come again in exactly this way.

When he drew her against him, Cara closed her eyes, feeling the rumble of the thunder, hearing the crack of lightning, knowing the depth of his need and the answering need within herself.

His mouth captured hers in a kiss that bruised her lips and sent her blood roaring in her ears.

He picked her up, his mouth never leaving hers, and strode through the forest toward their shelter. The fragrant cedar bed crackled beneath their weight as he laid her onto the bear pelt, then joined her. Lowering the skin that covered the opening of their shelter, he cast them into the ghostly glow of the fire, which popped and snapped on fresh wood.

"I . . . have never done . . . this," he whispered into her hair, laying bare his soul as he drew her into his arms. The admission sent queer tremors to the pit of Cara's stomach. "I want a part of you to carry with me."

"And I you," Cara answered, marveling at how her body arched toward his without conscious thought. She laced her fingers through his hair. Gone was the paralyzing fear she had experienced before, replaced now by a deep, smoldering want and a burning curiosity. A sense of power filled her as he trembled under her touch.

Sliding her hands into his hair, she let them glide the full length of it, moving out onto his bare shoulders and back, where moisture still clung to his skin.

"Are you sure?" He pushed away from her, kneeling on the pelt they shared.

Cara hesitated for a second, reading his eyes. "Yes."

His body was lean and firm, the tattoo of the Raven vivid against his brown skin. Pausing, he let his eyes move over her. His hands followed, cupping her rib cage and gliding down to her waist, over her hips, down to the tips of her toes, as though memorizing every detail.

"I've loved you from the first time I saw you," he said breathlessly. His tongue moved up the side of her neck to her ear, then flicked across her earlobe.

Sliding her fingers across his temples, she smiled as his lips moved over hers, drowning the words she had been about to say. Cara closed her eyes and let the emotions wash over her, feeling his whole body shudder beneath her fingertips.

In his arms she lay soft and warm, just as he had imagined for weeks she would. Her touch, her kiss drove him to a nameless madness. As he slipped his arms beneath her, her body rose up to meet his. He closed his eyes, remembering the stories the other men told around the fire on hunting trips. All the erotic images their words had conjured up floated free in his mind, colliding in a mass of confusion.

He pulled away from her and drew a deep breath. Her emerald green eyes stared at him, open and trusting, reminding him of deep ocean pools where he swam as a boy. Like those pools left by the evening tide, her eyes drew him under their spell. He searched for the panic and fear he had so often seen in their green depths, but saw only the same desire he felt in every bone of his body. "Don't be afraid," he mumbled.

"I'm not afraid."

He drew a shaky breath. He was terrified. What should he do next? As if reading his thoughts, she slipped her arms around him and pulled his chest down against hers. One hand tangled itself in his hair; the other glided down the small of his back, sending little ripples out across his skin like a stone thrown into a tidal pool. Desire roared into his veins. His doubts disappeared and an age-old urge took over.

They lay still and damp, clasped in each other's arms. His heart hammered against her ear and hers against his chest. Rolling to the side, he gathered her to him and rested his chin on the top of her head.

"We will never be like this again," he murmured, his words sweeping away their warm cocoon.

"I know," she whispered.

"I will always carry you in my heart."

Tears coursed down her face. He had given her a precious gift and she had none to give him except her love. Her innocence had been lost years ago.

Tall Dancer rolled her to her side and slid his arm from beneath her head. He stood and moved to the fireside. Snowflakes made dark circles on the surface of the orange coals as they fell and melted with a hiss.

Behind him, Cara wept into their furry bed, and the dark night suddenly seemed lonely. He closed his eyes and called up the image of her face, soft and tender with passion, then etched every detail into his memory. On long, cold nights while he lay by Kaskoe's side, it would be Cara's face he would see.

"I'm going to have to keep you tied like this."

They were standing on the beach beside a wide cove. Tall Dancer had explained that beyond a forested spit of land jutting out into the cove was his village. The overcast sky had lowered, threatening to dump more snow onto the foot already on the ground. He stood in front of her, threading the leather thong through his fingers.

"From here on, someone will always be watching us after we enter the cove." He slipped the thong over her head and pulled the knot snug around her neck. His fingers brushed her skin and he paused. Their eyes met, but neither spoke. There was nothing to be said. They had said it all last night.

"You can ride here, though." Moving around to the front of the sled, he hollowed out a small nest in the piles of furs. "If we're stopped, I'll explain you couldn't keep up and were slowing me down."

Cara nodded numbly and climbed into the sled. They swung inland, away from the coastline and her father's threat, and entered a world she instinctively knew belonged to Tall Dancer. The twisted, gnarled trees struggling for existence on the shore were replaced by towering, lush cedars. Dead vines twined around the knobby tree roots, hinting at the thick underbrush there in the summer.

For several hours, neither spoke. Each time Cara looked back at him, Tall Dancer's jaw was tight, and his eyes were on the trail ahead. Her stomach flip-flopped every time she thought about his wedding. Their time together had been too short.

She noticed when the dogs changed their gait. They swung

around a last point of land and a village magically appeared. Long plank houses lined up side by side, bordering a smooth sound filled with clumps of ice. Curls of gray smoke snaked out of smoke holes and quickly disappeared into the sky. Wooden piers lined with men in pointed hats and long garments jutted out into the water.

Behind the first row of houses sat another with a wide dirt path between. Children and dogs ran and wrestled in the dirty snow, which was rapidly melting into brown slush. One of the men looked up, dropped the long pointed pole he held poised above the water, and ran inside the nearest house.

Before Tall Dancer could stop the sled, they were surrounded by people. They all chattered at once, but Cara caught several references to his impending marriage.

Despite the fact he towered over them, his affection for the villagers was evident in his eyes and words. Young women in the crowd watched him enviously and hid their giggles behind their hands. As she watched the girls flirt with him, Cara was again reminded that in a few days he would be a married man with family responsibilities.

The old familiar fear returned. Without his presence, she no longer felt safe. He had stood between her and death and had risked his own standing with his neighbors, the Tsimshian, for her.

Tall Dancer returned to the sled and they began to make their way through the throng of people, but were stopped by three young warriors halfway across the open area ringed with houses. They welcomed him home and admired Cara, poking and prodding at her. She shrank away from them and pressed closer to Tall Dancer's side. Finally, their curiosity sated, they stepped out of the way.

Tall Dancer dragged one foot in the snow to stop the sled in front of a long wooden house where totems with grinning ravens guarded the door. The house was built of long, thick beams. Ridge poles ran from the front to the back, supported at each end by a post. Planking covered the sides. There were no windows; the only ventilation was a smoke hole in the roof. Carefully cut joints made the dwelling's corners tight.

Tall Dancer untied Cara's leash and led her inside through a circular door carved as the open mouth of a raven. A group of women squatting around a sunken firepit rose as they entered. The smell of smoke and grease was overwhelming. On four sides of the sunken area rose rows of benches marching up to a wide ledge. On these ledges sat individual living quarters partitioned off with hides, blankets, or planks. A woman straightened from the fire as a man entered the house and pushed past them. Regally, he climbed to the highest ledge and went into the first dwelling. The woman hurried after him.

"Who's he?" Cara whispered as people scurried out of the man's way.

"He's the head of the highest ranking family in this house." Tall Dancer whispered back. "Don't speak again until I tell you."

His sharp words stung, but Cara remained quiet, nervous under the curious stares cast in her direction. Tall Dancer did not acknowledge the other women who looked up at them, and they continued through the house until he reached the back wall. Climbing up to the top ledge, Tall Dancer pushed aside a ragged blanket, the pattern of a raven nearly faded from it. An old woman sat hunched over a partially finished basket, straws strewn about her as she worked intently on a difficult design. She did not notice them until he touched her on the shoulder.

" '*Atle?*''

The woman looked up and her brown eyes sparkled out of a face the color of worn leather. Rows of wrinkles crowded around her eyes. A smile spread over her face and affection made her eyes misty.

"Tall Dancer!" She rose, spilling the straws and unfinished basket to the floor. "You have come home safe." She caught his cheeks between her palms and patted his face as she would a child's.

Tall Dancer caught her hands in his and kissed their tips. "Are you well, mother?"

She withdrew her hands and waved him away. "Well except for an old woman's complaints." She groaned as she bent to pick up her spilled work.

Tall Dancer laughed. "You're the youngest person I know."

She straightened, and her gaze fell on Cara. She narrowed her eyes when she saw the leather strap around her neck. "What's this?" she demanded.

Tall Dancer fidgeted and looked like a scolded child. "This is Cara. She is a slave."

The old woman circled Cara, poking at her body and lifting her garments to have a better look. She took the seams of the new leather clothes in her fingers and felt them. Throwing him a telling look, she continued her examination.

"So this is the slave I have heard about. You and she have been well discussed over the fires at night."

Tall Dancer's cheeks turned red. "Klaida gave her to me at the potlatch. What else could I do?" he said with a shrug.

Cara looked between the two of them. The old woman narrowed her eyes, he fidgeted his feet. He had lied to his mother, and she knew it.

She scolded him with a look and continued. "Kaskoe is very upset over this. Word reached us that you would not sell this slave to some men of the Kagwantan band. You said she satisfied your needs."

Tall Dancer looked more uncomfortable. Cara smothered a giggle.

"Young men often want what they should not have, but so close to the wedding?" The old woman spread her hands palms up. "Could you not wait?" She leaned closer and winked at her son. "Kaskoe has surprises planned for you, so the women say."

Tall Dancer looked chagrined and his mother smiled. The warmth between them was palaptable in the air. Cara liked the old woman instantly. Then, suddenly, the air chilled.

A tall, dark man pushed his way into the room. He wore a

stained set of sealskin clothes. His long, black hair was clubbed at the nape of his neck and his skin was leathery. He didn't speak as he let the blanket fall closed and coolly regarded Tall Dancer.

"Noisy Feather." Tall Dancer's hand flew up to cover his mouth as he addressed the man in front of him.

"*Kalk,*" Noisy Feather replied with a nod.

"I have brought you much wealth."

Eyes as dark as the older woman's swept Cara, but she felt none of the warmth she felt from Tall Dancer's mother. "I see what you have brought. The Kagwantan men told us of your slave."

"I have brought her for my mother."

Noisy Feather fixed Cara with his gaze until Tall Dancer saved her. "Come outside and let me show you your pelts." Tall Dancer tugged at his uncle's arm. Noisy Feather turned to go slowly, watching her until he ducked beneath the blanket.

With him gone, Cara suddenly felt alone and frightened. She tried to ignore her fear and concentrate on her surroundings. The large house was incredibly clean, even though numerous children scampered back and forth. Like the Tsimshian village she had spent the last few months in, all the members of one clan lived in one house. Several women sat in front of their dwellings working on baskets or preparing food to cook for supper. She leaned her head back to look at the smoked ceiling. Magnificent totems graced the beams that held the roof erect.

The men returned, and Noisy Feather's arms were loaded with furs. This time he had a more pleasant expression.

Tall Dancer tugged on her collar, and she followed him down the ledge to an empty compartment. He pushed aside a ragged blanket and pulled her in behind him. A pile of blankets filled one corner and a table occupied another. Once inside, he made sure the blanket was securely closed before removing the thong from her neck.

Cara rubbed at the chafed area. "Is this your house?"

"Yes," he said, swiping at a spider web. "This is where I stay when I'm here."

"Did you convince them I'm your slave?"

Tall Dancer shook his head. "I'm not so sure they believed the story. Especially my *kak,* Noisy Feather." He picked up a blanket and shook it. Dust billowed out. "Stay in here out of sight." With no more explanations, he ducked under the blanket and was gone.

As he stepped outside, he drew a deep breath of the smoke-tainted air. Around him swirled the sounds and smells of home. Children raced by, splattering dirt-tinged snow with their feet. By the side of the next house, a group of children played in a snow bank. Conversations among family members drifted over from neighboring houses. Somewhere someone was crying, but another voice soothed with calm words.

He bent down and ruffled Buck's fur, then led the team around the back of the house and put them into a special pen. He wedged the sled underneath the overhang of the house and gathered up his furs and his leather pack.

Curious eyes followed him as he entered the house and hurried toward his living quarters. Two women stood in front, peeping through a tear in the blanket. They started and hurried away when he stepped up behind them.

Before he could go in, his mother came up and tapped him on the shoulder. Without a word, she motioned him to follow to her house. Once inside, she pointed to a corner filled with neatly folded blankets. He obliged and, with much grunting, she positioned herself across from him cross-legged on the floor.

"What is between you and this slave?"

Her question was blunt, but he knew he wouldn't have to respond. His face told the whole story.

"Where is *kak?*" He glanced around for his uncle.

She shrugged. "Gone to brag on your furs. Answer my question."

Tall Dancer glanced away, but watched her face from the corner of his eye.

She studied him silently for a moment, then slowly shook her head. "You love this girl."

It wasn't a question. It was a statement.

"I saw her at Klaida's potlatch and recognized her for a white girl. I asked Klaida for her, and he gave her to me." He leaned forward. "You know what the Tsimshian do to their slaves. They had gotten her trading with the Haida. Her life must have been horrible. All I could think about was freeing her." Tall Dancer raised his head and stared into eyes that knew him all too well.

"As a child, you brought home injured birds and rabbits. But this white woman is not a rabbit," his mother said softly.

"I know," he answered.

"Do you love her?"

Tall Dancer closed his eyes. "Yes. I do." Speaking the words lifted a great weight from his shoulders, but he knew the weight was now on his mother.

"Does she feel the same for you?" She leaned forward to listen to his answer.

"Yes."

She laid a withered hand on his arm. "Does she know about the marriage?"

Tall Dancer jumped to his feet and paced the room. "I told her about Kaskoe. I explained how it has to be."

His mother's eyes softened as she rose, moved to him, and touched his face. "I want you to be happy, my son. That is all your father wanted for you, either here or with the whites, whichever you chose. But Kaskoe is like you. You and she have been raised with the same beliefs and customs. She will make you a good wife. You will learn to overlook her temper. After all, when it is dark, who cares about her temper, heh?"

He laughed, enjoying the flicker of youth in his mother's twinkling eyes. She could always make him blush with her forthright ways. "I am going through with the marriage. I know it is expected of me." He took her face in his hands. "Please don't worry."

"What will you do with the girl?" she asked, grabbing his shoulder as he was about to leave.

"I will take her to Fort St. Michael in the fall, when I go

south to set my trap lines along the sea, and leave her there with the Russians." He turned and looked down at his mother.

She made a sucking sound through her teeth. "Kaskoe will not like your traveling with a woman slave. There has already been much talk."

"I could not leave her there. Klaida would have killed her. To go to the fort then would have made me arrive here a month late."

"We will talk about this later. The important thing now is what to do with her until you can return her. You cannot keep her in your house with a new wife. I want her to come and live with me."

Tall Dancer smiled and put his hand on her shoulder. "You do understand she is not a slave? I plan to set her free. But I told her it would be safer for her to act as one as long as she is with us."

"And she and I will continue to do so." Her voice held an excited note as she anticipated the game of pretend. Tall Dancer gave her a final hug, then ducked beneath the blanket.

She looked after him, thinking how his broad back and loping gait were so like his father's.

Tall Dancer returned to his house and found Cara asleep on a pile of furs in the corner. He bent down to shake her awake and suddenly noticed how much she had changed in the past weeks. She had gained weight and the circles beneath her eyes had disappeared.

His heart beat faster as he watched her chest rise and fall. He longed to take her in his arms and love her again as he had last night. But tribal customs were stronger than his desires. He was to marry another, and he would abide by that agreement now that he was home. The confines of rules and traditions weighed heavily on him.

For one last moment, he closed his eyes and remembered holding her, loving her, remembered her softness and her moans in his ear. Perhaps he would never love that way again. Perhaps neither would she.

Gently, he shook her awake. She sat up and rubbed her eyes. "What is it?" she asked.

"We must talk," he said, getting to his feet and pacing the small cubicle.

Cara sat up, wondering what new turn her life had taken.

"The wedding will be in a few days. It would not be right for you to stay with me."

Old fears rose again and caught her around the throat.

"I am giving you to my mother."

She released her held breath. He had told her that from the beginning. Why was he telling her again?

"We must make a show of it, my giving you to my mother, so others will know this is how it is between us." He stopped pacing and looked at her, his eyes pleading for understanding.

"You will live with her through the summer until I leave to go south and set my traps in the fall. You are in no danger." He sat down on a woven mat, his back against the wall. " 'Atle understands our arrangement. You will not be her slave, but you must act as such when you are in view of others in the clan. She will teach you what you need to know."

Despite the fact she had liked his mother from the beginning, his assurances only made her feel more lonely. She was to be alone again for the better part of a year, expected to act and do as if she were once again a slave. Her lot hadn't improved, she thought dismally. It had worsened.

Chapter Seven

Tall Dancer delivered Cara to his mother before the evening meal. Cara kept silent as she followed him past blanket-shrouded doorways where curious eyes stared at her. Stopping in front of his mother's house, he held the blanket aside. Cara glanced up at him, then ducked under his arm.

His mother rose from her seat on the floor and dumped the basket and straw out of her lap.

"My mother's name is Marisha." He gave Cara a push forward.

"Put your things there." The old woman pointed to a corner. Cara deposited her blanket and the set of sealskins Tall Dancer had made for her on the trail.

"Fill this with water at the stream." Marisha shoved a tightly woven basket into Cara's hands. Cara glanced between the two. Anger was building on both their faces. With another glance over her shoulder, she ducked beneath the blanket and hurried away.

Marisha watched her only son stare after the young woman now weaving her way through the women squatted by the firepit. The women's eyes followed her until she left the house; then they whispered among themselves.

Helplessness replaced Marisha's anger. She had been one of the few Tlingit brides to marry a man she loved, and their love had sustained them through sickness and hard winters without enough to eat. The joy of their union was rare, and she wanted the same joy for her son with a woman of his choice.

But his impending marriage would benefit each family. It could not be helped. This was a fact of life among their people. To put the wedding off would insult the bride's family. Wars had been fought over such disagreements.

"You don't have to tell me what my obligations are, *'atle*. I know the good of the clan must come first, and I accept that. Next fall, I will deliver Cara to her own people."

Marisha looked closely at her son through dimming eyes. "Are you sure that will be the end of it for you? Will you carry her in your heart and into your marriage bed?"

Tall Dancer turned away and dropped the blanket back into place. He raised his eyes to hers and the depth of his feelings for the girl shocked Marisha.

"I will try to put her memory aside and honor my agreement with Kaskoe." Without another word, he turned on his heel and ducked beneath the blanket, leaving it moving with his haste.

Morning fog clung to the surface of the swift creek and patches of snow frosted the tops of gray boulders. Cara's knees sank into the mud as she knelt down and dipped the basket into the water as she had done every morning for a week. Spring was rapidly approaching, judging by the swelling buds on the trees. Perhaps warmer temperatures would raise her spirits, she thought with little enthusiasm.

Sprinkles struck her face as the water leaped and tumbled over moss-covered stones. She lifted the basket and took a long drink, then rose and started up the hill toward the village. A cold wind tugged at her long dress, and she was glad for the bear fur around her shoulders. Her feet slipped and water sloshed over the basket's rim. Last night's rain and snow had made the worn path slippery.

As she approached the big houses, she saw a crowd gathered at the edge of the sound. Tall Dancer stood at the front of the crowd, a head above the rest. Cara hurried into the house, but Marisha was gone, too, along with all the families.

She set the basket down by the firepit's edge and hurried outside, pushing her way through the crowd until she stood in the first row of people behind Tall Dancer, Marisha, and Noisy Feather. They stood side by side, a huge pile of furs in front of them. No one spoke, but all watched a barely visible spit of land jutting out into the water.

Then, through the fog, a canoe emerged. Cara squinted. Twenty warriors paddled the craft that sliced through the water, plowing a path through ice floes. In the bow stood a large figure shrouded in an enormous fur. Figuring him to be a visiting chief, Cara turned to leave.

"She's so big," someone whispered.

Cara glanced to her right. Two young girls huddled close together and spoke behind cupped hands.

"He hasn't seen her since her confinement," the other said, bobbing her head to see around the crowd now surging forward.

"The men are having to paddle extra hard. Look at them strain." Both girls covered their mouths and giggled.

A man in the rear of the crowd turned around and glared at the girls. They joined hands and ran away toward low bushes along the water, their giggles trailing behind them.

Cara's heart began to thump. Tall Dancer's intended wife had arrived. She pushed back into the crowd in time to see the craft scrape ashore. Five men jumped out of the back and attempted to shove the canoe onto the sand. They grunted and strained to no avail. More men joined the first. They succeeded in pushing up a ridge of sand at the boat's bow, but little else.

A distinguished man rose from directly behind the shrouded figure. He stepped out onto the beach, then held out his hand. Cara watched the chubby fingers that entwined with his. A

massive woman shed the long fur wrap and rocked the canoe
ominously. The men at the back clutched at the sides and tried
to keep the craft from tipping. She swung her leg, as large as
a sizable cedar stump, over the side. It thudded onto the sand,
and her other leg joined it. Tall Dancer stepped forward.

For the first time, Cara tore her eyes away from the woman.
Tall Dancer wore soft new sealskins. His long hair was clubbed
back, tied with a leather thong bearing a little shell ornament.
Red and blue beads sparkled in the sun as he stepped away
from Marisha, picked up an armful of furs, and stepped up to
the woman. The little gray man at her side moved forward.

"I give these to you, Big Rabbit, as a gift," Tall Dancer
said, his voice pouring over the crowd, melting the frigid air.

The little man grinned from ear to ear as his arms surrounded
the luxurious furs. Tall Dancer turned toward the woman. His
expression never changed, but his face blanched when she shyly
looked down and offered him her hand.

"I have not seen you in many years, Kaskoe," he said in a
voice barely audible to the crowd around them.

"I have been in my confinement," she said with a smile.

"I offer you these." He bent down again and picked up the
slick black furs he had used to cover Cara's feet.

Kaskoe grinned and accepted the pelts. "These will be added
to my wedding dress," she said, twirling two ermine tails while
she smiled coyly.

Tall Dancer returned to his family's side. Kaskoe's father
took her hand and guided her down the muddy street toward
the house at the end of the row. The crowd trailed behind them,
whispering and giggling. Cara shrank into the throng, but her
eyes locked with Tall Dancer's for a moment. He held his head
high, but his eyes told her he knew the whole village was
laughing at his bride. He looked quickly away and moved off
with Noisy Feather and Marisha at his side.

In a few moments, Cara was alone. Behind her she heard
the men finally beach the boat. They passed her and made for
the house, eager to partake of the food and drink offered there.

Why hadn't Marisha told her this was the day? She had barely seen Tall Dancer since their arrival a week before because he had been busy with the arrangements for his potlatch and wedding. She suddenly felt as dreary as the soft rain just beginning to pelt down.

"There is no more room in the slave quarters." Marisha stood toe to toe with a man in a pointed cedar hat. Her hands gripped her slim waist and her chin tilted in defiance.

The man stared down at her for a moment, then sighed and shrugged his shoulders. "You may keep her with you, then." He leaned forward and frowned. "But only until there is room for her in there." He thrust out his arm in the direction of the room beside the door.

Marisha didn't give an inch, nor did her expression change even when the man deepened his frown. Heaving another sigh, he turned and moved toward the door, shaking his head.

Cara peeped around the wooden partition that separated Marisha's house from those on either side. The confrontation had captured the attention of all the residents. Work stopped at the firepit as everyone looked toward the pair.

Cara had held her breath as the formidable man leaned toward tiny Marisha. They had been arguing for some time over where Cara would stay. Slaves lived in the front compartments nearest the door of the big house so they would be easily accessible for chores. But now, with the jammed quarters, Marisha was insisting Cara live with her.

Cara expelled her held breath when the man turned and moved away. Work in the house resumed, and Marisha came toward her wearing a triumphant grin. She motioned Cara inside when the women at the firepit stopped their work again and stared.

"Little-River-Underneath has agreed to let you live here with me until there is room in the slave quarters," Marisha said as she let the blanket drop into place.

"What will Noisy Feather say?" Cara bent down to pick up her water basket. Late afternoon shadows were slanting through the smoke hole and soon she should begin preparations for the evening meal.

"Pfft." Marisha made the sound through pursed lips and waved her arms at no one in particular. "My brother worries too much. Always worried about what someone will say."

Cara moved toward the door, but Marisha's bony, wrinkled hand on her forearm stopped her.

"I am sorry I did not tell you Kaskoe was arriving today." Her eyes were full of genuine concern, but the mention of Tall Dancer's marriage sliced through Cara.

"I did not want you to worry." Marisha smoothed Cara's arm, her eyes sympathetic and kind.

Cara nodded, even though the lump in her throat was choking her, bringing tears to her eyes.

"It is bad that her father has chosen to return to our village. All these preparations would be going on far from here." Marisha shook her head.

Cara turned away, ashamed at the hot tears suddenly washing her cheeks. For two weeks the house had been in turmoil while preparations were made for Tall Dancer's wedding and potlatch. She had seen very little of him, only fleeting glances as he passed through the house, always with Noisy Feather at his side. Yet with each passing day and each brief glance, her love for him deepened.

Marisha's grip on her arm tightened into a gentle tug. Reluctantly, Cara turned, and Marisha reached up to smooth back a wisp of Cara's hair. "When this is all over, I will take you into the forest to search for roots and herbs. I will teach you what to look for and how to use them."

Cara knew Marisha was trying to take her mind off the impending ceremony, and her heart warmed to the old woman for her efforts. But nothing would ease the ache. She turned as Marisha's hand slid away and hurried down the platforms before prying eyes saw her tears.

She ducked through the round doorway, down the steps of the porch, and out into the street. The air was brisk and salty, heavy with moisture from the breeze that blew off the sea. Her head down, she trudged toward the stream. As she neared, she saw a large group of young women gathered at water's edge. In their center was Kaskoe.

Cara stopped, tempted to turn back and go further up the stream to fill her basket with water, but they had seen her. Their chatter stopped and they turned in her direction.

Kaskoe rose from her seat on a large rock. Her straight hair hung down the sides of her round face and the recently placed labret swelled her bottom lip into a shelf. Long and intricately woven, her dress strained at the sides to cover her breadth. Strips of ermine fur proved the garment had been enlarged several times.

"What are you staring at, slave?" Kaskoe demanded, taking a step out of the circle of her admirers.

Cara glanced at the other young girls now assembling at Kaskoe's side. She was outnumbered, but before she could think of an answer, Kaskoe cuffed her on the side of her head, sending her flying into the freezing water. The breath rushed out of her chest and rocks scrubbed her back as she sank to the bottom.

The other girls howled with laughter when she rose, her hair matted to her head and her clothes dripping water. The brisk wind cut her to the bone. Kaskoe stood in the circle of her comrades, a wicked smile stretching the corners of her wide mouth.

Cara waded to shore and reached down to retrieve her basket. Kaskoe gave the basket a kick, sending it skidding into the swift stream. The red and green bands of cedar fiber bobbed along as the current caught it and washed it toward the sea.

"So you are Cara, the slave who has the village laughing at me." She shoved her face into Cara's. "You are the one Tall Dancer would not trade. When he and I are married, I will ask that you be given to me and I will make your life miserable for disgracing me." Her puffy face hovered over Cara as she growled the words. "I know he slept with you on the trail."

She moved a step closer and Cara could smell her foul odor.

"Some men came to my father and told him. Kagwantan

warriors told this village about the beautiful red-haired slave Tall Dancer owned. I will get revenge for my disgrace.''

She moved even closer. ''Tall Dancer is a good catch.'' She dropped her voice to a whisper. ''Many women have hoped to be married to him, but my family are the ones who made the arrangements. It is I who will bear his children and warm his bed.''

Cold, angry, and tired of being intimidated, Cara flung herself at the woman. Caught off guard, Kaskoe glanced around frantically for her friends, who were stunned into immobility. Cara wound her hand in Kaskoe's hair and yanked.

''Ow,'' the woman howled. Together, they stumbled backward, teetering dangerously close to the water. Eyes open wide, Kaskoe glanced over her shoulder at the rushing stream.

''In you go.'' Cara shoved against Kaskoe's stomach and they both flew into the stream.

Kaskoe hit with a huge splash. Flat on her back, she struggled to rise. Cara quickly scrambled to her feet and stood over her with fists balled. She leaned down, intending to smash Kaskoe's face, feeling the anger of the past year rise inside her like a demon. As she pulled back her fist, a hand caught her wrist and lifted her out of the water.

Tall Dancer set her down roughly, casting her a fleeting amused look. Then he waded into the water and offered Kaskoe his hand. Boiling mad moments before, Kaskoe whined her anger as soon as she saw him. Babbling and crying, she tried to explain how Cara had attacked her. Her friends shrank away after a comment from one brought a fierce look from Tall Dancer.

Bracing his feet against the bottom of the creek, Tall Dancer hauled Kaskoe to her feet. She scrambled out of the water, up the bank, and stomped away toward the village, her friends trailing behind.

Tall Dancer crossed his arms and waited. Cara looked down at the puddle forming at her feet where the water dripped off her clothes. A sudden, swift breeze cut through her.

"She started it," Cara mumbled, feeling like a disobedient child.

She moved away toward the long houses.

"Cara, wait."

She heard him, but she didn't stop. A small crowd had gathered. Winter camp was long and boring and everyone was hungry for some new bit of gossip to help them pass the long nights and brief days.

Cara climbed the steps to the house and pushed someone aside. When she ducked through the door, voices hushed and all eyes turned toward her. Families gathered at the hearth murmured among themselves as she hurried up the platforms, stepping over children and dogs. She rounded the wooden partition and slid through the blanket that covered the door. Marisha was gone and the room was dark and quiet. Cara shucked out of her wet clothes, then sat down on a pile of furs and rubbed her chilled skin with a coarse woven mat.

"So you have met Kaskoe." Marisha dropped the curtain into place and stood above her. "She has a bad temper. So do you, I see."

"How did you know?" Cara ceased scrubbing her legs and looked up.

Marisha shrugged. "Gossip travels quickly."

Chafed by Marisha's tolerance of the girl, Cara said, "She told me after she and Tall Dancer were married she was going to ask that I be given to her."

"No. You are mine, given to me by my son."

Alarmed by her tone, Cara glanced up.

Marisha smiled, pushing her face into a sea of wrinkles, and ran her hand under Cara's chin affectionately. "No one else need know the truth."

Tall Dancer smoothed the fur on a wolverine pelt and laid it atop a pile of others. He raised his head and breathed in the odors of home—the salty sea, the rank fur, the ever-present decaying wood and moss. He ran his hand over the pile of pelts stacked as tall as his waist—a generous bride-price for someone like Kaskoe. An involuntary shiver went over him as he thought of her bloated face and body in his bed.

Memories of Cara rushed to the forefront of his thoughts. He closed his eyes against the onslaught of emotions. Silky hair, green eyes snapping defiance, soft skin beneath his touch.

He took a deep and ragged breath. He couldn't break this marriage contract, no matter how repulsive he found Kaskoe. All his father had worked for depended on this alliance between the two families. Never before in the history of the clan had a white man elevated himself to a station of wealth. Never before had a white man married a woman of the people and offered her family wealth.

He opened his eyes, grateful for the cold wind that ruffled his hair and cooled his desire. He would go through with this marriage.

He scooped up the furs and strode toward the house with them. Tonight Big Rabbit would either accept or reject his bride-price for Kaskoe. Behind his back, the old man was called *Lukciyan kutici-yad,* Child of a Mink's Scent Glands, because he was so stingy. A mink's glands had to be carefully cut around to avoid spilling the stench over the fur.

As Tall Dancer ducked into the house, a wave of smells and heat struck him. Down at the firepit, women squatted on an area filled with rounded stones and busily fished hot stones out of the fire with long tongs. As the stones were dropped into watertight wooden boxes, the water inside hissed and sputtered. The mingled scent of porpoise, seal, and fish lay heavy in the air, and the smell of roasting bear meat made his mouth water as he climbed the platforms to his mother's house.

Skirting the wooden screen, he brushed aside the blanket. Marisha sat in the center of the floor chewing on a piece of buckskin. Tall Dancer tossed the last of the furs down on top of another pile and flopped down opposite her. She removed the piece of leather from her mouth and held out a pair of sealskin pants. The side seams were carefully sewn with porpoise sinew, and little smooth shells dangled down the front.

"You will be the finest dressed groom this camp has seen," she said with a smile and a caressing swipe to the garment.

Tall Dancer kissed her on the forehead, then took the pants from her and ran his hand over them. "Where's Cara?" he asked, glancing quickly around the room.

Marisha paused for a moment before answering, a pregnant pause that told Tall Dancer he was in for a lecture.

"I sent her to the forest to gather moss." She folded her hands in her lap and sighed. "I wish you would talk to her before tonight."

"I don't know what I can say." He rose to his feet and stepped over to a woven hanging on the wall. With one finger he traced the raven pattern tightly imbedded in the cedar fibers.

"You can release her."

He whirled around. "Release her? From what?"

Marisha looked up at him. "From your love."

He sighed and dropped his arm.

"The girl will live in torment when you and Kaskoe are married and living together."

His fingers entwined with the rough fringe edging the hanging until the fibers cut into his flesh. "What can I do?"

"Make her think you love Kaskoe. Make her think you want this marriage."

He shook his head. "She knows the truth. She sees it in my eyes."

Marisha suddenly appeared at his side, took his cheeks in her hands and turned his head so he stared directly into her face. "Then teach your eyes to lie."

Cara sat in the back row of people crowded around the firepit in Big Rabbit's house. The fishy odor of burning eulachon oil filled the air and smoke hung over the crowd. She peeped over their heads for a glimpse of Marisha and Tall Dancer. They sat together on the lowest bench. By their side sat Noisy Feather. A pile of furs lay at their feet, and they stared at the father and daughter opposite them.

Big Rabbit, his stomach protruding over the rope that held his bark apron onto his rounded hips, leaned back and seemed to be thoughtfully regarding the pile at his feet. Kaskoe took up the entire other end of the bench. Her dress slid tightly up her hips and her long straight hair was tied up with bones and shells. She smiled coyly at Tall Dancer, but he was studying the floor.

"These are fine pelts, Tall Dancer," Big Rabbit said, heaving himself to his feet. "Fine pelts and many of them." He grunted as he bent to pick up an ermine skin and rubbed it against his cheek. "But not enough for my daughter."

Tall Dancer jerked up his head. "Not enough?"

"No."

Tall Dancer leaped to his feet. He opened his mouth to speak, then clamped it shut when Noisy-Feather grabbed his forearm.

"What is your price?" Noisy Feather asked.

Big Rabbit dropped the ermine fur, crossed his arms over his chest, and looked up at the carved beams overhead. An expectant hush fell over the crowd as they waited, their eyes moving from the young man to the old.

"Give me these furs and"—he paused and glanced at the crowd—"the red-haired slave."

One huge gasp echoed against the sides of the house. Cara clapped her hand over her mouth. Tall Dancer's face turned to stone. Cara waited, her very existence hanging on his next words.

"No . . ." he began, but Marisha put one hand on his shoulder and slowly rose to her feet, the other hand on the small of her back.

"I beg you, Big Rabbit, do not ask for the slave. She serves an old woman well."

Big Rabbit glanced at Kaskoe. "The slave has embarrassed my daughter."

"The white girl does not know our laws. She is innocent. My son told the Kagwantan warriors that she was his woman only to save her life, for he was bringing her to me, help for an old woman."

Cara stifled a giggle at the piteous whine in Marisha's voice. Tall Dancer's mother was putting on quite a performance, although the pain in her lower back might be real from the game of shinny she had played that morning with a group of children. Cara smiled as Marisha limped forward to take Big Rabbit's hand, remembering her sailing the skin ball along the ground with a stick while the children around her cheered and dodged and tried to whack the ball away from the goal line.

Big Rabbit glanced at Kaskoe. Her lip, already protruding from the labret, stuck out further. "I will take these furs."

Marisha smiled, squeezed the big man's hand, and hobbled back to her seat. The crowd rose to its feet and dispersed to do bedtime chores. Two men from Big Rabbit's family picked up the pelts and carried them away. Hours and hours of care had gone into those skins, Cara thought as the last armload disappeared into a partitioned room at the end of the house. Kaskoe giggled, a high-pitched irritating sound, then waddled after her father.

One hand on his mother's shoulder and one under her arm, Tall Dancer escorted her through the door and down the steps of the house. Noisy Feather followed, frowning. When they were gone, Cara slipped out, avoiding as many people as possible.

The streets of the camp were almost deserted. A stray dog trotted between the houses, searching for a leftover morsel from supper. Cold moonlight flooded the earth and turned the totems guarding the house entrances into steely-eyed sentinels. Wrapping a bear fur around her shoulders, Cara moved toward the stream, seeking its monotonous gurgle to ease her mind.

At the end of the street stood a half-finished big house. Carved totems stared at her with unpainted, hollow eyes. The soft, pungent smell of newly stripped cedar beckoned her. She climbed up the steps to a wide porch, then ducked inside.

The vastness of the interior echoed back her breathing. Bedrooms were not yet partitioned off. In the center, scooped out earth represented where the firepit would be.

She breathed deeply, inhaling the fragrance of newly turned

earth and freshly cut cedar. Benches ran halfway around the firepit. She sat down on one end, feeling the splinters prick her bottom.

Years from now this surface would be worn smooth from hundreds of hands, feet, and backsides walking and sliding down its length, she thought, rubbing her hand over its roughness.

A shadow moved to her right and she jumped to her feet. Tall Dancer stepped out of the darkness and into the circle of moonlight pouring in through the unscreened smoke hole.

"It's magnificent, isn't it?" His voice reverberated through the empty house.

"Y-y-yes," Cara stammered, fear slamming her heart against her ribs. If she were caught with him, the entire camp would be on her. Her life wouldn't be worth saving.

His hair hung loose around his shoulders. He wore the sealskin pants, but no shirt. One hand grasped a fur around his shoulders.

"How did you find me?" she asked, then realized that was an arrogant statement. Perhaps he hadn't followed her. Perhaps they had stumbled onto each other.

He stepped down into the pit, then up onto the layer of smooth stones surrounding it. "I saw you walking this way and guessed you might come in here."

Cara was suddenly afraid. They were like strangers again, despite the intimacy they had shared.

"Cara." He put his hands on her forearms. "I want you to understand you will be safe here until fall."

Cara ducked her head. Looking into his deep brown eyes just made the pain worse. "I know," she murmured.

"I have to do this." He tightened his grip and she winced.

Cara raised her head. "You don't owe me any explanations."

"I think I do." His words hung on the cold air.

"No. We both knew that night would be all we would have." She turned her head as the first tear fell. "Please. Don't."

"Cara."

His lips caressed her name. He took another step toward her.

In a flash of intuition, she knew what would happen. Her blood rushed first hot then cold. Prickles ran up her arms as his hands entwined with hers. He kissed her again and drew her near, making words unnecessary. Liquid fire trailed after his finger-tips as his rough hands stroked her back.

''No.'' She jerked her face away and pushed against his chest with both hands. She had to get away from him. When he pulled her close, his very being devoured hers, engulfing her so she couldn't think.

''I love you.'' He caught her arm and spun her around to face him. His lips crushed hers as he kissed her hungrily.

Her blood warmed, blurring thought and guilt. She slipped her hands into his hair and ran her fingers through its silkiness. For this moment, he was hers.

''I love you.'' He whispered the words and pressed her cheek to his shoulder.

The soft words echoed in the empty house, bounced against the walls, then hung in the air . . . waiting. Desperation gave rise to panic. What would he do if she gave him the answer he wanted? Refuse his marriage vows? Leave his people for her? Where would they go if he did?

His eyes were dark and expectant when she looked up. She opened her mouth, then closed it. If she uttered the words, she might irrevocably change both their lives.

Without a word, he turned and disappeared into the darkness at the rear of the house.

The water, slushy with ice, took his breath as Tall Dancer dove into the ice-clogged sound. Down he plunged until his hands scraped the rocky bottom, then his feet. Crouching, he pushed off the bottom, shot back up through the water, and surfaced. Dawn blushed in the eastern sky, but the village was dark and quiet. Stretching out on his back, he floated, relishing the chill of the morning breeze against his skin. These few moments were his alone. Soon other young men would come down to the sound to take their icy plunges under the supervision of their maternal uncles.

Tall Dancer closed his eyes and thought back to his own conditioning with Noisy Feather. Some mornings he had been barely able to endure the cold swim each young man took every day to toughen him. On those mornings, all he could think about was getting out of the water and back into the warm house. Over the years, the morning baths became less chilling and more refreshing. Later, the icy swims helped him clear his mind when he was troubled, especially in the years after his father's death.

Now the cold water eased other achings, he thought, feeling a rush of desire for Cara. Today was his wedding day. Today he would fulfill his family's dreams and wants and marry Kaskoe, a woman he could barely tolerate. Yet with this marriage, he would consummate his father's hard work and ambitions. With this union, his family would be elevated in rank beyond their expectations, and they would move to the top row of sleeping quarters in the big house.

Words and laughter drifted to him from the village. He glanced at the sky. The faint pink was now a swirl of orange, yellow, and deep pink. It was time to prepare for his marriage. With long, languid strokes, he swam to the shore, shrugged into his sealskins, and set off toward his house with a heavy heart.

Chapter Eight

Cara wiggled in through the crowd gathered outside Big Rabbit's house and slipped unseen into the last row of benches surrounding the firepit. Craning her neck to peer around those in front, she saw Tall Dancer sitting cross-legged on a woven mat in the center of the house.

He wore a new ceremonial robe and a headdress of white ermine fur. Black-tipped mountain goat horns rose above the white fur and a carving of his family crest adorned the front of the headdress. More ermine tails hung down his cheeks and touched his shoulders. An elaborately woven blanket, a gift from Marisha, hung around his shoulders and fell in soft folds around his hips. Marisha sat on one side of him, Noisy Feather on the other.

Across the firepit, Kaskoe's relatives sat with stern, expressionless faces. A hush fell over the crowd and those still outside walked in quietly and filled the empty spaces.

Little-River-Underneath entered the house's round door and moved down the wooden platforms to stand in front of Tall Dancer. He nodded and everyone in the house began to hum and sway, then to sing.

"Heyuwa, helqwyuwa. 'i, 'i, 'i, 'i, 'i."

They repeated the verse three more times, and Cara recognized the wedding song.

Tall Dancer stood and turned toward the back of the house. The blanket covering Big Rabbit's sleeping quarters parted and Kaskoe stepped through. Her clothes were as elaborate as Tall Dancer's and covered her from neck to ankle. Woven from cedar fibers, the material was covered with images of killer whales, seals, and ravens cavorting across her spacious stomach. Spruce roots had been woven into her dark hair and the two ermine tails Tall Dancer had given her on the beach dangled from the edges of her hair.

The song grew louder, and Kaskoe began to sway with the rhythm. Cara stood numbly as the crowd rose to their feet, although tears blurred her vision. Kaskoe moved forward, lifted the edge of her dress, and carefully planted each large foot on a flat copper plate lying on the floor of the house. She whirled, stumbled and the crowd caught their breath. Then, she quickly righted herself and the song continued.

" 'i, 'i, 'i, 'i, 'i."

Copper plate by copper plate, she moved down the house until she stood at Tall Dancer's side. Although he was taller than she by a head, she was more than twice as wide. She nodded, then sat next to him, looking shyly downward. Tall Dancer did not return her greeting and sat stone-faced, staring at the floor.

The crowd sat and the chief began to explain each one's responsibilities. He charged Tall Dancer with providing for his family, with protecting his family's name, and with fidelity. He entrusted Kaskoe with family duties and the rearing of the children. All through the speech, Tall Dancer kept his face forward and did not once glance at his bride. Cara closed her eyes and remembered how he had looked last night, how he had tasted and smelled and felt. Then she carefully tucked away each memory.

When she opened her eyes, Tall Dancer was handing the furs over to Big Rabbit. He accepted the pelts, then placed his daughter's hand in Tall Dancer's. The crowd began to sing again.

Cara could stand no more. She crawled around behind the benches and ran out the door, down between the houses, heading for the privacy of the forest beyond. Brambles tore at her face and stones cut the bottoms of her feet, but on she fled. She ran until the canopy of trees darkened the forest floor with a premature dusk.

Her chest heaved when she stopped and braced with one hand against an ancient, moss-covered cedar tree. Overhead, the branches moaned against each other and the wind sighed. Cara fell to her knees on the spongy carpet and covered her face with her hands. Hopelessness was consuming her, roasting her alive in its dry sorrow. Try as she would, she could not erase from her mind Kaskoe's face as she looked up at her husband.

Tall Dancer forced a smile as people thronged around him and his bride. At his elbow, Kaskoe chatted and giggled with the other women, blissfully ignorant of what was in her husband's heart.

Occasionally, she laced her arm through his and held him possessively. His nephews were showing the honored guests to their places, and everyone waited anxiously for the potlatch to begin. In his mind, he ran over the words he planned to say, but faltered when he came to the place to extol the virtues of his bride. From the corner of his eye he could see her scratching at her hip through the itchy dress. He scanned the crowd for Cara, then scolded himself. A slave would never be permitted at a wedding feast. He sighed and willed his lips to say the words he must.

As the ceremony began, he looked out over the now-quiet crowd. Raven women sat together on his left, Raven men on his right. Wolf women sat on the same side as the Raven men; the Wolf men sat on his left. He raised his head and looked to the back of the house, where Big Rabbit sat with the two chiefs

of the Raven and Wolf clans. He drew a breath and heard
himself begin to speak.

"Thank you for coming today to my marriage and to this
celebration. I am the son of Vasili Zaikov, who was the son
of Mikhail Zaikov." He waited while the crowd buzzed expectantly and the two chiefs at the back nodded and conferred.

"My father was a brave man who chose to live among the
people instead of his own people, the *tsatyka*—cruel men who
take our women and our furs and trade them for beads and
looking glasses. He escaped these people and came here to
work and trade until he was a wealthy man and could marry
my mother." Again the crowd buzzed and Kaskoe elbowed
him in the side.

"I am proud to be his son, and I challenge anyone to say
bad things about him." He waited, but drew no response.

"This is my wife, Kaskoe. Her father, Big Rabbit, is chief
of this house." The crowd settled down as he moved into more
familiar territory. He heard himself bragging about her virtues,
while his insides roiled with thoughts of what was expected
later.

Cara's chest ached from sobbing. The sun was sinking in
the sky and the deep forest seemed even darker. She rose from
her seat on the damp moss and stumbled back to the camp.
Between the houses trudged guests, their arms loaded with pelts
and blankets.

From the porch of one house came the slurred voices of two
men intoxicated on the juice of Dead Person's Berries. "Well,
he married this woman named Kaskoe," one mumbled. "She's
almost as big as a tree. She's the biggest girl I've ever seen. I
don't know how many men are needed to marry her." The
men laughed and slapped each other on the back.

The potlatch must be over, she surmised and slipped into
the shadows to prevent being seen. As she crept from house
to house, desperately working her way back to Marisha's and

her own private corner, she saw the last of the guests congratulating the newlywed couple.

Kaskoe was leaning on Tall Dancer's shoulder and they smilingly endured the ribald remarks tossed at them by friends. Those living in Big Rabbit's house warned the couple not to awaken them with lovemaking, as happened many nights in the thin-walled compartments.

Hot tears rolled down Cara's cheeks as she stood in the shadow of the house. She furiously wiped them away and bolted down the street toward Marisha's. She walked in unnoticed, crept down the line of benches, and ducked in under the blanket.

She pulled the blanket closed, shutting out the faint light from eulachon lamps and casting herself into darkness. She grasped the coarse blanket and wadded the material tightly in her hands. Burying her face in the fabric, she cried for the loss of the only person who could have made her stay here bearable.

Marisha found Cara asleep on the floor, her face stained with tears, her basket unfinished. She knelt and looked into the girl's sleeping face. Sadness was etched across her cheeks even in sleep. The months would be long until fall.

She sighed and sat back on her heels. Perhaps she had been wrong to instill so deeply in her son the ways of the people. He would honor his marriage at the expense of his own happiness. She should take joy in that, she told herself, and be proud of a son so loyal to his people. But the thought did little to cheer her.

She smoothed back a lock of Cara's hair. Kaskoe did not love Tall Dancer, but she would cling to him to elevate herself and her family. *This girl loves him,* she thought, pulling a blanket over Cara. She would have made her son a good wife. Marisha sighed again and crawled onto her own sleeping platform.

* * *

Tall Dancer lay on his back and stared up at the strange faces on the carved beams over his head. At his side, Kaskoe snored loudly and deeply. She shifted her position, and her flabby rump rubbed up against the side of his leg.

She hadn't put up much of a fight over his refusal to consummate the marriage. She had only shrugged, lamented the loss of their furs at the potlatch, and swiftly fell asleep.

Tall Dancer sighed and pulled the itchy mat over his chest. He ran his fingers over the edge and thought wistfully of his mother's smooth, soft blankets.

How would he escape his wife tomorrow? He had often laughed at the young men who married older widows and found themselves little better than slaves. Now he was no better off than they.

Kaskoe could be formidable when crossed, but she couldn't control his thoughts. Those were his own. Another snore erupted and grumbling filtered in from an adjoining partition. He closed his eyes and thought of Cara and how she had looked in a circle of moonlight in a half-finished house.

"You dropped a thread there."

Marisha bent over Cara's shoulder and pointed a bony finger to a flaw in the blanket. Cara sighed and pulled out the threads all the way back to her mistake. A blast of wind swooped through the house as someone came in and slammed the door against a hail of snowflakes.

"Keep your thread tight," Marisha ordered, pulling at a loose loop.

Cara shifted on the hard wooden bench. Behind her, conversation at the firepit settled into a low, familiar buzz. She resumed weaving and marveled at the red and black killer whale emerging beneath her hands. A fiber of cedar bark sliced her finger. She shook her hand irritably, then picked out a snarl in the goat-hair and cedar-fiber yarn.

Overhead, the smoke hole screen rattled against the roof. She turned and looked toward the fire as a shower of flakes drifted down, then fizzled away in the fire's heat. The storm outside had raged for three days, and she had spent almost all her waking hours weaving.

She glanced at the pattern board beside her. The faded wood was cracked, but the red, blue, and yellow colors persisted. She reached out and ran her fingers over the design and thought of the generations of Marisha's family represented in these bits of dried paint. The family's history unraveled down the length of the board. Included was the adoption of Tall Dancer's father into the tribe and Tall Dancer's birth. At the end in bright new stain was the story of Tall Dancer's marriage.

The knot untied, she wound the thread around her hand and continued to dip in and out of the warp fastened to a board above. This pattern had become her only link to Tall Dancer, as she hadn't seen him in days. He and Kaskoe were living in Big Rabbit's house and the storm had stopped everyone from visiting.

Another gust of bitter wind cut through the house. The door banged open and everyone turned to look. Kaskoe grunted as she stomped through the opening, her head and ears wrapped in a huge black bear fur sprinkled with snowflakes. Behind her Tall Dancer's arms were loaded with household things. Kaskoe straightened, shrugged out of the fur, and threw it on the floor. She swung her head around, surveying the house. Cara returned to her weaving, but felt the woman's eyes on her back.

The wooden bench groaned as Kaskoe stepped on it and walked down its length. Cara heard her stop behind her, but she didn't turn. Then Kaskoe snatched up the pattern board and studied the paintings. She leaned forward and stared at Cara's blanket.

"Marisha!" the woman bellowed at the top of her lungs.

Marisha came out of the bedroom, frowning at her daughter-in-law. "I am here. Why are you making all this noise?"

"What is this slave doing with the pattern board?"

Cara's head flew back as Kaskoe grabbed a handful of her hair.

"She is weaving, daughter." Marisha fixed the big woman with an even stare.

"Why is she using our board? This should have been passed on to me."

Marisha's frown deepened and she planted her hands on her hips. "You have never shown any interest in the blankets. Your mother told me during your seclusion, she could not get you to weave from your own family's pattern board."

Cara jerked out of Kaskoe's grasp and Kaskoe drew back to slap her, but Tall Dancer grabbed his wife's hand.

"Let the girl be," he rumbled.

Her anger now transferred to her husband, Kaskoe whirled on him. "Why did you not see that I received this board?"

"It is as *'atle* says. You were not interested in making the blankets."

"I am now." Kaskoe clasped the board close to her chest with both beefy hands and tilted her chin like a defiant child.

Tall Dancer's complexion changed from brown to bright red. He opened his mouth to speak, but Marisha stilled him with a touch. "Let her have it. I have many more patterns." She stared into her son's eyes, communicating a silent message.

Behind them, the house had grown quiet as every eye watched. Cara looked between the three. Tall Dancer glanced down at her and then looked quickly away. His face lost its ruddy glow, and Marisha let her hand slide off his arm.

"Why are you here in this storm?" Marisha asked, possessively resting her hand on Cara's shoulder.

"We have come to live here," Kaskoe answered haughtily.

"Your father asked you to leave his house," Tall Dancer corrected. "He said his ears had grown weary of your whines and complaints."

Kaskoe glared at the people who stopped and openly stared. "We have come to live here," she said with a note of finality. "I want that bedroom over there." She pointed to a bedroom two doors down from the chief's.

"No," Marisha shook her head. "That is Little Beaver's house."

"Well, he'll have to move. I want it." Before anyone could stop her, she stomped off toward the chief's room. She entered without announcing her presence. From inside the partition, her voice carried as she made her demands. Little-River-Underneath's voice was a monotonous low rumble. Suddenly, the blanket burst open and Kaskoe strode out.

"Bring the things here, husband." She waved at them from beside Little Beaver's door. Little-River-Underneath went into the man's house, reemerging in moments with the whole family following, their arms loaded with blankets and wooden boxes.

Little Beaver was a stooped, short man who carved beautiful war canoes for the village. Soft-spoken and timid, he offered no defense against the bullying. Little-River-Underneath escorted them further down the row to a tiny, dusty bedroom recently deserted by a family whose daughter had made a favorable match to an older, highly ranked man. Little Beaver seemed not to mind that his displacement was an insult to the station of his family.

Kaskoe smiled a satisfied smile as the last child scurried out, throwing her a terrified glance. Tall Dancer colored again, bent down, and retrieved two ermine tails from the pile of furs at his feet. He followed Little Beaver inside his new residence, then returned without the furs.

Kaskoe scowled at him as he passed. "Silence, woman," he said from between gritted teeth. Kaskoe started to speak, then apparently thought better of it. Instead, she turned on Marisha.

"You will have to learn that I am your daughter now." Kaskoe gave Cara's hair another fierce yank.

Cara rose to confront her, but Marisha pushed her back down with one hand.

Suddenly, the house shook with the force of another buffet of wind. The low buzz of conversation ceased. A shrill whistling filled the air. Heads snapped around toward the door. Crying children climbed into their parents' laps. Kaskoe's face blanched.

"Just today someone said they heard whistling down near

the sound,'' Marisha leaned forward and whispered. ''They said it was not the wind, nor a branch scraping on the roof.''

Beads of sweat broke out on Kaskoe's upper lip and her darting eyes conveyed her fear.

''Little Beaver said he saw a long mark in the snow coming out of the woods and ending at the edge of the sound.'' Marisha leaned closer still. ''Something broke the ice and dived in. He heard the splash.''

Kaskoe's chest rose and fell in irregular gasps. She glanced nervously to where Little Beaver smilingly caressed the ermine furs while he chatted with Tall Dancer. People had gone back to their chores and conversations.

''You don't think tomorrow Little Beaver will speak to the Land Otter Men of me . . . do you?'' Kaskoe asked.

Marisha frowned, and Cara stifled a giggle. ''*Kucda* would love to get you and take you to his den. Maybe he would make you marry one of his brothers to break you of your selfishness.''

Kaskoe glanced again at the little stooped man talking to Tall Dancer. Cara smiled to herself, watching this bit of drama play out. Rumor had it Little Beaver had been captured by the Land Otter Men last year when his canoe overturned while he was searching for the perfect tree for a canoe. *Kucda* had captured him and almost turned him into an otter, but he got away and ran all the way back to the village. Now it was said the Land Otter Men came around during a storm and whistled for him, hoping he would return.

Cara glanced at Marisha, whose eyes twinkled as she enjoyed Kaskoe's distress. The big woman wrung her hands, then turned and hurried to Little Beaver's side. Beneath her breath, Marisha chuckled.

''Marisha? Do *you* believe in *Kucda?*'' Cara asked as she picked up her weaving again.

Marisha shrugged. ''Who can say? In the forest are many things we do not understand.''

Cara closed her eyes and let the stories she had heard of the

Land Otter Men run through her head. She remembered the story of the young man who was forced to spend the night on a coastal island and slept under his canoe. All night long *Kucda* whispered to him, imitating the voices of the boy's parents, and knocked on the canoe. When he flipped the canoe over, nothing was there. A Russian tale also ran through her mind, a similar story where a youth was spirited away.

She sighed and looked at the spot where the pattern board had rested. No matter that Kaskoe had taken it. The design was burned onto her memory. Every figure and every color change was clear in her mind. She would best Kaskoe and finish the blanket without the board.

As she wove, she glanced to where Kaskoe was talking to Little Beaver, her grip preventing his attempts to escape. Tall Dancer had moved away and was striding down the bench toward his bedroom. He stopped in front of his door. His eyes locked with Cara's for a moment before he pushed the blanket aside, entered, and let it fall closed.

The house was already awake and stirring when Tall Dancer opened his eyes. On the sleeping pallet at his side, Kaskoe snored peacefully. As he did every morning, he wished the woman beside him was Cara.

He rolled to his back and stared up at the smoke-stained beams over his head. Morning noises blended into a comforting murmur, and he tried to guess which voice was Cara's. He imagined her laughing at the firepit with his mother, going out into the cold for water, returning with her cheeks rosy and someone's child romping at her side.

Kaskoe snored loudly, caught her breath, and sat up. She turned toward Tall Dancer and smiled slowly, spreading her wide lips. A chill ran over him. The thought of making love to her mound of flesh turned his stomach. He rolled to his feet and moved as far away from her as the cramped quarters would allow. Behind him Kaskoe grumbled as he quickly slipped into his sealskin pants and shirt and left the bedroom.

His eyes swept the house, and he spied Cara already seated in front of the half-finished blanket. Curly auburn hair now hugged her head and little wisps of it tickled her ears. She bent over her work, her tongue tightly clamped between her teeth.

After glancing around, he paused to watch her. Her nimble fingers passed the yarn back to front through the hanging threads. At the top of the work was a row of fur, just right to snuggle against one's neck on a cold night. Passion stirred to life at the thought of lying with her beneath the blanket. Desire roared into his veins, so intense his head spun for a moment.

Behind him a sharp thud sounded, followed by a long string of curses. Kaskoe must have stubbed her toe on a wooden box. The sound had the same effect as a dip in cold water—a routine begun the morning after the marriage. Now the morning ritual meant to toughen young men became his only salvation from thoughts of Cara.

Quickly, he moved down the opposite side and hurried out into the bright morning. Patches of snow still lay on the shady sides of the houses. As he strode toward the forest, he looked over his head at the bare branches bearing rapidly swelling buds. Spring was not far away, then the busy summer. Before long he would be on his way to return Cara to Fort St. Michael.

He pushed his way through the last line of dense, scrubby trees and emerged onto the beach. Waves crashed on the white sand, then slithered back into the sea, their energy spent. Brisk sea air caressed his face with salty moisture. He shouldered his bow and arrow and trudged down the beach, his beaded boots crunching in the sand.

A looming pile of rocks beckoned him. Out here where the air was devoid of smoky haze, he could think clearly. He took a deep breath and faced the decision he had to make. Life with Kaskoe was becoming unbearable.

He could divorce her simply by denouncing her, but the shame would be a part of his ancestry forever. He closed his eyes, and his father's words came drifting back. *The air was thick with smoke. The smell of the fight was sharp and burned my nose.*

He could hear his father's voice, carefully converting the story into Tlingit for the listeners around the firepit.

Then there she was, hiding in the forest, peeping around a rock. He remembered seeing his father reach over and squeeze Marisha's hand. In his memory, she was years younger, the same young woman who played skinny with him and his boyhood friends. Even now he could see her braids swinging wildly as she scrambled for the hide-covered ball.

I felt a hand over my mouth and I was afraid. His mother's voice had chimed in, a voice loud and strong, not cracked with age as now. *He whispered in my ear in our language. He told me he wouldn't hurt me. He wanted to save me from the Russians. I saw his skin was white and his clothes were ragged. He said the Russians wanted skins and women and I thought he would drag me out to them. Instead, he shared my hiding place until the fight was over. We went back to the village and I explained how he had saved me. They welcomed him into our home.*

Marisha had beamed at her handsome husband. *He worked for many years, trapped and traded. One day he offered my father a bride-price for me.* She had blushed a pretty pink. *My father said yes and we were married.*

A step in the sand brought him back to the present. He jumped and grabbed for his bow. Cara stood at his side, a basket hanging from one hand.

"I c-c-came out to gather seaweed," she stuttered, her eyes wide with surprise.

Obviously, she, too, had sought solitude here.

He took a step toward her. She cast a glance over her shoulder before backing up.

"Cara." He saw the fear in her eyes.

"I don't want there to be any trouble."

"I think I've caused enough trouble for myself."

The wind caught a wisp of her hair and coiled it round and round in a tantalizing dance. With a rush of heat, he remembered why he had come out here. She looked at the ground, and he resisted the urge to take her in his arms. "I was out here trying to decide whether to divorce Kaskoe."

Her head came up and her eyes widened. "Oh, no. You mustn't do that. It would be a disgrace on your family."

"Which is better? A disgrace on the family or my misery?"

The touch of her hand on his arm sent his thoughts back into dangerous territory.

"I'm sorry you're unhappy," she whispered.

"What about you? Are you unhappy, too?"

She didn't answer and glanced at the ocean. He dragged her into his arms before she could protest. Her lips tasted salty, and he wondered if he was kissing away the sea air or tears.

She relaxed against him, returning his kiss, warming to him as he had to her. She was food for a starving man. The torment returned—exquisite joy edged with profound pain.

As her body molded to his, forbidden memories rose again, as vivid as they had been their one night together. He was past the point of caring who saw them. A demon was in possession of him now, a demon that sat on his shoulder and drove him on to feel more of her, taste more of her.

Then she stepped coolly out of the embrace, her eyes cold and hard as she looked up at him. For an instant, he wondered if the Land Otter Men had taken his Cara and left someone else in her place.

"You are married now. You must honor your people's ways." The words could have been his own, except he no longer believed them.

A tear glistened at the corner of her eye, but none fell and her face remained stoic. "We won't meet again like this."

"Cara—"

She turned on her heel and started away.

"Cara."

She stopped, but didn't turn.

"I have to make a choice."

She didn't acknowledge that she'd heard. Instead, she moved off down the beach, passing pile after pile of seaweed.

Her heart still thudded in her chest and the blood raced

through her veins. She'd wanted him like a wanton woman. Had she stayed a few moments longer, she'd have let him take her there in the cool recesses of the rocks.

Other women coming to the beach to gather seaweed gave her tears curious looks. Looking down, she concentrated on placing one foot in front of the other until the sound of the surf faded.

Chapter Nine

Spring came early. Buds burst forth. The snowcaps of the western mountains shrank, and trickling streams became rushing torrents. The savage crashing of the waves just beyond the sparse line of trees settled into a smoother, melodious surge.

Cara stumbled over two little boys chasing a buff-colored puppy with a piece of rag in its mouth. She laughed and swung her basket as she headed to the stream for water.

With spring had come an increase in village activity. The deep spruce forest was coming to life with tiny green buds and chartreuse fern fronds. Already the gathering for next winter was beginning.

"Are you coming to the storytelling tonight?" a voice behind her asked.

Startled, Cara turned. Silver Eyes, a young woman living in their house, approached her, also with a basket in her hand.

"Yes." Cara continued toward the stream as the young woman fell in beside her.

"The children are looking forward to it. Tall Dancer is the best storyteller in the village."

Cara kept her head down, hoping Silver Eyes wouldn't see the blush that covered her cheeks. "I have heard he is." Secretly, she dreaded spending the evening so near to him, yet unable to touch him or speak to him.

"I do not think he is happy with Kaskoe," the girl continued.

From the corner of her eyes Cara saw Silver Eyes shake her head.

"He does not laugh as he did, and this is the first time he has told stories. Last winter it was almost every night. Kaskoe is not a good wife for him."

Cara felt her blush deepen, and her skin burned again where he had touched it that early morning on the beach.

"I think he wanted another for his wife."

Cara slowly raised her head and stared into the gentle gray eyes.

Silver Eyes smiled slowly. "Do not worry. No one knows but me."

Cara swallowed down rising panic. "How—"

Silver Eyes shrugged and again started toward the forest. "Tall Dancer and I were children together and lived in the same house. I know him well."

If she knows, who else has noticed? Cara's mind raced back to the morning on the beach when she had all but given herself to him. Who had seen them? She tightened her hands into fists. How could they have been so stupid?

Trudging along looking at the ground, she didn't see Silver Eyes stop and plowed into the back of her.

"You should encourage him to leave Kaskoe." Silver Eyes had dropped her basket and clasped Cara's arms with both hands. "She is not a good wife for him."

Cara shook her head. "No. It would bring shame to his family. I will be gone soon."

"If you leave, his love will leave with you. You are a stranger here among us, but I have watched you. You are kind and gentle and deserve his love," Silver Eyes said gently, then turned on her heel and disappeared into the trees.

* * *

The crowd sitting on the wooden benches fidgeted and quieted fussy children. The fire leaped and cracked, voracious on the new wood recently fed it. The faces nearest the flames glistened with perspiration. Then Tall Dancer walked into their midst. He wore the same soft sealskins Cara remembered in her dreams, but tonight his dark hair was loose and flowed about his shoulders.

"Tell about Fog Woman," a little boy sitting between his father's legs cried.

"Yes, yes," the crowd echoed. "Tell about Fog Woman."

Tall Dancer smiled and Cara felt its warmth all the way to her seat far at the back, even though his eyes were on the children on the front row.

"Raven was fishing with his two slaves Gitsanuk and Gitsa-qeq," he began, clasping his hands behind him and moving to stand and stare into the flames, "when a thick fog rolled in and they could not find their way out. Suddenly, a young woman appeared from nowhere." His voice rumbled over the crowd.

Cara smiled, watching the youngsters' spellbound faces as Tall Dancer acted out his words. Raven was considered to be the ultimate trickster in Tlingit folklore, a crafty creature who often got the best of his victims, but sometimes fell victim to his own greed. It was Raven who was credited with the creation of many facets of Tlingit life.

"She had long, flowing hair and gray eyes and she was very beautiful, like Dust here." He touched the nose of one of Little Beaver's children, a tiny bright-eyed girl firmly wedged between her father's knees, and she giggled.

" 'Give me your hat,' Fog Woman said." Tall Dancer snatched off Little Beaver's spruce root hat. "Now, Raven was usually quick-witted, but this time he just stared. 'Give me your spruce root hat,' Fog Woman insisted. So Raven gave her his hat. She turned it over and all the fog flowed into the hat. 'How did you do that?' Raven asked."

The children laughed again as he exaggerated Raven's exasperation. Cara noticed Kaskoe for the first time. She sat directly behind where Tall Dancer stood, a scowl on her face while she searched the crowd.

"Raven fell in love with the beautiful Fog Woman and married her."

"Like you married Kaskoe, Tall Dancer?" little Dust piped up.

He paused and looked into the tiny girl's dark eyes. "Yes," he said slowly. "Like Kaskoe and me."

The little girl squirmed and stared at him adoringly.

"They lived at the head of the creek, and during the winter he entertained her with tales of his great deeds."

Cara watched him and smiled. He was totally enthralled with his own story and so was his audience, judging from their faces.

"One day Raven went fishing and left his servant Gitsanuk at home with Fog Woman. She ordered him to go down to the river and fill her hat with water. When he brought it back, guess what was in it?"

"A fish!" the children chorused.

"That is right. And she named the fish in her hat a salmon. 'We must cook this fish before Raven gets back, for he is so greedy he will eat it all and leave us none,' she said. She thought about all the tales he had told her of his big appetite and about how cruel he had been. Fog Woman told Gitsanuk how to cook the fish. When it was baked, she ate some and gave the rest to the slave. She told Gitsanuk—"

"Put the bones in the stream," the children shouted.

He smiled at their enthusiasm. " 'Put the bones in the stream so they will return to the place of their birth and there will be plenty of fish for next year.' He had barely finished when Raven returned."

Tall Dancer paused dramatically, letting the tension build. The children's eyes never left his face.

" 'Ah, I see we are having halibut for dinner tonight,' Raven said. 'You're going to have to eat kelp and berries, though, for I have had a hard day and deserve all the fish.' "

Unanimously, the children groaned.

"Then, Raven spotted meat between Gitsanuk's teeth. 'What's that?' he demanded. Gitsanuk blurted out the whole story. Raven called his wife to him and demanded to know where the fish had come from."

"That's a secret," Dust spouted.

" 'What do I have to do to know this secret?' Raven said." Tall Dancer put his hands behind his back and bent over to look into the children's faces.

He must have told this story to them many times, Cara thought.

"He had to build her a smokehouse," a little girl at the back shouted.

"Right. Now Raven did not like to follow orders, especially his wife's, but he wanted the salmon badly, so he spent three days building the smokehouse. On the fourth day, he went to the stream and found it filled with salmon. Fog Woman told him they would need to catch and dry fish for the winter. Soon, Raven grew bored with his wife. He was mean to her and she ran away. Realizing he had made a mistake, he chased after her, but she slipped through his fingers each time. Then she drifted out over the water and was gone."

The house was still, with only the crackling of the fire. The children leaned forward in anticipation of the ending they knew by heart.

"Raven had his riches to comfort him. He had boxes and boxes of dried salmon, enough for himself and a new wife for the winter. Suddenly, he heard a swishing sound." He cupped a hand behind his ear.

"All his dried salmon came back to life and slithered down to the water where Fog Woman disappeared. All he had left were the drying racks and the smokehouse. Then the next spring, fishermen saw the little salmon all headed for the sea. The next fall, the stream was choked with adult salmon. The men caught all their canoes could hold."

The children heaved sighs of relief and leaned back against their parents. Eyes drooped and mouths yawned. People stood and carried already sleeping children up to bedrooms.

Cara peered over the rows of heads toward Tall Dancer and for an instant their eyes met. Despite the distance and the crowd between them, it was as if a bolt of lightning had struck her. In his look he conveyed the same depth of emotion she had felt in his arms that night on the trail.

Boxes clattering to the floor awakened Cara. She turned over on her sleeping pallet just in time to dodge one that plunged from a pile over her head. It fell with a thud and the lid burst off, scattering a layer of fine, brown powder onto the wooden floor.

"Ah!" Marisha fell to her knees and began to scrape up the powder. "Devilclub bark. Not easy to find." She worked at the spill until only a fine layer was left. Struggling to her knees, Marisha dusted off her hands. "We will go to the island today and collect my medicines. You will come with me and learn."

Cara threw off the heavy cover, grateful for the cool air that dried her sweaty skin.

Marisha stuffed small baskets and wooden boxes into a large sealskin sack. She hauled a skin tent and poles from behind another pile, then slung the parcels over her shoulder, slid her feet into a pair of beaded moccasins, and headed out the door.

Cara scrambled to her feet, grabbed two conical spruce root hats and two long capes woven of cedar bark and goat hair. She barely had time to shrug into her own clothes before Marisha was across the house and ducking out the door. Cara ran to keep up with the old woman's strides.

"Why are you in such a hurry?" Cara panted.

"It is a beautiful day." Marisha pointed over her head to where two fluffy white clouds melded together against the backdrop of a blue sky. "It would be a shame to waste it inside that stale house." She drew a long deep breath of salty air and swung into a ground-eating stride.

At the edge of the sound, several canoes were beached on the sand. Marisha stepped into the last one, threw her pack to the floor, and picked up a broad oar. ''Be careful,'' she warned as the craft tipped crazily when Cara stepped into it.

Marisha steadied the craft before backing it expertly out into the sound. With swift, quiet strokes, she guided the boat across the water, breaking the thin layer of early morning mist.

Cara piled the wraps behind her and leaned against them. She glanced over her shoulder toward the horizon and drew a deep, relieved breath. No ship rode there at anchor. Perhaps Tall Dancer had been wrong. Perhaps her father had given up his search, damned her to the bottom of the sea, and returned to Russia in glory.

Despite the beautiful day and hopeful thoughts, her heart sank at thoughts of Tall Dancer. Laying awake on her pallet, she had heard his footsteps on the wooden platform and the gruff greeting he got from Kaskoe when he returned home late. Their muffled voices had risen in argument, then fallen off in silence.

''Would you like me to paddle a while?'' Cara asked Marisha.

''No, child. I enjoy slipping along through the water myself.''

''How long has your husband been dead?'' Cara asked.

Marisha's bright dark eyes blinked in her leathery, wrinkled face. A quick tear glistened in her eyes, then vanished. ''Many years. Since Tall Dancer was a boy.''

''Have you always lived alone?''

''Yes. Since my son went to live with my brother to learn the ways of manhood, I have been alone.''

''Aren't you afraid, living by yourself? Couldn't you live with Tall Dancer and Kaskoe?''

Marisha replied with a snort. ''Live with that sack of seal blubber? Never. I will look after myself until I am no longer able. Then I hope death will take me swiftly.''

Her words chilled Cara and she shivered before turning back toward the front of the canoe to watch the forest slip by.

They paddled north for a few miles before Marisha beached the canoe on a pebbly beach. They stepped out and dragged the boat up on the shore. Cara carried the supplies as Marisha led the way into a seemingly impenetrable wall of forest.

Tall cedars loomed above their heads and crowded so close together that it was almost dark on the forest floor. Shadows and cracking branches made Cara jump. What if another clan lurked nearby? They might be taken hostage.

Marisha led her further and further into the forest until they came to a clearing. Saskatoon bushes weighed down with blossoms abounded in the small open area.

"This is my favorite place to gather these berries in the summer. We will come back here when they are ripe," Marisha said as she bit into one of the little green balls.

Pushing on through the brush, she directed Cara to set up camp on the far side of the clearing so the backs of their skin tents would be against the dark forest. Cara piled rounded stones in a circle for a firepit and placed the packed boxes and baskets inside the tent.

"Come with me." Marisha crooked her finger at Cara.

Marisha lead them deeper into the emerald cedar forest. The trees stood tall and skinny and little feathery branches of needles waved in a gentle breeze far above their heads.

"See here? Mountain ash." Marisha touched the delicate leaves of a tiny bush growing between two cedars. "We want the roots," she said, falling to her knees to dig at the base of the plant.

"What do you use it for?" Cara said, holding out a basket to receive the roots.

"It cures the lung fever." Marisha put her hand to her chest.

She dumped the handful of roots into the basket and scrambled to her feet.

Next, she stopped before a low shrub with dark green, leathery leaves. Marisha pulled a handful and rolled the leaves between her palms. Cupping her hands, she inhaled deeply, then offered Cara a whiff. A sharp but pleasant aroma arose from the crushed leaves.

"Boil this, then drink the water. It goes well with seal blubber.'' She snatched off handfuls of leaves and crammed them into a thin sack of seal bladder.

As they moved along, Marisha regaled her with remedies and treatments. Cow parsnips for soreness of the joints, blue currants for bad eyesight, yarrow for boils and infections, lichens for sores. When they came to another partial clearing, Marisha led her to a tall plant with dark green spiny leaves. Others grew profusely around them.

''Goatsbeard,'' Marisha said, touching the plant almost reverently. ''Take care with this one. It will cure the white man's sickness when it comes. Boil the roots and drink the tea. At first the patient will ask 'Why do you give me something to make me worse?' But then he will feel better.''

Cara touched the tough, spiny leaves and felt a tug of regret. Her people had brought the white man's sickness—smallpox— to the Tlingit. The word still produced panic in St. Petersburg.

''Are you listening?'' Marisha asked, frowning.

''Yes, I am.''

''This root might save your life one day.'' Marisha dropped to her knees and grubbed at the base of the plant.

By sunset, they had filled half of their baskets and boxes with plants to be dried for food and others to be stored as medicines. On their way back to camp, Marisha produced a stone ax and began to hack at a small cedar tree. Cara took the tool away from her and finished the job while Marisha supervised. They stripped the bark from the felled tree and split some long pieces from the trunk. They made several trips until the whole tree lay in planks by their firepit.

At dawn the next day, they returned to the forest. As they picked berries, dug roots, and stripped leaves, Marisha explained their uses and history. Leaves of the bearberry were used to treat kidney and bladder infections. Those of the peppermint were dried and crushed and used to relieve gas. Cow parsnip leaves were cooked and eaten along with the stems or dried and used as seasoning.

Afternoon shadows were lengthening and their boxes and baskets were bulging and heavy by the time they returned to camp. Marisha snared a rabbit and they ate the meat cooked with fresh herbs and sprouts. After dinner, she showed Cara how to unravel threads of wood from the innermost part of the cedar tree. She twisted the flexible fibers into a long string and wound it around a branch.

As the two women sat by their fire, twisting the wood fibers, the light stretched only a short distance into the dark void beyond. In the forest behind them, nocturnal animals began to move and hoot and rustle. Cara watched the shadows.

"Why are you so nervous, my child?" Marisha finally asked.

Cara stared into the dark, seeing shadows and movements behind every tree. "Are you not frightened out here all alone?"

Marisha snorted her response. "No. I have been here many times all alone and stayed for many days. This is our land. We have nothing to fear here."

Cara's dread drifted to her father. Had he truly given up the search for her? Or did he still ravage the coast, taking out his anger and revenge on any he encountered? Did he somehow know she was here on the island?

"How did you come to be with the Tsimshian?" Marisha asked, her fingers flying.

How many more times must she tell this story? Cara wondered. Surely Tall Dancer had already told his mother. Or was Marisha asking for other reasons? Did Marisha know the most hated man in *Aliaska* was her father? Did Marisha know she fed and sheltered an offspring of The Butcher? She closed her eyes and drew a shaky breath. "My father is a Russian trader."

When she opened her eyes, Marisha's expression remained the same.

"I ran away from him and the Haida found me wandering the woods. They made me a slave," Cara blurted before she lost her nerve.

Marisha stopped twisting the thread and dropped her hands to her lap. "Why did you run from your father?"

Cara looked down at her work. "Because he is a cruel man."

"Many men are cruel," Marisha said, her eyes on the work in her lap.

"He is more cruel than most."

Before Cara could explain, Marisha raised her head and gazed out at the forest.

"What is it?" Cara whispered urgently, fear prickling the nape of her neck.

Marisha shook her head and motioned for her to be quiet. After a moment, she said, "Tall Dancer, come into the light."

"How did you know it was me?" he said, stepping into the midst of their camp. He wore a fringed shirt that hung down past his hips. Slick sealskins hugged his long legs, and his hair flowed freely down his back.

"Do you think I don't recognize my son's footsteps after I've heard them for so many years? Why are you here—and where is your wife?" Marisha narrowed her eyes at him.

He grew uneasy under her scrutiny. Sometimes, he thought, she knew him too well. "I came to see if you and Cara were safe. You're a long way from the village."

His mother's expression did not soften as she watched him steadily. He began to feel like a child caught with his hand in the berry bowl.

"Come and eat." Marisha nodded toward the rabbit carcass roasting over the fire.

Tall Dancer glanced at Cara. Tiny tendrils of her hair coiled against cheeks pink from the fire's heat. Her skin would be soft and warm, fragrant in a way that was hers alone.

Marisha took the rabbit off the spit and divided it three ways. From a covered basket, she produced steaming cow parsnips. They ate in silence, but he was aware of his mother's furrowed stare. She finished the last bite of rabbit, wiped her greasy fingers on her dress, and scrambled to her feet.

"Come with me." She looked at Tall Dancer and jerked her head toward the forest. Marisha led them out of hearing range of the camp to a lone boulder with small, low bushes at its base.

"Why have you come here? Not to see if we were safe."

Marisha turned to face him, her head tipped back to look up at him. "I have been here many times and you never came. You have come to see Cara, haven't you?" She leaned close and peered into his face. "Where is Kaskoe? Did you bring her or leave her home alone?"

Her glare could still disarm him, and he knew he was in for a scolding. "No, I did not bring Kaskoe with me, and I think you know why I'm here." He took her frail hand and kneaded her fingers. "Allow us this time together."

Marisha shook her head. "I knew there would be trouble."

He squeezed her hand. "Have you forgotten how it felt when you wanted Father so badly and he was denied to you?"

Marisha searched his face. Cheeks that were once round and chubby were now lean and angular. Hands that once clutched hers with fat little fingers now gripped with a man's strength.

But his eyes were the same—deep brown eyes that could sparkle with mischief or darken with rage. Now he stared at her with all the innocence of a child, and in that innocent gaze burned something she had once seen in his father's eyes.

Her son was right. She, too, had wanted someone denied to her. She knew she should send him back to his wife and his vows, but her heart ached for him. He was trapped in a loveless marriage with a woman he could not bear while loving a woman he could not have.

Marisha smiled slowly and touched his cheek. Without another word, she turned and walked back toward camp. She brushed by Cara and went into the tent without a word of explanation.

Cara looked back at Tall Dancer. He stood a few feet away, the twinkling firelight shooting his raven hair full of streaks of blue.

"Why are you here?" Cara asked, her heart already knowing the answer.

He stared at her, his eyes darkening. "I came to see you."

Chapter Ten

He stepped into the fire light. Cara swallowed the fear rising in her throat. He seemed taller, more frightening than before. A long, slim braid hung down in front of one ear and a new earring accompanied the braid on the right. He held out his hand to her, and she knew she must go. Their fingers touched, and, without a word, he led her away.

Nighttime fog blanketed the ground in a fluffy layer that swirled around them as they walked.

Hoo, hoo-hoo, hoooo-hoo. The owl's cry vibrated the air around them; a distant female answered.

Past the clearing full of goatsbeard he lead her, until they came to a bare spot sheltered by huge cedars. Bare trunks soared toward high branches that intertwined to shut out all but a sliver of the night sky. Soft cedar needles blanketed the ground and a huge, rotting cedar log stretched across the clearing.

"I've missed you," he said.

"I've missed you, too," Cara answered, willing her hands to stay at her sides.

Cool dampness caressed her cheek as he stepped forward, swirling the mist in front of him.

"This is all I will ever have of you, isn't it?"

His hand stopped inches from her face, then dropped to his side. "I should not have come."

Warring emotions raged in Cara. She wanted to go into his arms, to press her cheek against his shirt and feel his hands caress her back, but she knew that each touch, each kiss belonged to another woman.

Clouds moved across the sky and moonlight found a niche in the thick canopy above and slanted down to light their faces.

"Why do you come here? What do you want from me?" Cara fought the tears building behind her eyes. His presence only made the emptiness that consumed her greater.

"I wanted to see you, to know you are all right."

"Your mother takes care of me."

"I knew she would." He smiled, and she thought her heart would break.

"What about your wife?"

At her words, he moved away, his arms crossed over his chest, and sat down on the rotting log. "She is my wife only in name."

"You don't sleep with her, yet you come here to me."

Abruptly, he rose to his feet and stepped into the shaft of light. "I have entered into an agreement with Kaskoe that I must honor, but you never leave my mind or my thoughts. My heart will always belong to you."

"What about the rest of you?"

He stared down at the neatly stitched toes of his moccasins.

"I can't live like this, Tall Dancer—stealing away, hiding, meeting in secret places. We both know I will be gone this time next year and you will still be a husband."

He raised his head and stared straight at her. "I cannot offer you what no longer belongs to me. My life is not my own. I owe my loyalty to my clan, to all the people my actions affect, those who have raised me and taught me our ways." He moved forward and took her elbows in his hands.

Cara turned her head to avoid his scent, the soft aura of

cedar and muskiness that surrounded him like the mist at his feet.

"The clan controls my life, but not what I think and feel. I love you, Cara. That I can offer you."

While her pride screamed at her, Cara stepped into his embrace. Oh, she was such a fool for doing this, she told herself, yet she pressed her cheek against the front of his shirt as his arms encircled her.

Tilting her head up, she found his lips lowering to meet hers. Gathering her to him, he kissed her as if he would devour her soul. His hands found the string of her bark dress. It slithered to the ground and settled at their feet with a gentle sigh while the mist chilled her skin. An inner voice urged her to pull away from him, he belonged to another, but his hands roamed her back and his lips searched her mouth, stilling her thoughts.

Moving her fingers across his skin, she found the string that held his breechcloth around his hips. The coarse material grated as it slid out of the knot. He stepped away enough for the garment to fall to his feet, then removed his leggings. They stood naked against each other.

His long, dark hair spilled across her arms as she slipped them around his neck, entwined her fingers, and brought his cheek to hers. He caught her face in his hands and brought her lips to his. His kiss, gentle at first, tentative and exploring, deepened. His breaths grew ragged and labored, sounding hollow in his chest.

A pleasurable panic spread throughout her as she realized he was out of control and there was no stopping the inevitable. She sank to the ground with him, the layer of needles cushioning her back, all around them the swirling mist and the scent of leaf mold.

Pushing her guilt away, Cara threaded his hair with her fingers, combing the dark length away from his face. Maybe this was all she would ever have of him, but at least this part was hers alone.

* * *

The waning moon peeped through cedar branches that sighed on a gentle breeze above their heads. He lay on his back, looking up at the stars that flickered above while Cara slept on his shoulder. He had failed, failed in the promise he made himself when he left the village to come here, failed to keep the vows he made to his uncle and Kaskoe.

He turned his head to watch Cara sleep. Moonlight flooded her face as she lay on her side, one arm pillowing her cheek. Her lashes were dark moths resting on her cheeks. Running his fingers over the contours of her body, he marveled that she had given him so much pleasure. Countless nights they had lain under the same roof. She had been so close, yet societal order kept them apart.

The wind moved through the overhead canopy and its gentle sigh now seemed menacing and scolding. A faint whistling filled the forest. Goose bumps rose up on his flesh. He had defied years of tradition, defied his father and his uncle. What would be his punishment?

This must never happen again. But he lied to himself. Already he wanted more of her. His uncle's pleading words whispered on the wind, begging him to accept Big Rabbit's daughter as his wife and make the union that would elevate the family standing.

"Will it ever be like this again?"

Her voice startled him. He rolled his head to the side. She gazed evenly at him, the flush of passion still on her cheeks.

"No." He turned his head away. "We will never see each other like this again."

Her silence was loud and when he looked, she stared straight at him. "You are thinking about your family."

He nodded and cringed at the sorrow that crossed her face.

"I hoped . . ." She let her words drift away.

She had hoped he would leave Kaskoe and love her.

"I cannot." Having to say the words pierced him like a knife. "Not now."

"Ever?"

"I don't know." He rolled to his feet and picked up his leggings.

She leveled him with an emerald stare, coolly cutting him to his soul. Without a word, she pulled her clothes on and disappeared into the forest like the mist, leaving him standing alone in the clearing, naked against the gathering chill.

Marisha heard Cara enter the tent and lie down on her bed. Cara's breathing was irregular and Marisha knew she lay awake with a heavy heart. Marisha smiled, remembering a stolen night many years ago when the soft needles of the cedar and a warm bare shoulder had also been her bed and pillow. By allowing Tall Dancer and Cara to be alone, Marisha knew she had aided a serious infraction of clan law. But the guilt was easier to carry knowing her son had known love for one night.

Cara heaved the skin pouch over her shoulder and stumbled as the load settled. Her feet sank deeper into the beach sand and she struggled to walk the distance to the beached canoe. Today she and Marisha would leave their camp and head back to the village. A cloud of sadness passed over her at the thought of leaving the idyllic setting.

Bittersweet memories of her night with Tall Dancer rose, but she pushed them away. She couldn't think about that now, she decided as she dumped the load into the boat. The craft wallowed sloppily and Cara eyed the water line along its body. Many more such sacks and there wouldn't be room for them. Behind her Marisha scrambled into the boat, crawling over two weeks' worth of dried herbs and twisted yarn.

"Are you ready?" she asked, taking up the wooden oars.

Cara turned for one last look at the wall of dark cedars pushing each other toward the surf. Somewhere in the dark fortress was the clearing where Tall Dancer had lain with her and broken her heart. Stubbornly, she shut out the thought, shoved the canoe into the water and jumped aboard.

As they approached the ragged coastline of their sound, they noticed unusual activity on the beach. A crowd of people gathered on the sand, all looking out toward the ocean. A prickle ran down the back of her neck and she glanced toward the horizon, but found it empty.

The keel of the canoe scrubbed on the coarse sand as Marisha sent the craft ashore with a powerful pull of the oars. She stowed the oars in the floor and stepped out. Cara hopped out behind her, struggling with the heavy sacks of yarn.

"There she is!" someone down the beach shouted, and the crowd rushed in their direction. As they neared, Cara saw the anger on their faces and began to back away. A man with huge earrings dangling from his earlobes reached her first and grabbed her arm. "Find the Russian hunters!" he shouted. "Tell them we have the red-haired girl."

The same people she had eaten with and laughed with now milled around her in a blur of bodies. Another hand grabbed her hair and yanked her forward. Cara pitched face first into the sand. She raised her head, spit out the grit, and stared at two immense bare feet. She followed the tree-trunk legs up to equally large thighs and eventually to Kaskoe's grinning face.

"Take her and trade her for the other girls," she said, kicking Cara's ribs.

Cara saw dots of light as all the air went out of her body.

"This slave is mine and I will do with her what I wish." Marisha's shadow covered her as she stepped between Cara and the crowd.

"Give her to the hunters! Some men are going out after the girls! Let them take her with them!" someone shouted.

"No. No one will take her. I am an old woman and I need her strength. I will not give her up," Marisha insisted.

Suddenly, a wild man jumped into their midst. Black hair hung down his back in a single long twist matted and clogged with filth. "She will cause us all to die," he shouted and pointed to her with a dirty, twisted fingernail several inches long.

Cara recognized Tek-'ic, the village shaman. Some said his power was great, that vivid images came to him during his dreams.

"She is evil. We must give her to the Russians. I see great trouble for us." He rolled his eyes back in his head and three young men immediately appeared at his side.

"Tek-'ic sees it coming," his three assistants chanted. The shaman fell to his knees in the sand and began to dig, throwing a spray of dirt between his legs.

The crowd hushed and fell back. When Tek-'ic spoke again, it was in grunts and snuffling sounds. Tek-'ic was getting his *yek,* the spirit of the bear.

Prickles rose on Cara's spine as the shaman contorted in the sand, swinging his head back and forth like a bear ready to charge. She backed up until she bumped against a body. Firm arms went around her and she inhaled the faint odor of cedar. Tall Dancer pulled her against him and held her there until the shaman collapsed face down in the sand.

The crowd murmured and Kaskoe glared, but Tall Dancer kept Cara snugged against his body. Then the shaman moved, struggled to his feet, and raised his arms to the sky.

"*Hak!*" he proclaimed. "The spirit has told me the people are in great danger. He says men will come and take our furs and our women unless we kill the red-haired slave." He swung his gaze to Cara and grinned with yellow, broken teeth.

"It is as my mother has said," Tall Dancer declared. "This slave is her only help. As you can see, I have a wife and father-in-law to provide for."

The crowd murmured, but the shaman had locked his chilling gaze on Cara. Still on all fours, Tek-'ic moved around them, sniffing at their feet like a bear after a rotten log. Then he rose up on his knees, his hands in the air like paws.

"Something is wrong here," he growled low. "This woman is more than a slave."

Cara felt Tall Dancer's muscles tense against her back. She glanced at the crowd, then realized they had not heard the comment, that the shaman had intended the words only for the two of them.

"Kill her!" Kaskoe lunged forward out of the crowd.

"Wife, go back to your cooking." Tall Dancer's voice was low and barely controlled.

All eyes turned toward Kaskoe. The throng of people were now more interested in the war between man and wife than in the shaman's predictions. The pair stared at each other for several more moments. Then Kaskoe dropped her gaze and shuffled away toward home.

The shaman suddenly rose to his feet. With a last glowering look he hurried away, his thick mat of hair dragging in the sand behind him, his three assistants trotting at his heels. One by one, the people drifted away to their chores.

Marisha sat down on the front of the canoe and sighed. "What has happened here?" she asked.

Tall Dancer released Cara so quickly she stumbled. He backed away and stuffed his hands underneath his armpits. "Two days ago, two Russian hunters stumbled into the village. They were drunk and said they were from a ship." He glanced at Cara. "They went into all the houses looking for a red-haired girl they had been told was here."

"Who told them?" Marisha asked.

"The Kagwantan. They saw Cara with me on the trail."

Marisha shook her head slowly and looked at her feet. "What about the two girls who were taken?"

"Some men have gone after them. If they don't catch up, the hunters will probably use them as prostitutes, then take them down to Fort St. Michael and sell them."

Cara glanced up at Tall Dancer. As he stood with arms crossed, he looked nothing like the tender man who had loved her a few short nights ago. Now he was a warrior and a husband.

"I am going to look for them," he snapped, then turned on his heel to leave.

"Let me go with you." Cara sprang to her feet.

He turned on her a glance so cold Cara swore she could feel it creep across her skin.

"No," he said shortly, then strode off toward the village.

Even the roar of the waves seemed to mock Cara. She sat down beside Marisha on the edge of the canoe. Out beyond the mouth of the sound, no mast bobbed with the swells, no telltale circle of gulls pinpointed a ship.

He must be along the coastline, she surmised. Down the rock-strewn beach she saw no one except a group of young girls searching for seaweed. But he would come. He would question and torture until someone told him where she was.

Tarakanov lowered his spyglass and watched the little boat frantically rowing toward his ship. The rope ladder sailed overboard, and the two men barely waited for it to hit the water before they dived for the wooden rungs and scrambled aboard.

"Where is my daughter?" he asked the men, who trembled before him.

"We didn't see her," one answered, glancing at his companion.

Tarakanov stepped closer and wiped at Eben's cheek with his finger. A trickle of blood oozed from a red scrape on his skin.

"This looks like it was made by a woman's nails."

Both men exchanged looks. "We pretended like we were drunk, just like you said, Captain. Only we didn't see no red-haired girl. We looked that whole village over. Nothing."

"Then how did this happen?" He pointed to long welts on one sailor's cheek.

"Well, we didn't say we didn't see *no* women. There was these two gals, real young and real pretty. So we took 'em."

Tarakanov fought against the urge to strangle both of the English sailors. While each had a strong back and able hands, neither had any sense. He had easily convinced Baranov to release the pair from the brig at Fort St. Michael and impress them into his service.

"Where are the women? You were paddling for the ship like the devil himself was after you."

"He was a devil," the men chorused.

"We had the girls in a thicket on the edge of the beach, and they were coming around to our way of thinking." Eben poked Charles in the side.

"Then this big brute busted in through the bushes and yanked them girls plumb out of our hands. He picked us up by the backs of our pants and throwed us out onto the beach. Well"— Eben shook his head solemnly—"we weren't 'bout to wait around and ask him what his name was. We set out to running and him pounding behind us. Barely got the boat in the water."

Raising his glass again, Tarakanov moved to the rail and searched the beach. A tall, wide-shouldered man was just entering the woods, the two girls shuffling along behind him. From the expression on the man's face and the way the girls hung their heads, he guessed the man was chastising them about their choices in company.

Quickly, he scanned the man. So this was Cara's protector, the one the Kagwantan braves had warned him about—Tall Dancer. His anger fired as in his imagination the big man held Cara, caressed her, stripped away her clothes. Abruptly, he lowered the glass.

"Weigh anchor!" he shouted. His crew scrambled to obey.

"You and I will meet again, Tall Dancer," he murmured as the ship slowly turned away from shore.

Marisha picked up a bag of yarn and set off toward the house. With a final glance at the ocean, Cara picked up another sack and started the uphill climb behind her.

Silence greeted them when they entered the house. Eyes followed them until finally they were shut away in their own bedroom. Marisha flopped down on a woven mat and peered up at Cara.

"We're going to have to do something about that hair of yours," she said decisively.

Rising from the floor, she took down a small basket with a fitted lid. Inside was the brown powder derived from black spruce cones used to dye goat hair. She poured a small amount into another basket and poured in water. Swirling the mixture with her finger, Marisha made a thin paste.

"Bend down," she ordered, then poured the mixture over Cara's hair and massaged it in. Under curious glances, they left the house and went down to the stream. Cara dunked her head under the clear water and ran her fingers through her hair. When she looked down at her own reflection, a brunette looked back at her.

"There," Marisha said with a smile. "No one will find you now."

Cara stared at Marisha's distorted reflection in the swirling eddy near the stream's edge.

No, no one would find her.

She would have to find them.

The firepit burned brightly and sparks fluttered heavenward as Little Beaver threw on another log.

"Why have you called us together?" Little-River-Underneath asked, drawing his bear fur tighter around him.

Tall Dancer tilted back his head and stared up at the unfinished beams stretching above. What he was about to do would shame his family, mark his clan and his lineage for all time. He had thought long and hard about his decision, but there seemed no other solution.

"I want to divorce my wife," he blurted.

Little Beaver and Little-River-Underneath drew in their breath sharply. The other elders murmured among themselves. Only Noisy Feather remained quiet. He picked up a stick and jabbed at a burning log until the dark exterior fell away, revealing the heart of orange glowing embers.

"Why do you wish this divorce?" his uncle asked, squinting up at him through the smoke.

Centuries of tradition were carved on the bronzed, wrinkled faces before Tall Dancer—faces that had weathered lean winters and disease-filled summers, faces that relied on instincts and beliefs to bind the many clans together.

Tall Dancer searched for an answer. They would not understand if he said he loved Cara, but despised Kaskoe. Many long marriages existed between a man and a woman who could barely stand the sight of each other.

How could he tell them that memories of his parents' love made him long for more than other men were willing to settle for? How could he tell them he was no longer one of them, content to believe in the Raven and the Land Otter Men and live their lives as generations before them had?

"I do not love Kaskoe," was his feeble answer.

Loud guffaws burst from the old men sitting cross-legged around the firepit.

"What has love to do with marriage?" Noisy Feather asked. "I do not love Picking Strawberries, but she cooks good seal."

The elders laughed again and elbowed each other, enjoying the inside joke shared with the entire village. Picking Strawberries's temper was outdone only by Kaskoe's.

"I cannot tolerate her temper, her constant whining and bullying. I cannot stand to see her face!" Tall Dancer shouted at them, his hands clenched into fists at his sides.

His outburst shocked the men, and they stared at him with open mouths. The silence in the empty house was overwhelming, broken only by the cracking of damp firewood.

Noisy Feather rose, pulled his bear robe tighter around him, and stepped up to Tall Dancer. "You are acting like a child, *kelk,*" he said softly.

His uncle's quiet voice and probing look made Tall Dancer uncomfortable. He knew he was being selfish, knew he was making a fool of himself, but his words were true. He didn't think he could spend one more night with Kaskoe's rump grinding into his groin while she slept.

"You cannot have all you want. No man can. Have you thought what a divorce would mean to this family?" His uncle's words were soft, but his voice was firm. Over his shoulder, Tall Dancer could see the other men straining to hear.

"Yes, I have."

Noisy Feather narrowed his eyes. "Is there another?"

Tall Dancer glanced away. Noisy Feather knew. He grunted softly and laid a hand on Tall Dancer's shoulder.

"No," Tall Dancer whispered.

Noisy Feather's gaze heated Tall Dancer's cheeks. "What about the red-haired slave? Tek-'ic says you love her. He says she makes medicine for you to make you love her."

"Tek-'ic is lying." Tall Dancer met his uncle's gaze unwaveringly.

"She could be a witch," Noisy Feather whispered.

"She's not a witch." So Tek-'ic was spreading lies about Cara. The old man wanted her dubbed a witch so he could kill her with good reason and prove himself right about her bringing the Russian hunters to them.

"No. No divorce," Noisy Feather stated loudly. He shuffled to his seat, flopped down, and stared at the ground.

Each elder in turn nodded agreement. Tall Dancer threw his head back and again looked at the totems grinning from the newly carved cedar. There was no honorable way out of this, no way he could have Cara and still live here in the village. He had to choose—Cara, or everything he had ever held dear.

Chapter Eleven

Cara sat on a rock near the door of the house and watched a group of bare-chested men wade out into the stream with huge lattice fish traps. Stumbling and staggering against the current that bubbled with the exuberance of spring, they secured each end of the traps to boulders in the water.

The tree buds had burst into life, sprinkling the ground with their discarded protective coats. She calculated it was The Month of Green Leaves.

April.

The joy of the day dimmed. Only four months until Tall Dancer would take her down to Fort St. Michael and step out of her life forever.

Suddenly, a cry went up from the crowd at the river bank. *"Tsuk! Tsuk tan!"*

People pointed at the stream. A salmon jumped out of the water, clearing the surface with his silvery body and flashing an underside of red as he flopped back into the water.

Men hurried to the shore's edge and waded in with long, sharp spears to herd the salmon into the traps. Several women ran back into the house and slammed the door.

"They have their monthly blood," Marisha said as she slid onto the rock by Cara's side. "They will spoil the catch if the salmon see them." She elbowed Cara and nodded toward Kaskoe, laboring up the hill from the stream at a fast trot. "No baby this moon."

Other women hurried outside with their drying racks and set them up far from the water's edge for fear of insulting the salmon. Women were not allowed near the water during the salmon run.

Cheerful voices behind her caught Cara's attention. Silver Eyes raised her hand in greeting, then quickly resumed her conversation with the girls walking at her side. Before midsummer Silver Eyes would be married to a young warrior named Making a Nice Cave, and she would have no more time for cozy chats by the trickling stream. Cara watched them until they disappeared into the trees toward the beach.

A sudden breeze ruffled her hair, and Cara ran her hand through her now brown tresses. The dye Marisha used had made her hair dry and brittle and she came away with a handful of broken ends. She glanced back toward the stream, where a crowd of men had gathered at the nearest end of the fish weir.

Tall Dancer stood ready to take the first salmon, an honor he had been granted. He reached down and scooped a salmon out of the weir, held the fish over his head briefly, then handed it over to Little Beaver, who was in charge of the sacred rite to ensure next year's catch would be as good as this year's.

As the group of men gathered around, Little Beaver sprinkled the fish with eagle down and placed it on a special altar with the fish's head pointing upstream so the rest would know the direction in which to swim. He gave an elaborate speech of welcome. When the ritual ended, they began a chant that continued as the fish roasted over the open fire.

The odor of the roasting flesh made Cara's mouth water. When the skin cracked open, revealing the pink flesh underneath, Little Beaver carefully removed the meat, split open the skin, and dished out a tiny piece to each man on the end of his bone knife. The ceremony was now finished. They were free to continue fishing. The salmon had been honored and would return next year.

Cara glanced at the knot of women gathered near her. They whispered behind their hands and looked in her direction. The village had shunned her since the day hunters took the two girls. Even though the girls had been found, unhurt but frightened, the belief was spreading that Cara was a witch.

"Why don't you join them?" Marisha asked as she shifted her position and groaned.

"I don't want to cause any trouble."

"Pshaw." Marisha spat onto the ground at the base of the rock. "Old busybodies spreading stories."

"Some people believe I am a witch," Cara said looking straight into Marisha's eyes. She looked tired today. In fact, she had looked more tired every day. An inkling of fear worked its way into Cara's mind.

"So let them think it," Marisha answered with a shrug. "It will give them something to do. Look—Tall Dancer comes with our first fish." She slid off the rock like a young girl, but groaned again and stumbled as her feet touched the ground. She waved Cara's help away and set off toward the drying rack at a fast walk.

More men waded into the water with spears, driving the salmon into the weirs. Further downstream from the main trap, Tall Dancer leaned over and untied a rope wound from cedar bark fibers. He pulled and tugged until the top of the trap cleared the surface of the water. He hauled it out of the water and started up the hill with his wiggling treasure.

Marisha went down to meet him. As he handed her the trap, it slipped, fell, and burst open. They scrambled and laughed, trying to grab the slippery fish flopping their way back to the river.

Marisha grabbed the last fish, stuffed it into the trap, and slammed shut the lid. Suspended between them, the trap swung and dripped and bounced as they trudged up the hill to where Cara had already set up a drying rack.

Tall Dancer set his side down, avoided Cara's eyes, then

headed back for the stream. Marisha reached inside and grabbed a large fish, laid it down on a flat rock, and sliced off its head with the edge of a finely honed bone knife. Then she flipped it over and sliced off the tail and fins. Carefully, she cut open the belly. A handful of orange roe spilled out, which she caught in a watertight basket. Then she split the fish in half and hung it over a block of wood. One sweep with a crescent-shaped knife disposed of the entrails, and then the fish was ready to hang on the drying rack.

Cara and Marisha cleaned fish while Tall Dancer hauled full baskets up the hill for both them and Kaskoe, who had set up her drying rack beside them. Minutes melted into hours as the sun moved across the sky and the stench of raw fish hung heavy in the air. Behind and to the side, other women slashed off fish heads and scraped entrails while keeping up a steady chatter of village gossip.

A great bustling to Cara's side caught her attention. Kaskoe, along with several young girls, were chattering in whispered voices. Cara tried to concentrate on her work while resisting the temptation to push Kaskoe's precarious rack to the ground. As she stared down at her bloody board, their prattle stopped abruptly. From the corner of her eye she saw Tall Dancer stride up, a basket of fish in his arms. He said something to the girls that set off a gale of giggles, then turned and went back for another load.

Cara glanced up when she heard raised voices. Down the hill, Marisha and Tall Dancer challenged each other across a trap full of fish. One would jerk on the wooden bars then the other would, sawing the trap back and forth between them.

Cara caught enough words to know Marisha was refusing any help. She frowned. Lately, Marisha had refused help of any kind from anybody. Just this morning, she had sent her brother scurrying from the house when he suggested his wife should do enough drying for both families' winter stores.

A sharp snap and a thud made her jerk her head up. Tall Dancer sat on the ground with a pile of flopping, wet fish in his lap. In front of him his mother was doubled over with laughter. Others joined in. Then she heard the roll of Tall Dancer's laughter as he tossed a small trout at his mother.

Cara smiled and ducked her head. She couldn't remember the last time she had heard him laugh. Lately he had scowled and gone about in deep thought. Rumors flew behind cupped hands that he had asked the council for a divorce from his wife and they had refused.

Marisha brought an armload of fish to her and spilled them on the ground. Then she sat down to repair the trap.

At her side, Kaskoe greeted Tall Dancer affectionately as he brought another load of fish to her. Cara scraped at the fish furiously, hoping to drown out the words obviously said for her benefit.

She heard the sharp smack of a hurried kiss, then saw Tall Dancer head back down the hill. The young girls helping Kaskoe giggled and cooed over him. Cara couldn't resist one glance and found Kaskoe grinning at her.

Cara breathed in the lingering scents of the day and the far-off scent of rain. The sun had slid behind the trees and evening was casting an orange light over everything. She curled her bare toes in anticipation of her favorite part of the day.

At her side, the drying rack was full of salmon. Wood smoke drifted slowly through the glade of trees. All around, others were lighting small fires by which they would guard their day's harvest of fish from marauding animals.

Overhead, stars were just popping out of a clear purple sky and the first breeze of evening was cool and scented with spring flowers. Happy voices blended together, making the nightlong chore a reason for celebration. Cara rested her chin on her drawn-up knees and wondered if she could ever again live a dull life of candles and laces and wine.

From the shadows, Tall Dancer watched Cara draw her shoulders up as the breeze ruffled her hair. Her once-short tresses now hung down her back in two, fat braids. The throat-to-toes dress clung to her figure. He closed his eyes and saw her the way she had looked when they made love weeks ago, and his arms ached to hold her again.

He glanced around the glade. Marisha was supposed to be out here tonight. Why had she and Cara switched watches? Again, he glanced around. No one was paying him any attention. Should he approach her?

Cara jumped when he touched her shoulder. She turned, and all the feelings she had denied for weeks came rushing forward. Painful memories forced themselves into her thoughts. Abruptly she turned away.

For that brief few minutes in the forest he had been hers, only hers. Here she had to share him with Kaskoe, his mother, the whole village. Ever since that night, he had made no advances toward her, not even to speak a friendly greeting.

"Is Kaskoe with child yet?" The question popped out, and Cara was as surprised as his look said he was.

"No," he answered stiffly. "She has no child yet."

They were silent as Cara pondered the unasked question between them. Had he slept with Kaskoe? She sneaked a glance at him from beneath lowered lashes. He squatted beside her, yet he stared out into the night. A burning desire to know gnawed at her.

"I love you, Cara," he murmured and scratched absently in the sand with a stick.

Cara glanced around quickly. One person guarded each rack, but most were old men already asleep by their fires. No one seemed to have heard.

"You belong to her and you always will." Cara waited, hoping he would deny her words, but he remained silent.

Her words stung, but her soft lips invited him closer. As he looked at her profile, the breeze blew across her cheeks, softening her expression with errant tendrils of hair. He was leaning toward her when a snapping twig stopped him. He turned and saw Big Rabbit waddle up to a nearby fire. His father-in-law greeted two other old men huddled at the fireside, then launched into a story about one of his hunting trips. Tall Dancer's heart thudded at what he had been about to do.

"What do you see out there?" he asked Cara, nodding to where the silvery ocean was barely visible beyond the tiny grove of trees.

"Nothing," she answered.

"Thinking about your father?"

She turned and studied his face. His expression was blank and gave no indication as to what thoughts lay behind his dark eyes.

"No." She turned back toward the ocean. "I don't think about him anymore."

"When are you going to tell me what happened?"

Cara sighed and watched a wave crash on shore, spewing its energy in a silver rain. Every heave of the surf reminded her of her father, and that gave life to other unpleasant memories— beatings, neglect, cruelty.

The sky had been clear the night she escaped. Brilliant stars had glistened overhead as she slipped from her cabin, up the steps, and quietly into the dark waters. Memories of the cold slipping up around her made her shiver again. Absently, she massaged her arm muscles, remembering the long, silent swim to the beach.

"Cara?" He watched her with a worried expression.

She shrugged. "Someday."

Before he could ask her more, a form moved behind them and Marisha stepped out of the dark.

"I came out to see if you were cold," she said to Cara, looking pointedly at Tall Dancer.

He met her eyes and knew she had been watching them, determined not to leave them alone together again.

She squatted between them with a groan. "It cannot happen again," she stated, looking from one to the other.

Their eyes met over Marisha's head. Then Cara looked away, tears glistening on her lashes.

Cara gagged at the vile odor coming out of the canoe. She covered her nose with the sleeve of her dress and stirred the foul mess. Right after the salmon run died out, Marisha began to catch eulachon, a small fish used for lamp oil. For days Cara had pounded the little fish into mush and dumped the slurry into a half-buried canoe. The village men added water and heated stones to boil it.

Cara took a wooden ladle and scooped out the oil that floated to the top and poured it into a box. At her side were three other boxes in various stages of cooling. She dropped the oar, scooped out the congealed oil, and dumped it into yet another box. She glanced over her shoulder. Someone should be coming to relieve her soon. She picked up the oar and stirred the mess again.

Spring was well established now. Birds sang overhead, new leaves fluttered in the breeze, and the tall cedars at the back of the village sported dazzling green new growth, a sharp contrast to the dark green of their mature branches.

But all the sights and smells of spring did little to lift her spirits. Only two more months, she told herself, until Tall Dancer would take her away from here.

Tears sprang to her eyes at the thought of leaving Marisha. She was fast becoming feeble. This spring's work had proved too much for her, and reluctantly she had consented to let Cara and Tall Dancer do most of the work after the salmon run.

Cara dipped off more oil. It splattered her legs as she poured it into the box. Tall Dancer spoke rarely now, even to his mother. On the times he helped Cara with the harvest, he did so with tightly pressed lips and few words.

His nightly fights with Kaskoe echoed through the house, and gossip flew. Half said Kaskoe was pregnant, the other half speculated why not. Cara thought her head would burst if she had to hear the possibility debated one more time.

A soft hand on her arm stopped her stirring.

"Come, child," Marisha said. In her hand she held a large basket with a handle.

She lead them with faltering steps to a beached canoe. They climbed in and Marisha directed Cara to the island they had visited in early spring.

"Pull the canoe up over there." Marisha pointed to a sheltered cove on the coastline of the island.

Cara gave a hard push and the canoe's bottom scraped on the sand. She hopped out, then reached back to take Marisha's hand. Bony, cold fingers wrapped around hers, and Marisha groaned as she stepped out. Clutching a basket tightly in her hand, Marisha set out for the forest with faltering steps.

Following the same path as last winter, they soon came to the clearing filled with saskatoon bushes. The bushes now drooped to the ground with tiny red fruit. All around them bear spoor, wolverine tracks, and bird droppings announced the popularity of the berry patch. Wading out into the thicket, Cara ignored the brambles that scratched her and the insects buzzing around her head as she filled her basket. Marisha grinned at her over a bush and began to stuff her mouth full of the berries while she picked.

Cara continued to pick, but her gaze was drawn to the wall of cedars and the clearing hidden within it. Just as her mood began to dip, a wet blob splatted against her cheek, then another.

She peered across the bush and found Marisha grinning, her arm drawn back for another throw. For the next few minutes, the patch was a hail of ripe berries sailing back and forth.

"Enough. Enough," Marisha said, covering her face with her arm and plopping down on a rock.

Cara sat down beside her, breathless from laughing.

"It has been a long time since I have done that." Marisha set her basket down and wiped at her face with both hands to remove the pits clinging there. "I have not had so much fun since I was a child." She flicked a pit off Cara's cheek.

A rosy color had returned to Marisha's face. For weeks now, she had been pale and drawn, but today she seemed almost girlish. Cara looked down as Marisha's hand covered hers.

"I have not had such a good friend in a long time, either. Not since my husband died." Marisha's eyes crinkled into a smile as she gave Cara's fingers a squeeze.

A warmth flowed into Cara's veins. She felt she truly belonged here. How long had it been since she had thought about Russia and all she'd left behind? She looked down at her hands, tanned brown from the summer sun. Marisha's skin tone was the same as hers, but Marisha's fingers were covered with tiny blue lines showing through the transparent skin.

A breeze rippled through the patch, signaling the approach of evening. They made camp on the beach, just inside a grove of cedars. Cara walked along the shore, placing hemlock boughs in the surf to catch herring roe as it washed up and gathering seaweed. Then she collected wild celery and cow parsnips from the woods.

As the velvet of night pushed aside the light of day and blended the ocean and sky into one, they sat side by side on the beach and ate fish roe and seaweed, roasted celery and parsnips.

"Tell me the story of *Lqayak*," Marisha asked, wiping her fingers on her dress.

Cara glanced up at the night sky. The Milky Way stretched over their heads. She smiled. Marisha was testing her, trying to see if she still remembered the story of how *Lqayak* made the Milky Way with his snowshoes.

Cara began, "*Lqayak* was one of four brothers and a sister, half dog and half human." As she related the age-old story, the sky above them seemed to expand until there was nothing else—no sea, no forest, no one but them and the twinkling stars overhead. She took Marisha's hand in hers and squeezed, hearing her own voice drone on about how *Lqayak* found himself in the sky. As she spoke and the night deepened into velvet, she began to believe the tale she spun.

The constant chop, chop grated on Cara's nerves. Inside the house, the heat was stifling. She longed for the cool outdoors where the evening breeze would blow through her hair and dry her perspiration. Other villages had moved to a summer camp of tents and outdoor living, but their village was located near the ocean and near a stream, so there was no reason to move.

Cara reached up to wipe perspiration from her forehead. The

fire in the firepit added to the heat. A basket tipped precariously and she reached out to grab it, but it slipped and her finger struck a hot rock.

"Ouch!" She popped her finger into her mouth.

The door opened, letting in a whiff of cool air laden with the scent of red cedar. The chopping grew louder.

Little Beaver scurried through the house, ducked into his bedroom, then hurried out again, an ax in his hand. He was carving a war canoe. Little-Lake-Underneath had ordered a new one made when he received word there had been another skirmish between the Kagwantan band and Russian hunters further south.

An ominous feeling crept up her spine every time the Russians were mentioned, especially when anyone brought word that the Russian ship scouring the coastline flew a black flag. Only her father's ship flew a black flag.

The basket at her feet bubbled and hissed as water sloshed over the edge, jerking her back to reality. As she adjusted the basket's position and pushed another smooth stone into the flames, she glanced up at her sleeping quarters.

Marisha had gone in and laid down, something she never did. For days now she had denied that she felt ill, but her lagging gait and short breaths told Cara something was wrong. Marisha had dosed herself with a cup of skunk cabbage tea, to no avail.

Despite her energy and bright eyes, Marisha was sick. She had begun to walk slower and had to rest more frequently. The cool, damp nights caused her pain in the morning as she tried to rise from the floor.

Lost in her thoughts, Cara did not notice several more women had joined her at the fire, including Kaskoe. Cara caught and righted her basket as Kaskoe pushed other baskets aside to situate hers. Cara glanced at the faces across the fire. The other women shot Kaskoe covert glances, but none dared cross her. Lately, her violent temper erupted faster and lasted longer. As she pushed Cara's basket over for the fourth time, Cara shoved back.

"Watch out where you're putting your things. I've picked up this basket three times before," Cara snapped.

"So the slave girl speaks," Kaskoe said haughtily, flinging back her braids. "Take your things away until I have finished my supper."

Heat rushed to Cara's cheeks. "I will not move. I have as much right to cook dinner here as you."

"You are a slave and no better than the sand under my feet. You will obey my orders." Kaskoe stomped her foot, sending several of the rocks around the firepit skittering across the tops of others.

"I am not your slave. I answer only to Marisha." Cara stood, both hands clenched tightly at her side, aware that the conversations around them had hushed and everyone was watching.

"You will answer to me, girl." Kaskoe lowered her voice and stepped closer. "I will have you as mine sooner or later and I will do with you what I will. When the old woman dies, you will belong to Tall Dancer and I will make him give you to me. Then we will see to whom you listen." Kaskoe leaned closer until their noses almost touched, her face contorted in anger.

Cara put both hands on the woman's chest and pushed. Kaskoe stumbled, then fell backwards, flopping down in the food she had been about to cook. Behind her, Cara heard muffled giggles. By the look on her face, Kaskoe had heard them, too. Cara expected her to retaliate, to lunge up at her. Instead, Kaskoe began to cry pitifully, sitting among the crushed baskets.

From the doorway of his bedroom, Tall Dancer watched the drama, but made no move to interfere. He had wondered when Cara would hit back. Kaskoe's wails grew in intensity. He sighed, pushed away from the partition, and started down to the firepit. He stepped over the spilled meat and parsnips and hauled Kaskoe to her feet. Sputtering and blubbering, she docilely followed him to their room.

Cara watched until the couple disappeared, then removed

her baskets from the fire and retired to Marisha's house, closing the blanket as she entered. Marisha lay on her bed asleep. Cara readied their meal, then shook her awake. Marisha picked at the food, then went back to bed, saying she was tired. After Cara had cleaned the dishes and tidied the house, Marisha still snored gently on her bed of furs, so Cara decided to take a walk along the beach.

The afterglow of sunset lit the beach as Cara strolled down the shore, picking up pieces of seaweed and putting them into the basket she carried. Herring roe clung to the seaweed and would make a good meal for tomorrow. Before she realized it, she had gone down the beach into unfamiliar territory.

Darkness was falling as she turned to go back, but she was engulfed by the dark before she was halfway home. Little flecks of light were reflected by the waves as they churned toward shore and gently lapped at Cara's feet. She stopped to admire the beauty of the ocean at night. The tide was out and the beach stretched endlessly beside the water's edge. Small ocean birds ran along the edge of the surf, picking at tiny bits of food washed up by the waves. To her left, a large group of boulders stood shadowy guard. Cara seated herself on one of the rocks and watched the mesmerizing undulations of the sea, her thoughts drifting in disjointed bits and pieces.

Suddenly, a slight noise behind her brought her to attention. She turned quickly to see a shadowy figure dodge behind one of the large rocks. Fear gripped her as she worked her way down from the boulder and prepared to bolt down the beach toward the village. She had never been this far away before without Marisha, and she did not know which tribe lived close to them.

As she peered into the night, squinting to see where the figure had gone, a hand went around her mouth and dragged her into a dark crevice. She tried to scream, but the fingers held her lips shut. She struggled and tried to bite the hand that held her, but his grip was too tight. Her captor put his mouth close to her ear, and his warm breath ruffled her hair.

Chapter Twelve

"You've lost your fight, Cara," her captor whispered.

He released his grip on her and she turned.

"Tall Dancer! You frightened me! What are you doing here?"

His hands lingered around her waist. "I followed you when I saw you leave the house."

"Someone will see." Cara pushed away as he gently drew her near.

He lowered his lips to her neck and lightly touched her skin. "I want you."

His murmured plea shot straight through her. She closed her eyes and begged her body to resist, silently reciting the impossibilities of their situation over and over again. But her knees weakened and she leaned against him, drawn there by this bond between them.

He fumbled with the back of her dress, untied the leather thong, and slid the coarse fabric slowly over her shoulders, down her arms, and across her hips until it glided into a pile at her feet. A brisk breeze made shivers spider-walk up her back. He drew her deeper into the crevice of the rocks and pressed her against the cool stone.

"Do you think of me at night when you're alone?" He kissed the wisps of hair at her temples. "Do you remember the night in the cedars as I do?" His tongue flicked against her ear, then moved down to the base of her neck. "Do you want me now as you wanted me then?"

The crashing of the waves became a sensuous background to his lovemaking. He dropped to his knees and laid his cheek against her bare stomach. "Love me, Cara."

His words were more a plea than a seduction, but they robbed Cara of the last remains of her will. She tumbled to the damp sand beside him at the foot of the great boulders.

The day's heat was gone, replaced the chill evening breezes, but Cara felt no cold as his body covered hers. Before, he had been a tentative lover. Now he was a demanding one, already pushing her body beyond its limits. Fire replaced the blood that coursed through her veins. His heart pounded in rhythm with hers.

"Please stop," Cara begged, digging her nails into his shoulders and hoping he wouldn't.

He raised his eyes to hers. "Do you really want me to?" His voice was labored and shaky.

"No," she answered, pulling him tight against her.

Something was tickling her toes. Cara cracked open an eye and stretched. A warm, rough body lay next to hers and a sense of well-being fogged her thoughts. A tinge of pink was showing over the wall of cedars behind them. Another wave broke, throwing foam on shore. Her eyes wide open and consciousness slamming into her, Cara sprang to her feet.

In the dim light of dawn, she could barely discern Tall Dancer's body lying beside her in the sand. He still slept, one arm tucked under his head, completely naked. Memories of last night rushed into her mind. Quickly, she scanned the dark beach. No one was about yet.

He grabbed her ankle. She looked down and found him grinning, slowly devouring her naked body with his eyes.

"What have we done? How long have we been here?" she cried, grabbing at her bark dress.

"All night, it appears." Nonchalantly, he stretched, then leaned back on his elbows.

Cara began to panic. There would be people up in the village now; they would surely see her return and would wonder why a slave girl was sneaking around in the predawn light.

Tall Dancer swung his legs around and sat up in the sand. He smiled, watching her snatch her clothes on and mutter to herself. She had reason to fear and so did he, but for the moment, he pushed that to the back of his thoughts.

In the pale light her figure was soft and curving and the passion that had possessed him the night before overtook him again. He caught her hand and she looked down at him, pausing in her frantic dressing. And then, without words, she was in his arms again.

Frantically, they made love as the last vestiges of night disappeared and the waves washed over them, obscuring all signs of their sin.

Cara returned alone. She crept along low to the ground, hoping not to be seen. Dawn was just breaking and the murmur of voices came from the houses she passed. As she entered the house, all was quiet. She tiptoed along the ledges until she came to Marisha's bedroom. Silently she slipped under the blanket at the door and found Marisha sleeping soundly on her bed. Cara removed her sandy, damp dress and lay down on her sleeping mat.

As she waited for full daylight to come, she noticed Marisha's breathing was irregular and shallow. Cara crawled over to her and laid her hand on the withered forehead. Laboring for breath, Marisha was burning with fever. Cara threw on her clothes, hoping Tall Dancer had crept in behind her.

"Tall Dancer!" She whispered frantically at his door, in between Kaskoe's thundering snores.

After a long pause, he pulled the blanket aside and smiled at her. Then the smile faded to a frown. "What's the matter?"

"It's your mother. She's very sick. You must come quickly."

Tall Dancer dashed across the distance between the rooms. Those sleeping on the wooden ledges stirred and asked questions. Kneeling by Marisha's bed, Tall Dancer laid his hand on her forehead.

"She's burning up. I have to go for the shaman." He rose and hurried out.

Cara pushed Marisha's blanket away and shuddered at the thought of the wild man putting his hands on her. He and Marisha barely endured each other. She scoffed at his mysticism and claims to commune with the spirit world, and he accused her of witchcraft each time she dispensed an herbal cure that worked.

In a few minutes, Tall Dancer arrived with Tek-'ic, arrayed in his finest gear. An apron of moose hide hung to his knees, then curved up on the sides and was girded at the waist with a belt of braided roots. Hanging from the bottom of the apron was an array of tinkling bones dangling from leather thongs. A shoulder robe with the image of a grinning raven covered one shoulder and dragged the ground on the other side. Around his neck hung an amulet, a leather pouch containing the tongues of land otters Tek-'ic had killed during the days he was receiving his call. This, Cara knew, was his most powerful weapon when treating the sick.

By now, word had spread of Marisha's illness. Neighbors filled the door in preparation for the performance by the shaman. Cara inched back until she was wedged into the corner. The shaman gave orders for Tall Dancer to carry Marisha out into the center of the house and lay her down beside the firepit. Several men helped, lifting her sleeping mat and all. Tall Dancer kindled the fire, then built it up with wood until it leaped upward, casting eerie shadows against the walls in the early morning light.

Tek-'ic crossed his arms and waited. Tall Dancer approached him and there was a whispered conference. Then Tall Dancer disappeared into his house, reappearing a few minutes later with an armload of silky ermine furs, the last ones of the previous year's crop. Without asking, Cara knew the shaman had exacted an exorbitant price for his cure. Coupled with his own greed was the fact he was treating a rival. Cara watched the furs change hands, then Tek-'ic began his performance.

He wore his long, matted hair swept up on top of his head and secured by an elaborate comb carved in the shape of a bear. He removed the comb and let his hair flow down his back and onto the floor. Then, he removed the shoulder robe and his apron, leaving him nude except for a small pouch in front fastened to his waist by a thong that ran between his legs and up his backside. He placed over his face a skin with fur clinging to it in the shape of a man's beard. Over that he strapped a carved bear face.

Tek-'ic crossed his legs and sat down beside Marisha. In each of her hands he placed the carved image of a bear, Tek-'ic's own *yek*. He produced a small engraved box which, when he lifted the lid, contained soft white eagle down. He blew the down into the air and let it fall on Marisha's face and body.

Tall Dancer stood on the other side of the room from Cara, but she could read his frustration in the tense muscles in his neck. He didn't believe in the shaman's magic, but he was following tribal custom. Kaskoe moved to his side until her hip touched his. He moved away from her, crossed his arms, and frowned at Tek-'ic.

Little Beaver produced a drum formed by a hide stretched over a hoop. He began to pound on it vigorously, and the sound echoed against the plank walls as he tried to frighten away the evil spirits that hovered over Marisha and made her worse.

Other men retrieved drums from their houses and began to beat them and chant in a monotonous tone. All the while, Tek-'ic was leaping and jumping around Marisha until a thin sheen of moisture covered his skin.

The incantations and drumming lasted for two hours. Her

head ringing, Cara worked her way down the ledges to Marisha. When no one challenged her, Cara moved to her side and took her hand. A slow, steady pulse throbbed in Marisha's wrist. Cara dropped her arm and moved away before Tek-'ic turned on her.

As she resumed her seat in the back of the house, Tall Dancer stepped up to the shaman, whose chest heaved from his exertion. They whispered among themselves, then Tall Dancer left and went to Marisha's house. He returned with a small box.

The shaman opened the box and took out a pinch of powder. He mixed this with water in a basket, then bent over Marisha, forcing the liquid through her lips. She coughed and sputtered, then fell back. Her chest ceased its jerking and moved up and down rhythmically. She was in a deep sleep.

The shaman donned his clothes, gathered up his furs, and ordered Marisha moved to her own house. As the men gently lifted her and carried her away, the shaman turned to Tall Dancer.

"There has been a serious *chlakass* in this house. This sin is the cause for the old woman's illness." Tek-'ic leaned closer and raised his voice. "My spirit told me terrible things will come to the clan unless this wrong is corrected." In a flurry of hair, he disappeared out the door.

Tall Dancer leaned against the door frame and watched the shaman hurry down the street. How could he have known about him and Cara? Did the old man really have powers to see and know all?

Cara poured a spoonful of thin broth made from aspen bark and dried fish into Marisha's open mouth. Part of the soup went down the corner of her mouth, but she swallowed and Cara knew she had gotten some of the dose. She sighed, set down the basket, and took up Marisha's frail hand. Cara smoothed the skin, then gently tucked the older woman's hand beneath a bear hide.

The blanket rustled behind her and Tall Dancer filled the

door. Without a glance at Cara, he moved to Marisha's side. He laid a hand on her forehead for a moment, then straightened.

"Has she been awake?"

His tone was matter of fact and impersonal.

"No, not yet."

He stared down at Marisha's face for a moment, then frowned. "Come for me if she does." He turned on his heel and left.

Cara felt the chill left in his wake. Did he somehow blame her for Marisha's illness? What had the shaman said to him that made him act this way? She sighed and smoothed the hide again.

"Here. Let me."

Cara turned. Little Beaver's wife, Brass, reached down and took the basket from her.

"Go outside. I will watch her." Her tone said she would tolerate no argument, so Cara gladly let her take over for a while.

As she stepped onto the porch, Cara breathed in a lungful of brisk air. She hadn't been outside the house for nearly two days. In that time, summer seemed to have arrived in its full glory. Birds chirped from the thicket and the insects hummed from the forest, but none of the sounds held joy for her.

She clasped her hands behind her back and moved off the porch and down between the houses. Watching her feet scuff the dust on the packed ground, she followed the sound of chopping. Little Beaver was working on another canoe. Little-River-Underneath had decided one war canoe wouldn't do. The village needed two.

As she walked, she thought about Marisha—kind, gentle Marisha. Would she ever know how hungry Cara had been for the compassion and love she gave? Cara chuckled over the irony that the only compassion she had ever known had come from the hands of a Tlingit woman, a member of a group of people her father despised and felt should be wiped out.

Marisha's hands looked so frail, but were so strong. Those same hands had cared for Tall Dancer when he was a boy.

How she must have missed him when at ten he went to live with Noisy Feather and his wife so his uncle might teach him the ways of manhood.

The chopping grew louder, interrupting her thoughts. She found herself in a shower of wood chips. She reached down and caught up a handful of the fragrant bits.

"How is Marisha?" Little Beaver stopped his work long enough to ask.

"There is no change," Cara answered, then noted his disappointment. "Maybe tomorrow."

Little Beaver nodded and continued hacking away at the bark of the giant cedar. Cara let the chips fall between her fingers as she circled the half log. Only special people were allowed to build a canoe of such importance. She ran her hand over the curved bow of the boat. Little Beaver had already flattened the bottom and shaped the sides. Now the log had been flipped over and he was digging away at the insides, sending out a shower of chips with each swing of his mallet. Occasionally, he stopped and carefully measured the inside thickness with two fingers.

Cara left him to his craft and strolled down to the stream's edge. She sat down on a worn stump and stared into the water. Tiny minnows darted in and out between the rocks, constantly swimming to keep their noses upstream.

She empathized with their plight. She, too, felt like she was swimming upstream—fighting her love for Tall Dancer, fending off Kaskoe's attacks, hiding her identity from the rest of the village, worrying about her father ransacking the coast looking for her. All were taking a toll.

She slid to the edge and dropped her feet into the water. It was icy cold and made her toes tingle. She lay back on the mat of moss and put her arms behind her head, cataloging the sounds of summer—except for one.

From a thicket on the other side of the stream came the buzz of human voices. Cara tried to focus her hearing on that sound alone, tried to shut out all the other sounds of the forest. The buzz became a giggle, then the unmistakable sounds of love-making.

Cara jerked her feet from the water, embarrassed at having walked up on a tryst. Suddenly, she thought she recognized a voice. Kaskoe. Relief flooded her, then guilt, then curiosity.

Nimbly she tiptoed across the stones in the stream and stole to the edge of the clearing. She parted the branches until she could make out Kaskoe's huge form flat on her back. Perched on top of her was Tek-'ic, the shaman. The shock of seeing him in such a position made Cara gasp.

The pair stopped writhing and Kaskoe snatched for her clothes. Cara ducked low and hugged the ground. The shaman rustled the bushes on the other side of the thicket, threatening the unseen offender with the worst kinds of ailments. He thrashed the undergrowth, and Cara held her breath as he neared. Then, when he was no more than a few feet from her, he stopped and turned, lured back by Kaskoe's erotic promises. As he whirled around, the tail of his knotted hair swept across Cara's face.

Days passed and Cara diligently tended Marisha. Then, one evening just at dusk, Marisha opened her eyes for the first time. She looked around the room and seemed bewildered until her gaze fell on Cara.

Smiling slowly, she reached up to stroke Cara's face. "Have I slept long?" she asked.

"You've been asleep for days. The shaman came to you."

"That old liar." Marisha tossed her head from side to side and frowned. "I should have taken more devilclub."

She turned back toward Cara and her frown smoothed away. "I dreamed I died and walked in the village as a spirit. Then I came to this big river. There was a village on the other side. I called to the people there and they came after me with a canoe."

Marisha gripped Cara's hand tightly. "I saw my husband,

but a big tree grew out of his head and his face was covered with moss."

Cara smothered a laugh, then realized Marisha was deadly serious.

"Then I saw my mother," she continued.

Before she could go on, Cara heard a soft footfall behind her and turned. Tall Dancer stood at the end of the sleeping mat, smiling down at his mother. When she smiled back, he hurried around to the opposite side of the mat, dropped to his knees, took her hand, and held it to his lips. He closed his eyes and kissed her fingers.

"I thought we had lost you," he said softly after a few moments.

Marisha turned her head and covered her son's hand with hers. "I will not be with you long, child. I have seen my death, my burial and"—she raised her head off the bed and gripped his arm tighter—"I have seen your father."

Cara wasn't expecting the stricken look that crossed Tall Dancer's face.

"Where did you see him?" he asked.

"In the village with the old ones."

He closed his eyes and kissed her fingers again. "Cara will care for you. I will be back later." Abruptly, he dropped her hand and left.

"Go to him," Marisha begged, catching Cara's elbow.

Cara turned. Every inch of Marisha's face begged her to obey. "Why was he so upset? It was only a dream."

"No." Marisha shook her head. "I have seen my death and he knows it is true. He will need you when I am gone. He is alone here."

Marisha let her hand slide away and her eyes drooped. Before Cara could ask any more questions, Marisha's chest fell and rose rhythmically in sleep. Cara stood, her legs trembling from squatting so long. After checking Marisha's forehead once more for fever, Cara darted beneath the blanket and hurried down the ledges toward the door. Counting on Tall Dancer's not going home to Kaskoe, Cara ran between the houses, heading for the beach.

She broke out of the trees and into the glow of sunset. She looked up and down the beach. Tall Dancer sat atop a pile of boulders and stared out at the red sun sinking to a watery death. Cara approached him quietly. Although she knew he heard her footsteps, he did not turn or acknowledge her presence. She climbed up on the huge gray boulder, and still he stared out at the heaving waves.

"Your mother will get well soon. The worst is past," Cara said with as much surety as she could muster.

When he turned to face her, she was taken aback by the sorrow in his eyes. "She will die." He said it as if it were already fact.

"How can you talk like that? It's almost as if you're wishing her in the grave." His refusal to see hope in his mother's condition both angered and frightened her. He and Marisha seemed so certain the end was near.

"She will die and go to the Spirit Town to be with my father." He turned back toward the ocean, now darkening with approaching night.

Cara sat silently by his side as the last desperate rays of day stretched above the surface of the water, then slowly disappeared. Bands of color arched across the sky, shimmering and wavering, appearing and disappearing. In the dusk, Cara could barely make out Tall Dancer's face, but she saw him smile as an unusually brilliant band of color burst forth.

"That's my father," he said, pointing to the night sky. "Up there in *Kiwa'a*. He's playing skinny with the other dead warriors."

Cara continued to watch him, having heard from her Tsimshian captors the story of the dead's playing causing the colors that flamed against the night sky.

"Did your father die by violence?"

As soon as the words were said, Cara knew the answer had something to do with her. Tall Dancer drew in a breath and turned to face her. Even in the dark, she could see and feel his eyes burning into hers.

"He was killed by Russian hunters while defending our village."

Chapter Thirteen

"Please, Marisha. Don't talk like that. What would I do without you?" Cara mopped soup from the edges of Marisha's mouth and sighed in exasperation.

All morning Marisha had drifted in and out of consciousness and talked of dying, trying to exact a promise from Cara to take care of Tall Dancer when she was gone.

Cara looked down into Marisha's drawn, gray face. How swiftly a few months could change one's life, Cara mused. Then she couldn't imagine life such as she had been living. Now she couldn't imagine living any other way.

But soon she would leave this life behind forever and the past months would be only vague memories. She brushed aside a wisp of Marisha's hair, but the old woman did not stir. How could she look after Tall Dancer when soon she would be back aboard her father's ship?

"How are you, *'atle?*" Tall Dancer swept into the room and knelt down on the floor by his mother's side. "You've had us all worried."

Marisha opened her eyes, smiled, and laid a withered hand

on his cheek. "I am fine now you are here. Cara, run and bring me some cool water from the stream," Marisha asked.

Cara looked at Tall Dancer. He stared at her for a moment before nodding and diverting his eyes. Cara gathered her baskets and went out of the house.

Marisha rose up on her elbows. "My time here with you is nearly done. I have dreamed of death, of the Spirit Town."

Tall Dancer felt a chill crawl up his back. "Mother, please do not talk like that. You have many years here with us yet."

"No." She shook her head stubbornly. "Don't try to avoid what I am telling you. I only regret I will not be with your father. He is in *Kiwa'a* and I will go to *sege qawu 'ani* because I have not died a warrior's death."

She gripped his arm tightly with her fingers. "I have grown very fond of Cara, and I want to make sure she will be treated well when I am gone." She nodded in the direction of the curtain, still swinging from Cara's exit.

As Tall Dancer stared down into her face, he knew she spoke the truth. She would not see another winter, and he wondered if he could face the loss. She was the only thing binding him to this village. Without her, he would drift like the ocean foam that washed up on shore every morning.

"I will take care of Cara until I can return her to Fort St. Michael," he said carefully, reminding his mother of his obligation.

Marisha lowered her voice to barely a whisper and pulled his face closer. "I am not talking about taking care of her. I am talking about loving her. I would be pleased to know you have each other when I am gone. Sometimes, my son, you have to take your happiness where you find it."

Tall Dancer sat back on his heels. Did his mother know about the nights he and Cara had spent together, nights filled with a passion so strong it took his breath? Did she know he had given his virginity to Cara and not to his wife?

"You wonder if I know you and Cara have been together. You wonder if I know you do not behave like a husband to Kaskoe. Yes, I know."

Her eyes glittered with mischief, and he was reminded of the times she had read his mind when he was a small child.

"I love Cara, Mother," he whispered as he kneaded her fingers, "more than I ever thought I could love a woman. But I am bound to Kaskoe, bound by the vows I said."

Tenderly, she caressed his cheek. "The life of the Tlingit is changing, *'ax yit.* More Russian hunters come and take more of the seal and the whale and the otter. We cannot fight them all. Your father used to tell me of the many Russians in their village, all eager to come here. We cannot fight them and win. We must learn to deal with them. You are the man to do that."

Her fingers trailed down his arm, coming to rest on the fur cover. The effort of speaking had drained her. She closed her eyes and her breaths evened out in sleep, leaving Tall Dancer to consider her words.

Cara dipped the basket into the water, waited for it to fill, then lifted it and replaced the tight lid. She glanced over her shoulder toward the house, but Tall Dancer still had not emerged. Wanting to give him as much time alone with Marisha as possible, she left the stream and strolled through the village.

Little Beaver was almost finished with the second war canoe. Now workers were filling it with water and dropping in hot rocks to boil the water and soften the wood so they could broaden the sides with wooden braces.

Cara ran her hand over the bow of the canoe and thought how frail it would look on the water compared to her father's ship. Little Beaver grinned at her, and the thought of a confrontation between her father's cutthroats and these men made a shiver pass over her.

When Cara returned to the house, Marisha was sleeping peacefully and Tall Dancer was gone. She began the preparations for dinner and carried the meal down to the firepit to cook. Across the fire, Kaskoe was preparing dinner for herself and Tall Dancer. Cara moved her things to the other side. She wasn't in any mood to exchange barbs with the woman tonight. But Kaskoe saw her and crossed the pit.

"The old woman is dying," she said, pushing her way through the other women. "When she is gone, you will be mine. Tall Dancer will get all her things, and that includes you." Kaskoe poked a finger in Cara's chest.

"Marisha is not dying." Cara pushed Kaskoe's arm away. "She's getting better. I will never be your slave."

Kaskoe bunched her brows into a frown, leaned forward, and shoved her face into Cara's. "I will get what I want, and I want you."

Kaskoe stalked away back to the other side of the pit. Cara raked her food out of the fire and returned to the house with a terrible sense of foreboding. Marisha opened her eyes as Cara entered. Smiling weakly, she held out her hand.

"Come here, my child. I need to talk with you."

Cara set down the baskets of food and knelt at Marisha's side.

"I have asked Tall Dancer to care for you when I am gone." She gripped Cara's hand and squeezed it.

"You are not going to die. Look here what I have made for supper. It will strengthen you." Cara pushed the basket of deer stew under her nose.

"No," she said, shaking her head. "I will never again roam the forest with you in search of berries as we did this summer."

Something in her voice rang with a note of finality, and Cara's sense of foreboding increased.

"You have brought me much joy, Cara. I had no daughter, but you have been that daughter to me." With trembling hands, she caressed one of Cara's fat braids. "Tall Dancer has promised he will see you are treated properly and returned to your people as soon as possible."

Cara felt the sting of tears, but blinked them away.

"I will go to Spirit Town, but my ghost will walk in the gravehouse behind the village. Do this for me." She tightened her grip on Cara's upper arm until Cara silently winced. "Tall Dancer will need you then. He has traveled among the white and learned their ways. Now he must find his own path in this time of change for our people. He will need someone to guide and love him.''

Cara smoothed Marisha's forehead, feeling for a moment the loss of her own mother so many years ago. ''Don't talk anymore about dying. You will live a long time and spend many summers yet gathering berries in the forests.''

Marisha's smile came and went slowly, then she slept.

Cara awoke the next morning to a slow, drizzling rain that beat a gentle staccato on the roof. The damp, moist air coiled through the house, chilling all it touched.

Her heart pounding, she crawled from beneath her furs and lit the lamp. The flickering flame illuminated Marisha's face. She lay on her back, her eyes open, a smile curving her lips. Cara touched her cheek, then yanked her hand away. Marisha's skin was cold.

Stroking Marisha's hair, Cara let numbness devour the pain that warred within her. She sat back on her heels. Marisha had smiled in her last moments of life, and that brought Cara some small comfort. As she closed Marisha's eyes, Cara wondered what she had seen in those final seconds.

Cara lingered over her body as her tears began to fall and pain overcame disbelief. Gone was the only person aside from Tall Dancer who had ever shown her love.

She covered Marisha's face and left the bedroom to fetch Tall Dancer. Kaskoe pulled the curtain aside and drew her lips into a surly snarl when Cara asked for Tall Dancer, but he stepped between them.

''Your mother is dead,'' Cara said simply, drained of the strength to soften the blow.

Tall Dancer stared at her a moment, then turned toward the front of the house and thundered, ''Open the door.''

A man just coming in threw the wooden door open wide.

Tall Dancer rushed past Cara and leaped the ledges to his

mother's room. Others in the house, seeing Tall Dancer's haste, jumped up and followed. He stepped into the quarters and yanked the fur from Marisha's face. He turned his back to the door, filled now by curious neighbors, and stooped over Marisha's body.

"She told me last night she believed she would join your father after death," Cara said, moving to his side.

Tall Dancer turned and closed the blanket, shutting out the curious stares of the other residents. Then he crouched down on one knee over Marisha's body and cradled his chin in one hand.

"She always believed she would see Father again." His voice trembled slightly. "She refused to believe he would live in a place meant only for warriors and she would live somewhere else." With shaking fingers, he gently smoothed the skin of her cheek. "Did she die during the night?" he asked without turning.

"Yes."

"I hope her spirit escaped," he murmured.

A crowd of people suddenly forced their way into the room. Members of the Eagle clan, the opposite clan from Marisha, descended to prepare her body. Tall Dancer rose and disappeared through the swinging blanket. Pinned in the corner, Cara watched the preparations.

The women wrapped Marisha in the blanket Cara had made and placed her ceremonial headdress upon her head. Then they pulled gloves onto her hands and thick skin boots onto her feet so when her spirit struggled through the thickets of nettles, devilclubs, and bushes, it would be protected. A fur was placed over her face and she was carried to the far wall of the house and propped in a sitting position.

Her belongings were carried from the tiny cubicle she'd called home and placed at her side so she might not enter the spirit world empty-handed. Several Eagle women took over the house and readied things for the watch they would keep all night on the body.

* * *

Cara heaved a huge basket away from the firepit and the lid slipped off, sloshing hot water over her hands. She cried out and dropped the basket.

"Don't I have enough to do to feed these lazy people without your wasting food?" Kaskoe shouted and cuffed Cara on the ear.

Intense pain shot through the side of her head and red splotches sprang before her eyes.

"Bring another basket of water." Kaskoe shoved a basket into Cara's midsection.

Cara glared at the puffy face in front of her. Kaskoe's hair hung down in straggly wet strands. Members of the Eagle clan watching Marisha's body expected to eat well, and the responsibility fell to Kaskoe to do the cooking.

At first she had cried and whined and appealed to her father. But Big Rabbit, tired of Kaskoe's complaints, had stated flatly this was her responsibility and then refused to hear any more.

Cara swallowed her anger, turned on her heel, and hurried away, all the while telling herself the reason she refrained from giving Kaskoe the smacking she deserved was because of Tall Dancer.

A sharp wind blew dried cedar needles and boughs across Cara's path. Overhead, gray clouds scurried across the sky before a cold wind. The brief summer was over and winter was not far away. The change in seasons would mark the time Tall Dancer would once again leave the village to trap all winter.

Head down against the wind, Cara hurried toward the stream. But she stopped when she saw Tall Dancer moving between the two new canoes still up on logs, awaiting the ceremony to launch them. He moved slowly down the length of one, his hand caressing the carefully honed edge. He circled them absently, his thoughts obviously somewhere else. He wore a breechcloth, sealskin leggings, and moccasins, and his chest was bare against the morning cold. Little sprinkles of water fell from his hair, still damp from his dawn plunge into the waters of the sound.

Cara paused and watched. They had not spoken since the morning of Marisha's death. He rarely came home and was never at meals because of the fasting that was part of his mourning.

Watching his absent circling, Cara sensed his loneliness. He did not feel a part of these people. Marisha had been his only link to the teachings of his childhood. An overwhelming empathy for him suddenly overtook her. The man who had protected her, saved her, comforted her like a child now needed that same comforting.

She stepped forward, then stopped. No. She wasn't allowed. Comforting him was Kaskoe's job. Cara tore her gaze away, ducked her head, and headed toward the stream.

Bypassing the well-worn place where she usually drew water, Cara moved further upstream where the water leaped over two large boulders, then fell with a deafening roar that muted all other sounds. Here she could think, undisturbed by village noises. She sat down on a mossy shelf and closed her eyes. Deep woods always reminded her of Marisha and the times they picked berries and dug roots.

A hand touched her shoulder. Startled, she scrambled to her feet. Tall Dancer faced her, his eyes full of pain, gray hollows shadowing his cheeks. Appearances and clan allegiances suddenly seemed unimportant. She went to him and encircled his waist with her arms, feeling his heartbeat against her cheek. After a moment's hesitation, his arms drew her near. Cara tried to cry quietly, but her frame shook with released sorrow, sorrow she could share only with him.

"Do not cry, or else it will rain and sleet on *'atle's* spirit as it tries to find its way home," he said, his voice breaking at the end.

"I can't help it. I miss her so already." She buried her face against him and felt his breath grow ragged.

His pain had become a shadow being that followed him

everywhere. He was a man adrift in his own time, torn between two worlds, two bloods that converged within him.

She started to move away, but he held her close. "Not now," he whispered into her hair. "Don't leave me yet."

Cara stayed.

The fire crackled and caught, shooting orange flames high into the night sky, illuminating the cedar-log pyre awaiting Marisha's body. The smell of burning seal oil floated heavy on the air, forever embedding itself in Cara's mind. Tentative flames licked at the spruce branches and brush like tiny demons.

The entire village ringed the pyre, but Tall Dancer stood alone in silhouette against the flames. Fists clenched, he stood rigid while his unbound hair floated around his shoulders in curly dark wisps.

The Eagle clan approached from the left with a wrapped bundle hefted high on their shoulders. They stopped at the edge of the fire, raised their burden, and tossed it onto the flames. A chorus of shouts, sobs, and weeping rose as the flames caught the blanket, devouring it happily while tiny orange fragments floated skyward.

Cara huddled at the back of the crowd, covering her nose and mouth and burying her face in the newly fallen leaves that littered the ground where she sat. She gagged as the scent of burning flesh worked its way through her fingers.

Then a new cry joined the others, a sound that ripped through her heart. She jumped to her feet and pushed her way through the people.

Tall Dancer leaped forward and whirled his long hair through the flames. He yelped as the scent of singed hair covered the odor of burning flesh. Dousing his hair with a basket of cold water, he shook his head. His long mane was now a crop of short, frayed tufts.

Cara's breath caught in her throat as he thrust his hands into the ashes at the base of the pyre and smeared his face with the soot. As the last fragment of Marisha's blanket disintegrated and the roaring flames hid her body from view, tears ran down his cheeks, leaving white tracks in their wake.

The circle of mourners broke up quickly, eager to return to their daily lives. As the number of people around her thinned, Cara moved forward. The once huge pyre was now a smoldering pile of coals, glowing red-orange with their heat.

Tentatively, she reached out her hand to touch Tall Dancer, then quickly drew it back when she saw his eyes stared at the flames and his face was contorted in anguish.

Someone grabbed her hair from behind. Kaskoe yanked Cara around to face her. "This slave is mine now," she snarled at Tall Dancer as he moved to step between them. "She is a witch. She has used a love potion on you that she got from Marisha, and you have been unfaithful to me. I know about the night on the beach."

Tall Dancer stared at her in disbelief. Kaskoe smiled, realizing she had the upper hand. "Someone saw you rolling in the sand with this slave. He will go with me to the elders."

Still stunned, Tall Dancer made no response.

Kaskoe took his silence as submission and plunged ahead. "You want her. You have wanted her since the first time you brought her here, but you cannot have her." She shook Cara as she talked. "You want to divorce me, but I will never let you go. Not until she is dead will I release you, and that will be a long and miserable life from now." She curled her lips into an evil smile and shook Cara again. "You cannot divorce me because my father will not pay you your inheritance."

Tall Dancer's face slowly changed from bewilderment to rage. Her smile disappeared as she saw the fury in his eyes.

"I do not want the payment from your father," he growled. "I have rank and wealth of my own, and I do not need his if you are the price."

He towered over them both. Kaskoe stumbled back a step, dragging Cara along with her as Tall Dancer took another pace forward. For a moment Kaskoe's countenance dropped, then she regained herself and spat back, "If I go to the council, there will be gossip. The shaman will torture her to make her confess she is a powerful witch. Then he will kill her.''

Tall Dancer clenched his fists as he fought the impulse to pound her leering face into pulp. As angry as he was, he knew Kaskoe was right. She had more than enough evidence to convince the elders that Cara was a witch. They had long suspected Marisha of witchcraft, but no one had ever had the courage to accuse her. The torture of witches was horrible.

Anger rapidly replaced his fear. Despite the pain Kaskoe was likely to put her through, at least she would live if she continued as Kaskoe's slave for a few days until he could ready his sled. Then he would take her to the fort. If he defied his wife, the entire village would side with her because of their fear of witchcraft.

Reluctantly, he watched as Kaskoe dragged her away, the image of Cara's face etched into his memory.

Cara struggled against the woman, but found that despite her obesity, Kaskoe was strong. The more Cara struggled, the more Kaskoe's hold on her hair hurt. Other residents of the house had heard the angry words spoken in the yard, and they gathered in the doorway as Kaskoe approached with Cara.

She shoved them aside, dragged Cara past Marisha's old house, and shoved her into her bedroom. At once, Cara felt Tall Dancer's presence in his belongings that dangled from the walls. Kaskoe pulled the blanket closed, shutting them into the semidarkness together.

''I will enjoy making your life miserable,'' Kaskoe said as she approached Cara. ''When I tire of you, I will kill you at one of our potlatches. That will give me great pleasure,'' she growled. ''Do you know why? Because your death at my hands will prove you are a witch, that you bewitched my husband, flying to him in the night. Killing you will bring me great respect.''

Cara felt her blood run cold as Kaskoe threw the damning words at her. She had seen a witch tortured and killed in the Tsimshian village. A young girl in love with a young man already promised to his uncle's wife had been labeled a witch by the old woman, then killed slowly and cruelly.

"For now, you will attend to my personal needs day and night. You will sleep here beside us. I want you to lie there and watch as I make love to him night after night, knowing you can never have him again."

Cara hated herself for the tears that rolled down her face. She feared feeling helpless more than the pain she knew was imminent. Kaskoe controlled her destiny. She could either kill Cara or let her live.

The next morning, Cara awoke on the bare floor, curled into a ball for warmth. Kaskoe had refused to give her any furs, instead piling them on her own bed. Cara stretched, slowly emerging from her pleasant dream of gathering berries in the clearing. Suddenly, Kaskoe jerked her to her feet.

"Go and fix breakfast for my husband and myself," she said, shoving Cara toward the firepit.

Cara stumbled forward. The baskets sat by the fire from the night before, and she had to carry them outside and scrub the dried food from them with coarse sand before she could prepare breakfast.

Tall Dancer had not come home last night and now, as she crossed the ceremonial grounds, she saw him squatted, digging through the remains of the funeral pyre. His hair lay in uneven layers above his ears. Occasionally he picked up a black object and dropped it into a small wooden chest. Cara shivered. He was raking Marisha's bones out of the ashes and putting them into a basket to place in the gravehouse. She glanced back toward the house, wishing she could go and relieve him of his burden. But her hopes were dashed when she saw Kaskoe standing on the porch.

By the time she returned from the stream, Kaskoe had placed food on the hearth for Cara to prepare. One by one, Cara shoved round stones into the fire. She was just beginning to rake them out of the flames when Tall Dancer entered the house.

His face was still streaked with black and his hair was unnaturally mussed. Others gave him room, but he passed among them looking neither right nor left. With labored, slow steps he climbed the ledges of the house until he reached the top row. He brushed by Kaskoe as she came out to greet him and went, instead, to Marisha's vacant house. He stepped inside and pulled the blanket closed behind him.

Cara shivered by the edge of the stream as light snowflakes drifted down, sprinkling her face and hair. Kaskoe had taken away all her warm clothes and insisted she wear instead torn garments with sleeves that dangled over her fingers. She massaged her temples with both hands. Her head still rang from last night's fight between Tall Dancer and Kaskoe. Threats and rebuttals had flown back and forth, and Cara didn't remember ever seeing him so angry as when Kaskoe again threatened to accuse her of witchcraft. Marisha had been dead only half a moon, but it seemed like years.

Cara stuck out her tongue and caught a fat, drifting flake. It quickly melted and she savored the fresh taste. For weeks, the weather had grown steadily colder, but today was the first snow. Behind her, she heard the excited shouts of the village children as they ran with their tongues out to catch the flakes. A chubby toddler tripped and fell, then wailed loudly. His mother hurried outside, picked him up by the back of his dress and dragged him back inside.

A pang of regret struck her. How she had once longed for children of her own. She touched her abdomen and wondered if she might be pregnant with Tall Dancer's child. Shaking her head, she tried to dispel all thoughts of that. A pregnancy now would surely brand her a witch.

Tall Dancer stepped out of the house and pulled a thick bearskin around his shoulders. He quickly scanned the village and saw Cara standing by the stream watching the children play. He saw her touch her stomach and his heart fluttered. Was she thinking the same thing as he? Was she wondering if his seed had been planted within her?

He closed his eyes and tipped his head back to let the cold

flakes plop upon his cheeks. How he wished Cara would conceive a child from their union. They would leave the village and live alone in a house he would build.

He opened his eyes and looked around the village again. He no longer felt any ties here. Even his people supported Kaskoe's belief that Cara was a witch. They didn't say so, but there were whispered rumors around the fires at night. Some said Marisha had been a witch and had passed her knowledge on to the girl slave she treated as a daughter. He hefted a bundle more firmly onto his hip, stepped down off the porch, and set out toward the stream. He smiled, thinking of Kaskoe's reaction when she discovered her favorite wrap gone.

As he reached the outskirts of the village, Cara started back from the stream, walking with her eyes cast downward. She only looked up when he stepped into her path. She was thinner despite the food he slipped her unnoticed. Only a few more hours, he told himself. Then he would take her away from this.

He settled the robe over her shoulders and let his fingers linger on her neck. "It is cold today," he said with a smile.

"Kaskoe will be angry," Cara said as she slid her hand across the silky fur.

He touched her shoulders lightly. "We leave tomorrow."

"So soon?" Her head flew up and her eyes brightened.

He let his hands slide off her shoulders. "I have already stayed too long. The dogs are ready and we must go before bad weather comes. This snow will last all night. Tomorrow there will be enough for the sled to run."

Cara smiled radiantly, but then her gaze darted to the house behind them. Her eyes full of dread, she shouldered the large basket of water and sidestepped him.

He turned in time to see Kaskoe hurrying toward them, her face bunched in anger. When she reached Cara, she cuffed her on the ear. Cold water splashed onto Kaskoe's feet and wet the hem of her dress. She drew back her hand to slap Cara across the mouth, but Tall Dancer stepped between them and grabbed her arm.

"If you ever strike her again, I'll kill you," he growled

between clenched teeth. He spoke the words slowly and evenly, enjoying the emotions flickering across Kaskoe's face.

"She is mine to do with as I wish," Kaskoe answered, her face now expressionless.

Tall Dancer swallowed and took a deep breath to control his temper for fear of smashing her face. "Soon," he said slowly, "I will return her to her people and you will have to do your own chores."

Kaskoe's face was stone. She neither blinked nor swallowed. She stared at him as evenly as he stared at her. "What makes you think the witch will live that long?"

Chapter Fourteen

Snow and bits of ice flew up from the sled's runners. Tall Dancer ducked to avoid a cedar branch bearing down on him. Cold wind whistled around his ears as the dogs sped across the new fall of snow. The brisk air, the smell of fresh snow, the thrill of effortless speed combined to exhilarate him.

He leaned to the side, swinging the dogs into a wide turn, then followed the bed of the stream. It had been much too long since he'd done this. Life in the wilderness beckoned to him now as never before.

He squinted up at the sun dipping low in the west. Night was approaching, and it was time for him to get back to the village. Reluctantly, he swung the dogs around and headed back, slicing over his previous tracks. Mentally, he ticked off his equipment. His traps were oiled and ready. A large sealskin bag held dried fish. New arrows hung in his quiver, and his bow had been restrung with fresh sinew. Tomorrow they would leave.

A pang of sorrow dampened his mood. Once they reached Fort St. Michael, she would be gone. How he wanted to disappear into the wilderness with her and never return to the stiff social requirements of his people.

As he approached the outskirts of the village, he saw a crowd gathered before his door. Instantly alert, he dragged one foot and brought the sled to a halt. The crowd surged forward, struggling and shoving to get inside. He left the sled and elbowed his way through the group.

At the center of the house, Little Beaver's youngest child lay on the lowest wooden ledge, covered with a deer hide. Gathered around were the boy's mother, father, and other relatives. Tek-'ic, regal in his ceremonial costume, stood alongside the child. Spectators filled the rest of the ledges. Tall Dancer scanned the crowd until he spotted Kaskoe and Cara not far from where the child lay. Suspicion filled his thoughts.

The hum of the crowd stilled as Tek-'ic threw his head back and began to jerk and chant, putting himself into a trance. Stragglers outside the door hurried in to get good seats. The child on the bed began to convulse and moan.

Little Beaver stepped forward and handed the shaman an armload of furs. Tek-'ic paused in his chanting and carefully inspected the pelts. He ran his hand across the silky furs, then placed them on the floor and began to wail in earnest.

The shaman fell on all fours, swinging his head back and forth in imitation of a bear, his *yek*. The ermine tails dangling from his headdress flew back and forth, and shells attached to the headpiece rattled. Slowly, he circled the firepit, stopping at each person.

When he reached Cara, Tall Dancer glanced at Kaskoe. She smiled slightly, watching the shaman bawl and swing his head. Then, he began to bounce on his hands like a bear about to charge.

Cara's face turned deathly white, and Kaskoe's plan became clear. Little Beaver's youngest child, Someone Bites Her, had always been afflicted with a strange disease that made her fall to the ground and jerk and salivate. Many shamans had come from tribes far away to treat her, but none had ever succeeded in curing her of the terrible affliction.

"No," Tall Dancer cried, lunging forward.

Strong arms caught his, and he was hauled backward by two of the shaman's assistants.

"Let me go," he growled, trying to snatch his arms out of their grasp.

"The witch must die," one of the young men said in an emotionless voice.

"She's no witch. This is Kaskoe's doing." He tried to jerk away, but the men held him tight.

Tek-'ic roared. Kaskoe and another woman grabbed Cara and dragged her to her feet. They tied her hands together with a rope, then fastened it to her hair so her head was strained back. Cara cried out as they bent her body backward. Again Tall Dancer lunged forward, but was checked.

Tek-'ic fell to the floor and began to convulse. The women half carried, half dragged Cara to the door, passing within a few feet of Tall Dancer. They took her outside and tied her between two trees. Kaskoe braided a long, spiny devilclub into Cara's hair to pierce her scalp each time her head bobbed.

"Confess you are a witch," Kaskoe demanded.

Cara remained silent, her lips pressed together.

"No!" Tall Dancer cried, hot rage consuming him.

Cara's wide-eyed gaze met his, and his rage began to cool. To save her, he would have to think without anger. When Cara showed no signs of confessing, Kaskoe tightened the knot, pulling her head back even further. The two assistants eased their grip on Tall Dancer's arms. When he didn't struggle, they let him go and stepped back warily. Tek-'ic came out of the house and sauntered up to Cara.

"This witch has many lids," he declared, pointing at her. "It will take many days to loosen them all. She will not confess easily." He paced around her, his hands clasped behind his back. "Bring sea water," he called to his assistants.

One of the young men ran forward and handed the shaman a basket. He caught the back of Cara's hair and yanked. When her lips parted, he poured the salty water into her mouth. She strangled and sputtered. Tek-'ic stood back and smiled. "We will see if she is ready to confess in the morning."

When Tek-'ic made no more motions toward Cara, the crowd thinned. Tall Dancer hurried down the steps toward her. The shaman's two assistants were on his heels. But Tek-'ic himself stepped in front of Tall Dancer.

"You will not touch her," he declared, his arms crossed stubbornly.

"Cut her down, Tek-'ic. You know as well as I she is no witch."

"Ah, but I do not know that. She has been going around with men, married men, and she is not ashamed."

"Kaskoe put this in your mind," he growled, only loud enough for Tek-'ic to hear.

The shaman smiled. "Your wife is very convincing. You have not lain with her. That is your loss."

It took a few moments for the words to sink in. Then Tall Dancer lunged at Tek-'ic. He grabbed the shaman around the neck and squeezed.

Tek-'ic's eyes bulged and his long, curled nails bit into Tall Dancer's wrists. Tall Dancer squeezed tighter and Tek-'ic's face turned red. Then someone grabbed him from behind. One of the shaman's assistants hauled him backward and spun him around. The assistant's fist connected with Tall Dancer's chin and sent him sprawling back into the dirt.

"See!" Tek-'ic cried, clutching his throat with one hand. "She has bewitched her lover!"

Tall Dancer heard the sharp intake of breath all around him. Lying on his back, propped up on his elbows, he looked into the disapproving faces of his friends. Noisy Feather frowned and, even from a distance, Tall Dancer felt the pain of his uncle's disapproval.

The crowd began to rumble again. Those who had shuffled off toward home now returned hastily, eager not to miss any more excitement.

He glanced over at Cara. She hung by her arms, which were extended between two sapling cedars. Her head sagged forward, her hair falling in a cascade over her face. Her fate was sealed. Sometime during the ten days allowed for a witch's confession, she would be killed—unless she admitted her guilt.

The village was still, lit only by a feeble fire warming the two young men guarding Cara. Tall Dancer approached her with even, steady steps. One of the young men stirred, then leapt to his feet.

"Stop!" he cried in an unsteady voice.

"I want to talk to her." Tall Dancer nodded toward Cara, unsure if she was unconscious or asleep on her feet.

The young man quickly scanned the village. "Tek-'ic says no one is to talk to her."

"Well," Tall Dancer slurred with a slow smile, "he'll make an exception for me."

Again the young man glanced around, then looked down at his sleeping friend.

Seeing the man's indecision, Tall Dancer tried another approach. "If she is a witch and has been my lover, how do you know I'm not a witch, too?"

A deep furrow etched across the man's face. He moved back a step.

"I might help convince her to confess. Then you wouldn't have to spend another night out here in the cold."

That suggestion seemed to make a connection. With another nervous glance to assure no one else saw, he nodded in Cara's direction.

Tall Dancer hurried to her side and caught her cheeks in his hands. She stirred, mumbled something unintelligible, then opened her eyes.

"Cara."

She stared at him blankly.

"Listen to me, Cara." He said and shook her head slightly. "You have to confess."

She blinked and frowned. "What did you say?"

"I said you have to confess in the morning."

"They'll kill me." She ran her tongue over her cracked lips.
"Not if you do exactly as I say."

Morning's light brought another crowd of curious onlookers.
They gathered around Cara, each one hunched against the cold,
their wraps pulled tightly around them.

"Do you confess now?" Tek-'ic asked her, his face only
inches from hers.

Cara opened her eyes. Her vision was fuzzy and dim, but
she could make out Tall Dancer standing on the edge of the
crowd, his dog team already hitched to the sled. She blinked
and tried to clear her mind, to remember all he had told her
last night.

His whispered words had been in Russian, and over the
months she had forgotten much of her native tongue. After
licking her dry lips, she peered at the shaman again and sum-
moned her strength for the performance of her life.

"Yes, I confess."

Tek-'ic looked stunned and took a step backwards. "You
do?"

Then, she began to babble in Russian. At least she hoped it
sounded like babbling to the villagers. Word for word, line for
line, she recited her favorite nursery rhyme taught her long ago
by a woman now only a shadow of a memory.

The shaman backed up another step. "Cut her down," he
ordered.

Cara held her breath. If the plan were to go awry, it would
be now. Tek-'ic had the choice of letting her live as a confessed
witch or killing her. The two young men sawed through her
rope bonds with stone knives and stood back as her feet touched
the ground and she crumpled to her knees. She rubbed her
wrists and got to her feet. The crowd circled her. She glanced
at the wall of disapproving faces.

"You cannot live here any longer," Tek-'ic said with a quick
glance at Kaskoe.

"She is going with me." Tall Dancer stepped forward.

"Ah. Her lover." Tek-'ic smiled as again the crowd gasped at so blatant an admission.

"I am taking her back to her own people at Fort St. Michael."

"When you return, Tall Dancer, you must pay for going around with this witch."

Tall Dancer did not answer. He didn't plan to return. As he prepared, he glanced at Noisy Feather's face. It remained immobile.

Cara moved toward him and the crowd opened a wide path to let her through. Tall Dancer pulled aside a fur to reveal a warm nest of furs. She paused for one last look around the village before leaving. Despite the miserable days she'd spent here with Kaskoe, some of her happiest days had also been spent here with Marisha.

"I am going with you."

They both spun around at the sound of Kaskoe's voice. She stood behind the sled, bundled to the nose in a thick bear pelt and dangling a bulging sealskin bag.

"You didn't think I would let you go and leave me here ashamed and humiliated, did you?" she asked. "I have no place here now. Your unfaithfulness has seen to that. She is my property and I will not let her go. She will serve me while I accompany you to the fort and back." She leaned closer. "And I will conceive a child while we are gone, or I will have you tied up as a witch when we return."

Tall Dancer glanced at the condemning faces that surrounded him. All his actions the villagers had considered only odd while Marisha lived could well be interpreted as witchcraft. Kaskoe's threat was real, and not just in this village. Gossip would carry the story of a witch to other clans and other villages. Former friends would now be afraid and suspicious. Having enemies as enemies and friends as enemies could make the trip through dangerous country impossible.

"You leave me little choice," he said. "But you will have to walk."

"Walk!" she stormed, bunching her face into a frown. "I will not walk. I am your wife, and I will ride in this sled."

"You will not abuse my dogs. You are too heavy and I will not ask them to pull you. If you want to go, you will walk."

Kaskoe studied his face for a moment, then seemed resigned to the fact. Tall Dancer threw her sack into the sled and spread a warm wrap over Cara's shoulders.

They left the crowd far behind and trudged to the edge of the village where the lonely gravehouse stood. Tall Dancer issued a single command to the dogs, and they lay down in their harnesses.

"Why are we stopping here?" Kaskoe asked irritably, stamping her feet to keep them warm.

"I want to see my mother's remains one last time," Tall Dancer said firmly.

Kaskoe opened her mouth to reply, then snapped it shut.

The door protested on its rotting leather hinges as Tall Dancer pulled it open. A musty, moldy odor swept out. He lit the wick of a lamp kept by the door. The flame faltered, then caught, throwing eerie shadows upon the walls.

Elaborately decorated boxes sat on the uneven shelves that lined the walls. Inside each were the cremated remains of a villager. He went straight to Marisha's box and picked it up, swept the dust away with his hand, then traced the carved images with his finger.

When had he decided never to return? He thought about Marisha, remembering her laughter, her lighthearted ways. It seemed impossible she was reduced to what he held in his hands. He looked at the far wall. One box, covered with dust and long undisturbed, sat in a back corner. Carefully replacing Marisha's box, he moved across the house and picked up the box.

A cloud of dust billowed up as he blew away the grime. Faded paint adorned intricate carvings. He flipped up the lid and gazed down at a thin layer of ash—his father's remains. He closed the box, walked toward the door, then placed it on the shelf beside Marisha's. "Good-bye," he whispered. Taking one last look around, he backed out and closed the door.

* * *

They traveled until they came to another Tlingit village at midmorning. The sky had lowered and light snowflakes drifted down. Villagers poured out to greet the visitors. Refusing their offers of hospitality for the night, Tall Dancer walked a few paces away from the sled to talk to the village leader, a young, dark-haired man with a stern expression.

Cara, feeling uncomfortable riding while Kaskoe waddled along behind, had opted to walk, too. As the men talked, she strained to hear their conversation, but they spoke so quickly she could not catch the words. She glanced around the village. Several men squatted on porches as they whittled on new arrows. Stacked next to several doors were new spears and lances. She glanced back at Tall Dancer. He turned on his heel and strode back to the sled.

"What's the matter?" she asked, seeing the concern on his face.

"There have been some skirmishes with the Russians south of here," he said. "The chief said the Russians have been hunting deeper and deeper into our territory. Some of the clans have attacked their camps."

Kaskoe looked genuinely frightened. "You will take me home," she said, stamping her foot. "I do not want trouble with the Russians. Don't you remember how they took the girls from the village last summer because of her?" She pointed at Cara.

"I'm not taking you home." His face looked haggard and Cara could see dealing with Kaskoe was exacting a price. "I don't have time to retrace my steps. You wanted to come on this trip, so you will have to accept whatever happens."

Kaskoe pouted for the next few miles, granting them a few hours of peace. They made camp on the shores of a sound just as the sun dipped into the ocean. Concealed in a copse of trees, Cara built a small fire and cooked their dinner while Tall Dancer kept careful watch. Soon after they ate, Kaskoe rolled up in her pelt and began to snore. As dusk deepened into night, Cara and Tall Dancer sat across the fire from one another. He stared into the flames, seemingly lost in thought.

"Are you worried about what the chief told you today?" Cara ventured.

He shook his head. "I have heard rumors for months that the Tlingit nation will rise up against Fort St. Michael to destroy it and send the Russians from our land."

The hatred in his voice made her blood run cold.

"Some of the clans are against such action. Some want to destroy every white man who sets foot here. Either way, the Russians are here to stay."

Again, Cara felt a stab of guilt. Months ago he had ceased asking her about her home and her family. Many times she wondered if Marisha had told him her secret.

"Do you think we are in danger here?" Cara glanced out into the darkness.

Tall Dancer shook his head. "I think we are safe."

Kaskoe snored loudly and turned over onto her side. Silence stretched between them. The fire crackled and popped.

Somewhere deep in the forest behind them an owl hooted. The eerie call sent chills up Cara's spine.

"He says there is trouble ahead," Tall Dancer said without looking up.

Cara studied his bowed head. Rarely had she heard him subscribe to native suspicions.

The owl hooted again, a long *hoo-hoooo,* that reverberated through the forest.

"He says there will be much sorrow."

Never had she seen him so despondent. Cara rose and walked around the fire. Kneeling beside him she took his face in her hands. "I do not want to leave you."

He looked up at her and studied her face. "You have to leave. There is trouble in the wind and much killing to come. You will not be safe with me."

"I will always be safe with you." Gently, she touched his lips with hers.

Her kiss was like a spark touched to kindling. He crushed

her against him, willing that she stay there, firmly attached to his heart forever. Suddenly, Kaskoe snorted, gasped for breath, and turned over. The effect was like a splash of cold water. He released Cara, jumped to his feet, and walked away into the darkness.

Kaskoe was still snoring peacefully when he returned. The fire had burned itself into a pile of embers. Pointedly, he rolled out his furs and lay down as far from both women as the warmth of the fire would allow.

On the other side of the fire, the sled dogs stretched out around Cara. Occasionally, she rubbed them behind the ears.

What would she do once they reached the settlement? Wait for her father to come and claim her? Get aboard the next Russian ship and sail for home?

Either thought seemed as impossible as this life would have seemed only a year ago. Tears squeezed out between her lids. With Kaskoe's snoring as cover, Cara sobbed her dismay into the silky fur of a bear pelt.

Two days later, they crossed into the territory of the Kagwantans. Everyone's nerves were stretched tight. Stories of skirmishes were repeated as they met other natives on the trail.

Tall Dancer walked cautiously behind the sled, his knife prominently displayed at his belt. Kaskoe complained constantly, and his patience with her had begun to grow thin. Finally, he thundered at her to remain silent. She obeyed without comment.

All along the way, he had paused to set and retrieve traps. New pelts were piled into the sled, then stashed beneath rocks and fallen trees carefully marked with piled stones or hash marks.

Kaskoe trudged along, holding them back with her slowness. Tonight they would stay in a Kagwantan village for fear of attacks by straggling Russians ransacking the countryside.

They entered the village about sunset. The big houses lining the shore of a small sound looked much the same as the village they had left behind. Tall Dancer halted the sled in front of the chief's house and went inside.

Cara and Kaskoe were left outside to endure the curious stares of the villagers. A group of half-naked women approached. Their lips jutted out, misshapen by labrets. Carrying short sticks in their hands, they circled, poking at Kaskoe's body as if they could not believe all that bulk was her. Angrily, she swung a beefy arm. They moved a safe distance away, but kept up their stares.

When Tall Dancer came out, he motioned them to follow him through the village. An abandoned house stood at the edge. One end was crushed by a large cedar that lay across it. The end nearest the door was still sturdy, and there in the dark they made camp.

The firepit was unusually small, but still intact near the center of the house. Tall Dancer pulled the sled inside and tied the dogs outside. Cara unloaded their supplies and prepared to cook, while Kaskoe sat by the fire warming her hands.

The inside of the house seemed enormous, its family dwellings all vacant. Fat totems told that this had been a wealthy family, and Cara wondered if they had escaped safely.

After their meal, Cara spread her fur by the fire. Tall Dancer moved to put his blanket away from his wife, but Kaskoe followed him and lay down by his side.

Far into the night, something woke Cara. She lay still, listening. Kaskoe was snoring loudly, but Cara was sure that was not what had awakened her. She sat up and looked around.

The house was completely dark except for the small glow coming from the embers of the fire. Tall Dancer's still form lay rolled up in a bear fur beside Kaskoe. Outside, the dogs whimpered and whined.

She got up and pulled the robe around her. An eerie yellow light filled the crack beneath the door. She cracked the door open and peeped out. Yellow flames lit the night sky.

"Tall Dancer, get up! The village is on fire!" Cara shook his shoulder.

He threw aside his covers and leaped to his feet. He shoved open the door, then threw his arm over his face against the wall of heat that hit him. Silhouetted against the flames that leaped and consumed the cedar houses, a band of men ran from house to house. He squinted against the snowfall of ashes. Russians!

"Go to the back and hide beneath the rubble. Quickly," he commanded. Then he disappeared outside.

"Come, Kaskoe, we can't wait! They're almost here!" Cara scooped up their pelts and hid beneath the fallen timbers and planks. Peeping out of her hiding place, Cara saw Kaskoe still looking out the crack in the door. Opening her mouth to call to her again, Cara was silenced by the scrape of a door opening, the scuffling of feet, and a dull thud.

"What do we have here?" a voice said in slurred Russian.

Cara peeked out. The men surrounded Kaskoe, poking and prodding her and laughing as she swatted at them. They were obviously drunk.

"She is a big one, eh?" They laughed hilariously.

Cara ducked as one man held a lamp aloft and looked toward the back of the house. She heard the sounds of a scuffle and Kaskoe's oaths. The sounds dimmed and the door scraped shut. Cara waited a few moments, then peeped out again. The house was dark and empty.

Hours crawled by before she finally emerged from her hiding place. She crept forward in the dark and listened. The crackling and screaming and popping of guns had quieted.

She opened the door a sliver. The houses stood in half-burned skeletons, embers glowing in their hearts. An unearthly quiet possessed the village. There was no sign of Kaskoe or Tall Dancer, no sign of the Russians. The sled dogs huddled beside the house and licked her hand as she reached down and rubbed them.

After commanding the animals to stay, Cara crept through the village, sliding along the sides of the houses for protection. Bodies lay everywhere. Blood spattered the few plank walls left standing and ran out into the street in puddles. Gingerly she stepped over the dead, holding her blanket over her nose to keep out the stench of burning flesh that permeated the air.

Twisted bodies lay where doors had once hung, their hands reaching for the latch. The Russians must have surprised the village and caught most of the warriors inside asleep.

Those who didn't perish in the burning dwellings had been killed as they fled. Cara frowned, noting most of the dead were men. The women and children had been taken captive.

She closed her eyes and remembered a night when her father had taken a large number of captives. In her mind she could still hear their screams and pleas as they were forced down into the hold of the ship.

Cara opened her eyes. A woman's naked body lay face down on the ground, her dress torn away. With horror Cara remembered the sounds and smells of her father's men abusing the women captives.

She glanced across the expanse of the village. Except for the flames still dancing on a few houses, there was no movement, no sign of Tall Dancer or Kaskoe. Cara crept back toward the abandoned house and wondered why this house had been spared. She slipped through the door and took a dying ember from the firepit to light the end of a stick. Holding it aloft as a lamp, she scanned the walls of the house. Suddenly, her light caught a terrible face, contorted in agony, the lips drawn back in a snarl.

Chapter Fifteen

Cara screamed and dropped the firebrand. No hands encircled her throat and no knife pressed cold against her ribs, so she picked up the burning branch and held it over her head. The face she had seen grinned at her from a shelf along the wall, a wooden mask that rested beside a small carved box. Cara gasped. They had spent the night in a gravehouse!

She sat on the edge of the firepit and tried to collect her thoughts. Where was Tall Dancer? Had he been killed? She took up the lighted stick and moved again toward the door. As she slipped outside, a hand clamped over her mouth and a voice whispered in her ear.

"Don't be afraid, Cara."

He eased his hand away and she turned and threw her arms around Tall Dancer.

"I thought you were dead." Relief flooded through her. She raised her head and looked into his eyes. "They took Kaskoe."

His lips were drawn into a tight line. "I know," he said with no emotion in his voice. "I had a few close calls myself. They have captured all the women and children and are taking them to a ship waiting off shore. I heard some of the men say they are to be used as hostages against the Tlingits at Fort St. Michael.''

A shiver shook Cara's body. Was it her father who had rained death and destruction in these villages? Where was he now? Could he have known she was here in the village? Was he sorting through the captives right now searching for her? Or was he still here?

''What do we do now?'' Cara whispered, eyeing every shadow.

Tall Dancer looked down on her auburn head, which leaned against his chest. Gently, he pushed her away, then wiped at a streak of blood smeared on her cheek.

Guiltily, he felt no loss at Kaskoe's disappearance. No pleasure, but no pain either. All his thoughts had been centered on Cara.

Later, when he had seen her sneaking through the village, his heart had leapt into his throat and his eyes had constantly scanned, looking for the red-haired Russian captain who had swiftly dispatched so many Tlingits.

A crash echoed through the dark. The remains of another house fell, sending a shower of orange sparks into the night sky. An evening breeze brought the pungent scent of blood and death.

''We have to leave here.'' Without another word, he collected their things from the house and led the dogs into the dark, quiet woods. They found a rock outcropping on the side of a hill. There they spread their furs for the night.

''What will we do now?'' Cara asked as she pulled another fur over her.

''I can't take you into Fort St. Michael now. Looking like you do and being with me, they would be upon you in a minute. I have a friend who lives near there. I will take you to him. He will see you get back home.''

Cara's heart sank. So he still intended to return her. She turned onto her side, her back to him. Until now, she had hoped some miracle would prevent her from being delivered into the hands of the Russians. ''What will you do about Kaskoe?''

Silence met her question. She turned onto her back to look at him. His head drooped and he looked at his hands, turning them over and over.

"After I leave you, I will try to get into the fort and get her out." He glanced up. "She is my wife. It is my responsibility to care for her."

Before dawn, they piled the bodies one on top of another, covered them with brush, then set fire to them. The sun was just clearing the trees when they left the village, and the stench of burning flesh followed them for miles through the forest.

Tall Dancer crept to the edge of the clearing on his belly. He lay still, his cheek pressed against the cold snow. Cara lay beside him and waited until he raised his head before she, too, peeped over the bushes at the Russian fort. She gasped and his hand on her head crushed her face to the ground.

"Shhh!" he hissed and lay perfectly still.

After a few minutes, Cara risked another peek. Across a clearing sat the formidable Russian fort. The two-story fortress seemed a part of the forest except for the bare, packed slope that ended at the edge of the sound. An unfinished sloop bobbed at anchor. On the second-story parapet, a man sat casually smoking a pipe, a wreath of smoke over his head.

Cara lay back down and turned her head in Tall Dancer's direction. His short, dark hair lay in curly wisps on his neck. She reached out and twirled a strand between her fingers. His hand closed around hers and squeezed briefly. Then he started to crawl back down into the forest.

She thought to beg him to let her stay. For a moment she considered throwing herself at his feet if that would prevent his leaving her sight, prevent the impending separation. But without a word, she climbed into the sled as he held back the furs.

They skirted the fort on the west side, then reached a clearing. In the center sat a small, cozy house of stone. A rock-strewn path led to the front door and dead vines curled around a trellis on either side. Tall Dancer stopped the team at the back of the house and stepped off the sled. Cara climbed out, amazed at the tiny bit of civilization perched in the middle of the wilderness. For all the world, she would have sworn she was back in St. Petersburg.

"Who lives here?" she asked as Tall Dancer strode to the door and rapped sharply three times.

"This is Byron's house. He and I have been friends for many years. He buys furs from the Russians and sends them to England."

They waited in silence. Then the huge door swung open a crack and a tiny, wrinkled face poked out.

"May I help you?" the man asked, eyeing their ragged appearance. "All trading for blankets is done down at the fort. I suggest you attend to your business there. Now be gone."

"We are not here to trade, Claude. I am here to see Byron. Don't you recognize me?"

The little man rummaged in his vest pocket and produced a pair of spectacles. "Upon my word. Tall Dancer," he said after situating them on his nose. He swung the door open wide and a host of delicious smells poured out.

"Tall Dancer! No other Kolosh would risk coming here now." A young man stepped into the doorway and threw his arms around Tall Dancer. They embraced. Then the young man dragged them each by a hand into the house and kicked shut the door. The stranger, too, was tall, his dark hair drawn back into a queue. He wore a beautiful red waistcoat and black leggings that ended in black buckled shoes.

"And who is this?" he asked, taking Cara's hand in his. His fingers were soft and his touch warm. "Don't tell me this is Kaskoe. You have indeed won a prize, brother."

Cara's glance flew to Tall Dancer's face. He looked away. "Cara, this is my brother, Byron."

"Your brother?"

"Yes." Tall Dancer flopped down in a chair next to a table hewn from rough lumber. "And, no, Byron. This is not my wife."

"She lets you run about the woods with someone of this beauty?" He kissed her hand and his brown mustache tickled.

"My wife was captured by a Russian raiding party many days ago." Tall Dancer passed a hand over his eyes as he spoke.

Byron immediately dropped Cara's hand and went to Tall Dancer's side. "They are raiding deeper into Tlingit territory?"

"Yes. They killed all the men and took the women and children captive."

Cara compared the two men. Byron was as light and friendly as Tall Dancer was dark and brooding, yet in each was an uncanny resemblance. How could these two men be brothers? Marisha had told her her family's story. It didn't include a brother. The pattern board had not included siblings, especially two so different. Byron was obviously culturally refined; Tall Dancer wore the trappings of his Tlingit heritage. She glanced up and realized they were both staring at her.

"Are you wondering how we could be brothers?" Byron asked, his arm resting across Tall Dancer's shoulder. "Well, my dear, that is a long and twisted story. Perhaps you would prefer to tell it?" He poked Tall Dancer in the shoulder blades.

"I thought your father lived with Marisha and her family," Cara said.

"He did, my dear," Byron said. "But that was after my mother's death. You see, our father lived another life before he came to this fair land." As he spoke, he thumped Tall Dancer on the back.

As Cara watched them, it seemed impossible they could come from two so completely different cultures, then blend together so perfectly. Byron's eyes sparkled with amusement at his own clever words, but Tall Dancer's brow was furrowed in a frown and Cara knew he worried that he should be searching for Kaskoe.

"Come, let me make you more comfortable." Byron pushed away from Tall Dancer's chair and made for the next room, his buckled shoes clopping against the stone floor.

He led them into a cozy room that Cara fell in love with

immediately. From the gray stone floor to the stone hearth that held a roaring fire, everything in the room was put there for comfort. Bear, deer, and mountain goat hides were strewn across the floor. The man who had answered the door, Claude, tended the fire. Cozy fabric-covered chairs surrounded the hearth.

Byron motioned for them to find a seat. Cara timidly sat on the edge of one of the upholstered chairs, aware it had been a long time since she'd sat in a real room with furniture and rugs, yet Tall Dancer seemed completely at ease in these luxurious surroundings. He settled back in one of the chairs, crossed his legs and graciously accepted the glass Claude brought. Cara couldn't keep her eyes off Tall Dancer. He amazed her with his ability to blend into a culture she would have thought foreign to him. What other secrets did he hide?

Claude brought them a tray with biscuits and warm brandy. Byron passed the first glass to Cara and smiled warmly as her eyes met his. As the fire crackled, Byron and Tall Dancer settled into a discussion about the Tlingit resistance to the Russians, and Cara was left to her own amusement. She wandered about the room admiring the pictures and maps that adorned the walls.

Byron listened to his brother explain the Tlingit side of the issue, but all the while he watched Cara. Her green eyes were exquisite. He had seen many Indian women since coming here, but there had been no other with beauty like this. Tall Dancer had introduced her simply by name and had given no details about her.

His curiosity was aroused. Where was the woman Tall Dancer had traveled home to marry after Byron had tried to convince him to stay here and oversee the fur-trading business?

Tall Dancer noticed Byron's interest and felt an edge of jealousy. The attraction between his brother and Cara charged the air. And why not? Neither one had a vested interest in the turmoil gripping this land. Cara had announced her independence from her father and all his dealings. Either she or Byron could leave and return to their other lives in the civilized world and never look back.

He looked down at the brandy swirling in his glass. On the other hand, he was part of the conflict right at their door. The path of his life was changed each time another gang of drunken Russians decided to raid and destroy a village.

Then there was Kaskoe. He had to try to rescue her from the Russian fort. Much as he would like to leave her there and disappear back into the forest, he knew he could not.

He looked up. Cara stood across the room examining a picture, and Byron's eyes were sweeping her from head to toe. What would happen between them once he was gone? Tall Dancer shook his head slightly and tried to concentrate on the conversation. After all, he had made his decision last spring when he married Kaskoe. When he walked out these doors, he would never see Cara again.

"Claude, take Cara into the bedroom and see she is settled," Byron instructed the old man as he brought in more wine.

"Yes, sir," he responded with a chagrined glance at Tall Dancer.

"I forgive you for not recognizing me at the door." Tall Dancer smiled at the old man's discomfort.

"I am sorry, my boy. You're here only once a year and my eyes aren't what they used to be."

Tall Dancer patted the old man on the back as he turned and motioned Cara to follow him into the adjoining room. Byron's eyes followed her until she disappeared.

"Tell me about her," Byron said, leaning forward. "By God, how did you find such a beauty? What tribe is she? Is she your mistress?"

"No." Tall Dancer shook his head. "She is white. I found her tied up in a Tsimshian village about a year ago and took her back to my mother's village until I could return her here this winter."

"She is a rare beauty." His eyes strayed to the bedroom door.

"She's Russian, Byron."

"Russian?" He flopped against the chair back and whistled low.

''That's not all. I think she's the Butcher's daughter.''

Byron's eyes grew round. ''How do you know?''

Tall Dancer swirled the brandy in his glass, then downed it in one gulp. ''I knew she was Russian from the first and suspected there was more to her story than she was telling. Then Russians raided our village, searching for a red-haired slave. The ship that was scouring the coastline has disappeared, and I believe he thinks her dead.''

''If he even suspects she's still among the Tlingit . . . ''

''He'll raid another village, then another, and he won't stop until he finds her.''

''What are you going to do with her?''

Tall Dancer leaned forward, his elbows on his knees, his hands clasped between them. ''I want to leave her here with you and I want you to return her to St. Petersburg, without her father's knowledge.''

Byron rose from his chair and went to stand by the hearth. One hand propped on the mantle, he stared into the flames. ''Well, I don't object to having her company for a while, but Tarakanov—the Butcher—is sure to find out she's here. This is a small place, Tall Dancer, with bored men and little else to do except gossip.''

Tall Dancer spread his hands. ''I want you to use your connections to see to it she is returned to Russia . . . and placed in some suitable situation there.''

Byron whistled low. ''That's a large task, brother. Tarakanov knows everything that goes on in the fort, every ship that arrives and departs. His cruelty is exceeded only by his ego.''

''I'm entrusting her safety to you.''

Byron studied his brother's face. When he looked at Cara, there was something in his eyes, something he tried to hide behind that bloody Tlingit mask of indifference.

''The trappers say he's a madman—cruel, savage. Besides, she might not be his daughter. She could be anyone. She could have confessed in fear,'' Byron suggested.

''But she isn't anybody. She's the daughter of the man intent on destroying my people.'' Tall Dancer got to his feet and walked over to the window.

Byron crossed the room and placed a hand on Tall Dancer's shoulder. ''What is it about this girl you have not told me?''

Tall Dancer turned and looked into his brother's face. ''I love her.''

''But?''

''But I'm married.'' Tall Dancer crossed his arms and looked out at the beginning snowfall. ''And my wife is a hostage in the fort.'' He nodded toward where a thin trail of smoke went up into the low clouds.

Byron sat down hard in one of the chairs. ''Your wife has been taken by the Russians? When?''

''We spent the night in a Kagwantan village two weeks ago, and there was a raid. The Russians burned everything to the ground except the house we were sleeping in. They captured my wife, but missed Cara. The captives were herded onto a ship.''

''I take it things did not go well in your marriage?''

Tall Dancer sat back down in one of the chairs and shook his head. ''I knew when I married her I did so only to preserve the clan. I was already in love with Cara. I fell in love with her the first time I saw her. I asked the elders for a divorce when I realized the situation was hopeless. They refused.''

''And you feel obligated to abide by their decision?''

Tall Dancer nodded.

Byron sat down in the chair opposite him. ''Things are changing for the Tlingits. The old ways are disappearing. More Russians are coming, more English. You will have to change too, brother.''

Tall Dancer shook his head. ''I cannot. The traditions go too deep. I do not fit into the white man's world.''

''You're half white, Tall Dancer. Have you forgotten that? Soon all the land we see will be the white man's land.'' Tall Dancer looked up and Byron felt a stab of guilt. ''I'm sorry, but you know it's the truth.''

Tall Dancer rose again and walked to the window. Snow

pelted down in gigantic flakes that pressed patterned faces to the glass for a moment before melting and running down the pane. "Then I will no longer be a part of this land."

Cara followed Claude into the tiny bedroom. A bed sat in the center of the room and a colorful Chilkat blanket covered the foot. Furs were strewn across the cold stone floor. Claude fiddled with the fireplace until a tentative flame licked at the logs. The window looked out over the hill between the house and the fort beyond.

"Is there anything I can get you, Miss Cara?" Claude asked from the door.

"No, Claude. Thank you."

Claude disappeared, shutting the door behind him.

Cara ran her hand down the bed, wondering how long it had been since she had felt a feather mattress under her fingers. The murmur of voices filtered through to her from the other room. She picked out Tall Dancer's deep murmur and tried to understand his words, but the men lowered their voices.

The crackling of the fire, the warmth of the room, the lure of the bed combined to make her suddenly sleepy. She crawled beneath the blanket and fell fast asleep.

A hand shaking her shoulder awakened her. She rose on one elbow and stared into Tall Dancer's face.

"It's time to eat," he said shortly and turned to go.

"Wait," she said, her hand outstretched. "When will you leave?"

He faced her. "In the morning."

"Will I ever see you again?" The words stuck in her throat even as the answer rang in her mind.

He stared at her a long minute, slowly shook his head, then disappeared out the door.

They ate a silent supper together in the cozy kitchen. Claude fiddled at the hearth, clanking together pots and pans. Tall Dancer pushed the food around on his plate, but Byron ate heartily. Cara took tiny bites of the food, trying to fill the emptiness rapidly consuming her insides.

"Excellent, Claude," Byron said between bites. "Don't you think so, brother?"

"What? Oh, yes. Very good, Claude." Tall Dancer chewed a bite of venison.

"My brother tells me you are Russian, Cara."

She glanced up to see Byron watching her closely.

"Yes."

"And your father is a Russian ship's captain?"

"Yes." Cara rubbed her sweaty palms down the side of her dress.

"What is his name?"

Cara hesitated, glancing from one man to the other. Byron studied her face, but Tall Dancer concentrated on his plate.

"Alex Tarakanov." There, the evil words were said.

"The Butcher." Tall Dancer shoved his plate to the center of the table.

"Yes. The Butcher," Cara murmured and lowered her gaze.

A warm hand closed over hers. She looked up. Byron smiled at her and patted her fingers. "Do you want to return to your father?"

She glanced at Tall Dancer, but he refused to meet her gaze. Suddenly she was angry—angry he offered her no alternative, angry he seemed to value his traditions over her love, angry he didn't leap up and beg her to return to the forest with him.

"No," she said with a deep breath. "I want to stay here with you."

Tall Dancer raised his head. His gaze was cold and lifeless as he studied her face. Abruptly, he pushed his chair back and strode from the room.

"Then you shall stay." Byron patted her hand again, pushed his chair back and followed his brother.

Cara looked down at her plate, but her food had turned tasteless. She pushed back her chair and hurried to her room. As she passed through the main room, she saw Tall Dancer standing in front of the window. *No doubt looking out onto his precious wilderness,* she thought as she slammed her door shut.

She sat down on her bed and looked out. She was seeing the same thing as Tall Dancer, but were his thoughts the same as hers? She doubted it. Finally, she had admitted her identity. But what would her father do once he knew of her whereabouts? Would he take her back and try to force her into his bed again as he had done so many times before? Would he make her watch again as he slaughtered women and children, killed the men and split them from crotch to neck?

Outside, the stars shone out of a darkening sky. Tomorrow morning Tall Dancer would be gone, back to the dense forests of the Tlingit nation and back to his wife. When he walked out of the gates and into the forest, she would never see him again.

Byron and Tall Dancer sat by the fire sipping brandy.

"She never told me his name," Tall Dancer said as he swirled his drink in the glass. "Not in all the time we've been together." The motion of the brandy was mesmerizing, lulling.

"Tell me about your wife," Byron suddenly asked. "Is she beautiful? Did you bed her right away?" he asked, a mischievous edge to his voice.

Tall Dancer laughed weakly, "No, our marriage was arranged by our families. She was from a high-ranking family and so was I. I married for the good of both families and she was interested only in her elevated position."

"You never loved her?"

"No. We barely tolerated each other. She is spiteful and cruel, filled with hatred for all things. Except for the obligation I owe her, I would let the Russians keep her and pity the Russians."

Byron laughed. "And would you then make Cara your wife?"

Tall Dancer looked quickly at Byron and his brother smiled slowly as he read Tall Dancer's face. "In all the years we have known each other, I have never seen you look that way at any woman. Are you going to walk away into the forest and leave her here?''

"I am leaving her in your hands."

"Then you are a fool." Byron flopped back in his chair and downed his drink.

Tall Dancer sighed. "I had to make the decision years ago whether to live as a white man or as a Tlingit. I chose to live with *'atle's* people. If I am to continue to do that, I must abide by the traditions and laws. My mother helped to arrange my marriage, and, as she pointed out, Kaskoe and I have lived a common life and can share a home and children and raise them in the ways of their people."

"You would bring children into a loveless home, mothered by a woman whom you despise, only to raise them in a culture suspended in time? Your children must know how to live in both worlds and use this knowledge well. I know you, brother. If there were any good in Kaskoe, you would be scratching at the fort walls at this moment, demanding her release."

"I cannot live with Cara in a Tlingit village. She would not be accepted, and our children would be taunted—as I was. No, our father worked hard many years before he was accepted into the tribe, and I inherited his honors. I cannot betray that, not even for Cara."

"How many more years do you think the Tlingits can live a normal life, unaffected by the white man's ways? That time is short, and things will never be the same again. Take Cara, go someplace, and make a life with her."

"You always look at things so simply. You don't have the weight of hundreds of years of ancestors looking over your shoulder."

"Make your decision, old man." Byron sat his glass down beside the chair and rose to his feet. "Because I'm not sending her back to that demon father of hers. If you don't want her, I do."

Chapter Sixteen

Cara lay awake in the huge bed. An eerie light illuminated the room, the reflection of a full moon on new snow. She stared up at the ceiling of rough timber and wondered why Byron had built this house here, so far from any civilization. The fire popped, tossing orange embers out onto the floor. She slid out of bed, took the hearth broom from its hook and quickly swept the glowing coals back into the fire.

She looked down at her feet, swathed in one of Byron's nightshirts. Not even the tip of a toe showed from beneath the yards of fabric piled around her ankles. Maybe she couldn't sleep because the bulky material wound around her as she tossed in bed, she mused, knowing she was making excuses to appease her aching heart. With a sweeping motion, she pulled the gown over her head and tossed it over a straight-backed chair.

She went to stand in front of the window. Softly, the big flakes plopped on the glass. Memories, sweet and bitter, tumbled into her mind.

She remembered the first snowfall only a few short weeks ago and how the children ran and laughed, chasing the flakes with outstretched tongues. Warm, wonderful people had surrounded her then.

She remembered the nights she and Marisha had spent gathering roots and herbs. They had talked of the first snow and provisions for the winter.

She closed her eyes as bittersweet memories of Tall Dancer arose—the feel of his skin warm with passion, the scent of the damp forest, the softness of the rotting wood beneath her back.

Tears squeezed out from beneath her lids and dropped onto the window sill. A dry sob caught in her throat. She would never be happy anywhere but at his side. But he was not free to choose her.

He had made his position quite clear. He owed his loyalty to Kaskoe, whether or not she deserved it. She was his wife and would eventually bear his children.

Cara had no doubts Tall Dancer would get her back. He never failed at anything he attempted. Together, they would return to their life in the great cedar forest, and she would never see him again.

Cara turned from the window and crawled into the feather bed. Tears wet her pillow and she buried her head in its softness to muffle the sobs that jerked her chest.

Her sleep was fitful and filled with bits and pieces of dreams. Then something awoke her. She pushed herself up on her elbows. There it was again—a soft scraping noise.

Throwing the big gown over her head, Cara opened her door a crack. The house was quiet and dark. She padded down the hall and into the kitchen. Dark, wet spots stained the floor in front of the door.

Cara ran to the only window, which looked out toward the back. The edge of night was receding, tinted with a fringe of pink in the east. A lone figure wrapped in a fur was pulling away from the house on a sled. Her heart flew to her throat.

He was leaving without even a good-bye.

Her fingers fumbled with the latch on the door. A nail scraped her knuckles, but she pulled on the latch until it sprang open. Cold air rushed in. Cara leaped outside, but his name died on her lips when she realized she might place him in danger if she alerted the fort. The sled tracks merged with the forest and were quickly obliterated by the falling snow.

Tall Dancer pressed his cheek into the snow and peered over the edge of a fallen log. Guards paced the upper wall of the fort. Two, three, four, he counted. *Why so many?* The last time he was here, there were barely enough sober men inside the fort to have one for each corner. Now they walked the wall like soldiers.

He rolled onto his back and propped his head against the rough bark. How was he going to get inside when it was so heavily guarded?

Suddenly, shouts burst forth. He rolled onto his stomach and peered over the log. Two men leaned over the edge of the side wall and threw something at a large brown dog.

Obviously heavy with milk, the dog hesitated, a puppy hanging from her teeth. One of the men shouted at her again and threw a stick at her. She ran away a short distance, then turned again and crept back. At the base of the log wall, a long spray of brown dirt marred the smooth surface of the snow. Tall Dancer smiled as the men turned away and the dog slipped beneath the wall of the fort.

Dusk fell quickly. He tossed his sled dogs an evening meal of dried salmon, then removed the amulet from his neck and the earring from his ear. After stuffing them both into a sealskin bag, he pulled the top closed.

Satisfied he now looked like a hunter instead of a Tlingit just in case he was caught, he turned up the bottle of brandy Claude had given him and took a deep drink. Then he sprinkled a little on his clothes.

Tilting his head back, he checked the sky. A few stars dotted the wide expanse of darkness and a new moon dangled above the horizon. He skirted the edge of the woods, then set off across the cleared field, hoping his gait appeared drunken. No one paid any attention.

How easy it would be to wipe out the whole fort, he thought as he slid along the wall. He found the dog's hole and crouched down. It looked big enough for him to squeeze through, but where would he come out? He bent down and looked in once more before crawling through headfirst.

He emerged behind what looked like a storehouse. A soft growl and tiny whimpers from a dark corner greeted him. He peered into the dark and saw the mother dog, her tail thumping on the ground.

Crouching low, he skirted the storehouse. Loud, raucous snores split the air. He glanced up at the wall again in time to see one of the men tip a crockery jug to his lips, then wipe his mouth on the sleeve of his shirt.

Tall Dancer crept from house to house, pausing only to look inside briefly. There was no sign of Kaskoe or the other women and children. Had they already been put on board ships?

When he reached the last house, he noticed a door ajar. Quietly, he pushed open the door. Sleeping men were scattered across the floor. He stepped carefully over each one until he reached a partition at the back. Groans and squeaks came from inside.

He poked his head around the corner. Outlined by the faint light was the form of a large woman astraddle a man. She rocked back and forth and the man beneath her groaned with pleasure. She wore a bark dress with ermine hides sewn into the side seams and she wore no bonds. As Tall Dancer watched, the sounds reached a climax. The woman rolled off the man and motioned for him to be on his way. He handed her a coin, rose from the bed, and pulled up the pants dangling at his ankles.

Tall Dancer flattened himself against the opposite wall as the Russian staggered past him, adjusting his pants. When he peeped back around the corner, the woman sat on the bed turning the coin over in her hands before depositing in into a jar by the bed.

Another man staggered past Tall Dancer and into the cubicle. In no time, the woman was upon him in the same fashion and the sounds that had lured Tall Dancer commenced again. *So Kaskoe has become a concubine.* Rage rose in him. She had bargained for her life with her body and had done well.

Tall Dancer turned, the bitter taste of anger in his mouth. Stealthily, he made his way out of the building without notice, then slid along the fort wall until he came to the loose dirt marking the hole under the wall. He dropped to his knees and was about to crawl beneath when a hand on his shoulder stopped him.

"Why do you crawl in and out like the Kolosh, Tall Dancer?"

Tall Dancer froze as he recognized the voice. He backed up, stood, and turned. Aleksandr Baranov stood behind him. A short man, he barely reached Tall Dancer's shoulders. His light hair receded from an ample forehead, but as he stood with arms folded over his elaborate coat, his eyes remained fixed on Tall Dancer's face.

Tall Dancer stared at the most powerful *promyshlenniki* in this land. Once a commander of other men, Baranov was now governor of the Russian-American Company that owned the fort and encouraged the hunters to rape the oceans and the shores. With Baranov's unwavering gaze fastened on him, Tall Dancer searched for an explanation. Rejecting all that came to mind, he opted for the truth. "I came for my wife."

"Is she in there?" Baranov jerked his head toward the house.

"Yes."

"I am sorry," he said, his expression softening for a moment. "Was she taken by my men?"

"She was taken by *promyshlenniki* at a Tongass village."

"I will see she is returned." Baranov turned to go, but Tall Dancer caught his arm.

"No."

Baranov turned with a quizzical expression.

"She was not much of a wife. She makes a better whore."

Baranov's eyes crinkled and his lips turned up in a small smile. "Come to my office before you are seen."

He took a step away and Tall Dancer hesitated. One word

from Baranov and the guards would be on him. He glanced up again at the men on the corners of the fort.

"You will be safe with me," Baranov said, catching Tall Dancer's arm.

They moved through the sleeping fort and into the bottom floor of the larger building. Large piles of shredded rope lay scattered about. Two Aleut girls slept curled up on a walrus hide.

The steps groaned as the men climbed to the second floor. Baranov pushed open the door to his office, then closed it once Tall Dancer was inside. Circling the office, Baranov lit a lamp on the desk. The faint odor of fish came from the smoking light.

"Tell me, Tall Dancer, what do you hear from the Tlingit?"

Tall Dancer sat down in the chair Baranov offered. He poured two drinks from a bottle of clear liquid and handed one to Tall Dancer.

"They are angry," Tall Dancer answered, then tasted the liquid in the glass. It was bitter and burned his throat.

"I hear they are planning an attack." Baranov reached to a picture on the wall and took down a metal cross hung from a ribbon. He paused, caressing the grooved surface a moment, then he dangled the object over Tall Dancer's head. "This is the Cross of St. Vladimir. It is a token of my homeland's faith in me, their faith that I will govern this wild land and the savages that live in it."

Tall Dancer stared at the medal slowly turning on the ribbon. He pushed back the rough timber chair and stood. "The Tlingit wish the *promyshlenniki* would leave this land."

Baranov smiled and slowly lowered his medallion. "Their wishes will not come true, Tall Dancer. The *gus-kiya-qwan* are here to stay, and every year more and more of us will 'come straight out from under the clouds.' "

Chafing from Baranov's ridicule of one of his people's stories, Tall Dancer planted both hands on the wobbly table between them. "I do not wish a war with *gus-kiya-qwan*—but Ska-out-lelt does, and he has many men and many weapons."

"And so do I."

Baranov didn't explain, but Tall Dancer knew the fort had a cannon that would wipe out Ska-out-lelt, the most powerful Tlingit chief, in open battle.

"I don't want to argue with you." Baranov leaned closer. "Come into the fort. Work for me and I will make you a wealthy man. I will give you otter hides, coppers, *baidarkas,* anything you wish."

A flush of anger burned Tall Dancer's face. Without another word, Tall Dancer turned on his heel and left the room. As he crept down the stairs, he half expected to feel cold steel slice through his back.

He hurried through the bottom floor and out into the night, pausing as he reached the stockade wall. Glancing back over his shoulder, he saw Baranov silhouetted against the yellow light of his lamp. He raised one hand in salute. Tall Dancer watched for a moment, then slipped beneath the wall.

A crescent moon glowed in a cloudless sky. On the wall behind him, the once-attentive guards snored softly in a liquor-induced sleep. Taking care to appear drunk as well, Tall Dancer staggered across the open area to the welcoming depth of the woods beyond.

As he sat down in the snow and his back settled against a log, the reality of what he had seen hit him. Kaskoe had willingly chosen the life of a concubine. She was not bound or forced to do what she did. He would attempt no rescue. She was no longer his wife.

But, he thought, rising to load the sled, he was no better than she. Hadn't he, too, been unfaithful? Hadn't he broken his promises as a husband?

He stepped onto the runners of the sled and turned the team back north. He would set his trap lines as planned, then return home. He would say Kaskoe had been killed and spare her family shame.

But as he set off, the taste of the wind in his mouth, he couldn't resist one last swing past Byron's house.

There, in the woods and out of sight, he watched the lighted window where Cara slept. He thought he caught a glimpse of someone. Then the candle was extinguished.

Snow fell thick and fast against the windows in Cara's room. Claude had already announced supper was ready, but her heart wasn't in eating. Instead, she stood and watched the snow deepen. How many hours had she spent here, watching the tree line, praying Tall Dancer would change his mind and come for her? But he had not, and no one had seen him since the morning he left. A thin line of smoke reminded her where the fort was, and she thought of Kaskoe, wondering if he had rescued her and if they had returned to their life in the village.

Cara sighed and turned away from the window. She and Byron had discussed her situation and he had carefully laid out her options, which she already knew. She could stay here with him, Byron had offered, politely not mentioning the possibility Tall Dancer might change his mind, but there was the probable chance her father would find she was here and come to claim her.

Or she could allow Byron to arrange passage back to Russia for her, sending her with enough money to start a new life. But no one waited for her in St. Petersburg. She had no family other than her father, no skills with which to support herself.

Then there was Byron's suggestion she go to England. He had friends there who would be willing to see she obtained a position as governess for a titled family's children. But even that prospect dulled as she thought of the miles that would stretch between herself and Tall Dancer.

As long as her father was out there, his very presence was a shadow over her life, threatening her happiness. She would know no peace. She had to confront him, declare to him her wish to be free. Perhaps by now he had tired of the search and would be willing to leave her to her own desires.

"Byron," she called, entering the kitchen.

"Yes." He lifted his head and wiped at the corners of his mouth.

"I want to go to the fort."

Byron frowned and glanced at Claude. "Why?"

"I want to find out about my father."

Byron hesitated a moment. "Do you think this is wise?"

"I can't run away from him forever."

Byron studied her a moment. "All right. You shall go," he said, and turned back to his soup.

Surprised he had capitulated so easily, Cara frowned. "When?"

"Today, if you like." He took a sip and wiped the corner of his mouth again. "Yours is getting cold." He pointed with a spoon at the bowl opposite him.

Cara sat down and began to eat. She felt Byron's gaze move over her and she avoided meeting his eyes. He was attracted to her, she could feel it in his gaze, but he had said nothing, nor had he touched her. She felt a pang of regret as she stared down into her soup. Even a small flicker of love could cause pain, and she knew that on some level Byron would be hurt, for her heart would always belong to Tall Dancer.

Cara drew in a deep breath, then wished she hadn't. The ankle-deep mud covering the tops of her shoes stank. The men who surrounded them, swathed in heavy furs, smelled even worse. Cara wrinkled her nose and hurried to catch up with Byron, wondering why the Tlingit men never smelled so bad. Or had she just never noticed?

Promyshlenniki newly arrived from the Aleutians strode around the fort half drunk. Aleutian women clung to their arms and stumbled after them. Aleutian men hurried by with bales of sea otter pelts. Tlingit masks, blankets, and other goods were carried out through the gates and down to the edge of the water. Cara wondered how they had been separated from their owners.

Bewhiskered and dirty, the trappers followed her with their eyes. Byron held her gently by the elbow and guided her through the crowd. Inside the trading post more trappers milled about, waiting their turn to be served. The men bumped and jostled her as they passed. Finally, Byron put Cara on his other side and walked between her and the men.

"I beg your pardon," a man said at her elbow.

Cara raised her eyes. A graying, distinguished man bowed slightly and nodded in her direction.

"Where did you steal this prize, Byron?"

Possessively, Byron slipped his arm around her waist. "Commander Medvednikov, this is Cara."

He took her hand and touched his lips to the tips of her fingers. "My pleasure, my lady." His eyes examined her, and she knew her image would be burned into his memory—possibly to report to her father?

"Cara, this is Vasili Medvednikov, commander of Fort St. Michael."

His intense stare unnerved her, yet somehow she managed to reply in a civil manner.

"Where have you been keeping this beauty, Byron? Perhaps rumors of your reclusive lifestyle have been exaggerated." He raised his eyebrows in a silent accusation.

"She was recently ransomed from the Kolosh," Byron offered.

"Ah, so she is not Kolosh?" He touched her hair and Cara recoiled against Byron.

Byron's grip on her tightened. "No, she is Russian."

Medvednikov's eyebrows shot up. "Indeed? Come. I'm sure the young lady would like a glass of wine." With a sweeping gait, Medvednikov turned away from them and headed deeper into the fort.

They entered a large residence. Colorful rugs padded the floor, rich wood gleamed from the paneled walls, and the dwelling smelled of tobacco.

Medvednikov moved aside a smoldering pipe, then took two wine goblets, the stems suspended between his fingers, and filled each of them with the burgundy liquid.

Cara inhaled the fragrance as he handed her hers. How long had it been since she'd tasted wine? She took a sip and felt a warming sensation stream down her throat and into her stomach.

"So, Cara," Medvednikov said, sinking into his chair. "How long has it been since you've seen your father?"

The wine's warmth turned to ice and Medvednikov's eyes bored into her. She'd been found out. "Two years."

"And how did you become separated? You were kidnapped, I believe."

He was waiting for her to acknowledge his story. She glanced up and found him watching her intently over the rim of his glass. "Yes, I was kidnapped."

"And how did you get away?"

Cara swallowed. "I was ransomed by an Aleutian man."

"Ransomed. With furs?"

"Yes."

"Now." Medvednikov stroked his chin and looked up at the ceiling. "Why would a stranger ransom you from the Kolosh? Why would he trade his valuable furs for a stranger?"

Was he trying to catch her in a lie? she wondered as she watched his face. Or was he just curious? "I suppose he hoped to be paid by my father."

"But he did not wait." Medvednikov frowned and leaned forward.

"The man is an acquaintance of mine," Byron inserted. "I will see he is paid for his sacrifice once Cara is returned to her father."

Cara hoped her sigh wasn't audible. Medvednikov and Byron stared at each other as if each was measuring the other's integrity.

"And so he shall be. I will send word to your father's ship at once." He shoved the chair backward and set his glass down. Byron and Cara did the same and stood.

"Perhaps Byron will be so good as to give you a tour of our fort."

With a curt nod, Medvednikov rose and strode out of the room.

The confrontation Cara had wished for was to be reality.

They stepped out of the cozy room and back into the chaos of trading post life. Immediately, the stench intensified. Overhead steel traps dangled, their jaws tightly shut. Piles of colorful Chilkat blankets rested on wooden shelves. Wooden barrels held coffee, sugar, and flour.

Byron moved behind the counter and picked up a pencil. Cara followed, eyeing the Tlingit women who hung on some of the men, concubines who had been captured from their villages, then stripped of their dignity and offered weevily food and dirty water in return for their favors. They leered at Cara and slung insults in Tlingit.

Cara ignored them all until one huge woman lumbered into the store. The men parted to grant her passage. She was drunk and dirty, her hair matted. Muttering unintelligibly, she shoved her way to the counter, reached over and began to pluck at Cara's dress. Byron came to her side and made a move as if to drive the woman away.

"Wait, Byron," Cara said. Then, to the woman, "What do you want?"

The woman muttered something about her dress and about a slave. Then she said, "Tall Dancer."

"What did you say?" Cara asked her.

The woman raised her head with effort. "I said you may be finely dressed now, but I still have Tall Dancer. He will never be yours."

"Kaskoe." Her lips formed the words, but no sound came from her mouth. The woman before her was a shadow of the buxom woman she had know in Tall Dancer's village. Hardly an attractive woman then, now she was dirty and thinning.

"Have you seen him?" Cara asked, hating the eagerness in her voice.

"Seen him? No." She wagged her head back and forth.

"He was going to come for you."

Kaskoe raised her head a little more. "He has not come for me. And I see he has left you, too. Now you are no better than me." She cleared her throat and spat a long line of saliva on Cara's dress front.

Byron pushed in between them. Tossing instructions to the clerk behind the counter, he led Cara away while she looked back over her shoulder. Kaskoe followed them until she slipped and fell in the deep mud. Men gathered around her. Two hauled her to her feet and another began to fondle her breasts, now hanging out of her torn bark dress.

"That was Kaskoe, Tall Dancer's wife," Cara said as Byron half led, half dragged her through the front gates. "He never found her. He must still be here."

Byron stopped halfway up the hill in front of his house. He grabbed her shoulders and spun her around. "When will you see he belongs to neither of you? He belongs there." He pointed toward the formidable wall of trees and underbrush just feet from his front door. "He belongs there and he always will."

"No," Cara insisted. "He loves me."

Byron loosened his grip on her shoulders and let his arms drop to his sides. "I wish I could make you see. I wish you knew him like I do. My brother is part of this land. He doesn't merely live here, he is part of all this. And all this is changing before our eyes. A few years from now, houses will stand here. Russians will raise families here. The Tlingits will be pushed further and further north, and Tall Dancer will go with them."

"No." Cara's voice broke and she cursed the tears that blurred her vision.

Byron reached out and drew her into his embrace. "I wish I could make you see," he whispered.

Chapter Seventeen

When Byron and Cara reached the house, a man stood on the doorstep, a fur hat in his hand. He nodded to Byron, but avoided Cara's eyes. As he passed her, she caught a scent she hadn't thought about in years—pine pitch.

The two men went into the kitchen and shut the door behind them, leaving Cara alone. Their voices came through the door as a hum. Cara went to her room and removed her coat. Shaking off the snow, she hung the coat behind the door. When she looked up, Byron stood in the doorway, his face ashen and his eyes large and dark.

"Your father has returned," he said in measured tones.

Cara suddenly couldn't breathe. A heavy weight crushed her chest. "Where?" she choked out.

"His ship is anchored in the sound. He has returned with a load of pelts and prisoners."

Cara nodded, her mind a blank where before it had been filled with things she wanted to say to her father.

"I've invited him to dinner. Perhaps we can work out something."

* * *

Cara fidgeted in the chair by the hearth. Byron paced the room. The elaborate clock on the mantle ticked, ticked, ticked until the annoying sound echoed in her head. When was he coming? She wanted to get this over with.

Dozens of incomplete plans floated in her mind. Would he demand that she return to him? How could she defy him? Where would she go? Would she ever get another chance at freedom once she was back under his control?

She looked up at Byron. He stared into the fire, frowning, and hadn't said a dozen words since this afternoon.

A pounding at the door interrupted both their thoughts. Claude hurried by them to answer it. A large man wearing a huge fur coat and matching fur hat stood in the yard. Snowflakes covered the shoulders of his coat, making him look like a grizzly surprised out of hibernation. As he removed his hat and stepped into the room, he smiled.

Cara caught her breath and her heart began to pound. Just seeing his face now, flushed with exertion of the climb to the house, reminded her of the nights the same face had sweated and grunted above her, holding her mouth shut with one hand.

All the terrible memories came flooding back, as did the details of the night she had escaped. The desperation, the hopelessness of her situation came back with vivid clarity. The world darkened and turned cold. Cara fainted, falling with a thud onto the stone floor.

She awoke in her bed. Claude hovered over her with a damp cloth, cursing Byron, her father, even the weather. Cara caught his hand as he started to lay the cloth across her forehead.

"How long was I out?" she asked.

"Oh, praise the Lord." Claude's voice trembled. "You've been out so long, Miss Cara, I thought you would die."

"Is he still here?"

"Your father?" Claude nodded and frowned. "He's in there with Master Byron."

Cara put her feet on the floor and tried to stand. She wavered for a moment, then regained her balance. "I think I can make it."

"He's a bad one." Claude shook his head. "I've heard talk."

Cara didn't comment. She stood, pulled her dress straight, and marched through the door. But her blood chilled when her father turned slowly in the chair and his eyes swept her from head to foot.

She had filled out some since the last time he had seen her. Now she had the curves of a woman, he thought. He had bedded many women since the little bitch jumped overboard, but none excited him like she did. He wondered how she had survived and noticed the hints of dark dye in her hair and the tan on her face. He traced the lines of her hips beneath the dress fabric.

Word had reached him that a red-haired slave was living with some Tlingit in a village down from Yakutat. The sources said a handsome buck guarded her.

That had planted the seed of jealousy, he admitted, made him livid with rage to think of another man owning what should have belonged to him. That's when the search had begun. The more he searched in vain, the angrier he became.

The vision haunted him day and night, the vision of some Tlingit bastard feeling her soft, white skin beneath brown rough fingers. The hunt for her had consumed all his energy. When he didn't find her, he had made them all pay. He couldn't wait to get her back on his ship.

Cara cringed inwardly at the way her father was assessing her. His thoughts were mirrored in the bright light in his eyes. She glanced at Byron, who was thinly disguising his disgust with short, clipped answers.

"You do not know the sorrow I felt when I thought you were dead." Vlad spoke in Russian, rising from his chair with outstretched arms. "I searched and searched for you. Did you suffer much at the hands of the savages?" His hands touched her forearms and she shrank back. "How did you get here?"

Cara couldn't bring herself to embrace the man. She dodged his grasp, sat down in a chair, and again related the story of her capture and rescue. Vlad listened with interest until her story was finished, then he pushed up out of the chair.

"We must go back to my ship. My men are waiting. We set sail in the morning for Russia."

Cara's heart bounced into her throat. If she let him get his hands on her, she'd have no chance to escape. She threw a desperate glance at Byron.

Byron pushed away from the hearth and went over to put his hand on Cara's shoulder. "Cara has consented to become my wife, Mr. Tarakanov. We will be married soon, and she will be staying here with me."

Cara tried to smile, but her shock made her speechless. What was Byron up to? She looked up at him, but he smiled innocently down at her. She looked at her father. His rage was evident in the rosy color sweeping down from his hairline.

"I see," he said evenly, with a sly smile. "Then if my little girl is not to return home with me, could I bother you for a night's boarding?"

Cara lay awake long after the household had gone to sleep. Every little night noise made her jump. The thought of her father sleeping right across the hall chilled her blood. Every time she closed her eyes, she saw his face, his sweaty, puffy face above her.

A small scraping noise made her eyes fly open. The night was moonless and the room was completely dark except for dim starlight. Then a hand covered her mouth. She tried to scream, but the hand pressed harder against her lips.

"Shh, girlie. Let your father show you how glad he is to see you." His one knee sank into the feather bed at her side. His other pressed her legs together, and he settled his weight onto her thighs.

"Easy now," he soothed as he pulled the blankets down.

His rough hand reached inside her gown. His cracked fingers massaged the tender tissue as she writhed against him.

"I'm going to kiss you now. One sound and these hands

can snap your neck." He leaned so close she could smell his foul breath.

Slowly, he removed his hand and lowered his lips to her mouth. Her teeth sank into his lower lip.

"Ouch! You bitch!" He slapped her.

Cara's head spun from the lick, but she knew this would be her only chance to get away. She drew her legs out from underneath him and rolled out of bed. Her fingers had just closed over the latch when he snatched her backward. He caught her forearms and flung her onto the bed.

"Still like it rough, eh, girlie? How did that buck give it to you?" He fumbled with his trousers as he fell on her.

Cara squirmed and kicked, making his task as difficult as possible. Her gown wiggled up to her hips and she felt the rough hair of his legs as his thigh rubbed against hers.

His touch made her more frantic.

Intent on his arousal, he had returned to torturing her mouth, careful not to let her bite him again. His knee parted her thighs and she tasted the bile that rose in her throat.

Suddenly, his weight was lifted off her and she opened her eyes in time to see blood from his nose spatter the wall beside her. Byron stood in front of him, one hand clasping a lamp and one hand on Vlad's shirt.

"Have you no decency, man? I should kill you right here for what you've done."

Vlad wiped at his nose with the back of his hand, then glanced at Byron and back at Cara. "She screws as good as her mother."

Vlad hit the wall with a thud. Slowly he slid down and fell in an unconscious heap.

When he awoke, Byron handed him a brandy and his hat and coat. With muffled curses, he donned them both and hurried away down the hill toward the fort.

Byron stood in the open door, one arm braced against the facing, and watched him scurry away. Suddenly a Tlingit warrior appeared from the shadows. He poked a piece of paper at Byron. His heart flying from the scare, Byron wordlessly accepted the note. He unfolded it, scanned the contents, and when he looked up, the messenger was gone.

"Go down to the fort and tell Mr. Medvednikov I wish to see him. It is urgent," Byron said to Claude, who had stepped up behind him.

Claude pulled on a coat and hurried out into the snow. Byron went into his room and put on a shirt. Then he checked in on Cara. She lay turned on her side, her cheek pillowed on her arm, pretending she was asleep.

He closed the door and went to the kitchen. Claude had left coffee on the hearth. As he poured a cup, he heard the door open and shut. He walked to the door in time to see Vasili Medvednikov throw back his fur hood and shake the snow from his hair.

"This had better be important to make me come out on a night like tonight." He stamped snow from his snowshoes.

"There is a resistance mounting among the Tlingits," Byron said, tapping the note against his hand. "They claim Russian hunters are ranging further and further into their hunting territory. Did you know about this?"

Medvednikov grinned at him and spread his hands. "You know I have no control over where the hunters get their furs and goods. They may be going further north, but what does it matter? There are plenty of furs for everyone."

"Well, the Tlingits think it matters. You are risking a war. There have already been skirmishes further north between isolated villages and hunters. One village was burned to the ground and all the women and children taken. I believe some of those captives are in the fort this very minute."

Vasili's big grin disappeared and he looked uncomfortable. "You know how it is to be a man far from women." Vasili held his hands out in a helpless gesture. "They must find pleasure somewhere, and most of the women brought in are very willing."

"Of course they are willing, Vasili, for the price you pay them. These people put great emphasis on wealth. You are taking advantage of their ignorance of us."

Medvednikov slapped Byron on the back. "You come down sometime and sample their wares. Then you decide the right price."

Byron squirmed inside as the big man made him feel like a child. Without another word, Vasili left the room. As the door closed behind him and Byron stared at the nails holding the boards together, he was overcome with the helpless feeling that disaster was imminent.

Tall Dancer trudged along the trail toward Fort St. Michael, groaning under the weight of the furs on his back. Pelts had been plentiful this year, and he looked forward to getting a good price for them now spring had arrived. By now he should have already traded his furs and headed home, but he had put off going to Fort St. Michael as long as possible. He dreaded seeing Byron again, dreaded the reminder Cara was gone from his life forever.

He glanced at the side of the trail where devilclub and salmonberry flashed their colors against the dark green backdrop of the forest. Bunches of bright ferns crowded at the foot of a rotten stump. The forest was filled with sights and smells of spring, but the joy was lost on him. All he could think about was last summer and his days with Cara.

As the morning sun dusted the dense forest with a sprinkling of sunlight, he paused beneath the branches of a low-sweeping cedar. He groaned as he lowered the bundle of furs to the ground, then slid down the tree trunk until he sat. His stomach rumbled, but he was too tired to eat. He was drifting off to sleep when faint voices broke the silence of the forest.

Instantly alert, he crept from beneath his protective canopy and back down the trail to a thicket of young cedars. Careful to make no sound, he pushed aside the concealing branches and peeped at a camp of Tlingit warriors painted and adorned for war. He strained to hear what they said.

His blood chilled as he caught a few of their words. He had stumbled upon the force intending to attack Fort St. Michael.

Threats had circulated all winter; clans had been organized. As he spied on the camp, an older man rose, waddled to the edge of the clearing, and began to relieve himself against the side of a tree. Ska-out-lelt! Tall Dancer thought as the man took off his mask and let it drop to the ground.

The man bent on destroying every Russian stronghold.

As quietly as he had entered, Tall Dancer backed out of the thicket and hurried back to his camp. He shoved his bundle of furs further under the cedar canopy. If they meant to attack the fort, he had to be sure Cara was indeed gone and Byron was safe with him.

It was midmorning before Tall Dancer reached the woods behind Byron's house. He had given the fort wide berth lest he be mistaken for a hostile, but the maneuver had cost him precious time. As he stood on the edge of the clearing, Byron's house looked peaceful. The yard had been swept clean and the dead vines had been trimmed away from the back door.

His heart fluttered with hope. Was it possible she was still here? Then he sternly reminded himself of Byron's words. The thought of her lying in anyone else's arms, even his brother's, pricked Tall Dancer's anger. Shaking his head, he reminded himself all that was important was to see everyone safely away.

He sprinted across the clearing and did not stop until the stone wall sheltered him in its shadow. He rose on tiptoe and peered in the kitchen window. The room was empty except for a low fire burning on the grate. He tried the latch and found the door locked. Grabbing the sill of the window, he hoisted himself up and into the room.

The aroma of roasting goose whirled up to greet him, and he felt a pang of jealousy. Claude never cooked like this. At the same time both a sense of dread and a premonition hit him.

No voices hummed from the other rooms. He crept into the main part of the house and peered down the hall. All the room doors were closed. The sense of foreboding grew deeper. He stepped first to Byron's door and put his ear against it. Nothing. Then he listened at the room Cara had occupied. Again nothing.

He placed his hand on the latch and lifted, dreading what he would see.

But when the door swung open he saw . . . nothing. The bed was neatly made, with a quilt thrown across the foot. A cotton dress hung from a peg on the wall. He stepped inside and took the garment down. Pressing it to his nose, he breathed in Cara's sweet scent. The relief he felt weakened his knees, and he sat down on the bed.

Distant shots rang out. Someone shouted from the fort. Tall Dancer sprang to his feet and fled the house. He stopped in the yard and looked right and left. If not in the house, where could they be? The shots grew louder and more frequent. The single shout he had heard grew into a steady chorus.

The fort! They were at the fort! He charged around the side of the house and ran smack into Byron, knocking him to the ground. For a moment, Byron's eyes widened and he reached for the pistol in his belt.

"Easy, brother." Tall Dancer held up both hands.

"Tall Dancer!" Byron scrambled to his feet, then turned to look at Cara.

She stood two paces behind the men, staring in shocked silence. Then she glanced at Byron, and Tall Dancer felt his anger surge again. The look that passed between them was intimate, a reading of one another's thoughts.

"Come. We must go. The fort is under attack." Her skin was soft as he took her elbow.

"I know. We heard the shots." Byron sprang for the open door.

"No. We don't have time to get anything." Tall Dancer grabbed his arm.

"Claude." Byron pointed toward the woods on the far side of the house. "He's down at the end of the clearing picking berries."

Tall Dancer looked between his brother and Cara. Byron took Cara's other elbow.

"I will go after him," Tall Dancer said, his throat tight with suppressed anger. "You take Cara into the forest."

He sprinted away, leaving Cara in a whirl of emotions. Before she could think, Byron dashed off, dragging her behind him. They ran through the underbrush, the brambles ripping at their clothes until they reached a rock outcropping rearing out of the forest floor. Unceremoniously, he stuffed her under the rock, then crawled in behind her. He pressed close against her and she felt safe.

Footsteps pounded outside, drawing nearer and nearer. Byron crawled outside and she followed. Tall Dancer flew through the woods, his hair streaming out behind him, Claude clasped tight in his arms, one around Tall Dancer's shoulder like a child.

"Who's attacking the fort?" Byron asked as Tall Dancer put Claude onto his feet.

"Tlingits under the command of old Ska-out-lelt."

"I have suspected it would come to this." Byron shook his head. "The Tlingit women have been disappearing from the fort lately, and the Russians have been dipping deeper and deeper into Tlingit territory."

As Tall Dancer and Byron conferred on the best escape route, the woods were suddenly filled braves in hideous paint and masks. Cara heard a scream split the air, then knew it was she who had screamed. Tall Dancer shoved Claude to the ground behind him and leaped between the attacking Tlingits and the old man. Byron jerked Cara behind a huge rock, hissed at her to stay, then leaped to his brother's side. Cara peeped over the rock and watched the two men dodge from tree to tree, turning back the Indians. Smoke from Byron's pistol filled the forest as he reloaded time and time again. Tall Dancer was fighting hand to hand with the ivory-handled war knife Cara had seen so often. Red blood dripped from its tip as he sliced at his fellow tribesmen.

As suddenly as they had appeared, the attackers disappeared, fading into the forest like phantoms. Tall Dancer and Byron, their backs together, heaved for breath in unison as their eyes darted left and right, tensed for another fight. Suddenly, from behind a tree stepped a lone warrior. A scream caught in Cara's throat. Tall Dancer was looking the other way, but Byron saw him.

"Look out!" Byron shouted, shoving his brother to the side and trying to get aim on the Indian.

Tall Dancer stumbled and fell. Byron fired, but not before the brave's war knife found its mark. Byron fell backward, the knife protruding from his chest. Tall Dancer quickly regained his balance and buried his own knife deep in the attacker's chest. The brave's face froze for moment, then he slumped to the ground.

Cara stumbled over to where Byron lay. Blood oozed from the wound and his eyes were closed.

"Byron! Byron!" Cara laid her head on his chest and heard a faint heartbeat.

Byron raised his hand and caressed her hair. He smiled at her and squeezed her hand. Then his breathing fell silent and his eyes closed.

"Byron!" Cara shook his shoulders, then burst into tears.

"We must go. The other warriors will be back." Tall Dancer tugged on her arm.

Cara wrenched her arm from his grasp. "We can't just leave him here."

"We don't have a choice." He grabbed her arm again and hauled her to her feet.

She stumbled after him, her vision blinded by the hot tears that coursed down her cheeks. How could he be so callous? There had been no sorrow, no regret in his eyes at his brother's death. Sobs shook her chest, but she stumbled ahead.

Claude, unaccustomed to walking in the rough underbrush, lagged behind and slowed their progress. They crept through the dense forest until Tall Dancer signaled them to stop.

"Over there by that fallen tree is a cave. I use it occasionally to hide my furs." He pointed at the huge rotting body of a magnificent cedar. Moss grew thick on its sides and ferns waved in the slight afternoon breeze.

"I want you to hide in there until I come for you. Pull some branches over the mouth of the cave and be still and quiet."

He put his hands on her shoulders and with his thumbs lifted her chin. "Are you all right?"

She nodded and then he was gone, blending into the underbrush. Cara led Claude into the dark, damp interior of the cave and covered the door as Tall Dancer had ordered.

The sounds of battle grew louder as Tall Dancer reached the edge of the clearing surrounding the fort. Smoke from the fort's one cannon hung heavy on the air, its acrid smell burning his nostrils. Screams split the air and the Tlingits scaled the log walls like a column of ants.

The cannon belched fire and smoke. A high pitched whistling filled the air, then a hole appeared a few feet in front of him. Dirt showered down on him as he threw up his hands. From his side, Tlingit warriors dashed across the clearing, fogging like mosquitoes out of the woods. On the bottom level of the fort, a man struggled to shut a window. Frantically he tugged at the hinged shutter, but a warrior caught him with a long knife. The man yelped, then slumped over the window sill. The Tlingit yanked him out of the way and climbed inside.

Ska-out-lelt ran out of the woods ahead of a group of warriors carrying burning branches. He stopped halfway atop a knoll and began to direct the attack. The warriors passed him, ran up to the fort gates, and hurled their burning brands at the roof. The flames wavered, caught, then blazed into an inferno. A frantic clanging entered the battle, and Tall Dancer remembered seeing the iron ring hanging inside the fort.

Down at the sound, a man paused in his task of laying fishing nets. He stood stock still, gaping at the attack with open mouth. Then he started to run, but his feet caught in the nets. A shot whined and he fell headlong into the foaming surf.

Tall Dancer noticed no one was paying him any attention. It was too late to help the fort, so he sank to the forest floor and covered himself with thick layers of leaves. He closed his eyes against the dirt and tried to sort things out as the din of battle thundered in his head.

Part of him was happy that the Russians were overpowered, but he knew they would be back in greater numbers, with heavier weapons. This battle would not be the great victory Ska-out-lelt wanted. It would be the beginning of the end.

He didn't know how long he had lain buried, but suddenly he realized silence had replaced the furor. He poked his head up above the leaves. The afternoon sun was slanting through the trees, bathing the forest in golden light.

Only a burned skeleton remained of the fort. Thin tendrils of smoke drifted lazily upward from the blackened mess. He stood, shook off the leaves and dirt, then stepped out into the edge of the clearing. Spread before him were bodies—twisted, mangled bodies. Down in the cove, the ship under construction lay on her side, her timbers broken, burned, and bent.

Tall Dancer moved across the clearing, carefully stepping over bodies. When he stepped inside the burned walls of the fort, he faced horrors like he had never seen. Decapitated heads stared at him from poles. Beneath lay the bodies, naked and broken.

He moved from burned foundation to burned foundation. In each one he found the same. Then he faced the house where he had last seen Kaskoe. He stepped over the door frame, the only thing that remained of the front wall. Two bodies lay across each other in front of him. He stepped over them and moved to the back.

There lay the body of a large woman. She was stripped naked and her hair was matted with blood. At her side lay a Russian hunter, naked from the waist down, but bundled in his sealskin coat from waist up. Beneath them both was the crushed frame of a bed.

Tall Dancer picked up Kaskoe's wrist to feel for a pulse, but she had already grown stiff. As his stomach roiled, he turned and walked away from the stench of death—through the burned gates, past the cannon barrel, and across the body-strewn clearing. He never looked back.

He circled back to the cave by a different route. Twice he encountered stragglers in the woods, but they were drunk and busy sorting through their booty from the fort and paid him no attention. When he reached the rocky outcropping, he crouched down and peered into the opening. Claude was asleep in the corner, but Cara sat with her arms around her knees, staring into space. Tall Dancer pulled the branches aside and entered.

"Everybody in the fort is dead," he said, sitting down at her side.

Cara did not respond. He leaned forward to peer into her face.

"Cara, did you hear me?"

"Yes," she answered tiredly. "What did you do with Byron's body?" She faced him, her eyes hollow and dark.

"I didn't do anything with it. The woods are full of drunken warriors. It would be too dangerous to bury him now."

"I want him buried in his yard," she said flatly, turning her eyes back to the cave floor.

Another pang of jealousy, followed by deep guilt, ripped through him. Byron's death hadn't seemed real until now.

"It's too dangerous to go back now. Judging from the whiskey that was in the fort, by now they're all roaring drunk."

Without warning, she threw herself at him. With flailing fists she beat against his chest.

"I want him buried," she sobbed. "If you won't do it, I will."

He caught her hands, and she slumped against him and sobbed. She had found in Byron what he himself could not offer. Two kinds of pain swirled in Tall Dancer, making him lightheaded with their combined intensity. He shouldn't be surprised, he told himself. Hadn't his brother warned him? His heart plunged. Now he was truly alone.

"We'll bury him." Tall Dancer dropped his arms, stood, and moved away toward the cave entrance. He propped one hand against the cold stone and stared out at the deepening shadows.

Chapter Eighteen

Cara opened her eyes to darkness and panic hammered in her veins. Instantly alert, she remained on the bed of leaves, listening. Dawn had not yet come, she determined by the heavy quiet that blanketed the forest.

"Claude?" she called softly.

"Here, Miss Cara." His voice beckoned from somewhere in the darkness.

Cara peered in the direction of the voice and could see a dim light through the branches covering the cave entrance. She emerged from the cave, and the aroma of roasting rabbit filled her nose. Tall Dancer squatted beside a small campfire holding the skinned carcass of a rabbit over the flames. Cara rubbed her forearms against the cold dampness that had settled over the forest.

"That smells good," she said.

Tall Dancer's eyes flitted to the encroaching shadows and he didn't answer. Cara knew it was risky lighting a fire, but she suspected he had done it for her.

As if in answer to her thoughts, he pulled off a back leg and held it out to her. She reached out to take it and their fingers touched. He hesitated for a moment, then withdrew his hand, pulled off another piece of meat, and held it out to Claude.

"Where will we go now?" Claude bit into the juicy bit.

"First we will return to my village. They are peaceful people and not involved in this. Then I will take you both north to Yakutat Bay. Russian ships land there frequently to pick up pelts. I'm sure one of them will see to it you get home." He tore off a tiny piece of the meat for himself.

Cara watched as his white teeth delicately nibbled at the meat. He had said, "You both." Anger warmed her face. He was still set on getting rid of her. Well, so be it. She'd not fight him any longer.

Tall Dancer tripped and stumbled, his feet tangling in a form in their path. He whipped his knife out of the leather pouch on his belt and held it in ready, shoving Cara and Claude behind him. The new moon offered little light and they felt their way along. After they buried Byron, they had moved at night to avoid the braves slowly working their way back to their villages.

Tall Dancer reached down and poked the lump at his feet. It moved, then rolled over onto its back and began to snore. Tall Dancer leaned forward and sniffed.

"Drunk," he said and poked at the man with his toe.

The disgust in his voice was evident. He had said little about the attack, and Cara wondered about his thoughts. Was he glad the Russians were wiped out? Did his disgust extend to her?

"We have to keep moving." He sheathed the knife and stepped around the sleeping warrior.

Just before dawn, he led them into the heart of a thicket. Coral pink, bell-shaped flowers hung from the tall skunkbushes they passed through. They didn't stop until they were deep inside the ring of plants and only the star-studded sky above them was visible.

In the center of the thicket was a small house. Even in the dim light, its state of disrepair was evident. A large piece of the roof sagged precariously over the side. The door hung askew, one piece of leather serving as a hinge. In fact, the whole house leaned at an angle. But guarding the entrance was an intricate totem, topped by the image of a brooding raven. As she moved closer to the door, she thought she felt the creature's eyes on her.

Soft fur brushed against her leg and she started and squealed softly. Yellow eyes peered at her, then a pink mouth opened and the familiar panting of a dog broke the silence.

"Buck," she breathed, ruffling his soft hair.

"I left the team here." Tall Dancer yanked the door open and looked inside. "It's safe," he said, and pulled the door open wider.

Claude staggered inside, flopped down on a rotting mat, and fell fast asleep. Cara stepped in behind him and expected Tall Dancer to follow. When he didn't, she turned to look back at him.

"I'll be in in a minute," he said, then swung the door shut.

Cara stared at the closed door. Cold crept in as the last of his voice faded. Dropping to her hands and knees, Cara felt her way to the other side of the room, remembering the layout of the houses in Tall Dancer's village. As she suspected, her fingers touched another sleeping mat thrown in the corner opposite Claude's. The wood fibers scratched her face and it smelled musty and old, but in seconds she was asleep.

Tall Dancer started a fire in the firepit and added a few sticks. Smoke stretched up and out the hole in the ceiling. By now the warriors would be intent on getting home. Smoke in the forest would be seen as other souls making their way back to their villages.

He turned to the salmon he had caught. Quickly, he gutted and decapitated it, then scraped out the orange roe. He jammed a green branch through the fish and held it over the fire to roast. As the meat sizzled and dripped, he stared into the fire, trying to get his emotions under control. Just the sight of her had brought back everything he had struggled for months to forget.

She stirred behind him and he turned. Raising up on her hands, she shoved the hair back from her face and sniffed.

"It's almost done." He held out the fish and she smiled. Immediately, he hated the way his heart tumbled.

He turned back to the fire and heard her move up beside him and sit down. Why did she make him feel like a young boy again, nervous and jittery around a girl? "Why didn't you go with your father?" he asked, avoiding her eyes.

"Byron told him we were to be married and he left."

She didn't look at him as she spoke the words that broke his heart. His brother, a man not driven by generations of ancestral pride, had prevailed and stolen Cara's heart.

"I never thought you'd come back," she whispered.

Her voice echoed his own thoughts. He hadn't thought he'd come back, either. She was the reason he'd avoided going to the fort to trade, the reason he'd tramped around in the forest long after the trapping season was over.

She was why he couldn't go home, and the reason he didn't want to.

Tall Dancer woke them early and headed them north, deeper into Tlingit territory. They left behind the small, cozy house and the dogs, who watched with lazily wagging tails until they were out of sight. Cara had despaired leaving them, remembering their soft fur and understanding silences. But there was no snow for the sled to fly across. Tall Dancer assured her he often left them there and they fended on their own, always returning to greet him when he arrived.

As the sun climbed in the sky, mosquitoes spawned in puddles left by the spring rains rose in thick, dark clouds. He insisted they travel just inside the trees and well out of sight from the beach.

The cedar forest they traveled through rose straight out of the sandy beach, a forbidding wall of green standing tall against the onslaught of the salt and surf. Spring flowers bloomed in the woods, and Cara snatched a few as they passed.

As she raised the blooms to her nose and inhaled their fragrance, memories of her days with Marisha came back in startling clarity. She picked saskatoon berries whenever they passed a thicket and filled the tail of her skirt with those she didn't eat. By the time Tall Dancer signaled to stop for the night, Cara had enough berries for supper.

That evening, after a cold supper of berries and dried salmon, they curled up in dry leaves blown against a line of young cedars. Cara lay on her back and looked up at a star-dazzled sky that winked and flirted with her through the canopy of the trees over her head. Claude snored softly from his bed of cedar boughs.

His hands clasped around his knees, Tall Dancer stared off into the night, reminding her of the man who had freed her from bondage and led her all those miles through forest and thicket. He'd been a mystery then and was more of one now.

As she watched, a soft evening breeze ruffled his hair, memories of another clear, starlit night surfaced. In that soft evening, his cape of mystery had dropped to the forest floor, revealing his heart.

Kaskoe. He had not mentioned her. Had he rescued her from the fort and was she waiting for them even now? He'd spoken only a few words since his return, and then only when necessary. He had built a wall around himself, a thick wall of silence.

Tall Dancer lay back onto his blanket, clasped his hands behind his head, and closed his eyes. The cool of the forest and the solitude of the night were his only weapons against the desire rising in him. Cara's closeness was as palpable on the night air as the scent of wildflowers that wafted in from the deeper forest. If he reached out he could touch her, feel her velvety skin beneath his hand again. He shuddered as memories washed over him, images as vivid and real as they had been that magical night a year ago.

Suddenly, a twig snapped in the darkness beyond the camp. Tall Dancer quickly rolled to his feet.

"What is it?" Cara whispered.

Tall Dancer shook his head. Motioning for her to stay, he crept forward. Then they were upon him. About twenty warriors in battle armor and paint appeared out of the dark. Two men grabbed Tall Dancer's arms and took the knife in his belt. Cara bolted into the forest, but she was quickly outdistanced and carried back to the fire by a warrior with a hideously painted face. Claude trembled in another warrior's grasp.

"Kendo! What are you doing here?" Tall Dancer asked a small man who emerged from behind his companions.

The big man holding Cara ran his hand through her hair and excitedly spoke to Kendo. The man holding Tall Dancer turned him over to another brave and he, too, examined Cara. Kendo stepped forward and picked up a strand of Cara's hair.

"So, Tall Dancer, we have captured not only you but the red-haired woman slave we have heard so much about. Our chief will be pleased at the slaves we will bring him."

"Slaves? Kendo, you and I are family. Why do you take us as slaves?" Tall Dancer struggled against the arms that held him.

Kendo stepped forward and pressed his face close to Tall Dancer's. "You took my sister to wife and when she was captured by the whites, you did nothing. This woman"—he indicated Cara—"has filled your mind. Now you and she are my slaves to give to our chief."

"Kaskoe had become a concubine to the Russians by the time I found her. She was willingly staying with them for the money. I saw her with my own eyes."

"Yet you did not attempt to take her away from them."

"No. She is dead."

Kendo looked surprised for a moment. Then the warrior's mask froze his face again. "Then you, too, will die."

Kendo led his prisoners single file through the forest, their hands tied behind them. The terrain over which they passed grew more rugged with each mile they traveled inland. Huge cedar trees towered above them, trees not bent and twisted like those along the coast that were constantly buffeted by sea gales. The forest floor was dark and damp. Giant ferns intertwined with exposed tree roots.

Cara slipped and fell to her knees. Someone grabbed her forearm and hauled her to her feet. Ahead of her, Tall Dancer's square shoulders bobbed in the half light.

She glanced at the man walking by her side. His face was painted with streaks of black and red. A wooden mask covered all but his ears and part of his chin. A raven with dark painted eyes glared at her from the top of the headdress. He was the man Tall Dancer had recognized and called Kendo, the man claiming to be Kaskoe's brother.

Deeper and deeper into the forest they traveled until, by the end of the third day, they saw the houses of a village nestled by a swift running stream. The people stopped their work and stared as the party passed. Cara raised her eyes and gazed ahead at a great house at the end of the first row. A carved openmouthed eagle, its talons exposed, covered the entrance.

Kendo spoke softly to his companions. Then, after a glance at Tall Dancer, he ducked through the door.

The crowd surrounding them consisted of men wearing only pointed hats. A few women gathered in a small knot near the back, their bark dresses covering them from neck to toes. A few carried baskets and shifted them to another hand to whisper behind a cupped palm to their neighbors.

Mixed in with their woven garments were pieces of Russian clothes. One woman wore a man's waistcoat over her bark dress. Another had a gentleman's pocket watch woven into her black hair. Cara looked back down at her feet and heard in her head the sounds of battle.

Kendo reappeared, motioned the captives inside, then waved his warriors away. As they scattered toward their own homes, their families met them with whoops of delight over the additional booty from the fort.

The moment she entered the house, Cara knew she was in the presence of a great and powerful chief. Never before had she seen such opulence.

Elaborately carved bowls, dishes, and combs wrought from yellow alder were polished to a gleam and hung on the wall. Piles of Chilkat blankets filled the corners of the room. Ceremonial dress lay across a bench on one side of the room, topped with a gigantic headdress larger than the man who would wear it. As they entered, a woman who had been weaving a blanket quietly rose and slipped out of sight.

In the center of the room sat a wizened old man. His hair was gray and hung down past his shoulders. Naked except for the pointed hat perched on his head, he rose as they entered.

"Kendo, my brave warrior." He patted the young man on the shoulder. "What have you brought back to us from your raid on the white settlement?"

"Many furs, Talko, much whiskey, and these slaves." Kendo gave Tall Dancer a sharp poke in the ribs.

"Divide the whiskey and furs among the people, but these slaves are mine." He stepped forward and peered into Tall Dancer's face.

Kendo nodded and bowed slightly before exiting the house. Talko began to circle them. He poked at their legs, crammed his finger in Claude's mouth to look at his teeth, and pulled at the dress Cara wore. Tall Dancer looked neither right nor left, keeping his eyes straight ahead. Finally, his curiosity sated, the old man stopped in front of them.

"So we have here one white slave, a brave, and"—he pressed closer and shoved his face into Cara's—"you look like a Tlingit woman." He ran his hand through Cara's long red hair. "But no Tlingit girl has hair this color. Who are you?"

"I am Cara Tarakanov." Cara tipped her chin up as she said the words she had long denied.

"You are Russian." His words fell with the thud of a death sentence. "You will be valuable additions to my possessions."

He walked up to have a closer look at Tall Dancer. Tall Dancer did not meet his eyes but continued to look at the wall beyond.

"A proud warrior. Where is your village? Who is your chief?"

Tall Dancer did not answer. Then the chief leaned closer and peered into Tall Dancer's eyes.

"You are the son of the witch Marisha and the white man who lived with her clan."

For the first time, Tall Dancer looked directly at the old man, surprise showing in his face.

"Your father's deeds of bravery were well known to us. A remarkable man to have worked his way into the clan, all for the love of a woman."

Tall Dancer looked away. The old chief smiled and raised one finger. Behind her Cara heard scurrying feet and saw a woman hurry out the door. When she reappeared, she held a basket of fresh water and some dried salmon.

"Put the old man with the rest of the slaves, but I want the woman with red hair and Tall Dancer to stay here with me tonight," he said to her.

She nodded, then grabbed the sleeve of Claude's coat and tugged. He followed her out, looking back over his shoulder. Another motion of Talko's hand and a younger woman brought two new blankets. Tall Dancer spread his on the floor and sat down cross-legged. Cara did the same and slid closer to him. Talko groaned and sat down across the firepit. He studied them for a long time before he spoke.

"I will give the two of you the opportunity to earn your freedom."

Cara glanced at Tall Dancer, but his face was unreadable. She had never heard of slaves being freed except at a potlatch. What was the old man up to?

"I have heard much about you. I know you"—he indicated Cara—"have lived with the Tlingit for many months and that Tall Dancer brought you from the Tsimshian to live with his mother." He shook his head. "There was much talk. Kendo was very angry." He paused again and watched Cara's face. "I think you and I can help one another."

Cara glanced at Tall Dancer and wondered why he didn't speak. The woman who had brought them blankets reappeared with a long knife and sliced through the leather straps that bound their hands. Cara rubbed her wrists where the leather had bitten into the flesh. The woman returned with an herbal salve for their wounds.

Talko watched patiently. As soon as the woman left, he began to speak again.

"During the winter, our village was raided by your village, Tall Dancer. Many of my people were taken as slaves. We have ransomed most of them at great expense. However, a valuable copper was also stolen during the raid. This copper belonged to my father and has never been given at a potlatch. I want you to get it back for me. If you are successful, I will grant you and the girl your freedom . . . and the old man's."

Tall Dancer stared, no longer wearing his mask of indifference. "My village made war on your people? We are so far away, and we have not been involved in war for many years."

"You have been away from your home a long time. Your chief died early in the winter and was replaced by a younger, more ambitious man."

"Little-River-Underneath is dead?"

Cara longed to reach out and take Tall Dancer's hand, but something in his expression stopped her.

"He was taken by the Land Otter People while hunting the killer whale."

"Who is chief now?"

"Wolf Eyes, the chief's *kelk*. He married Little-River-Underneath's wife. He was new to the village, having come to live with his *kak* only a few months before."

"I have not been home in many months. Why did they attack your village?"

"This young chief hopes by his deeds and by acquiring wealth he will become powerful. I believe he attacked us only to steal the copper. With it in his possession, his wealth will be great. People will want to follow him when he drives the Russians out of Yakutat."

Tall Dancer paled. "He is planning to lead another attack?"

"Not soon. He plans to approach the northern tribes, once our enemies, and urge them to join with him."

Cara felt terror pouring into her veins. If all the Tlingit united, they could very well drive away the Russians, but the price of such victory would be measured in blood.

"Will you retrieve my copper?" Talko asked.

Tall Dancer looked at Cara. Their eyes met. She could read the urgency in his expression. This might very well be their only chance at freedom and surely their only chance to unseat Wolf Eyes.

"Yes," Tall Dancer answered. "We will get the copper back."

"I want to take Cara with me." Tall Dancer and Talko sat cross-legged beside the firepit. Dust floated on the sunbeams coming down the open smoke hole. Cara tried to keep her attention on the meal she was helping to cook, but her eyes kept straying to Tall Dancer. He and Talko had been discussing the plan to steal back the copper since daybreak.

"She will help my disguise. The villagers know her as my slave and will not suspect."

Talko took a bite of the mush his wife offered him in a basket. As he chewed, he frowned. "Maybe you will not come back," he said, then swallowed.

"You have the old man. I will not leave him here."

"Perhaps you are tired of him. He is not a very good worker." Talko crammed a handful of mush into his mouth.

"No, but he is valuable to me."

Talko scraped the last of the mush from the edges of the bowl with one finger and popped it into his mouth. "You may take her."

"We will need supplies to get us back to the village and suitable clothes for Cara."

"I will have one of my other slaves bring what you require. I wish you good luck."

The old man grunted and struggled to his feet, then spoke to the woman who waited at his side. As she moved away, he climbed the ledges to the top row and disappeared into the first room.

''We leave at first light,'' Tall Dancer said shortly, then strode away. There was no emotion in his face, no flicker of the passion he had felt for her. He had not spoken of their love, nor had he attempted any intimacy, but Cara believed he still loved her. She had to believe—it seemed the only thing stationary in her rapidly changing world.

Cara watched him until he turned between two houses and vanished from sight. Before she could follow, Talko's wife shoved a skin and an awl into her hand. Indicating that Cara was to scrape the hide, the woman went back into the house, leaving Cara alone.

The same trail they had taken into Talko's village now led them toward the sea. The huge trees darkened the ground below, and Cara had trouble seeing the roots that lay in the path they followed. She stumbled and regained her balance a dozen times.

She scratched her neck where the bark dress chafed her skin. Over the past months, she had forgotten how uncomfortable the dress could be. Over the winter, she had lost some of her tan, but days of walking in the summer sun and heat would darken her before they reached the village.

They backtracked for three days before they came again to the house in the thicket of wildflowers.

''Do you think Claude will be safe?'' she asked as she put down her heavy pack.

''Talko will care for him. He is not a cruel man and, besides, Claude is the reason we will return.'' Tall Dancer dropped his pack as well.

''How do you plan to get the copper?''

His brow creased slightly and she knew he had no plan. But she had to ask, had to keep him talking. His deep silences were unbearable.

''When we get to my village, I will find out all that has happened. I will meet with this new chief and find out what kind of man he is. Then I will decide what to do.''

Once again the awkward silence fell between them. Tall

Dancer wanted to ask her what had happened in the months they had been apart, why she had stayed. But he couldn't speak the words, and the distance between them widened. Pushing aside the thoughts, he tried to concentrate on the dogs that had followed him inside.

"What will happen to them?"

He glanced up. Cara was stroking the furry coat of one dog that had wrapped himself around her legs.

"I will let them run free until I return."

"Aren't you afraid they'll run away?"

"Maybe they will, but I can't take them along. We need to be able to move quietly and quickly."

Cara glanced down into the heart-shaped faces and felt a lump grow in her throat.

Tall Dancer laid a fire and produced pemmican from his sack. He fed each dog a chunk, patted each in turn, then turned his back on them. Accustomed to lying at his side, they remained close to the fire as night fell, but when wolves began to howl deeper in the woods, they moved toward the door, nudged it open and, one by one, melted into the night.

Chapter Nineteen

The only constants in the lonely, fear-filled days that rolled by were heat and mosquitoes. Clouds of the tiny, black insects fogged up from standing water to torment Cara and Tall Dancer as they forged through thick underbrush.

Nights brought relief from the insects' torture, yet produced another misery, one deeper and not so easily avoided—Tall Dancer's impenetrable silences. The connection between them was gone, his mind closed to her. He was not unkind, pausing often to allow her stumbling steps catch up with his, yet deep within him a chunk of ice threatened never to melt.

They camped beneath a large cedar whose sagging branches formed a natural shelter. They were within a day's walk of his village, and smoke from a fire would not seem unusual along the well-used trail. Tall Dancer caught a fish in a small stream that trickled nearby. Cow parsnip and some berries added to the meal that filled them both.

Cara had dyed her hair again, and now her eyelids drooped as she leaned back against the trunk of the great tree and watched him moving about the camp, a chilly presence at the edge of her consciousness. She dropped off into a deep sleep.

A loud snap nearby awakened her. She started, and saw Tall Dancer crouched in the underbrush. When he caught her eye, he put his finger to his lips and motioned for her not to move. Holding her breath, she watched two men pass by her, talking softly to each other as they disappeared into the woods beyond the camp. Tall Dancer crept forward, looking for followers. When none appeared, he indicated for Cara to emerge from her hiding place.

"Who were they?" she whispered.

"They were from my village. Wolf Eyes plans to attack a group of Russians further up the coast." He stared at the spot where the men had disappeared into the forest. "I wonder why the tribal elders are allowing this man to endanger the lives of our people." He shook his head slowly and his eyes grew sorrowful. "For every *promyshlenniki* they kill, four Kolosh will die."

The path once so familiar to Cara was now beaten and muddied from a steady flow of people. She and Tall Dancer blended into the stream of humanity rapidly filling the village.

The village looked much the same as Cara remembered it, but a new chief's totem stood in front of the house she had shared with Marisha. As they moved with the throng of people, Cara searched for Little Beaver or Brass or Silver Eyes, but she saw no familiar faces.

The horde stopped at the far end of the village in front of a new house. On the porch stood a man dressed in a fine ceremonial shirt. His headdress was choked with many spruce roots, testifying to his youth and experience. He began to speak, encouraging the gathered men to follow him into battle against a Russian encampment on the shores of Yakutat Bay. They would be easy prey, he said, a large number of women and children to kill and capture, as the *promyshlenniki* had done to their people.

The crowd responded to his words. Soon they were shouting

and waving their weapons, pouring out of the village into a cleared area beyond, where food and drink waited.

Tall Dancer found himself alone in the muddy street. Puzzled, he walked slowly through the nearly empty village. Where were the people he had known all his life?

Wandering aimlessly, he noticed the totems guarding the doors of every house had changed. Little Beaver's canoe-making spot near the edge of the water, once littered with fragrant curls of cedar wood, was now bare, and undergrowth rapidly reclaimed the spot.

The stream where he had helped his mother and Cara dry salmon had been dammed and diverted to another route, one that bypassed the stones that had created cheerful songs when the stream tumbled over them.

At the end of the village was the gravehouse, still intact, but long neglected. The door groaned a dusty protest when Tall Dancer pulled it open. A curtain of green velvety moss had grown over the door and now hung like a hide ripped from a tortured beast.

Inside, new boxes lined the shelves, pushing the older receptacles to the back. Tall Dancer stepped inside, his gaze hurrying to his mother's spot. Her box sat as he'd left it, his father's remains at her side.

A small sigh of relief escaped his lips. He'd begun to think he'd been the victim of one of Raven's tricks and was dreaming the strangeness he was now experiencing.

But he *was* here. The truth of the changes in the village stared at him from the cluttered shelves. Many people had died and their deaths had been close together. Now he had to find out why.

As Tall Dancer moved away from her, walking as if in a trance, Cara felt the chill between them deepen and settle into her bones like a damp, cold day. She watched his steps falter and meander, then turn toward the gravehouse. Fearing to intrude, she set up camp in a dense thicket of cedars on the outskirts of the village.

As she went about the tasks of establishing a temporary home, she nervously glanced over her shoulder, but saw only the forest beyond. She felt as if she were in a ghost village, where only the souls of the miserable and the lonely remained.

"The village was raided by a clan from further north." Tall Dancer's voice startled her and she whirled, heart pounding. His face was gray and drawn and he looked like one of the ghosts her imagination had just conjured.

"Most of the men were killed, the women enslaved, the rest sold to the Russians. Once they were settled, they attacked Talko to collect greater wealth than they found here."

"What about Little Beaver and Brass and Dust?"

He eased his tall frame down and sat cross-legged by the fire. "Gone. Little Beaver is dead. Brass and Dust were captured and sold to the Russians."

The quavering hoot of an owl deep in the woods behind them lent a mournful note to his words. Tall Dancer stopped talking and stared in the direction of the sound.

"What is it?" Cara asked, well aware of the Tlingit beliefs about an owl's cry.

"He tells of terrible sickness," he replied, still staring at the curtain of dense trees.

A chill ran over Cara. Seldom had she heard him give voice to tribal superstitions. Maybe the loss of his friends influenced his words. Her mind flew to Marisha. She would have known what to do.

"At least this makes things easier for us," he said as he handed Cara a piece of smoked fish off the spit. "We can mingle among them without their realizing why we are here. I can pass as a warrior, here for the next raid on the Russians, and you can pass as my wife."

Cara raised her head to meet his gaze, hoping for some flicker of suggestion to accompany his words, some hint that what had once been would be again. But his gaze was flat and dead and Cara felt the ghostly chill return.

* * *

An unseasonable fog crept through the forest, snaking close to the ground and muting the usual morning sounds. The sky overhead was leaden, pregnant with morbid expectation. As Cara emerged from her lean-to, her uneasiness returned and foreboding darkened her mood.

Days had passed, and no one had challenged them about their presence, accepting them with cool disinterest. Wolf Eyes did indeed have the copper and made no secret of proclaiming its worth while boasting of the many scalps he had taken during its theft. This morning Tall Dancer had announced the best time to take the copper would be after the warriors left for the planned attack on the Russian encampment.

Cara approached the stream through the fog-smothered forest, feeling the fingers of moisture wrap around her arms, then slide away unseen. When she knelt to fill her basket, she noticed no one else was there. Odd, she thought, as she rose and started back for their camp. The usual morning village sounds were absent from the forest today. No children played just beyond their elders' sight, no ax bit into tough cedar wood, no voices drifted to her with half-understood words.

As she skirted the village, she thought she heard a wail and voices edged with worry. Ascribing it to the unsettled weather, she walked faster until she left the village behind and was once again safe in their camp. Tall Dancer was already gone, so Cara raked stones into the fire to boil the water.

At mid morning, he returned to the camp, his face white and drawn. He stopped across the firepit from her and stared, his eyes hollow

"What is it?" she asked, rising, all her irrational fears crowding in to sit upon her shoulders.

"The people are sick. They have the white man's disease."

"Smallpox! How do you know?"

"I saw some of them. The whole village was stricken almost overnight. The Russians brought it here."

Terror covered the accusation she thought she heard in his

voice. She'd seen smallpox wipe out entire crews on ships. Those few who survived bore the marks of their victory for the rest of their lives.

As Cara lay on her mat that night, wails of mourning filled the quiet forest. She covered her head with a blanket and tried to sleep, but the sounds of misery worked their way to her. Sometime during the night she awoke and found Tall Dancer gone from his sleeping mat on the other side of the shelter. She lay awake listening for his steps, but it wasn't until dawn that he returned with a bundle under his arm.

"Where have you been?" Cara asked, rising to her elbows.

"I have the copper. Now we can leave." There was no joy in his face, illuminated by the faint light, nor in his voice.

"You stole it by yourself, right out from under his nose?"

"He has been spending most of his time assessing the number of braves he is losing and leaves his house unguarded. His two slaves died last night, and I walked in and took it."

Cara scrambled to her feet and began packing their things. The sooner she was away from the sight and smell of death, the happier she'd be. The smell of it lay heavy, as smoke from funeral pyres filled the air day and night.

"No." Tall Dancer caught her arm as she was about to roll up her mat. "If we leave now, he will know we took it. We have to stay for a few more days."

Cara shuddered against a sense of foreboding. She raised her eyes and met his. He drew her close, encasing her in his arms as if to erase her fear. She pressed her cheek against his chest, grateful for the brief intimacy, even if it only lasted these few seconds.

"Don't worry. We'll be gone soon." His hand stroked down her hair and encircled her waist, bringing her close against him.

She waited, letting him decide the next move. His grip tightened on her back and his arms grew rigid. Then, his lips were on hers, crushing the breath from her with his urgency.

His lips moved from her mouth to the top of her neck, to

her ears, down to the dip at the edge of her shoulder. Cara closed her eyes and sighed. She had waited so long for his touch.

Then, suddenly, it was over. He pulled away from her and stepped back. Cara opened her eyes. He stared at her, his eyes still dark with passion.

"I can't," he said with a shake of his head. "I have no right."

"You have every right." Cara stepped closer to him and slid her arms around his waist.

Gently, he took her arms and set her away from him. "No."

"Why?"

Tall Dancer turned his back to her.

"Is it Byron?" She saw his muscles tense.

"At first. But now"—he paused and turned to face her—"there is too much difference in us. You are Russian. I am Tlingit. Our people are about to engage in a bloody war. Nowhere would be safe."

Cara felt a flicker of panic. He was slipping away from her just as the sea slipped away from the shore, and yet her heart lightened. He still loved her. "I don't care. We'll live somewhere deep in the forest, away from what is coming."

He shook his head. "We cannot survive alone."

Cara took a step forward, then stopped. She had been about to beg him, to plead with him to stay, but pride welled up in her. She'd beg no man to have her. Raucous memories spun in her head. She was a young girl on her knees at her father's side, begging him not to hurt her, begging for her life.

Cara shook herself. "When this is over, will you take me to Yakutat Bay so I can return home?"

He looked at her a long, heavy second. "Yes," he answered.

They scooped out a shallow depression in the thin soil, placed the copper in it, then scattered dirt, leaves, and debris over the area. Next, they spread Cara's blanket out over it. Tall Dancer made several trips through the village to gather information, but there was no mention of the copper missing. Everyone was too concerned with the disease destroying families and lives.

He returned to the camp after dark, but Cara was rolled up in her blanket asleep. As he sat down by the fire, he noticed he had a slight headache. Looking toward the village, he saw a heavy layer of smoke. He sniffed and acknowledged that as the cause of his pain.

During the night, Cara awoke to hear him moaning softly in his sleep. She crawled over to his blanket and laid her hand on his forehead. He was hot and dry. As he tossed in his delirium, he muttered unintelligible words and grabbed at the air.

"Nik yagu," he said. *"Nik yagu."*

"The Canoe of Sickness," Cara murmured, cold fear coursing through her. Marisha had told her when a man saw the Canoe of Sickness, it had brought disease and was awaiting the souls of those who died.

His face was pale. Occasionally his eyes flickered open, but they were wide with fright and she knew he saw only the evils in his mind. As Cara bathed his forehead, stories she had heard about death came back to her, stories of people fighting their way through brambles and thickets of devilclub to find their way to *sege qawu 'ani*—the land of the spirits.

For a moment, her thoughts were scattered by the fear of losing him. Then she heard a quiet, gentle voice, the words so clear they might have been spoken out loud. Her mind cleared and she remembered Marisha's careful, detailed explanations of how to prepare medicines.

"You're not going in that canoe," she told him as she covered him with her blanket.

Skirting the village, Cara worked her way down near the beach, just inside the line of trees that muffled the crashing of the waves. Plunging through the thickets of cranberries and salmonberries, she reached a low, swampy area ringed by trees that swayed like ghosts just above the surface of the still, stagnant water. Around the edge of the standing water grew tall, spike-leaved goatsbeard sporting long, white beards. She fell to her knees and raked at the spongy soil with her fingers until she had filled her basket with roots. Then she hurried back to camp, careful to avoid the village and the layer of smoke that reached out into the forest.

With shaking hands, Cara threw wood onto the embers of the fire and built it into crackling flames. She pushed rocks into the fire to heat, then covered Tall Dancer with the blanket he had thrown off. The basket that had been full of water last night was empty. She had to go for more. With a final look at him, she set off toward the village.

Wails of mourners mingled with the moans of the dying. Cara shook off her fear and hurried along.

Suddenly, her way was blocked by a huge warrior. He stood directly in front of her, his hands on his hips, and showed no signs of moving. As soon as she looked at his face, she knew this was Wolf Eyes.

His eyes were an odd shade of brown, almost yellow, and his glance was piercing, bordering on madness. His bronze skin was reddened by the sun and his thighs were as large as both her legs. He wore no clothes except for his knife and a pointed wooden hat. Cara looked up into his face and saw a hatred there she could not describe.

At first she thought it was directed at her, but then she realized he was looking over her head. Turning around, she saw another dead body brought out of one of the houses and laid on a funeral pyre built outside.

He has lost another soldier. Cara gingerly stepped around him and hurried away. She wondered if he had yet missed the copper.

When she returned to the camp, Tall Dancer had thrown off the blanket covering him and had torn at his clothes until he was naked. His blanket was soaked through with sweat and urine. Delirium possessed him as he tossed and groped with his hands. Cara boiled and steeped the roots until they made a tea. She spooned the liquid through his lips and further soaked his blanket with what dribbled out of his mouth as he lolled his head from side to side.

And then all that remained to do was wait.

Cara soaked a piece of moss from the swamp in cool water and laid it on his forehead to keep his raging fever down. Weariness overtook her and her eyes drooped. She stretched out on the ground beside him and slept, dreaming of Marisha and their ramblings through the woods.

A far-off sound nagged at her. They were in the swamp and Marisha was pointing out a plant to her, urging her to use the roots to treat smallpox. But it wasn't goatsbeard, the roots she had used. She was arguing with Marisha and Marisha was shaking her head. Someone called her. Marisha faded. The sound became louder until it penetrated her sleep. Cara shook herself awake. Sunlight was slanting through the trees. She must have been asleep for several hours.

"Cara," Tall Dancer mumbled in the voice of a child.

She leaned over him and recoiled when she saw his face. Hideous pockmarks marred his skin. His body and the blanket on which he lay were soaked in foul urine.

"Oh, God, I used the wrong plant," she whispered.

Cara bent over Tall Dancer's body and felt his forehead. Prone on a ragged sleeping mat, he mumbled and tossed his head at her touch. His skin was dry and feverish, and a thin line of saliva ran out of the corner of his mouth.

Grunting and pushing, Cara rolled him over onto his side, pulled out the wet blanket, and replaced it with dry moss. Then she pulled her sleeping mat over him to cover his naked body. In a few minutes, he was drenched again. As the long night wore on, his body rid itself of fluids at an alarming rate. Several times every hour she changed his bedding, soothed his fever with cool water, and prayed for a miracle.

His hallucinations became more violent, more disturbing. Sometimes his eyes looked directly into hers, but she knew he did not see her. His mind was far away, somewhere free of disease. It was then she remembered Marisha's dying words about dreaming of *sege qawu 'ani*. He had mentioned the name several times in his ravings. Could he really be seeing the land of ghosts?

Cara tossed another stick onto the fire and wrapped her arms around herself. Wails from the village increased, an owl hooted in the forest behind her, and Tall Dancer moaned until Cara put her hands over her ears and clamped her teeth shut to keep from screaming. Again, Marisha's quiet words came to her, words of encouragement, words of wisdom, assuring her she had done the right thing in choosing goatsbeard.

The moon set behind the trees, plunging the forest into the deep dark of early morning. Diligently, Cara tended him. Then, as the tendrils of dawn's light crept across the sky, he stilled. His breathing became regular and even. Only then did she lie down at his side and sleep.

Cara wiped her face with moss, then dipped it back into the basket and laid it across Tall Dancer's forehead. She coughed and wished a sea breeze would sweep away the smoke that clogged the forest.

The wails of mourning had grown fewer, but there was less activity in the village. Every door sported a branch of devilclub hung upside down to ward off the sickness. Every day as she went to the stream for water, more bodies were brought out of the houses.

The burials were simple and brief. There were no elaborate funeral potlatches. Too many had died and the survivors could only gather enough strength to pick up the dead bodies and burn them as soon as possible.

Smoke crept through the forest as cedar trees were felled to fuel the funeral pyres. An eerie stillness abounded—no children chattered, no women grouped at the stream. The silent village seemed populated by ghosts.

Cara trudged up the hill to their camp, wearily lugging another basket of water. She had existed on berries and roots, reluctant to leave Tall Dancer long enough to gather food, and her strength was waning. She glanced at him as she set down the water and was grateful to see that his bedding was dry. The red rash had spread over his face, shoulders, and chest. Some of the vesicles were filled with yellow pus.

She had dampened moss and was laying it across his forehead when his hand caught hers. Tiredly, she raised her eyes to his face and found him looking at her—not the muddled look he had given her before, but a bright, aware look. She caught her breath, anxious to speak, yet afraid he would drift away again to that mysterious place. "Do you know me?" she whispered.

He smiled and squeezed her hand. "How long has it been?"

"Two weeks," she said around a growing lump in her throat.

His eyes swept her. "Have you been sick, too?"

She shook her head. "I was sick with the pox when I was a child."

"You look thin." The hand holding hers trembled and he let it drop to the pile of leaves beside him.

"How do you feel?" Tears brimmed her eyes and coursed down her cheeks.

"Weak. Hungry."

She sobbed, then couldn't stop. Laying her head on his bare stomach, she cried until there were no more tears. His hand stroked her hair until she raised her face. "I don't have much except thin soup and some cow parsnips," she said in a hiccuping voice she hated.

He nodded and closed his eyes. As Cara started to rise, he grabbed her arm. "I love you," he whispered as Cara looked back at him. "Through the fever, you were there with me."

"I was here beside you."

"No, you were *there* with me. Wherever I was."

There had been times when he mumbled strange words and fought against unseen terrors, his body rigid with fear. His brain had sent his consciousness to some fever-induced hell she could only speculate about.

But she had been with him.

Her heart soared with the little strength she had left. "I love you, too," she answered, kneeling at his side. "I thought I had given you the wrong medicine."

"What did you give me?"

"Goatsbeard."

He smiled. "That explains why I feel so bad. How did you know?"

Cara was afraid if she answered him honestly, he would think she was as crazy as she did. "Your mother spoke to me." She watched his face for a reaction.

He only smiled and closed his eyes.

Chapter Twenty

"Now is the time to leave," Tall Dancer announced one morning, struggling to his feet.

"Are you sure you're ready?" Cara asked, catching his arm as he stumbled.

"Warriors in the village are scarce and those left are busy with the dead. Our absence will not be noticed."

Throughout the day, he puttered about the campsite, returning to his bed several times to conserve his strength. Cara snared a rabbit and caught salmon in the stream. She cut the fish up and smoked the pieces while roasting the rabbit over the fire.

"I'm going down into the village," he announced, holding onto a sapling tree for support.

Cara started to object, then changed her mind. This might be the last time he would see the village of his childhood.

Wolf Eyes was dead, along with the village shaman. Now the village was leaderless and rife with rumors it would be deserted and the survivors would move south and join with another village that had lost many people, too.

Tall Dancer turned and staggered down the hill. Smoke still obscured the bottoms of many of the houses and coiled around the village like a giant snake. Two funeral pyres smoldered in the center, still too hot for anyone to retrieve the ashes and bone bits left.

Hollow-eyed children watched him from the porch of every house. Some of their faces were spattered by deep scars, but all of them were silent and still, their innocent minds still trying to take in the horror that had left their homes in turmoil. He wondered how many of them were orphans, how many of them had lost their entire families. Of the few people who moved about, he noticed each one had a blackened face and shorn hair.

He stumbled and fell to his knees by the edge of the swift stream. Where before there had been grass and green moss beside the sparkling water, now there was only blackened ground, stained by the light dusting of cinders that covered everything. He ran a trembling hand across his eyes. Nothing was the same, nor ever would be again.

Gripping the rough bark of a sapling, he rose to his feet and made his way to the back of the village. Once covered by vines and edged with wildflowers, the gravehouse now sat on ground trodden and churned by many feet.

The door protested as he swung it open. The shelves were jammed with boxes and baskets of ashes placed haphazardly and piled on top of one another.

He shoved boxes aside until he found Marisha's and drew it out. He blew off the coating of dust and opened the lid. A few bone fragments stuck up out of the light gray ash and a great longing enveloped him again. He glanced around at the ill-kept house. Then he retrieved his father's remains and closed the door.

''What are you doing?'' Cara asked when he stumbled into camp and flopped down at the base of a tree.

He set the boxes down at his side and looked up. ''I want you to come with me.''

Afraid he was suffering a setback, Cara knelt at his side and gently took his arm. ''You need to rest.''

''No.'' He wrenched out of her grasp. ''I must do this now.''

Cara saw the trembling in his hands and felt alarm prick her scalp as she recognized the bone boxes. "All right," she said, straightening. "I'll come with you."

He shook off her hands, then braced his back against the tree and struggled to his feet. She followed him down into the village, through the silent streets and to the edge of the stream. He did not stop at the well-worn place where water was drawn. Instead he lead her further upstream, struggling through thick brambles and briars.

When he reached a clearing beside a large rock slick from cascading white water, he stopped. "Their way of life is gone," he said as he opened both lids. "And I think they will be happier here." He poured the dust into the racing waters, then tossed in the boxes.

He sagged against a tree, his face paling. He was in pain—whether emotion or physical, she couldn't tell. Suddenly, she saw him through the eyes of a Russian and not a woman in love. What had they done to these gentle people? This terrible disease that disabled and disfigured had wiped out almost a whole village of women and children and warriors. Tears stung the backs of her eyes and she felt a chasm open between them.

The next day they left their camp for Talko's village. Wordlessly, he led them through the dense forest, his steps often stumbling and unsure, but determined. The layer of ash muted the colors of autumn for two days' travel.

Relief flooded Cara and she felt her heart lighten when the last traces of cinders and smoke were left far behind. Along the way, she fished for the last few salmon flopping their way upstream and snared snowshoe hares whose coats were just beginning to turn from brown to white.

Tall Dancer grew stronger as the days passed. She could see the fatigue in the slump of his shoulders and the stumbling of his steps, but he wouldn't give in to exhaustion. At first, they only traveled a mile or two a day, and when they stopped he slept long and deep. Then his stride lengthened until Cara struggled to keep up with him. They reached his cabin just as snow began to filter down through the cedars.

Tall Dancer threw open the door, and Cara heard the scurrying of tiny feet as light spilled in on the dusty floor.

"Sit down," she urged. "I'll lay a fire." She pulled dry wood from the pile beside the firepit, and soon fragrant cedar smoke was drifting up toward the smoke hole. Tall Dancer squatted and stared into the flames, his hands clasped between his knees.

Cara watched him from the shadows as she drew preparations for supper from their packs. His lean cheeks were sprinkled with pockmarks, some with the scabs still attached. Her heart swelled with love for him. She circled around behind and touched him on the shoulder. Slowly, he turned and looked up at her.

"This is the beginning of the end," he said softly.

She could think of no words to reply, but questions tormented her mind. Did he think of her as one of *them,* the people who had brought this plague on his people? In time, would his bitterness fall on her?

He returned to staring into the flames. Cara pushed three smooth stones into the fire, rose, and hurried outside to fill a basket from the trickle of a stream that ran by the cabin. When she came back in, he was stretched out beside the fire, asleep. As soon as the stones were hot, she dropped them into the basket and added fresh rabbit and some roots.

The fire soon had the tiny house warm. When she stepped between him and the fire to rake out an errant stone, his hands caught her legs and pulled her down next to him. In one motion, he rolled her over until he lay on top.

The warmth of the fire and the long-desired closeness of him lulled her into a comfortable lethargy. He untied her dress and slid it down. Her naked skin basked in the warmth as his lips nibbled at her neck.

"It's been too long," he murmured between teeth clenched around her earlobe.

"Hmm," Cara answered.

Want for her suddenly seared red hot within him, quelling his resentments. Now, as his lips moved over her, his mind remembered having been this way before, remembered how and when he had loved her. The urge to possess her, to claim her again as his, overrode every other conscious thought.

Loving her emptied him of his small reserve of strength. As he lay exhausted, cradling her in his arms, she rose up on one elbow and leaned over him to smile down, her hair skimming his chest. The bond between them had never been broken, he realized, only stretched a bit. With their bodies they had reforged the union, consummated the link that bound them together.

She smiled again, a quiet, steady devotion glowing in the depth of her eyes. Then the edges of her eyes tipped down seductively. His fatigue forgotten, he shamelessly wanted her again.

Snow that heralded an approaching storm filtered lightly down through the giant trees as they approached Talko's village. People were hurrying to retrieve the last fish from the drying racks, but they stopped and watched. Tall Dancer was painfully aware of the scars on his face. As he and Cara approached Talko's long house, someone on the porch ran inside. In a few seconds, the yard swarmed with people.

He and Cara pushed their way inside and found the old man sitting just as they had left him, naked except for his pointed hat. He was licking the last of a stew from his fingers when he raised his eyes, saw them, and smiled broadly.

"So you have returned. Did you bring my copper?"

Tall Dancer pulled the bundle from his pack and unwrapped the broad piece of orange metal. "I have returned your copper. Where is the old man?"

Talko smiled. "He is here and well."

He signaled to the silent woman standing behind him. She disappeared into another room, then reemerged with Claude. He wore a long bark garment and smiled with relief.

"Have you been treated well?" Tall Dancer asked.

"I have been cared for and left unharmed," Claude replied.

Tall Dancer handed Talko the copper. Its burnished surface glowed, taking on the orange hues of the firelight. Talko's wrinkled fingers lovingly traced the grooves in the flat, hammered surface.

"My father gave this to me when I was named," he said, turning the treasure over. "His father gave it to him at the same time in his life." He raised his eyes to Tall Dancer. "I thank you for returning it to me. You are free." His eyes returned to the treasure in his lap.

"You are an honorable man," Tall Dancer said with a dip of his head.

"Are there many left in your village?" Talko's question stopped him from leaving.

Tall Dancer's hand went to his scarred cheek. "No."

Talko shook his head. "Ska-out-lelt was victorious at the fort, but I fear this is only the beginning of the *promyshlenniki*. There are many who have the white man's sickness," Talko said in a voice almost to himself. "Many who will die. They will come." He stretched an arm toward the door. "They will come and take our pelts until there are no more otter and no more Tlingit." Moisture glistened in the wrinkles around his eyes and his face reddened. Then he dropped his head and began to run one finger across the imprint of the copper.

Tall Dancer waited, but Talko said no more. Crooking a finger at Cara and Claude, he started toward the door. They rose and silently followed him outside.

"What do you wish to do now?" Tall Dancer asked Claude as they stepped outside into the fresh air.

"I wish to stay."

Astonished, Tall Dancer stared at Claude. "Are you sure?"

"I am an old man. If I live to make the journey to England, where will I work? Where will I live?" He shrugged his shoulders. "I am comfortable here. I have food and warmth . . . and a few friends."

"You could go to America. Many ships go there and take pelts to somewhere called Boston."

Claude shook his head. "No. It is a young country for young men. There is no place for an old man like me. All I want is a warm fire and a warm woman for the rest of my years." He smiled and slyly glanced down the village. "There is a young woman, recently widowed. Talko says she has no brother-in-law to take her in. He and I have reached an understanding."

"All this in so short a time?" Tall Dancer searched Claude's face.

"When you reach my age, lad, you cannot tarry over things as you did when you were young." Claude's eyes twinkled. "I was once quite a lady's man, you know."

They stayed with the village for a few days and were treated as family and not the prisoners they had been. Then Tall Dancer grew restless. The big house where they stayed was warm and cozy but crowded. Children played and cried all hours of the day. Husbands and wives argued, and Cara knew by the creases in his forehead he was ready to leave.

The light snow that had dusted the ground deepened into a swirling white cloud that engulfed the village and softened the lines of the houses' rough planks.

"It is time to go," he announced one afternoon as he stood on the porch looking toward the bay. A huge black bearskin wrapped him from head to foot.

Cara stepped to his side and followed his gaze out over the water. The surface was calm and swallowed the snowflakes that fell upon it. That was that. They would go.

The morning they left, the villagers loaded them down with dried meat, pelts, and new arrows.

"Much snow," Talko said, pointing a bony finger at the mountain towering over the tree canopy. "She wears a rain hat." A thick, dark cloud covered the very top of the mountain. "You must hurry." Placing a quivering hand on Tall Dancer's shoulder, Talko drew his bearskin tighter around him and shuffled back into the house.

Only a light snow fell, yet the thickening clouds and Talko's prophecy weighed heavy on them as they wound through the forest, heading for the coast. Snow plopped on dried leaves as the flakes grew larger, driven on a sudden breeze. Darkness came early. They made camp in a thicket and hastily put up a lean-to of cedar branches. After a quick meal of dried salmon washed down with water, they crawled inside and pulled a bearskin over the door.

Cara laid her head on his shoulder and listened to the snow pelting on the roof. He entwined his fingers with hers and pulled her hand to his lips.

"I want to take you as my wife," he murmured.

"Wife?" Cara sat up, her head brushing against the branches. "But how?"

Tall Dancer rolled over to face her. A little light crept in through the branches and illuminated his face. "Here. Now."

"But isn't there some ceremony necessary?"

He pressed her fingers to his lips. "Our worlds are no longer familiar. You are without a home. I am without people. But we have each other. Ceremonies are for those who watch, not for those who promise."

He squeezed her hand tighter. "I take you as my wife. I will provide food and clothing for you and I will care for you when you are sick, as you have cared for me."

There was no need for him to promise or say the words, she realized. The vows between them were unspoken and binding. "And I will care for you and bear your children and keep you warm on cold nights," she answered.

"Then we are husband and wife." He leaned forward and gently brushed her lips. "But our wedding night will have to wait until we are in our house where it is warm." He smiled and drew the pelt around her. Together, they rolled up in the furs and the pat-pat-pat of snowflakes lulled them to sleep.

The next morning, the snow was thicker and wetter as they approached the coast. Wind yanked at their clothes and ripped away their body heat. Just beyond the line of trees that broke the force of the gale, the surf roared on the beach. Cara licked her lips as she stumbled along and tasted salt.

At midday, they turned inland, passing through a copse of trees. There in the center, head raised, stood a deer. The roar of the ocean drowned out their steps and the storm whipped away their scent. Tall Dancer laid down his pack and pulled out his bow and arrows. He loaded a new shaft, one given them by the villagers. Motioning her to stay, he moved around behind the animal.

The buck raised his head, slowly chewing a mouthful of tree bark. His nostrils quivered and his ears swung forward. Through the snow, Cara could see Tall Dancer circling. He stopped, drew back on the bow, and let the arrow fly. The deer leaped. His head down, he pawed the air, then galloped a few yards and plunged to earth, plowing a trench in the snow with his nose.

Tall Dancer ran to the still quivering deer, whipped out his knife, and slit its throat. Blood bubbled onto the pristine snow, and Cara watched the light dim in the buck's large brown eyes. For a moment, she felt regret at having taken his life. Quickly, Tall Dancer skinned and cleaned the animal, carefully wrapping all the parts in skin and burying them in the snow to freeze.

"We will stay here tonight," he announced as he sliced another length of meat away.

A tiny stream trickled nearby. They washed the meat and the knives in the swift, cold water. By the time they were through, there was barely time to put up cedar boughs for cover before darkness set in. Tall Dancer lit a small fire that hissed and spit when snowflakes fell into the flames. Two hunks of meat speared through with a green stick sizzled over the fire.

"Here." He handed her the skin, carefully rolled up. "This is for our son."

Cara slid her hand over the soft fur, remembering the pliable pelts Marisha kept in a corner. She held the skin up to her cheek. A baby. His son. She met Tall Dancer's eyes. He smiled, and she wished home were nearer.

* * *

By the time they reached the cabin, the heavy snowfall had deepened into a blizzard, piling up against the long sides of the tiny house at an alarming rate.

They stumbled inside, and Tall Dancer lit a fire in the central firepit. Soon the house was warm, while outside the wind howled at the door and buffeted the walls.

Cara cut up two chunks of meat and dropped them into a basket along with some shriveled cow parsnips and wild celery roots she had dug up in the woods. All the while, she was aware of him watching her from a sleeping mat in the corner.

The rocks sputtered and hissed as she dropped them into the basket with the meat and vegetables. The mixture began to boil, and the aroma carried throughout the house.

Cara nibbled at her food. *Why am I so nervous? They had slept together before.* But this was different. He was her husband now.

Tall Dancer set his plate to the side and took hers away. "You do not eat. You worry the food."

Their fingers touched and a shock traveled through her body. He stood, took her hands, and pulled her to her feet. Then he scooped her into his arms and carried her to a pile of furs he had prepared by the fireplace. The silky hairs caressed her body as he slid her clothes off.

"We will make a son tonight," he said as his warm skin slid over hers.

"A son? What about a daughter."

"We will make a daughter after our son is born."

"You . . . seem . . . so . . . sure," she gasped as he ran his hands over her skin, tingles eddying in their wake.

"I will need a son to help me keep his mother out of trouble." He smiled at her, but his eyes were serious, darkened in passion.

And so began the marriage of two souls, an ancient ceremony without tradition or words, only emotion and instincts.

"I have planted a child in you," he said with a satisfied smile as they lay entwined by the fire.

Cara waited for a joking remark or a twinkle in his eyes, but there was none. "You're serious, aren't you?"

"Yes." He clasped his arms behind her and he rolled them to their sides. "In summer we will have a son."

Cara looked over his shoulder, where the fire danced in orange patterns on the walls. What if she could not bear children? Terrible memories rose to torment her, memories of pain inflicted in dark rooms. How would she tell her husband?

Winter raged on. Storms off the ocean pelted the land with snow and cold rain for days at the time. Tall Dancer hunted whenever there was a lull in the weather and Cara scraped hides, cooked, cleaned, and thought about her husband's prophecy. She was aware of each tiny twinge in her body, every phase of her cycle, hoping he had been right.

The sled dogs returned one by one as winter deepened. Tall Dancer ran his trap lines in the streams of the forest around them, never straying far from home. The cold winter produced thick, luxurious pelts. By Christmastime, they had a high pile of furs, and Cara knew she was pregnant.

"You don't have to look so startled," she scolded Tall Dancer. "You told me yourself you had given me a child."

"I never thought . . ." He let his words drift off.

Cara laughed. "You mean you didn't know?"

"Well, I hoped . . . thought . . . " He stepped forward and gathered her into his arms. Bits of ice and snow clung to the fur of his bearskin wrap, and he smelled fresh, like the outdoors.

"Are you happy?" she asked, burying her face in the pelt.

He drew back and held her away from him. Tenderness softened his features. "How could I not be happy?" he said softly. "But . . . do you never think about home?"

The question caught her off guard. She moved out of his arms, walked over, and poked at the fire. "My home is here with you."

"Do you never think of the town you left? An easier life?

Do you never want to get on board one of the ships that come here and sail away?''

"No."

"Good."

Something in his voice made her turn.

"Because tomorrow we will meet a ship that comes to trade for furs."

Cara caught her breath. What Russian captain would be foolish enough to brave the winter to trade for furs? She knew the answer before she asked herself the question. The Butcher would. She raised a hand to her hair. The dull brown dye had faded, and she wouldn't be able to dye it again.

"He will not see you. Only I will meet him."

"Why you? Why does he come now to get furs from only one man?"

"Other men will be there—men from Talko's village, men from the Tongass."

Alarm grew in her. "Why now, in the winter?"

"Russia is anxious for the furs. The long winter has made the supply small. Some men in Talko's village told me they trade for many things, things you should have."

"No!" Cara grabbed the back of his wrap and pulled it off his shoulders. "I don't want those things. You can get all we need with your own hands."

His jaw was set as he turned. "You are my wife now. I promised to provide for you. You should have a dress of soft cloth, warm blankets for the baby—things you had at home."

Fear nearly choked the breath out of her. Her mind raced ahead, seeing Tall Dancer approach her father. "Those Russian ships have nothing you cannot give me." She put her hands on either side of his face. "They are robbing you. Can't you see? The more you trade with them, the more often they'll come. Soon they won't wait for you to bring the furs to them. Soon they'll take what they want."

"I do not go only to trade." Gently, he caught her hands in his and lowered them from his face. "I go to judge their weaknesses."

"What do you mean?"

Tall Dancer moved away from her to the edge of the firepit and stared down at the flames. "If I am to destroy my enemy, I must know him, know his weaknesses."

"You're going to attack the ship?"

He looked up at her. "Not tomorrow or the next time, but when he is pleased with us and thinks we are only stupid savages."

The thought of her father's death becoming a reality brought mixed emotions. How many times had she wished him dead? How many hours had she spent planning his murder herself, laying out elaborate and impossible schemes? The thought brought a rush of joy, but then she looked at her husband's face. Her father proudly employed a group of ruthless men who would do whatever he ordered. They were seasoned fighters, men accustomed to brutally killing.

"Please, no. He'll kill you. You don't know him as I do."

Tall Dancer put his arms around her and drew her close.

"Talko's men will be with me. I will not argue about it anymore. We go tomorrow."

Cara laid her head against his chest and listened to the familiar thump of his heart. The beat quickened as he ran his hands down her back.

"Are you sure you want to raise a child here?" he murmured into her hair. "Here, with no other women around?"

She thumped the earring that dangled from his left ear, making the tiny bones rattle. "I can think of no better company than you."

He lowered his lips to hers and pulled her tight against him. She opened the fur wrap and wiggled inside.

"Careful, woman," he growled. "Are you sure this is wise?"

"The baby will be fine," she said against the neck of his shirt. "I hope you aren't going to run away from me until spring."

He threw off the robe and sank to the floor, pulling her down with him. "I will not run far," he promised.

Chapter
Twenty-One

The wind blew cold, cutting straight through the bear fur Cara held wrapped around her. Overhead, gray clouds scuttled along on swift wind, and the scent of snow was in the air. Peeping between the branches of a tree, she watched Tall Dancer and the other men, their heads bowed together in whispered conversation.

Beyond them, just outside the breaking waves, bobbed her father's ship. It was grayer than she remembered, but at the top of the mast flew the black flag she knew so well. There was no face on it, no emblem or clever motto, only the fluttering solid black field.

A small boat was lowered over the side, and its occupants began to paddle for shore. Cara shrank back into the protection of the trees and her teeth chattered as the craft scraped up on shore and the men scrambled out. Closely, she scanned the group, but her father was not among the men who carried guns cradled in their arms.

Tall Dancer straightened and strode toward the men, the other Tlingits behind him. The two groups met. The sailors nodded their heads and listened. Then they began to gesture and talk rapidly.

Tall Dancer nodded, and one of the Tlingit men ran back down the beach and picked up a bundle of pelts. He hurried back and held the furs out to the sailors. They ran their hands over the silky pelts and nodded again.

Waves crashed on shore and carried away the words Cara strained to hear. Every muscle in her body was stretched tight as one of the men stepped closer, his gun held ready in his hands. Tall Dancer stood his ground while the man silently looked him over.

Then he dropped a bag at Tall Dancer's feet, said something, and laughed. The sound of his laughter rippled over Cara. She closed her eyes against a flood of memories. When she looked again, the men were shoving their boat back into the water.

"Beads," Tall Dancer said as he ducked into the forest. "They offered us glass beads for the furs." He dropped the bag.

Cara knelt and pulled open the thong that held it shut. A rainbow of shiny beads spilled out onto the ground. When she looked up, Tall Dancer's jaw was set in anger.

"Let's go home," she said, rising to her feet. She took his arm and together they walked into the forest, leaving the beads on the thick pad of fallen leaves.

Vlad Tarakanov lowered his spyglass and smiled. She wasn't dead. The Kolosh's reports had been accurate. She was alive and well—very well, if he was any judge of women. He raised the glass again and trained it on the woman crouched at the edge of the forest. Adjusting for the swell of the waves that rocked his ship, he swung the glass around to scan the tall warrior talking to the sailors.

"Tall Dancer." He whispered the name, then spat on the deck. The tall Kolosh owned what should be his. He had raised the brat after her whore mother died on him one night. By all rights she should be here on the ship with him, doing his bidding, warming his bed at night. He ran his tongue over cracked lips.

His anger flared as he watched her drop the beads to the ground, take the Kolosh's arm, and lead him into the forest. *By summer's end, she'll be in my bed, I vow.*

Tarakanov collapsed the glass and shouted at his men to hoist aboard the small boat. Then he hurried to his cabin and cleared his desk with one swipe of an arm. An old and tattered map lay beneath the clutter.

He ran his finger down the coastline, then stopped where a small stream emptied into the ocean. He traced the stream back and smiled. "Raise the sails!" he shouted to his crew from the door of his cabin.

The first tentative buds of spring were poking their heads out of their protective sheaths when Cara's time came. She was sitting on the floor scraping a deer hide when the first pain hit.

She doubled over and, with fear gripping her throat, made her way to their sleeping mat. Contractions stabbed through her with growing regularity. She lay on her back and watched the afternoon sun move across the cabin floor, trying to remember what Marisha had told her about birthing.

Why didn't I remember some of this before? All afternoon she balled up the edges of the mat in her hands and fought against the pain that washed over her, leaving her damp with cold sweat.

Long after nightfall, Tall Dancer hurried down the trail toward the house. With every step he cursed the impulse that had made him follow an injured deer until dark. Now he was returning later than he wanted, with no deer meat to show for his efforts. As he stepped through the thicket of bushes, he noticed the skin-covered windows were dark.

He hurried to the door and flung it open. "Cara?" No answer.

He dropped his bow and arrow and hurried to the fireplace. He picked up a stick, lit the end, then held it high above his head. Cara lay motionless on their sleeping mat, her hands wound in the tattered edge.

Cold fear went through him as he approached her and dropped to his knees. Her eyes were closed, but as he neared, he saw her chest rose and fell with silent breathing. When he lay his hand on her brow, her eyes flew open, full of pain.

"How long?" he asked.

"Since early this morning. Something's wrong. The baby's stopped moving." Her eyes were as wide as those of the doe he had missed this afternoon, and her face was pale and drawn.

Quickly, he covered her with a blanket and stoked up the fire in the firepit. He heard her grunt and saw her knuckles whiten as another pain racked her. Before he could return to her side, another pain had gripped her. They were coming more frequently now, and her hands never left the balled up mat.

He raked his fingers through his hair. Her life was in his hands, and he knew nothing about childbirth. Only women were allowed in the birthing house, and it was never discussed afterward. He threw another piece of wood on the fire and paced back and forth. Marisha would know what to do. She had assisted in many births.

Cara cried out, pleading with him to do something. He pressed a palm to his temple and tried to think. What had Marisha said about births? Had she ever mentioned it to him?

Memories came back in bits and snatches. A calmness settled over him and he felt his mother's presence. With vivid clarity, he suddenly recalled a conversation he'd overheard between Marisha and another woman. They had been talking quietly and he had been a child, but now he remembered every word.

He strode over to the mat, dropped to his knees and ripped Cara's dress off. With both hands he felt her swollen belly, creeping across the skin with lithe fingers.

"What . . . are . . . you . . . doing?" Cara gasped between pains.

"Shhh." He concentrated on her stomach. "The baby's turned wrong."

Cara stared at him over her stomach. "Backward?"

"Feet first."

Her eyes widened. "Will we die?"

"No," he said with as much assurance as he could muster. "I'm going to turn it." He stood over her and took her hands. "Stand up."

Cara raised her head off the mat. "I can't."

"Yes, you can." With all his strength, he hauled her to her feet. She collapsed against him and he could barely reach around her. Moving around behind her, he clasped his arms across her chest. "Squat down," he commanded and pulled her down with him. "Lean against my knees and grab that pole." He moved her limp hands to the pole that supported the center of the roof.

She opened her mouth to disagree, but another pain cut off her words. Squeezing the pole, she groaned, a heart-wrenching sound, then would have collapsed to the floor had Tall Dancer not slid his knees under her buttocks. She was tiring and he had to work fast. Her head sagged forward to rest on her arms.

The water bag the baby's head rests on must break first.

"Hang on to that pole." He moved around in front, knelt down at Cara's feet, and began to probe her. She raised her head at his touch, but the effort was too much and she dropped her head. His fingers touched a membrane. He closed his eyes and gave it a pinch. A flood of water poured over his hands and arms.

Cara screamed. He probed further, putting her cries for help out of his mind. Something wiggled against his hand—a foot.

I grabbed one foot, then the other, and held them in one hand. Then I pulled one arm down.

He grabbed another wiggling limb that felt like a foot. A third member moved. Assuming it was an arm, he gently tugged. Nothing happened. He looked at Cara. Her eyes were wide with fear.

If the other arm had been down, the baby would have choked to death.

He tried again, but felt nothing. Praying he was right, he

tugged and the baby moved. Another tug and two feet poked
out.

"Cara! I can see the feet!" He raised up to look at her, but
her face was concealed by her hair. The pains were coming on
their own only a few minutes apart. When he felt the muscles
tighten against his hand, he tugged again. A bottom, two legs,
and two feet poked out.

"A son," he whispered. Tears blurred his vision as another
pain bore down. He tugged and a wet, bloody baby slid into
his hands.

I cut the cord and wrapped it around the mother's toe.

He pulled his knife from the sheath at his belt. Glancing at
the still baby lying on a mat at his side, he slashed through the
cord connecting the baby to Cara. Tiny, red, and wrinkled, the
infant fought for life's first breath. Tall Dancer picked him up
by the heels. A thin stream of liquid flowed from the baby's
mouth. His first cry was a weak meow, the second a lusty
scream.

Cara had collapsed on the floor, unconscious to her baby's
cries. Tall Dancer swathed the infant in a soft fur and quickly
wrapped the end of the cord between Cara's toes.

The afterbirth must come out and be burned.

He glanced from the baby to Cara.

If it doesn't come out on its own, you must pull it.

He grasped the end of the cord and tugged. A large, red
mass slid out. Quickly, he swept it up in leaves and tossed it
into the fire. He laid a hand on Cara's forehead and found it
cool. Her cheeks were turning pink again and her breathing
was even and regular. He pulled a bear pelt over her and let
her sleep.

By the fire, a basket of water warmed. He poured the water
into a larger vessel and eased the baby's tiny body into it. So
small, but so perfect—he had a tiny nose, a shock of black
hair, tiny fingers and fingernails, and tiny feet. "And his father's
heart," Tall Dancer whispered softly as the baby's hand closed
around one finger.

After lifting the baby out of the water, he wrapped him in

a soft ermine fur Cara had intended for his carrier and laid him in the crook of Cara's arm. The baby stared up at Tall Dancer for a moment, then closed his dark eyes.

Tall Dancer brushed back a damp ringlet of hair on Cara's forehead. She was beautiful despite the dark circles and traces of pain in her face, and he ached with his love for her. With one finger, he traced the outline of her lips before covering her and leaving her to sleep.

Back by the fire, Tall Dancer eased himself down on a mat near the flames. His hands shook as he pushed back his hair. Blood stained a path from his wrist to his elbow. The friendly presence that had calmed him during the birth seemed to subside, leaving in its place a chill, but a feeling of satisfaction. "Thank you, *'atle,*" he murmured to the dark corners of the room.

Cara opened her eyes to a haze. At a distance, someone moved slowly across in front of her. *Am I dead?* She moved her head and things came into focus. Tall Dancer stood by the fire, his back to her.

"The baby?" she asked.

He spun around and hurried to her side.

"You've been crying," she said, seeing the stains on his face. Panic hit her. "The baby died?"

"No, no. He's right here." He picked up a bundle and laid it in her arms. "He's hungry."

"He?"

Tall Dancer smiled. "You've given me a son."

Cara turned her head. The baby's soft black hair nudged against her side. She moved him closer to her breast and put the nipple to his mouth. Hungrily, he began to suck.

Cara frowned, trying to remember the birth. She remembered someone pulling her to her feet and pain—terrible pain.

"Was the birth difficult?" she asked, taking in Tall Dancer's ashen face and tousled hair.

"Not for the baby," he said with a crooked smile, "even though he came out backward."

Threads of conversation returned along with the memory of panic. "You turned him?"

"No. Just helped him along a little."

Cara closed her eyes, remembering tender, warm hands caressing her, soothing her, and his voice calmly encouraging her. And then she remembered another voice, a softer, gentler voice urging her to have faith in her husband.

Tall Dancer gently removed the baby and placed him in the baby carrier he had made when Cara fell asleep. As he stood over his son and laced the cover over his chest, he could again feel Marisha's presence.

It was the grandmother's job to make the basket for the baby carrier. She would help gather moss for the diapers and make the feather pillow for his head. But he had done it instead, hoping no ill would come of his doing a woman's job.

Then, in a sudden flash of memory, he saw the ship bobbing at anchor the day he met the Russians on the beach and a chill crept into his blood.

The morning was glorious, bursting forth in a chorus of bird songs and brilliant colors. Cara held her face up to the morning sun and tried to drag a bone comb through her tangled hair. A large rock propped the door open, allowing the fresh scent of spring to pour in, carried on a warm breeze. She looked down to where little Alexei slept peacefully in his carrier. She had named him after one of her childhood friends, but Tall Dancer had insisted on having a naming ceremony and giving his son a proper warrior's name when he was older.

A constant chopping worked its way into her thoughts and she rose from the floor and moved to the door to watch Tall Dancer. His shirt hung over the low branch of a tree as he hollowed out the heart of a cedar tree for a canoe. Blond curls of wood littered the ground and stuck in his dark hair. As if knowing she watched, he suddenly stopped, straightened, and turned toward the door. He gave her a slow smile, raised his hand, then picked up his stone ax and resumed work.

Behind her, the baby whimpered. She picked him up, untied the front of his carrier, and lifted him out. She pulled aside the neck of her dress and put him to her breast. They lay down together on a pelt on the floor. Cara closed her eyes and let a sense of well-being wash over her.

Suddenly the stillness was disturbed by the barking of a dog. Another joined in. Tall Dancer's chopping stopped. Cara sat up and the baby fussed. She shifted him to the other breast and listened. Tall Dancer's voice was muffled as he spoke softly to his dogs.

Birdsongs in the trees ceased and a prickling ran along her back. She frowned and shifted her position. The forest had grown abruptly quiet many times lately. Even the raucous squirrels would stop their scampering and barking.

The dogs would whimper and growl, often awakening them late at night. But each time Tall Dancer went outside to investigate, nothing was there. In the morning, there were never any tracks.

Wolverines often prowled around the cabin, but Tall Dancer thought even the presence of an unusually large one would not excite the dogs this way. They were accustomed to the scent of wolverine, often running across them either in the traps or along the trails.

As she listened, a bird sang tentatively, then another and another until the trees were again filled with song. She sighed and lay back down. Tall Dancer's feet scraped on the porch. He stepped inside, leaving a trail of wood chips behind him.

"Why were the dogs barking?" she asked.

"I don't know," he said, shrugging his shirt over his head. Then he bent and pulled his war knife from a wooden box by their sleeping mat.

Alarmed, Cara sat up again. "What are you going to do with that?"

"Hope I don't have to use it." He rammed the shiny blade into the beaded sheath that hung from his waist.

"What aren't you telling me?" She put Alexei back in his carrier, closed her dress, and rose to her feet.

"Something is out there. The dogs know it. The birds know it. What ever it is, it's cautious." His voice held a note of apprehension.

"Could it be a bear?"

He shook his head. "I would have seen tracks."

Cara stared out the open door. New growth on the cedars, the birches and the aspens had turned the forest into a magical place. Light green fern fronds dotted the forest floor and spring flowers topped bramble thickets. But out there somewhere, something stalked them. She could feel it, too.

"You owe me the truth." She turned to face him and read the indecision in his eyes.

"I think someone is out there watching us. I haven't seen any tracks, but from the way the dogs are behaving I think they know."

Terror gripped Cara's throat. Someone out there knew everything they did, yet left no tracks.

"I'll get some wood," Tall Dancer said, throwing the last small piece into the fire. "From now on, I want you to stay close to the house." He turned to leave, then paused and kissed her gently, letting his lips linger on hers before he strode out the door.

Cara turned her attention to the baby. He slept peacefully, the black birth fuzz on his head thinning to make way for slick, shiny black hair.

Suddenly, the door burst open. Two big Tsimshian warriors stomped inside, dragging Tall Dancer between them. One of his legs was twisted at an odd angle and a trickle of blood ran down his face and neck. The men dropped him, and he crumpled to the floor. Cara clutched the baby to her chest, wavering between rushing to his side or protecting her child. Another figure pushed in between the two warriors.

"Father!" She clutched the baby tighter and stared at the short, bowlegged man who leered at her.

"Yes, Cara, it is I," Vlad Tarakanov answered.

He spoke rapidly in Russian and Cara had to strain to follow him. It had been a long time since she had spoken or heard her native tongue.

"Did you think you had seen the last of me?" He strutted around her, circling closer and closer. "I have come to take you home."

Cara's eyes narrowed. "Why did you come all this way for me, Father? Why did you do this to my husband?"

Vlad moved a step closer, tugging at the elaborate waistcoat that barely covered his protruding belly. A long coat of otter pelts hung from his shoulders and swept the floor. He removed his leather gloves one at a time and carefully folded and put them away before he spoke again.

"I was afraid, my dear, that the Kolosh"—he kicked at Tall Dancer—"might try to prevent your returning home with me."

His eyes swept her from foot to head and his face took on an expression Cara remembered too well. She swallowed and moved back a step.

"Put down the brat." Her father moved a step closer.

"No!" She moved back another step and felt her feet tangle in the raveled edges of the sleeping mat.

"Put down the child and come with me." He reached for her, but she jerked her arm away.

He dropped his hands to his sides and nodded to the two men towering by him. One grabbed her arms. The other wrenched the baby away.

"No!" she screamed, as the warrior held the infant aloft with one hand.

"One word," her father said in a low voice. "One word from me and he will dash the child to the floor and crack his head open as easily as I cracked this Kolosh's leg."

Cara glanced down at Tall Dancer, his leg twisted at a crazy angle behind him. She closed her eyes to shut out the picture of her baby's head crashing to the floor.

"I will take no bastard home to the tsar," her father said.

Cara looked from her father to the Tsimshian to Tall Dancer. His eyes were closed in either pain or oblivion. She couldn't tell which. She swung her gaze back to her father. He smiled at her. No, he leered, his sneer full of dark teeth.

"I will leave him with his father." She took the baby out of the warrior's hands, bent, and placed the infant next to Tall Dancer's chest. If she cooperated now, maybe she could escape and work her way back later. As she straightened, she silently prayed that after she was gone, Tall Dancer would somehow be able to look after the child.

Her father nodded. The braves stepped forward, each catching her by an arm and lifting her feet clear of the floor. She struggled against them until Vlad stepped forward and cuffed her across the face. The salty taste of blood filled her mouth.

Vlad narrowed his eyes and lowered his voice to just above a growl. "You will come with me. I have come a long way to fetch you back with me. I won't let a half-breed and a little Kolosh bastard stand in my way. If you don't come, I'll kill both of them." He pulled a pistol from his vest pocket and made a great show of wiping it clean before pointing it directly at Tall Dancer's forehead.

Cara knew he would do as he threatened. "I'll go with you. Leave them alone."

He smiled victoriously and slowly repocketed the weapon. Tugging his coat tighter around his shoulders, he turned in a whirl of material. "Bring her." He arrogantly threw the order over his shoulder as he started for the door.

"Wait," Cara cried as the men carried her toward the door. "Please let me have a few minutes with them."

"You have spent all the time in their company that you will," Vlad said as they crossed the porch and stepped down into the yard.

They set her on her feet and tied a thong around her wrists. Then, with a shove that sent her stumbling, the men forced her to walk in front of them. She stumbled along, trying to get a final look at the cabin. They made a turn and the cabin disappeared from sight.

They traveled by foot until dark, then made camp alongside the trail. All afternoon the two Tsimshians had not spoken a word. When they made camp, one stayed while the other went hunting for game. Vlad seated himself on a rock and pulled his fur coat closer around him. Cara shivered in the cold. The brisk ocean breeze cut through her even though a line of scrubby trees shielded them from the beach.

"How did you find me?" Cara asked.

Vlad smiled into the flames. "I have been looking for you since the night you left my ship. For a while I thought you had drowned."

Cara snorted in disgust. "I'm sure you were grief-stricken."

"A man hates to lose a valuable possession, even one as much trouble as you have been."

"I'm nobody's possession, least of all yours." Cara felt her anger growing and vowed not to let him see how angry he made her.

"You didn't object when that Kolosh savage dragged you out of the Tsimshian village at the end of his thong."

He smiled, and Cara knew her shock registered in her eyes.

"Oh, I didn't know right away. At first I could find no red-haired woman. No one had seen her. Then, some of my men . . . convinced Ska-out-lelt to trap sea otter pelts for us. In the course of our dealings, they mentioned a white slave who had stood off a Tsimshian chief and all his men. I inquired and found that this slave had red hair. I knew at once you had gotten yourself into another entanglement. But by the time I got to the village, you were gone."

He shifted his position and glanced up as the Tsimshian warrior held aloft a squirrel, then skinned it in one swift slash.

"It was hard tracking you after that. You and your rescuer simply disappeared into the forest. I went back to the business of buying pelts. Then, while trading up and down the coast for pelts, some of my men went ashore near Dry Bay for some fun and kidnapped two young girls. They told an unbelievable story about a red-haired slave while begging for their . . . virtue."

Cara felt as though a black cloud had crossed the sun. All

those blissful months she had spent with Marisha, her father had been right off shore.

"I returned, but you were gone, disappearing into the wilderness again."

Cara fought against the urge to grab up the roasted squirrel her father held out to her. He shrugged and popped the brown meat into his mouth.

"Don't you wonder how I found you in that cabin with the Kolosh?"

Cara stared over his head, trying not to see the grease that ran into the hair of his long mustache and dripped from his chin.

"Now that was a piece of work. You see"—he leaned forward and clasped his hands—"I was a bit late for the massacre. I was out in the Aleutians when the bloody Kolosh burned the fort, but I sailed as soon as I heard. A storm delayed me and it wasn't until a few weeks ago I arrived. Then some Kolosh approached my men about trading in the winter."

Cara's heart plunged.

"Now, that day"—he smiled and inched closer to her—"I was watching the edge of the forest with my glass." His smile widened. "What did I see? A red-haired woman hiding in the forest." He wagged a finger in her face. "If you had left that dye on your hair a few more weeks, I never would have been the wiser, never would have known it was you. But that mane of yours gave you away." He lifted her hair and let it fall through his fingers, then sat back with a satisfied look. "After that, it was easy."

Cara sidled further away. "Where are you taking me?"

"Home. We are going home to St. Petersburg with a hold full of pelts." He drank from a flask that he pulled out of his coat. "I will be wealthy and the tsar will be pleased."

"What part am I to have in this? I have no interest in your wealth, nor in the tsar."

He leaned toward her until she could smell his foul breath. "Your part in this is personal. There are many long, cold miles between here and Russia."

Chapter
Twenty-Two

They reached the site of Fort St. Michael just as the sun
sank into the silvery ocean. Its blackened ruins reared up out of
the rocky outcropping on which they sat, looming in silhouette
against the lavender sky. A ship with its lights ablaze bobbed
at anchor in the cove. One of the Tsimshian lit the end of a
branch and held it high. An answering wave came from the
ship and a small boat was lowered over the side.

A cool evening breeze, rich with ocean scents, ruffled Cara's
hair and brought gooseflesh to her arms. She closed her eyes
and pretended she was walking along the surf with Marisha,
gathering herring roe. She inhaled deeply and could almost
believe she was really there.

The deep swoosh of the boat beaching brought her back.
Her father stepped forward and spoke to the men standing
alongside with oars in their hands. They laughed at his comments and cast sidelong glances at her.

One of the Tsimshian men grasped her arm and helped her
into the small boat, then pushed her to the floor. Her father
joined them, and she found herself sitting between his knees.
As the men shoved the boat off the beach, then jumped in and

began to paddle, he caressed her hair. She recoiled at his touch, and a thousand searing memories flashed into her mind.

He allowed his hand to slide down her hair and onto her cheek. She sank her teeth into the back of his hand. He retaliated with a slap that flung her head to the side and resounded in the stillness. Then his hand resumed its journey down the strands of her hair and onto her cheek.

"I see I shall have to tame you all over again, my pet," he whispered into her ear.

The little boat scrubbed against the large ship. A rope ladder struck the water at their side with a splash. Vlad heaved her to her feet and placed her hands on the slippery ladder rungs. When she started to climb, he cupped both hands beneath her buttocks and shoved. The men on deck backed away and stood silent as she stumbled aboard.

She scanned the faces around her. Her father had taken on a large complement of Aleuts, who did some of his dirty work among the Kolosh. They eyed her with suspicion; the Russian sailors regarded her with a deep disrespect.

Vlad stepped aboard behind her. He grabbed her arm and piloted her through the door that led down into the bowels of the ship. At the end of the dark hall, he stopped and unlocked a door. He shoved her inside ahead of him, then locked the door behind them.

On a table in the center, a lamp's wavering flame filled the room with the strong odor of burning oil. A bunk with filthy covers occupied one corner. The rest of the room was bare.

"These will be your quarters for the voyage," he said as he turned down the lamp, making the room bleaker than before. "I suggest you do not venture out on your own. My men have not seen, much less touched, a white woman for a very long time, and I fear you would not fair well in their hands. But then again"—he rounded the table and moved closer—"you have been living with a savage for some time. Maybe you could teach these men a thing or two."

Cara recoiled as he reached out for her. "He's not a savage. He's more civilized than you."

Vlad's face darkened and his eyebrows knitted together. Cara could see the rage building in him, and she smiled to herself. The barb had struck home.

"It is best you forget the savage," he ground out between clenched teeth. "You will never see him again even if he lives." He turned on his heel and swept out of the room.

The lock clicked as he removed the key. His footsteps receded. Cara sat down on the bed and felt the ship rocking gently as it crossed the waves and headed out to sea. Each pitch of the hull was taking her further and further away from Tall Dancer.

Waves of nausea raced over Tall Dancer as he pushed himself into a sitting position. On the sleeping mat at his side, little Alexei's face was red and bunched into a frown as he wailed his discontent.

How long had he been out? Tall Dancer wondered, dropping his head back against the plank wall and waiting for the world to stop spinning. He tried to move his leg, then gritted his teeth against a fresh onslaught of pain.

The ashes in the firepit were cold and black. Hours must have passed. Outside the open door, low clouds hid the sun and the first sprinkles of rain fell.

The baby wailed louder, and a sense of hopelessness washed over Tall Dancer. How would he care for an infant? His leg was broken. What would he feed the boy now that his mother was gone?

The thought of Cara's abduction drove into his midsection. Cara was gone, and he could not follow. Rain would soon wipe out her tracks.

His thoughts spun. The baby came first. Only another woman could give him the milk he needed, and the nearest village was Talko's. Tall Dancer rolled over onto his stomach. The pain almost took his consciousness again as he inched his way through the door and to the woodpile. Rain pelted on his back and muddy ground stung his face as it slid up his nose and into his mouth. Stacked by the side of the pile of dead branches were long strips of wood hewn from the body of his boat. He swung his broken leg with his hands until it was wedged firmly between two large branches. Then he threw his weight backward. He heard a sharp snap, and his vision tunneled into a tiny black dot.

Rain on his face awoke him. He tied two of the slats of wood to each side of his leg with strips torn off his shirt. Alexei was crying at full volume by the time he inched back to the cabin. He placed the screaming infant on a soft sealskin and rolled him into a bundle. Clamping the knot with his teeth, he dragged the child and himself out of the cabin.

The soft rain had become a pelting torrent. Fog rolled in and the clouds looked low enough to touch. Reaching the pile of wood again, he grabbed a branch and hauled himself to his feet. With the fork of the branch wedged firmly underneath his arm, he hobbled toward his partly finished canoe, now floating lopsided in the cove.

He lowered the baby into the bottom, where he was cushioned by a deep layer of shavings. Tall Dancer tossed his crutch in, then heaved himself into the bottom of the boat. The force of his body drove the canoe backward into the cove.

He reached out and clutched Alexei, who was now quiet with fear. The boat rocked precariously, then smoothed out and floated.

Tall Dancer pushed himself into a sitting position, sank a carved oar into the water, and propelled them along. The canoe skimmed through the water. If only he could make it to Talko's village.

The storm settled into a squall. Wind tore at the water, stripping mist from the tops of waves. The canoe rocked, listing to the thicker side. Tall Dancer willed himself to ignore the pain as each stroke of the paddle drove his broken leg against the bow of the boat.

Finally, as dusk was falling, he turned the boat into the mouth of the cove that ended at Talko's village. He put down the paddle and eased himself into the bottom. If he could just close his eyes for a few moments, he thought, dragging the baby closer.

Cara clung to the sides of her bed as the ship tossed and pitched in the storm-whipped sea. She had lain in the dark for days, too ill to get up and light the lamp. Vlad brought her an occasional greasy meal, which she threw back up if she got the first bite down at all.

The floor of the cabin was rapidly filling with water that sloshed from one side of the room to the other with the motion of the ship. She had lost count of the number of days she had been aboard. Each dark, lonely day melted into the next.

Only the sounds of boots on the boards over her head gave any indication anyone else existed in her miserable world. At night she still reached for Tall Dancer, but her fingers met only rough, cold boards. At times she thought she heard Alexei crying, then realized it was only the screeching of gulls over the ship.

Days later, the storm abated. The sea calmed, and so did Cara's stomach. A key rattled and her door swung open. Her father tossed some greasy clothes at her.

"Put these on," he said shortly.

Cara waited for him to leave. When he didn't, she shrugged and dressed quickly, too weak to care. As she finished with the shirt, he moved toward her and caught her arm in a viselike grip.

"I want to show you something," he said as he hauled her along behind him up the steps. The screeching of gulls met her as blinding light poured into the dark shaft when he opened the door. She squeezed her eyes shut. Her father pulled her onto the deck and she opened her eyes. Landmasses dotted the horizon and played hide-and-seek with a thick fog that rolled across the water. She breathed in the mingled scents of ocean and land.

The sensation of eyes on the back of her head made her turn. The crew was staring at her with open mouths. She looked down at the clothes that clung indecently to her body, then to her father. He, too, was staring, but his gaze held a menace that chilled her skin. He had left her alone until now, probably because she was so ill. Now, with fair weather that did not need his hand on the wheel, he would soon come to her.

She felt the ship swing about, and she moved to the railing. The dotted horizon was now a constant line, and one landmass loomed large. The ship nosed its way into a wide bay.

On each side of them, thick cedar forests grew down to the edge of the water. Dark, volcanic mountains reared out of the sea, crowned by thick clouds obscuring their tops. Herds of sea lion, sea otter, and fur seals frolicked amid the floating patches of seaweed, oblivious to the fact their very existence would soon be threatened.

In the masses of seaweed, sea otters floated on their backs, patiently cracking open shellfish with rocks, unaware of the ship that skimmed close to them. He father had also seen the otter, for he had released his grip and moved to the rail to stare hungrily at the little animals.

As the ship swung close to land, people emerged from the forest. Men, women, and children ran to the surf's edge and waved pelts and carved masks at the ship. Cara's heart sank. Little did they know that the Russian ship came not to trade but to take. Some of the crew hung over the side, shouting obscenities at the women, who smiled back in innocence.

They continued down the cove until they slowed and stopped in front of a peaceful village. The familiar scent of smoked salmon brought back vivid, tender memories. Plank houses surrounded the cove, their porches opening out at the water's edge.

"Man the cannon," her father boomed. His sailors grunted and pushed until the muzzles of the big iron guns were aimed directly at the chief's house. The crowd on the beach scattered. Women screamed and ran for the forest, jerking their children behind them. The men followed, looking back over their shoulders.

Small canoes filled with Aleuts were lowered over the side

of the ship. Swiftly, the men rowed to shore and jumped out
when they scraped on the beach. They disappeared into the
houses. Piercing screams and throaty cries rang out. Minutes
later the men emerged, their arms laden with pelts. They quickly
rowed back to the ship under a hail of arrows that fell into the
water behind them. Hoisted on board, they cast their loads
down at her father's feet.

He turned slowly, looked at her for a long time, then reached
down and jerked out of the pile a sealskin.

"Worthless trash," he said, then flung the silky pelt over
the side. "Otter fur." He picked up a skin and rubbed it against
his cheek. "This one will bring many rubles."

He laughed and the sound slithered down her spine. She
leaned over the rail and watched the sealskin sink slowly below
the surface, mentally counting the hours that had gone into the
skinning, scraping, and preserving of the hide.

The men returned to the village again. This time the village
men had mounted an attack. They waited in the edge of the trees,
then leaped out and grabbed the Aleuts. Her father watched the
struggle for a few moments, then raised his hand. One of the
cannon barked and belched a cloud of black smoke. The nearest
house exploded in a hail of debris. The Tlingit men broke off
the attack and ran for the forest.

"Run now, you bastards!" he shouted at the retreating men.
Another cannon fired and another house exploded. Throwing
his head back, he laughed loud and long as, one after another,
the houses were destroyed.

An acrid black cloud surrounded the ship and the scent of
sulfur was sharp. Cara coughed and tears ran down her face.
Did his cruelty know no bounds? She turned to move toward
the steps that led down into the ship, but he caught her arm.

"No, you don't. You'll stay here and watch, just like you
did when the savages murdered the good people at Fort St.
Michael. You didn't have any tears then, did you?"

Cara tried to wrench away, but he held a handful of hair.
The ship drew up anchor and slowly turned until Cara could
no longer see the Tlingit people scrambling over their destroyed

village. They sailed out of the mouth of the cove into a brilliant sunset. Cara stood against the rail, numb, and watched the orange orb sink slowly into the gray sea, wishing for a moment she could so easily ease her own torment. Yet in the north, clouds were gathering, forming a low black line that hugged the surface of the ocean.

Tall Dancer felt the canoe bump and then scrape against something in the water. He opened his eyes. The world was a blur, and his pain was intense. He pulled the baby closer and opened the sealskin wrap. Alexei's skin was translucent, but his chest rose and fell.

Weak with relief, Tall Dancer lay back down in the bottom. All he had to give the baby was a little water in a nipple made of supple sealskin. He had lost count of how many days they had drifted after his fever set in. How long had it been since either of them had eaten? One, maybe two days? No, longer than that.

Tall Dancer frowned and rose on his elbows to peep again over the side. Was he at Talko's village? In front of him was a looming wall of forest where the village should have been. He rubbed his hand over his face. When had he turned into the cove? He couldn't remember. Could this be the wrong cove? Pushing himself a little higher, Tall Dancer looked around. There was no sign of a village.

He struggled to sit up and picked up the paddle. There was nothing to do but go on and try to find a village—if not Talko's, then another. Fear began to prick his tortured brain. What if they were to happen on some other village, a village belonging to a warring clan—or, worse, a Tsimshian village?

He tried to plot out in his mind where the surrounding villages lay, but his thoughts were fuzzy. As the canoe moved along, he scooped water out of the cove and splashed his face.

The sky above was gray, threatening rain again. He raised the edge of the pelt that covered the baby carrier. Alexei was asleep, but not for long. Soon he'd be hungry again.

He paddled the boat out of the cove and through the breakers without seeing anyone else. Where was the cove? he asked himself, scanning the coastline. It looked all the same. Was he still in Tlingit territory? Or had they drifted into danger from the Tsimshians? They could be captured as slaves and Alexei would surely die.

Indecision struck him. He slowed his paddle strokes and let the boat drift. Maybe he should hide in a tiny finger of a hidden cove and wait until he saw someone. He leaned forward and pain shot up his leg and through his chest. He heard his own groan and felt the dull thud of the back of his head striking the bottom of the boat. Then darkness closed in around him.

"Oh, Lordy!"

The words popped Tall Dancer's eyes open. Was he dreaming? Where was he that someone spoke so?

The baby began to cry. He reached over to pull him closer and felt only empty space. He tried to think, but thought came slowly, stumbling and hesitating. Why couldn't he remember where he was?

"Come here and take this baby," the voice said again, this time with a ring of familiarity.

He tried to open his eyes, but they were so heavy. Too heavy. Hands slipped under his arms. He thrashed out, struck something, and someone yelped. More hands joined the first and lifted him up, then laid him down in luxurious softness. He opened his eyes a crack. A familiar face loomed over him.

"Claude." He said the name in his mind. His lips formed the words, but no sound came out. Cool, sweet water dripped onto his lips. He licked at the drops and strained for more.

"You can't have any more right now, Tall Dancer. It'll make you sick, it will. Take him to Talko's house and hurry."

Tall Dancer forced his eyes open wide. Ahead a woman was hurrying along with Alexei clasped in her arms. A broad-shouldered man stood at Tall Dancer's feet, another at his head.

They picked up the corners of the bear fur he lay in and lifted him, then entered the forest at a trot.

He forced his eyes to stay open and watched the bare branches rush by overhead. The familiar smell of smoke and burning fat curled though his thoughts as he raised his head to look around. His bearers were carrying him through a doorway guarded by a wide-mouthed salmon. They laid him by a fire so warm and inviting he wanted to crawl into the embers.

"How did he get here?" a cracked voice asked. "Send for Silver Eyes." A cold, bony hand closed over Tall Dancer's forehead. Talko's weathered face bent low over him. "How were you injured, my son?"

"*Promyshlenniki.*" The word came out as a rasp. "The baby?"

"The baby is fine. He is hungry."

Alexei's bundle was shoved into his arms. He pulled back the cover and stared into the baby's face. His dark eyes were wide and darting from side to side.

"Here. Let me have him." Silver Eyes reached down and took the baby.

Tall Dancer stared at the woman he recognized as Cara's friend.

"I thought you were dead," he said as she hugged the baby close. "Almost everyone died from smallpox."

"No," she said shaking her head. "My husband and I were at a potlatch when the sickness struck the village. My parents died, and my in-laws. Now we live here." She held up the baby and rubbed his nose against hers. "He is hungry. I will feed him. I have plenty of milk."

He watched as she pulled aside the long collar that covered her milk-engorged breasts. Alexei began to suckle eagerly.

"He is Cara's child?" she asked, caressing the baby's silky hair.

"Yes, hers and mine."

Silver Eyes smiled briefly, then frowned and knitted her brows. "Is she dead?"

Tall Dancer let his head fall back and closed his eyes. The word rattled around in his brain like a rock. "I don't know."

It was late in the afternoon when Cara felt the rhythm of the sea become erratic. Items slid around the cabin and her footing became unsure. She struggled to the door, pushed on it and found it unlocked.

He must think I won't try to escape. She pushed the door open and crept out into the hall. The ship lurched, throwing her against the wall.

Stretching out both arms to steady herself, she climbed the steps and pushed open the door to the deck above, catching her breath at what she saw.

Above them the sky boiled with low dark clouds. The wind tore at sails that snapped and fluttered, the masts bending under the wind's force. Her father and his men were drenched by waves that rose high over the side of the ship, then crashed down on deck with a roar. He had lashed himself to the wheel and fought the circle of wood with both hands while shouting orders that were snatched away by the wind.

From his scattered words, Cara determined they were dangerously close to shore, looking for a party of hunters he had dropped off earlier in the season.

A wall of water poured over the side, across the deck, and straight for Cara. She grabbed at the door with both hands as the wave swept her feet from under her and continued down the steps to add to the rising water below.

A sickening crack filled the air. The top of the center mast split and the sailcloth ripped. Cara stood frozen in place as the huge beam spiraled down, part of the sail fluttering behind it. Directly beneath stood her father's first mate. Cara screamed at him. He looked slowly upward in time to see the mast just before it pinned him to the deck.

She started forward, but the ship lurched and everyone standing was thrown down. The port side of the ship rose up and Cara fell and slid toward the opposite railing. She grabbed at the decking as she moved, splinters digging under her nails as she fought for a grip.

She struck the rail with a thud and wrapped her arms around it. Glancing back toward the wheel, she saw a huge crack split the deck in two. The gap between the two halves widened. The last time she saw her father, he was devoured by a looming wave.

She glanced around and found no one sharing this piece of the ship with her. Everyone must have been flung overboard. Another wave reared high. Cara shut her eyes and saw the image of Tall Dancer and Alexei.

The icy water snatched her breath as she plunged beneath the surface. Salt water burned her nose. The hard surface of a rock scraped her skin as the wave slammed her against it.

Suddenly, her head was above water. She gasped a breath, then was driven under again, tumbling over and over. When the wave abated, her fingers caught a notch on the rock. She heaved herself up, scrambling and digging into the stone with raw fingers that the salt water tormented.

She clambered over boulder after boulder while the surging sea snapped at her heels. Some sense told her she was heading for shore, but in the darkness of the storm, she could see nothing.

The rocks cut her knees and gouged her legs. When she thought she could go no farther, her bare toes dug into sand. With her last ounce of strength, she pulled herself out of the jaws of the sea and lay on the shore, her cheek pressed against the damp ground. Behind her the ocean roared its disappointment. Coughing and sputtering, she tried to raise her head, but she was too tired.

The chirping of beach birds awoke her. Sand crunched between her teeth. She spat and pushed herself up on her hands. The sun was high in the sky, but offered no warmth. There was no sign of the vicious storm of last night, only a beach littered with debris. Cara shivered and rolled over onto her back. The sky above was bright blue, but she was so cold her feet were numb. Lifting her head, she looked around her. The beach was long and deserted, made more ominous by the dense cedars crowding to the edge of the surf. She turned over and crawled further from the waves that lapped over her feet.

Shielding her eyes against the sun, she turned to where a snowcapped mountain dominated the sky behind the forest. A brisk ocean wind cut straight through her ragged clothes. Barefoot, she stumbled along, dodging pieces of wood washing ashore. Taking stock of where she was, she began moving south, down the beach. She had to come to a village sooner or later, she told herself.

Dragging her feet from fatigue, Cara pushed herself on until she saw a still form in the distance lying on the rocky sand. As she got closer, she recognized the first mate and began to run.

Reaching his still body, she caught his shirt and turned him over. A shaft of splintered wood stuck out of his chest. The wound was blue and puckered, with no blood oozing from it. His eyes were fixed, staring straight up. She let his head drop back onto the sand and stumbled backward, covering her mouth as she gagged.

Evening was upon her before she realized it. The fiery ball of the sun sank into the ocean and darkness soon followed, bathing the beach in hues of lavender. Cara shivered against the damp evening breeze and searched the rocks for refuge. Eroded from the stone by centuries of tides and storms, the mouth of a cave appeared. She clambered over boulders and crawled inside, where the noise of the surf was muffled. Faint light illuminated walls covered with etchings.

At least it was dry and out of the chilling wind, she decided, raking up a pile of dry seaweed scattered about on the cave floor. As she lay down on the fragrant stems, she vaguely wondered if the mouth of the cave was above the tide. She knew she should make sure, but fatigue bade her to stay. Outside, the surf pounded a steady lullaby and she felt her eyelids droop.

Chapter
Twenty-Three

The roar of the wind and the sea awoke Cara at daylight the next morning. Another storm churned just off shore, again threatening to devour the coastline. She sat up and watched as streaks of lightning stabbed into the ocean. She had to move inland. Here she was too vulnerable to the weather's tantrums. Somewhere to the south was Talko's village. Surely Tall Dancer would have gone there, she thought, pushing the possibility of his death from her mind.

Reluctantly, she crawled out of the cave and into the wind that churned the ocean to foam and blew a fine layer of moisture all over her. The beach looked unending, stretching away from her until it passed from sight into a foggy mist. With effort, she commanded one foot to step in front of the other while she watched the surf for washed up roe or edible seaweed.

With the approach of night, the winds settled into a mournful howl that made hair on the back of her neck stand up. She had been walking for hours, aimlessly following the shoreline despite her vows to turn inland. At times, the ocean almost seemed a friend, someone who walked at her side, constantly whispering in her ear. At other times it was a beast ready to spring.

She stumbled across something in the dusk and sprawled into the damp sand. Pushing herself up, she looked behind her. A body lay beside a blackened firepit of stones. She scrambled to her knees and crawled over to investigate. The stench made her recoil.

Holding her nose, she bent over for a closer look. The man was wrapped in a long fur coat and the top of his head was missing. Cara scurried backward, tripped, and fell again. Another body lay beneath her knees.

A scream rose into her throat, but she clamped her teeth shut and scrambled to her feet. More scalped bodies lay scattered about what had been a camp on the edge of a bay. Belongings and ruined pelts lay all about.

These were the men her father had been looking for the night of the storm, she realized. The Tlingit had found them first.

The waning light offered little help as she began to rummage through the camp for some remnants of food left behind by the attackers. She found nothing save the men's fur coats, overlooked by Tlingit warriors more interested in the pelts the men had hoped to transport back to St. Petersburg.

She approached the man she had stumbled over. Catching his sleeve, Cara tugged until his stiff arm slid out. Then she pulled on the other side and hauled the garment from beneath the body. Cara held it to her nose and sniffed. Only a faint odor of death clung to the fur. She slipped into the coat, which dragged on the ground but was warm. Shoving up the sleeves, she continued her search.

The Tlingits had stripped every man, and Cara despaired of finding anything useful. Then she spotted a knife sheath strapped to the swollen leg of one of the men. Cara pulled the knife and sliced through the strap that held the sheath to the dead man's leg. Once the knife and sheath were free, she took a leather belt off another man and strapped the knife to her waist.

Hunger and exhaustion took its toll all at once and she sat

down amidst the dead bodies. With her back to a large stone, she watched fog creep ashore, whipped into being by the roiling sea.

Her stomach rumbled, and she remembered summer meals on the beach with Marisha of herring roe and parsnips from the forest. She closed her eyes and could almost taste the delicacy. But with the surf pounding, there would be no roe today. Her eyes drooped, and she snuggled down into the coat, thankful for its warmth.

Cara was awakened by a strange silence. She cracked open an eye and saw the gentle sway of the sea. A blue sky hovered over her. The storm was gone. She struggled to her feet beneath the weight of the coat.

The camp was much larger than she had thought last night. Six more bodies lay closer to the forest. She rummaged through their belongings and found pants and shirts. Pushing nagging thoughts from her mind, Cara mechanically stripped the men of anything usable and piled the finds near the edge of the bay.

When she had finished, she sat down and wondered what to do next. How far from home was she? Nothing looked familiar, not even the mountain towering behind her. On the other side of the bay, a field of ice sparkled like diamonds in the sun.

She stared openmouthed. The slab of ice poured out from between two mountain peaks and ran like a river to the sea, where it ended in sharp cliffs. This was the glacier she had heard stories about, a slab of solid ice. As wondrous as the sight was, it stood between her and home.

Suddenly weary, Cara sat down on a rock and closed her eyes while the bright sunlight warmed her back. At her feet a small tidal pool moved in whirlpools from fish trapped by the outgoing tide.

Quickly, she started a fire, then removed her coat and pants and waded out into the pool wearing only a tattered shirt. A movement caught her eye. Her hands shot out and closed around an unsuspecting fish and tossed him onto the beach. The fish flopped, then lay still.

Remembering how she had seen Marisha do this many times,

Cara paused and waited again for a fish to swim close. A soft tail swept her hands. She grabbed at it and tossed it ashore, then waded out.

By the time she had dressed again, she was shivering from the cold. She poked a green limb through the fish and held it over the fire. Capturing the fish had been easy. Out of superstition, she performed the Tlingit rite, offering the first fish in thanks for her catch.

The food warmed her through and as she sat by the fire, a thought popped into her head. A boat! The hunters must have had a canoe. She jumped to her feet and scanned the shore of the bay. There, a good distance away, a clump of willows bent low over the water. Beneath the limbs, the outline of a canoe bobbed in the water.

Cara pulled the boat from under the willows and saw it bore the marks of the Whale clan, a clan she knew lived far to the north of Tall Dancer's village. She stepped in and paddled the boat to the point of land that separated the bay from the ocean. There she loaded in her fur coats and confiscated supplies.

Beyond the beach, waves rose up, then gently rushed to shore and slapped a kiss on the land. Cara pushed the boat out into the foam, then scrambled inside. She picked up an oar and began to paddle.

The pointed front rose and fell as waves moved beneath it. Her palms sweated and her heart thumped as she struggled to keep the boat upright while trying to envision Little Beaver expertly guiding his boat through breaking waves for hunts.

Only when she was afloat on the calm ocean did she release her grip on the oar and begin to row. The muscles in her shoulders and arms protested with each motion. But the wind was still, and the sun's warmth eased the soreness.

To her left, a sheer wall of ice towered over her head as she hugged the coastline. Fog rose from the water when stirred by an ocean breeze. Occasionally, chunks of ice broke off and crashed into the water, making waves that rocked the boat. But she dared not go further out into the ocean, envisioning the huge bodies of beached killer whales.

A loud crack made her jump, and she almost dropped the oar. A huge chunk of ice rumbled and shivered, then slid to its death into the ocean. Cara began to paddle furiously. Waves were speeding toward her, bearing on their crests chunks of ice large enough to smash the canoe to bits.

Closer and closer the swells came. She pointed the bow of the boat into the waves rapidly overcoming her, but still the surges buffeted her like a leaf on the water. She lost her balance, dropped the oar, and grabbed the canoe's sides.

Two waves passed successfully, then another loomed over her. Higher and higher it loomed, then crashed down on top of her. Tumbling and churning, the turbulent water pulled her to the bottom.

Her clothes twisted around her and the salty water stung her eyes and mouth. She couldn't tell if she was right side up or upside down, but she began to swim. Soon her head cleared the water. She coughed and choked. The cold of the water numbed her.

A large piece of ice bobbed alongside her. Beside it floated one of the fur coats. Cara grabbed the garment, flung it over the ice and heaved herself half up on it. Although the coat shielded her, a numbness crept into her limbs as she paddled for the distant shore.

The ice floe bobbed in the surf, and Cara crawled through the shallow water to shore. Her teeth chattering and her body shaking, she pulled herself along by clawing the sand until it sliced the skin under her nails. When she tried to move her legs, they did not respond. She had to find warmth or die.

A few yards away was the forest. She forced herself to crawl into it and used the first tree to help her stand.

Chunks of rosin clung to woodpecker holes in the bark. She dug several pieces out and held them in her hand until they gave off a pungent scent. Moss clung to the bark of the cedars and she pulled some away.

Then she picked up two stones, dug out an impression in the sand, and filled it with small sticks and dried needles. On top of that she placed the moss and on the very top the rosin.

Placing one stone close to the rosin, she struck the other against it. An orange spark flew, but missed the tinder. She tried again and missed the stone altogether.

Her hands trembled, and her clothes were growing colder. She closed her eyes and raised a prayer to the Spirit Above. Then she struck the stones together again.

A spark flew out, fell into the tinder, and a tiny tendril of smoke curled upward. A flame burst to life, sizzling on the rosin. Cara placed more needles and sticks on the flame until it ignited the firewood underneath.

Holding out her hands to the feeble flames, she sighed at the welcome warmth. When the sand was warm beneath the wood, she removed her clothes and gasped as the cold air hit her skin. Protected by the pelt's natural oil, the otter skin coat had repelled some water and was not quite so wet. She wrapped up in it and held her clothes out to the fire on a stick. By the time night fell, her clothes were dry and she was hungry. Loath to leave the fire, she curled up instead by the pit and slept.

Cara's eyes popped open and she lay still, wondering what had awakened her. The fire crackled and the waves slapped gently on the beach. Sounds from the forest behind her were magnified. The lonely hoot of an owl made the hair on her neck stand on end.

A sharp crack split the night, then the ensuing crash of falling ice. She smiled and snuggled deeper into the fur. Must have been the glacier, she told herself.

But as she was drifting off to sleep, a soft crunch woke her again. She was not alone.

Raising up on her elbow, Cara squinted to see down the beach beyond the glow of the fire. Something moved, something too large for an otter or a sea bird. Reaching for the knife at her side, she rose to her feet and crouched. An owl hooted from the forest again. Knowing she was at a disadvantage because of the firelight, she kicked sand over the precious flames. The damp cold of night wasted no time creeping into her clothes.

Before she could react, a gloved hand clamped over her

mouth. She sank her teeth into the grimy taste of leather. Russian curses filled the air.

Her attacker loosened his grip. With all her strength, she swung the knife behind her and felt the blade slide into flesh.

He let her go, fell down and grabbed his knee.

"Father!" she exclaimed, catching a glimpse of his face wrapped in fur.

"I'm not your father, you bitch." He struggled to his feet while a widening pool of red grew across his pants leg. "I found your mother pregnant and abandoned in an alley in St. Petersburg."

They circled each other, Cara with the knife in her hand. Vlad clasped one hand to his bleeding knee.

"I took her into my house and let her live there until her baby was born—in return for certain favors, or course." He grinned at her, and Cara felt gooseflesh rise up on her back.

He released his injured knee and hopped forward a step. "Unfortunately, she died in childbirth, and I was left with you."

Limping and leaving a red trail in the snow, he again circled her, his arms spread wide as though to engulf her. "I tried to give you away, but no one wanted you. My housekeeper raised you. One day I came back from sea, and you were a beauty." He pushed back the fur hood from his face and grinned at her.

"As you got older, I found out you had inherited some of your mother's talents."

The events of her life flashed before her eyes. Long forgotten memories rose. Cara shook her head to clear it.

Things made sense now. She had wondered why there were no pictures of her mother in the house, no clothes or other mementos of a lifetime. Images of the acts she'd been forced to perform with this man when she was barely thirteen rushed back, and she reeled with the reality.

"How did you get here? I thought . . ."

"Thought I was dead?" He laughed hoarsely. "No, I survived the storm. Only I washed up a little farther up the coast than you. I've been following you ever since." He lunged, catching her by the shoulders. "So you thought you would escape me again. Return to the Kolosh, is that what you want to do? You belong to me, and you will never be free of the obligation you owe me! For all those years I tended you and fed you and your mother, you owe me—and I intend to collect . . . in full."

Cara drew away in revulsion at the yellow teeth so close to her face. "Let me go. Return to Russia. I'm sure there are women anxious for the company of another man grown rich in *Aliaska*."

"Many of them, I'm sure. But, you see, it's *you* I want." He brought his face closer. "You I've always wanted."

Cara stepped backward. Dry sand shot out from under her feet, and she tumbled down. He pinioned her to the ground with his weight. Even in the dim light, she could see him leering at her, see the same light in his eyes she had seen when she was a child.

Rage took over. As he ceased struggling with her and began to nuzzle her neck, Cara brought the knife up and slashed his arm. Howling in anguish, he rolled to one side, and Cara sprang to her feet and began to run without regard to direction. When her feet crunched in the snow she stopped, realizing she was on the glacier.

All around her the ice gave off an eerie glow, reflecting the feeble starlight. She looked behind her and saw Vlad just moving onto the ice. Only leather moccasins separated her from the ice, while he wore boots designed to grip the deck of a ship.

As she turned to run, he caught the back of her coat and spun her around to face him. He clasped his arms around her and hauled her against him.

"You'll not get away so easily this time."

He leaned forward and Cara looked back over her shoulder. A chasm in the ice yawned inches from their feet. Another step and they'd plunge to their deaths. She faced Vlad Tarakanov and looked him directly in the eyes. Death here would be better than submitting to him ever again, but she wanted to take him with her, to see the look on his face as he plunged into the bottomless crack in the ice.

He took another step. Cara stumbled back, her heels hanging over the edge of the crevice. He stepped again. Surprise replaced his leer as he stepped out into space. He clung to Cara as he fell and she felt herself plunge backward.

Down they tumbled.

Suddenly, Cara was brought up sharply. The bottom of her coat was caught on a branch trapped in the ice. Vlad's hands gripped the tail of the coat, and tried to climb it hand over hand, but his gloves slipped on the slick otter fur.

Inch by inch, he slipped backward. For an instant, their eyes locked. Then his hands slipped off and he spiraled downward to a silent death.

Cara waited for the thud when he hit or a scream for mercy, but there was no sound—only the gentle, faint groan of the ice as it swallowed him.

Over her head, the surface of the crack was less than a foot away. She reached out her hand, but her fingers barely touched a large branch. She glanced up to where her coat was caught tightly, then began to move her legs, trying to swing over to the branch. The limb groaned when she moved, but she shoved against the side of the wall again. Her fingers closed around the limb. As she swung her other arm over, her coat gave away and she dropped, but caught by her hands.

She climbed hand over hand until her fingers dug into the snow above. Clawing with her fingers and pushing with her feet, she scrambled out of the crevice and sprawled on the ice. Her breath came in gasps as she pressed her cheek into the snow.

Rolling onto her back, she looked up at the stars, wondering why she felt nothing—not joy, not sorrow, just numbness.

After a bit, cold crept into her and she dragged herself to her feet and back to the fire. Uncovering the embers, she found a few still alive and fed them with rosin and bits of wood until, again, she had a bright fire. His words had left her numb. He

was not her father. All the guilt she had borne all these years
was lifted. She was not of his blood.

A dark form bobbed in the rushing surf. Her canoe tumbled
ashore, battered but usable. Again, unseen powers had provided.
The canoe would carry her home, home to her husband and
child.

Tall Dancer blinked against the haze that clouded his eyes.
People moved slowly around him, their faces hovering over
him for an instant and then disappearing. He felt as if he were
swimming in deep water, trying to reach the surface that was
just out of reach.

"Alexei?" Tall Dancer heard a voice say. Had he spoken?
He blinked again and the vision cleared. A woman stood over
him, a beautiful woman with long hair. "Cara?"

"No, it is not Cara. I am here. Silver Eyes."

He rubbed his eyes and the vision cleared more. Silver Eyes
opened her dress. At her breast, Alexei nursed hungrily alongside another tiny brown baby.

"My son," she said proudly, and pulled her dress closed.

The smell of roasting rabbit swirled around her and his mouth
watered.

"Are you hungry?" she asked.

His stomach rumbled and he nodded. She stepped forward
and laid Alexei on a blanket at his side, then left. Tall Dancer
turned his head. The baby waved both feet in the air and
crammed a fist in his mouth. Tall Dancer offered his finger and
the baby eagerly grabbed it and hung on. Tears stung the back
of his eyes as he saw the glint of red in the baby's dark hair.

"Where is Cara?" Silver Eyes asked, sitting down beside
him. She held a basket with steam rising from it.

"She's gone. Her father came back and took her away with
him."

Silver Eyes frowned. "He is bad?"

"Yes. Very bad."

''He is one of the men who rob our villages and steal our pelts?''

''Yes.''

She raised his head and tipped the basket so a thin soup ran into his mouth.

''I have to find her.'' Tall Dancer let his head fall back and swallowed the delicious broth, thinking rabbit soup had never tasted so good. ''How long have I been here?''

''Long time,'' she answered, raising his head again.

''I have to get up and find her,'' he said between gulps. As he struggled to sit upright, a sharp pain seared through him. He grabbed his knee and fell back against the soft furs that had cushioned his frustration for weeks now.

She shook her head and shoved his shoulders flat on the mat. ''You cannot go. Your leg is broken and your fever has been high. The shaman says you have a bad spirit within you that must be removed.''

''I don't have time for bad spirits. I have to find Cara.'' He tried to sit again. A sharp pain shot through him and he heard his own agonized scream.

The further south Cara traveled, the more signs she saw of movements of large numbers of Tlingit. Often she had to hide in the brush to avoid being seen by groups of warriors painted for war. She became more cautious in her travels. By day she stayed close to the tree line, and by night she slept without the warmth of a fire, deep in a tangle of vines or brambles.

The appearance of familiar territory took her by surprise. As she paddled her battered canoe around an island, suddenly before her was the northern border of Tall Dancer's clan. Stretched out before her was the beach where she and Marisha had dined on herring roe and seaweed and where she and Tall Dancer had made love.

She paddled until she reached the gentle cove that had protected the village from the sea. All that remained of the magnificent long houses were blackened skeletons, their charred remains clawing for the sky. She shivered, trying to fend off a rising sense of hopelessness.

She scanned what was left of the village and closed her eyes, peopling it once again with the happy faces she remembered. Then she turned her canoe toward the ocean and paddled out of the cove, leaving both it and her memories behind.

Perhaps Tall Dancer had somehow managed to save himself and the baby. Perhaps he had not been injured as severely as she thought. With each stroke of the paddle, Cara recited these things to herself, desperately confident that with enough repetition she could make them true.

Tall Dancer's cabin was deserted. Vines had grown up through the plank floor, possessively twining themselves around the things she had left behind. There were the baskets she and Tall Dancer had made, and, in the corner, the remains of their sleeping mat. Everything looked exactly the same as she had left it the morning her father had stolen her away. Tall Dancer had not entered the house again. That left two possibilities.

Cara glanced around the room, fear lacing itself around her throat. But there was no small body, no tiny skeleton. Allowing herself one tiny sigh of relief, she searched the area surrounding the house and, again, found nothing.

As she stood by the edge of the stream, she noticed the thick mat of cedar shavings where Tall Dancer had been carving out his canoe. Her gaze darted back to the water. The canoe was gone. Hope bloomed within her. The next closest village was Talko's.

She stood on the edge of the forest for a moment, eyes closed, trying to remember how Tall Dancer had led them back here. Landmarks passed before her mind's eye.

She plunged into the wall of trees.

The sounds of the village were like music carried on a soft breeze. Cara squatted in a thicket of brambles and listened to all the sounds she had learned to equate with happiness. Children squealed and ran close by, their tiny feet beating an uneven staccato on the earth. Somewhere voices were raised in good-natured arguing, and somewhere, deep within the village, a baby's cry was background to it all.

Some instinct within her stirred, drawing her to that cry. Casting aside the tiny voice that warned caution for her own safety, Cara stepped out of the tangle and headed for the village, following a well-trodden path.

"Promyshlenniki!" The cry went up from close by, but she paid the voice no heed. Her only thought was to get to Alexei and Tall Dancer, if they were here. If they weren't, then life held little purpose.

Hands grabbed her, pinning her arms to her sides, but she refused to resist, allowing her captors to bear her to the center of the village. She scanned the crowd that quickly formed, but there were no familiar faces.

The crowd suddenly quieted as if a hand had passed over them, and Talko pushed his way through the throng on short, trembling legs.

"Release her," he ordered in a voice trembling from age. "This is the woman who helped return my copper."

The crowd erupted, their words quick and unintelligible. She caught only bits and snatches of the words, but she recognized Tall Dancer's name.

"Tall Dancer. Is he here?" She grabbed Talko's arms but someone wrenched her away, spinning her around before she could hear his answer.

Again, she was born away by urgent hands, carried forward by an ocean of people. They steered her toward a plank house.

The darkness blinded her as she stumbled inside. Women cooking at the firepit stopped what they were doing and stared. A blanket door opened to a compartment on an upper room and a young woman stepped out, a baby in her arms. Tall Dancer stepped out behind her.

He'd taken another wife. Reality slammed into her, whisking away the last of her hopes. He'd assumed her dead or gone and followed the way of his people, a hard decision that put the good of the village first. Alexei needed a mother and Tall

Dancer needed a wife. So many had died that Talko would have urged him to remarry as soon as possible and begin a new family. But even logic could not stop the pain that arced through her, the feeling of utter worthlessness.

Tall Dancer started down the benches, his gait limping and stiff and his leg maneuvering at an odd angle. The woman followed close behind, one hand on his shoulder to steady him. Cara wasn't sure she could bear to have him so close and not be able to touch him. But she wanted to hold Alexei. He was her son and she intended to have him with her, she decided suddenly, even if she had to fight the whole village to take him away with her.

Tall Dancer stopped in front of her. His eyes teared and his lips moved, but no sound emerged. For a moment Cara wondered if his injuries had been worse than she knew. Then he moved forward and enveloped her in his arms.

"I didn't think I'd ever see you again," he mumbled into her hair. "How did you escape?"

"The ship wrecked in a storm north of here."

"You came all this way by yourself?"

"Yes."

"Your father?"

"He's dead."

He released her and stepped back. Alexei cooed and crammed a fist into his mouth. Cara didn't glance at the woman who held him.

Her hand trembled as she reached out to touch Alexei's silky, reddish hair. "I want to take Alexei with me."

Tall Dancer stumbled backward and sat down on a bench. "Where do you want to take him?" he asked, a puzzled expression on his face.

"He's mine, Tall Dancer, all I have. I want to take him away from here."

"I won't let you go again," he said softly and Cara heard the people behind them moving toward the door. The woman held Alexei out. When Cara took him into her arms, the woman quietly left. *Going for help,* Cara reasoned as Alexei snuggled

against her, the sweet baby scent of him swirling up to tease
her memory.

"Alexei's mine. You and your wife can have another child."
The harsh words stuck in her throat. She ignored the niggling
reminders that she had nowhere *to* go.

Tall Dancer frowned again. "What are you talking about?
You are my wife."

"I won't be a second wife, Tall Dancer." She raised her eyes
to his face and found his expression clouded with confusion.

"You are my only wife. I don't want another one."

Cara studied his face. "Then who's she?" Cara motioned
toward the door and noticed that the entire house was suddenly
empty.

"Didn't you recognize Silver Eyes? She has a baby of her
own and she nursed Alexei and cared for me after we came
here. Without her, he wouldn't have lived."

"I thought you had taken another wife." Cara's thoughts
tumbled and bumped into one another. Her words sounded as
if they came from far away, and fatigue began to crawl through
her, numbing every part it touched.

Tall Dancer rose and swept them both into his arms. "I
would have searched all of Russia for you. I was waiting for
my leg to heal. Then I would have gone to the ruins of Fort
St. Michael and asked every Russian who landed there if he
had seen the daughter of the Butcher."

Cara buried her face in his shirt, breathing in the essence of
him mingled with Alexei's sweet scent. "The Butcher and his
daughter died in a terrible storm on the north coast of *Aliaska.*"

The last stains of sunset faded in the sky above the bay.
Waves rushed to shore, kissed the sand, then slid back into the
ocean like forbidden lovers. Deep in the forest, a raven rasped
its love call to a mate.

Cara snuggled closer against Tall Dancer's shoulder and
sighed as the insects tuned up for their evening serenade. He
pulled the bearskin closer over them to guard against the chill

of the spring evening. With one finger, Cara traced a tiny pox scar on his left temple while her toes caressed the rough bump where his leg had been broken.

"Happy?" he murmured.

"Too happy," she answered.

He was quiet for a moment as the raven called again. "Listen. Raven is up to his old tricks."

Cara smiled. "Luring some maiden home, no doubt."

Tall Dancer's chest rumbled with his laugh. "Now that's an idea." He rolled over and pinned her beneath him. She could barely make out his face in the rapidly dimming light.

"Again?" she asked, playfully pushing at his shoulders.

"Ummm," he murmured into her neck.

"What do you think *Aliaska* will be like when Alexei is grown?" she asked.

Tall Dancer rolled to his side and propped his cheek on his hand, then grunted a little as he straightened his injured leg. "I don't know. Your people have come here to stay. Even if the Tlingit fight them, they will come back again and again."

"Don't call them my people. You are my people—you and Alexei."

Tall Dancer stared at her sternly. "You must teach Alexei about the *promyshlenniki*, Cara. You must teach him how they think and speak and how to live with them. Only that knowledge will save him."

"What if I teach him too well and he chooses one day to return to Russia and live as the *promyshlenniki* do?" Cara ran her finger down his spine and felt him shiver beneath her touch.

He pulled her into his lap with her bare back to his chest and wrapped his arms around her. "He has his mother's wisdom. He will choose the right path."

Cara smiled, feeling his hands sliding through her hair. Russia was a distant, faint memory. Here, love and sorrow were woven together into the fabric of life like strands of cedar bark into a blanket that would warm the weaver on cold *Aliaska* nights.